TOR ROMANCE BOOKS BY SUSAN KEARNEY

Island
Heat

Island
Heat

SUSAN KEARNEY

tor paranormal romance

A TOM DOHERTY ASSOCIATES BOOK
NEW YORK

ISLAND HEAT

Copyright © 2007 by Hair Express, Inc.

Excerpt from *Kiss Me Deadly* copyright © 2007 by Hair Express, Inc.

A Tor Book
Published by Tom Doherty Associates, LLC
175 Fifth Avenue
New York, NY 10010

www.tor.com

Tor® is a registered trademark of Tom Doherty Associates, LLC.

ISBN-13: 978-0-765-35666-6
ISBN-10: 0-765-35666-X

First Edition: February 2007

Printed in the United States of America

0 9 8 7 6 5 4 3 2 1

This is for the book wholesalers who work behind the scenes to bring books into the stores. A big thank you to Kent Haverman, Brad Wagoner, and Dave Van Overbeke at Anderson News, LLC, who went out of their way to make me feel welcome. And to all my new friends at Levy Home Entertainment, LLC: Pamela Nelson, Emily Hixon, Laura Pennock, Justine Willis, Abby Karlovitz, Jennifer Markowski, and Kathleen Koelbl. Touring on the LOVE Bus was a fantastic experience.

Acknowlegments

No one puts out a book alone. It's really a team effort. I want to thank my editor, Anna Genoese, for all her efforts on my behalf . . . and there were many. It's always a joy to work with you.

I also want to thank all the people who work behind the scenes at Tor: sales, marketing, publicity—you do a great job getting the book out there.

And a special thanks to Seth Lerner for his fantastic cover design and my daughter, Tara Kearney, for her photograph that ended up on the cover.

I owe my husband, Barry, and daughter, Tara, for sending out the ARCs when life got crazy. And to my son, Logan, who figured out how to get my TV interview up on www.susankearney.com.

And to my wonderful critique partners, Charlotte, Julie, and Jeanie, without whom I'd be lost.

Island
Heat

Prologue

After a two-year wait, Jamar finally had the opportunity to shoot his brother out of the sky. Now that the slime worm, Cade, had arrived, Jamar's cunning would pay off. Banking his spaceship to lock on his brother's craft, Jamar targeted Cade in his crosshairs. And fired.

"Got you."

Jamar's missile homed in on the ship breaking out of orbit. At this angle, it couldn't miss. But even as a thrill of satisfaction sizzled through Jamar, he noted three discharges and the pilot's ejection from the craft.

He checked the scanner and pounded his fist on the console.

Damn Cade. The man possessed more tricks than a dock rat. Instead of attempting to return fire, he'd ejected his precious cargo—along with himself. So when Jamar's missile struck and Cade's ship disintegrated into a ball of flames, the stubborn bastard hadn't died.

Jamar cursed and brought powerful scopes on line, watching as his brother plunged into the sea. He prayed to the Universal God that he'd soon be fish food. Cade should never have been allowed to leave the creche. But that slime sucker had fooled his educators and his taskmasters, hiding his minuscule measure of cunning behind a devious mask. Cade's deception was a blight on all Jamar held sacred—order and discipline. So when the rebel had secretly conspired to foment discontent and disrupt the economy, Jamar had sworn to crush the nuisance.

Yet, his brother still breathed. But not for long.

1

⚙

It wasn't every day that Shara Weston saw a man fall out of an otherwise empty sky. Back in her Hollywood days, she would have assumed coke and booze accounted for the strange sight of a man plummeting toward the sea. But Shara had abandoned her movie career almost five years ago and she hadn't sniffed, injected, or drunk herself into oblivion in almost a decade. She couldn't be hallucinating.

The sonic boom's echo that had drawn her attention from the Polynesian coral reef to the sky had been real. Lifting her head from the turquoise water, she'd anxiously thrust back her face mask and searched for the aircraft responsible for disturbing her late afternoon swim in her favorite island cove.

But she couldn't see any aircraft—just a body falling through clouds too wispy to hide a plane. Shara held her breath, watching him fall, waiting for his parachute to deploy. It didn't.

When the horrifying notion finally sank into her stunned brain that no canopy was about to flare open, Shara's adrenaline revved. Replacing her mask over her eyes, her snorkel into her mouth, she swam for her boat, using her flippers to propel her through the water. Years of swimming made her quick, powerful, and efficient.

As her arms churned the water in an effort to reach her boat, her thoughts swirled over the mystery of the man's fall. It didn't matter if he was a downed military pilot, or a stuntman, or a paparazzo come to spy on her in a plan gone terribly wrong—Shara couldn't survive another death on her conscience. Whatever his circumstances, she was the only person around who could help him. Her home on Haven Island in the South Pacific was wonderfully private—yet sometimes privacy could be damn inconvenient, especially if someone required medical care.

He crashed into the ocean about twenty feet from her and struck the surface with enough force for a backlash wave to tug her under. Spinning ninety degrees to the left, she searched for him in the clear water. Bubbles surrounded his body but she made out a golden flight suit and his dark hair.

Please, please let him be alive.

Praying he wasn't a dead body someone had pushed out of a passing plane to dispose of, hoping his limbs would begin to move and he'd swim toward the surface, she hovered a moment. But he remained as still as her heart that seemed to have stopped beating.

She'd heard of freak accidents where people had survived a fall from such heights. So if he was alive and the force of the fall had merely knocked the wind from his lungs, she might yet save him. Shara gulped a large breath of fresh air through her snorkel, then dived downward. He was about four meters below the surface, and with the sea calm and the sun bright, she had no difficulty snagging him. Grabbing his gloved hand, she tugged, kicking them both upward.

She burst back to the surface and gratefully sucked oxygen into her lungs. As she breathed, she turned him onto his back, slung an arm around his neck and shoulder, and staying on her side, swam him toward the stern of her boat.

There was no way from her position in the water that she could shove the man's large body onto the diving platform.

Somehow, she tossed her flippers into the boat, then climbed aboard with one hand while preventing him from floating away with her other. With both her feet planted on the decking, she hauled him up, first his powerful chest, then his muscular legs. She tossed aside her mask and snorkel, then, wasting no time, she rolled him onto his back. A pulse beat in the strong cords of his neck, but he wasn't breathing.

Tilting back his head, she pinched closed his nostrils, placed her lips over his mouth and blew air into his lungs. "Come on. Come on. Come on."

She exhaled more air into his mouth.

"Breathe. Damn you. Breathe."

Pale as a jellyfish, he didn't so much as flicker one black eyelash. Fierce determination compelled Shara to keep filling his lungs with air. No blood seeped from his nose, mouth, or ears. He had a pulse and he was not going to die in her puddle of the ocean. Surely he hadn't been under water long enough to drown.

"Take a breath. Come on, man. Stop being so difficult. One breath."

He coughed, spit out water. With a groan, he opened his eyes, sea-green eyes as deep as her lagoon. Bronzed skin tones replaced his former pallor. Relief washed over her, even as she noted his features. A bold nose and a strong jaw complemented his direct stare and made him as handsome as any of her former costars, if she discounted the twist of his lips that grimaced in obvious pain.

With another grunt, he clasped one hand over his obviously injured shoulder, while still managing to convey his interest in her with a piercing stare. The reminder that she wore only a minuscule bikini caused a smidgeon of wariness to trickle through her psyche. Now that she was fairly certain he'd live, she wondered if he posed a threat.

Was it simply coincidence that out of the entire Pacific Ocean, he'd crashed in her backyard? She had to consider if he'd deliberately sought her out. While the world hadn't forgotten Shara Weston the movie star, reporters came to Haven much less often now that she was merely a casting consultant. But she remained wary, knowing that one compromising photograph could sell for big bucks. One exclusive scoop could make any reporter's career.

"Easy. Don't sit up yet." Shara placed a hand on his good shoulder, pleased at the warmth that indicated he'd thrown off the chill of the deep.

"I'm fine." Voice tough, but threaded with pain, he ignored her instructions. Shoving his good hand onto the deck, he raised himself to a sitting position, shaded his eyes from the sun, and searched the empty sky. At his effort, sweat beaded on his brow. "Have you seen anything . . . odd?"

"Other than you falling out of the sky?" she cracked, and when he didn't react, she figured from the way he cradled his arm that he was in more pain than he wanted to admit. "After your swan dive into the ocean, you may have dislocated that shoulder."

He licked his top lip, apparently needing the taste of salt to believe he'd fallen into the ocean. Glancing sideways at her, he spoke carefully, almost as if he feared he might offend. "You have medical training?"

"You're holding that arm just like my stunt double did after Sweetie Pie bucked her off."

"Sweetie Pie?"

"Finest horse that ever made a movie." She bit her bottom lip. "Maybe you should—"

"I'm fine." The confident timbre in his tone suggested he was accustomed to giving orders.

He obviously wasn't fine. As he clutched his forearm to take the weight off his shoulder, his fingers trembled. Yet, with his gaze once more on the sky, he exuded masculinity, even as he again licked his top lip and a tiny smile of satisfaction curled his mouth. The breeze carried his tantalizing scent to her nostrils and sunlight glinted off his reflective gold flight suit that molded to his broad shoulders. His wet, dark hair, cut military short, spiked straight up and emphasized his chiseled cheekbones. A chest wider than the Pacific Ocean revealed the guy was in shape, possibly dangerous, reminding her that she had no idea of his intentions.

Shara stepped farther into her boat, opened a locker and tossed him a towel. Feeling too vulnerable in her skimpy bikini, she thrust her arms into a robe and tugged the belt tight.

Plucking two bottles of ice water from the cooler, she kept one, untwisted the cap of the second and offered it to her guest who had yet to make use of the towel. "Shara Weston."

"Cade Archer."

When Cade held her glance and introduced himself as if he'd never heard of her or the scandal, he raised her impression of him another notch. However, unless he was in too much pain for her name and face to register—or he'd grown up under a rock in a third-world country—he'd undoubtedly read her name and had seen her face plastered on any of a dozen magazine covers during her scandalous heyday.

"Thanks for . . . saving my life." Cade accepted the water bottle without letting his eyes drop to the open V-neck of her robe, winning another point in his favor.

"No problem." She twisted off the cap of her bottle, took a healthy swig, appreciating the cool liquid on her parched throat. Shara hated personal questions so she hesitated to ask them. But her curiosity got the better of her. "You a pilot?"

"It's one of my skills." He downed his water in several long gulps, then neatly recapped the bottle with only one hand.

When he didn't volunteer more information, she raised an eyebrow. "So exactly how did you end up here?"

A muscle clenched along his jaw. "I was shot down."

No kidding. And he'd survived a fall without a parachute. True, he'd landed in the water, but he'd fallen thousands of feet and the crash should have broken every bone in his body and caused all kinds of internal injuries. That he'd survived was a miracle.

But why hadn't she seen any burning metal falling into the ocean? "Where's your plane?"

"When another pilot locked onto me, I ejected before he got off his shot," he explained with a commanding air of self-confidence, as if he hadn't questioned his decision to eject for even a second. "The missile disintegrated my craft."

She hadn't heard of a war breaking out, especially over Polynesia. She didn't even believe any nearby islands possessed a landing strip long enough for military aircraft, either, but she supposed an aircraft carrier could be nearby.

"Where are you from? Who shot you down?" She shuddered. She knew all too well about accidents involving weapons. "Were you on a training mission that somehow went wrong?"

"That's classified." He craned his neck to search the sky yet again.

"Did you take off from a—"

"That's classified, too." The words sounded dangerous, menacing, but he delivered them softly, almost with regret.

"You're just full of secrets."

"You have no idea." Cade grinned, his smile all the more charming for his attempt to ignore the pain in his shoulder. It had been so long since she'd allowed a man to talk to her, never mind charm her, that the sudden warming heat in her core took her by surprise.

"Is your wingman coming to rescue you—"

"I'm alone." He had a solitary air about him, as if accustomed to the success or failure of a mission riding solely on his broad shoulders. However, she sensed no violence or threat coming from him and that eased her mind over her own safety. She didn't like the idea of bringing a stranger to Haven, but between his injury and the storm clouds moving in from the west, she saw no other choice.

"Let's get you back to my house and take care of that shoulder."

He turned irritated sea-green eyes on her. "You haven't been listening."

"Sure I have. You said that your shoulder's fine." Shara moved to the bow of her boat, pulled up the anchor and secured it on deck. Her sarcasm got the better of her. "In fact, you're in Olympic gold medal form, no doubt able to swim across the ocean back to wherever you came from."

He let out a soft chuckle, then winced. "I wouldn't go that far."

"Your pupils are dilated. When the shock wears off, the pain will likely increase." She started the engine, turned starboard, and set a course for her dock. When she noted his keen interest in a gorgeous stand of royal palms, she spoke with pride. "Haven's a tiny island, about one hundred acres of paradise, but I have my own water source and there's a surprising variety of flora and fauna."

"You own all of this?" Cade moved into the cocaptain's seat, careful to avoid jarring his arm.

She smiled with pride. "I bought Haven from a nervous seller. When the volcano at the south end rumbled and shot ash into the sky, I convinced him to sell the place to me."

Cade's gaze scanned the southern peak and returned to rest on her, his eyes full of curiosity. "You aren't worried the volcano will blow?"

She shrugged. "I had experts look over the place. They figure there's as much chance of an eruption here as there is of an earthquake taking out L.A."

As she navigated through the reef and along the shoreline, they passed papaya, mango, and breadfruit trees, several varieties of coconut palms, and dense tropical plantings full of ferns, palmettos, and banana plants. Wild chickens, iguanas, and turtles roamed the island, but Haven housed nothing more dangerous than an occasional mosquito that she could swat away—until now.

As an ex-actress Shara was good at reading people, but she couldn't get a bead on Cade Archer. Composed, intelligent, thoughtful, he kept his feelings checked. And he didn't talk about himself unless she pressed. Although he hadn't given her one solid reason to question his integrity, she sensed a well-hidden determination in the angle of his jaw and the glint in his eyes as he assessed his surroundings and took in the scenery with more than a casual eye.

"Would you consider selling your island?"

She shook her head. The first three years she'd lived here, she'd never left. Although during the last twenty-four months, she'd vacationed and had done some consulting abroad, Haven was not for sale. "This is my home. To me, it's paradise. No press. No trick-or-treaters. No nosy neighbors."

"You live here all alone?"

She hesitated, then nodded, seeing no point in lying when he'd see for himself soon enough.

His eyebrows rose in surprise or disapproval—she couldn't be sure. "Don't you fear pirates? Or storms? Or what if you get sick or hurt or lonely?"

"I have a satellite phone and a shotgun." And a vibrator, but she kept that fact to herself. In all ways important, she could take care of herself. "I also have medical books that will instruct us how to set your shoulder. Unfortunately for you, I don't keep painkillers on hand."

"Why not?" For an extra beat, he studied her face with an enigmatic expression.

"What I don't have, I can't ingest." She kept her tone light, noting a wry but indulgent glint in his eyes as her thoughts veered to the thirty-year-old bottle of scotch she kept on her mantel. Many a night she'd taken that bottle down, played with the seal—but it had yet to be broken.

She'd love a drink right now—to take the edge off a disconcerting day. No longer accustomed to sharing space with another human being, much less entertaining, she couldn't help feeling as if he'd invaded her world, her personal space. She'd moved to Haven in order to heal. And Cade's presence—and questions—were bringing back painful memories.

The Chivas had been a present from Bruce Langston, her leading man and husband. It had been his first-ever gift to her. During their four-year relationship, she'd never opened the bottle, and after his death, she'd kept her promise to him to stop drinking. She'd saved the aged alcohol as a memento, not only of their too-brief marriage, but also to test her willpower, to prove she was still strong enough to resist temptation, even without Bruce.

With the afternoon's sun setting into the west, thunder clouds moved in. The breeze kicked up and the ocean responded by spewing whitecaps. In deference to her injured guest, she kept the boat speed slow and the bouncing to a minimum. However, by the time she'd entered her tranquil and protected cove on the lee side of the island to dock, Cade's bronzed face had paled to a sickly white and he clenched his teeth against the pain.

After she secured the boat with a line at the bow and another at the stern, he carefully climbed onto her dock, his breath coming in sharp grunts accentuated by a soft hiss. He staggered and two deep lines of worry appeared between his eyes.

Taking a quick step to his good side, she slipped an arm around his waist and tried not to recall how long it had been since she'd last touched another human being. "Think you can make it to the house?"

His knees buckled, and she took the brunt of his weight on her shoulder. If she hadn't supported him, he might have toppled into the water or onto the dock and caused additional injuries to himself. Shoving her shoulder into his armpit, she half-carried, half-dragged him toward her home.

"You can make it to the porch, can't you?" she coaxed. "One step. That's right. Now another."

Between Cade's clammy skin and the shudders that racked his body, she feared he had internal injuries and was about to keel over. But without his help, she'd never make it from the dock and over the stone path along the beach, never mind carry him up her porch stairs. Cade was a big, rugged man. She gripped him tightly and her muscles ached and her legs shook from her effort. She needed him to remain conscious and keep his feet under him.

He spoke with calm and authority. "I must . . . rest."

"Not yet. Soon," she promised. "Soon you can rest." She feared if he collapsed, she might not coax him back onto his feet. Together they covered the last dozen yards but wobbled to a halt at the bottom of the steps. "We have to go up."

"Up," he agreed with a cross between a grunt and a groan and a curse.

Breath coming in pants, muscles quivering with effort, Shara urged him with words and pushed him with as much strength as she could muster to climb one step, then another. The ten steps seemed like ten miles. And when they reached her porch, his legs buckled. She'd barely lowered him onto a chaise lounge before he passed out.

Shara didn't attempt to wake him. If he'd suffered from internal injuries, there was nothing she could do to help him, but if she could find the medical book and figure out how to pop his shoulder back into place before he came to, it would be a blessing. Hurrying into her home, she automatically wiped her sandy feet on a braided throw rug before treading across her wooden floors into the library. This was where she read scripts for A-list actors to help them decide whether to accept or turn down a proffered role. This was where she corresponded with the world, where her satellite cell phone and the occasional mail boat's deliveries kept her in touch with friends and clients.

She'd stocked her library with hundreds of books and she'd catalogued them by categories. Gardening and food preparation took up one shelf of her bookcase. Engine repair, boating and navigation manuals shared shelving with carpentry and fishing books. Heading straight for the medical section, she removed a text from the top shelf and her first-aid kit from her bottom desk drawer. With a scowl, she stopped by the fireplace to pluck the Chivas bottle from the mantel.

She'd vowed never to break the bottle's seal.

But did it count if the hooch wasn't for her?

Shara snatched a glass from her kitchen and returned to her front porch to find Cade once again conscious, but lying in the exact same position in which she'd left him. The sun had set and she flipped on a light. He didn't turn his head, but followed her movements with his eyes. His chest heaved and his breath sounded raspy. His color remained wan.

Pulling up a chair beside him, she opened the Chivas,

poured three fingers into a glass. The rich golden color and the savory scent made her mouth water, but she ignored her burning yen for one quick sip.

Instead, she lifted Cade's head with one hand and tipped the rim of the glass to his lips with the other. "Drink."

He sniffed. Took a gulp. And sputtered. "Are you trying to poison me?"

How ironic that he didn't like the taste of the scotch that she had to fight against downing. "Chivas will help ease the pain."

"It's medicine?"

"Sure." His reaction and questions seemed peculiar. She placed a hand on his forehead to check for fever but his flesh felt normal to her. She held the glass to Cade's mouth again. "Drink some more."

He sipped and swallowed, screwing up his eyes but downing the alcohol. She kept the glass to his lips until he'd drained it. And when he lay back, he mumbled, his tone low and husky. "Mmm. That wassssn't ssso baddd."

Wow. The alcohol must have made a beeline from his gut to his brain. She supposed it was too much to hope the booze would work that fast on his pain as well. "How's the shoulder?"

"Goodd 'nuf to hold you." His voice, deep and sensual, sent a ripple of interest through her. A ripple she was determined to ignore. So what if lately she'd been yearning for conversation—one that wasn't by satellite phone. So what if she missed chatting about her day during a walk or over dinner with someone who cared. So what if she missed touching and being touched? Her recent yearnings likely meant she would be all-too susceptible to the first man she'd let set foot on the island in five years.

Annoyed she wasn't immune to his charms, Shara sighed, needing a distraction from the totally hot man on her lounge chair. She picked up the textbook and turned to the back where the appendix listed medical problems.

Cade hiccupped and then spoke slowly to enunciate each

word with the excess care of a drunk. "You're reading backwards."

Shara turned to the page she needed, consulted the diagram. Did she possess the strength to pull his arm straight then slowly release it back to the correct position in the socket? The medical text suggested the procedure should only be done by an expert, and her stomach rolled as she read how she could cause more damage. But her closest neighbor was a three-day boat ride away, and by sea, it could take a week to reach a real doctor. The text also said that the sooner the arm returned to the proper position, the sooner it would heal.

"Give me your hand." She moved her chair back to the correct angle.

Jaw thrust forward, Cade shook his head, his profile strong and rigid. "Don't want to."

She didn't argue. Leaning forward, she picked up his long, calloused fingers and gently raised his arm. Following the text's directions, she placed her bare foot under his armpit, on his ribs.

Two dimples appearing in his cheeks, Cade grinned at the sight of her foot. "Pretty toes."

"This may hurt." Betraying none of her uncertainty over the procedure, Shara slowly applied tension, tugging on his wrist and implementing pressure with her foot against his ribs to cause the necessary separation between his shoulder and the socket.

In fascination, Cade stared at her toes. Then he jerked up his head, his mouth twisting into a line of discomfort, his eyes hardening. "Ow. That hurts."

"Sorry." She kept right on tugging.

Cade grunted, his arms stiffened. His entire body tensed and bowed.

And something in his joint moved. Very slowly, she lessened the pressure. When she finished, she noted his hand had slipped into hers and his former grimace had relaxed noticeably. "How do you feel?"

Eager affection radiated from him. "Kiss me again."

Again? "We've never kissed." She attempted to draw back her hand.

He refused to release his grip. "You kissed me back to life. I tasted the salt on your lips."

He remembered her artificial respiration? How was that possible? He'd been unconscious. Shara didn't have to be a doctor to know Cade's reactions were all wrong. First he'd survived a fall from a plane without a parachute, without sustaining one broken bone and apparently no internal injuries beyond the dislocated shoulder. Next, he'd recalled events from when he'd been unconscious, and last, she'd never seen anyone who had gotten drunk that fast.

And his flight suit was composed of a very strange material. She could have sworn when he'd been in the water that the sleeves had covered his arms down to his gloved hands, but now the material was short, hugging impressive biceps.

Shara really could use a drink. She stared at the open Chivas. Licked her bottom lip.

He tugged her closer and she didn't want to risk hurting his shoulder by resisting. She sat beside him, close enough to inhale the scotch on his breath that taunted her, tempted her. If she kissed him, she'd taste the delicious liquor on his lips.

Stop it.

While the alcohol had clearly lowered his inhibitions, she didn't have an excuse for the sudden desire to kiss him that flooded her. She simply craved the booze—not the man.

Attributing her sudden fascination with his mouth and the yearning for him to the overload of leftover adrenaline from her taxing afternoon, she squared her shoulders. "How's your shoulder? Will you let me fix a sling?"

"So pretty." His tone was singsong but pleasant and musical and very powerfully male. "I'll let you do whatever you want with me."

Sheesh. One little drink and Military Man had turned into

charming Lover Boy. Wary, but amused, she finally disentangled her hand from his and opened the first-aid kit.

Cade raised his head. Catching her by surprise, he brushed back a loose lock of hair from her face and kissed her brow. "Thanks for making the pain go away."

"You're welcome." His eyes held hers, almost as if he knew exactly what he was saying.

Again she thought his reaction odd. She'd seen a lot of drunks, none of them got wasted as fast as he had. None of them recovered as quickly. It was almost as if his system worked at superhuman speed.

"I didn't mean for us to meet like this," he mumbled, his tone cagey.

"Really?" She dug through the first-aid kit, putting aside ointment, bandages, scissors. Behind a roll of tape, she found a folded sling.

"I was supposed to . . ."

She shook out the sling and adjusted the neck strap to the roomiest setting. "You were supposed to what?"

"Supposed to seduce you."

He wasn't making any sense. Obviously the alcohol was doing his talking and she took no offense. "You're a pilot and you've been shot down."

"But not in hostile territory." He seemed quite proud of himself and his gaze on her was as soft as a caress. "You like me, right?"

"Sure." She hadn't known him long enough to make a decision, but so far, so good. He'd piqued her interest, made her aware of him as a man. She slipped the material over his head, bent his arm and placed it into the sling. "I'm certain you're a really great guy. But you shouldn't get any wild—"

The roar of an aircraft cut off her words. A roar so loud it sounded as if the plane were about to crash into her home.

Tilting her head to search the night sky, she saw hellish sparks. Flames. Smoke. Surely two different people couldn't crash into her island on the same day?

Her porch shook as if sprayed with hail that ripped large

holes in the deck. Dust from the eaves rained down and her eyes teared.

What the hell was going on?

Cade grabbed her shoulders, tucked her against his chest. A strong, hard chest. "Get down. We're under attack."

2

Someone was attacking? Her? Shara tried to make sense of Cade's words, but between his yanking her against him, then tugging her off the porch deck, where a laser burst sprayed the wood and kicked up splinters, she could barely remember her name, never mind figure out what the hell was going on. As she peered at the holes in her porch where she'd just been sitting, fear paralyzed her. If Cade hadn't snatched her from her chair, she'd have been hit, lying on her front porch, bleeding. Or vaporized.

"Crawl inside," Cade ordered. With one powerful arm, he slung her toward the door.

On hands and knees, she scrambled inside, the fear riding up her throat, her mind numb with shock. Someone had attacked her home. Someone wanted her dead.

The ruthless violence fogged her brain cells, but at least one of them was thinking clearly. Cade had had the presence of mind to grab the first-aid kit, and he shoved it into her arms before slamming the door shut behind them.

Legs springing with catlike quickness, Cade stood, flicked off the lights, grabbed her shoulders and positioned her between him and the exterior wall. With his big body pressed against hers, shielding her, she couldn't move, could barely breathe.

Heart pounding in fear, she placed her palms against his back and pushed. "I've got a gun in the bedroom."

He didn't budge. "Will your weapon shoot down an aircraft?"

"An aircraft?" She'd forgotten the roar of the plane, and hadn't connected the sound to the attack.

"Those laser bursts came through the roof. Jamar fired them from the air."

"Jamar?"

"The pilot who shot me down."

"What should we do?" If the plane made another pass, he might hit them this time. Her wooden-shingled roof hadn't slowed the assault. Those shots had bit through her porch like a saw through plywood.

"We hide."

A blast, different than the roar of the aircraft, shook her home and rattled the glass. "What was that?"

She glanced at Cade. The man was grinning. "That was the sound of a fuel ejection. We should be safe."

The sudden turnaround confused her. "I don't understand."

"He'll have to leave—immediately."

"Why?"

"I'm not sure why Jamar dumped his fuel. Although malfunctions are rare—and this one is convenient for us, trust me—Jamar wouldn't have ejected his fuel unless he had an emergency on his ship. If he doesn't want to crash, he'll have to land somewhere else to refuel."

"How do you—"

"Shh. Listen."

She cocked her head and tried to hear anything beyond his heartbeat and her own blood roaring in her ears. "I don't hear—"

"He's gone." Cade released her.

She didn't dare move. "He might come back."

Relieved and shaking, she sank against the wall until her butt hit the floor and she drew her knees against her chest. She'd lived in peace for so long that the violence had seemed like a nightmare. But all she had to do was look at the holes in her floor to realize that she'd almost died, that Cade had brought danger to her and Haven.

"Jamar *will* come back," Cade corrected, "but we'll be ready for him."

Shara didn't like the sound of that. "This is *my* home, but he's after *you*. I want you to leave. If you aren't here, I'll be safe."

"I'm afraid not." Cade shook his head and peered out the window. Apparently satisfied, he flicked the lights back on. "But you're right that Jamar doesn't wish you any personal harm."

"You're contradicting yourself," she muttered, raising her chin to let him see the determination in her eyes. This was her island. He was trespassing. And she hated that Cade's presence had put her in danger.

"Jamar's mission is complicated. He needs to stop me. And one way he can do that is to return and destroy your island. But if you get in his way, he'll take you out with no more thought than you'd swat a mosquito."

"Destroy my island?" If she'd been frightened before, confusion choked her now. Either the Air Force had developed some extraordinary classified weapons or . . .

"It would be best if you'd sell me this island and leave immediately."

She folded her arms across her knees. "Haven is not for sale."

"I'll settle for a lease." He slid down the wall beside her and removed his arm from the sling. "And I'll try to keep you alive."

She ignored the heat in his eyes and the promise in his voice. "This Jamar—how can he destroy my island?"

Cade hesitated and spoke slowly, as if choosing his words with the utmost care. "We have sophisticated weapons."

"Who is 'we'?"

"We come from Rama."

"Where the hell is Rama?"

"What I'm about to tell you is confidential."

A shiver coursed down her spine. "In case you haven't noticed, there is no one else here but us." She refrained from mentioning her satellite phone, the computer uplink, or the mail boat that stopped by every few weeks.

"Rama is another planet."

"Uh-huh." Alarmed, she edged away from him. Apparently, he'd suffered more injuries than she'd guessed. The fall had scrambled his brain or he'd been delusional from the start. Either diagnosis was bad news for her.

Someone had just shot up her home and she was alone on her island with a crazy guy—a crazy guy who'd saved her life, she reminded herself.

"I came to Earth to build a portal between our worlds."

"A portal?" She blinked, her thoughts spinning. She'd almost died on her front porch and now he wanted her to focus on the most impossible of scenarios.

"Travel from Rama to Earth by spaceship takes too long. After I build a portal, travel will be instantaneous."

"I don't have a clue what you're talking about."

He reached out and fingered the hem of her robe. "Think of space as a robe. To travel from the hem to the collar would take many light-years. But if I folded the robe, the span between two points would shorten. When space folds, portals can narrow the distances between planets."

She glared at him. "You aren't pitching me some insane science-fiction movie script, are you? Because I won't attach myself to your script or recommend your work to my clients . . . so you're wasting your time trying to sell—"

"On Rama, my people are slaves. They are kept weak by Jamar and his ilk." His eyes glazed with hot intensity. She'd heard pitches before, but never with such desperate sincerity. Either he believed his story was real—or worse, it was. Clearly, he sensed her disbelief and tried to explain. "After I open the portal—"

"You intend for your people to come to my island?" she guessed, her eyes narrowed with suspicion.

"Haven is too small to house all my people. There are millions of us."

His story wasn't just outrageous, it was unbelievable. "Why would you build a portal if you don't intend for your people to come here?"

"Lack of salt keeps most of us weak. I plan to extract salt from your oceans and send it back to my world."

She recalled his licking the salt from his lips when he'd first recovered from his fall and his satisfied smile. Injured, shaken up, had he adjusted to his cover story that quickly? If so, he was a natural born liar. And his statement about being weak certainly made no sense at all. The man had muscles on his muscles. "You don't look weak to me."

"We planned for years for me to make this journey. Many people sacrificed their salt so I would have this opportunity."

"Opportunity?"

He arched a brow as if she was being dense. "With a portal I can send sea salt from Earth back to Rama. And I don't intend to steal it. The substance is so plentiful on your world that I'm sure we can reach a trade agreement."

He had it all figured out, seemed to have every angle covered. "And why do you need *my* island? Oceans cover seventy-five percent of the planet's surface. As you've noticed, there's no shortage of salt."

His expression stilled, his lips tightened in a serious tension. "Haven has two attributes that make it perfect for my purposes. It's unique because of your exact location on the equator. I must build the portal at a spot equidistant between the poles to create a proper balance. And your volcano is active. The portal requires a power source to tap and the volcano will supply that power."

She eyed him with suspicion. "You really aren't talking about making a science fiction movie?"

His eyes flashed with impatience. "I've come here to help—"

"Your people. How very noble." She rolled her eyes at the ceiling. "So tell me, Mr. Alien Spaceman—"

"Cade." He repeated his name through gritted teeth.

"How did you fool our radar? How did you sneak past the U.S. Air Force, the Hubble telescope, NASA, and the NSA? Surely one of our agencies must have seen you violate our airspace?"

Cade waved his hand, a dismissive gesture of Earth's defense systems. "Our technology's superior. We cloak our ships."

Her nerves tensed, determined to poke holes in his preposterous story. "And this Jamar, the guy who shot up my home, why does he want to destroy my island?"

"He wishes to stop me from building the portal." Cade showed no sign of backing down from his story. As he spoke his voice deepened with rigid determination, his eyes flashed with anger. "Jamar's people on Rama enjoy the current status quo. Their luxurious lifestyle of ease requires them to keep my people sick and helpless and dependent on the salt that they control. We are literally slaves. On Rama, salt is cherished and guarded like you protect diamonds. And there is never enough for all . . . so we searched for a planet where the supply was great."

Bent on remaining immune to his physical charm while she questioned his mental stability, she fought the sparkle in his eyes, the tenderness in his voice when he spoke of his people's plight. "Do you have one shred of proof that you are who you claim?"

Disappointment flickered in his eyes. "I had the verification you seek on my spacecraft."

How convenient for him that his only proof was gone but she refrained from pointing out the obvious. "You speak English on Rama?"

"I learned your language and your customs during my journey."

"How?"

"After capturing your radio and television signals, I taught myself your customs as well as English."

"Why not Russian or Chinese?"

"Haven was always my primary destination. The people on the islands around here speak mostly English."

"How long did your journey take?"

"A year."

She took a deep breath and altered her line of thinking. "So your plan, before Jamar shot you down, was to come here and . . . ?"

"Buy the island," he said matter-of-factly.

"And if I refused to sell?"

"I assumed you would accept an offer for more than the going price." He winked and shot her one of those charming, you-can't-rebuff-me smiles.

But she would reject him as well as his incredible story. Shara would never find another love equal to the one she'd lost with Bruce. Even Jules Makana, her friend and a powerful psychic, had reluctantly confirmed it. Shara and Bruce had shared a once-in-a-lifetime love. They'd had something unique together, more than most people ever dreamed. When he'd died, she'd wished she'd gone with him.

Over the years Shara had expected the stabbing pain of losing Bruce to lessen. It hadn't. But, like having a bad back, she'd learned to live with the constant ache, and the deep throbbing that penetrated straight to her soul. And yet occasionally, life threw a new twist at her, like her slowly growing yen for company. She'd been meaning to schedule another trip to L.A. for some face time with her clients to discuss their career goals. And of course, she'd stop in Hawaii to see Jules, maybe even ask the psychic for a new reading.

Oh God!

Memories flooded back. Jules's unusual warning. What had her friend told her exactly? Something about danger. A mission. So long ago. Back then she'd been in deep mourning over Bruce—but Jules's prediction of a man coming from nowhere, with a mission to complete had sounded so dire, so strange, so haunting, that the sudden need to find the tape from that session burned through Shara.

She'd learned the hard way that failing to believe in Jules was unwise—her past unwillingness to listen had already cost her Bruce. She could hardly ignore an earlier prediction that seemed to be coming true, no matter how bizarre.

Lifting her chin, Shara met Cade's direct gaze and ignored the questions in his eyes. "How long do we have until Jamar returns?"

Cade shrugged. "That's difficult to say. It depends upon his base of operations, his resources and how long he's been on Earth. He could return within days. Maybe hours."

"In that case," she struggled to her feet, knowing she needed time away from the so-called spaceman so she could think, "I'm going upstairs. The guest room's down the hall. If you're hungry, help yourself to whatever you find in the kitchen."

"What about you?" he asked, his expression concerned.

"There's something I have to do." She turned, glanced over her shoulder at him, sensing he wanted to follow. "Something I need to do alone."

Shara flung open her closet doors. After Bruce's death and the trial that followed, she'd fled to Hawaii and the comfort of Jules Makana's warmth. Thankfully, Jules hadn't ever said, "I told you so." Instead she'd wrapped Shara into an embrace and they'd cried in each other's arms.

For a while she'd stayed as Jules's houseguest. Later she'd leased a beach cottage down the street. When she'd healed enough to figure out she didn't want to return to Hollywood and resume her career, Jules had helped her find Haven.

However, during the time that Shara's mind had been numb with grief, shock, and the loss of Bruce, she'd begun to tape her sessions with Jules. She'd saved, dated, and lovingly stored each one in her bedroom closet.

It took twelve tries before Shara found the session she wanted. After popping the correct tape into her player, she leaned back, closed her eyes and let Jules's mesmerizing and alarming voice take her back to that day, until she recalled specific details.

Many psychics used crystals to help them focus, but Jules employed her outdoor patio, the sound of the ocean, the palm trees in the breeze and the birds that nested around her yard. Of Hawaiian descent, Jules wore her dark hair tied back in a thick braid. That day Jules had worn an old T-shirt with a picture of a red-and-blue feathered parrot, threadbare jeans, and pink beaded flip-flops. Thin, tanned, and physically fit from surfing, she'd picked up a plate of cookies and her brown eyes urged Shara to eat one of her delicious chocolate chip marvels.

"I've had a very strong vision about you." Jules set down the cookies, took a seat beside her, and sipped from her glass of sweet tea. The moment she sat, her cat, Kapuna, leaped into her lap, curled, and settled. Seemingly lost in her thoughts, Jules's eyes remained serious as she stroked the purring feline.

"And?" Shara prodded.

"It's so strange . . . that I hesitate to tell you more. Yet, the urgency that came with the vision will not allow me to keep silent."

Over the years Shara had learned how Jules worked. They'd met during a film she'd made on Hawaii and had immediately hit it off. Jules had an upbeat attitude and she only spoke about good things, about visions that could be altered. For example, if she saw incurable cancer, she didn't speak of it, believing that her power should only be used to give hope. However, if she saw a vision to help someone heal, she wouldn't hold back at all.

Shara leaned forward to make sure she didn't miss any of Jules's words. "Tell me."

"You're going to meet a stranger, a man, on a desperate mission."

"What's his name? When will I meet him? How will I know him?" Ever since Jules had told Shara to cancel her last picture and she'd disregarded her advice, inadvertently causing Bruce's death, Shara hadn't dared to ignore her friend's predictions.

"You know I rarely see the big picture. This time I only have three flashes."

"I'm listening."

"First, he'll tell you an outrageous story—one you won't believe."

"And?"

"He's for real."

"Great." Shara bit into her cookie and allowed the chocolate to soothe her. "You're going to have me believing every crazy person I meet. It's a good thing I left Hollywood—everyone there is nuts."

Jules grinned and then grew serious once more. "Second, only you will have the power to stop his mission and it's vital that you do."

Shara's stomach churned and she prayed that this was one of Jules's false predictions. Some flashes never panned out. Others were preventable due to Jules's foreknowledge.

"And third?"

"This man will find you extremely attractive. Use your wits and your beauty to stop him."

"Stop him from what?"

"I don't know." Jules set down her tea. She took Shara's hand in hers. "I don't like burdening you now, perhaps he won't seek you out, but you need to recognize him if he comes to you."

Shara caught a glimmer of secret knowledge hidden in Jules's eyes. As an actress she was good at reading emotion and she could see her friend holding back. "There's more that you're not telling me."

"Nothing else is clear."

Jules had shaken her head and they'd never spoken about the stranger again. It had been four years ago and Shara had forgotten the conversation until Cade's appearance had jogged the memory.

With a shaking hand, Shara pressed the "stop" button on her tape player. Another of Jules's predictions was coming true and Shara's stomach knotted and her mouth went dry at the idea that according to Jules, Shara was supposed to stop Cade.

She wondered if Cade had lied to her about his people.

For all she knew he wanted to open the portal so his world could invade Earth. He'd claimed his people were more technologically advanced. Perhaps he intended to send through a virus or a bomb or robot warriors or an electro-magnetic burst or . . . the possibilities were endless.

Taking a deep breath, Shara reminded herself that Jules was not always correct. Shara considered whether she should seek out her friend, make a trip to Hawaii for another reading. But if Cade was up to no good, if Shara truly was the one person who could stop Cade, she shouldn't let him out of her sight.

Perhaps she was meant to simply call the authorities—but who would believe her crazy story that a psychic had pre-dicted Cade's arrival and that she was supposed to stop him?

Most people didn't believe in psychics. Shara had gone that route before. When she'd tried to pull out of her last film, Bruce, her business manager, her agent, and even the director had told her she was putting entirely too much store in Jules's prediction of a terrible accident on the set. Then Bruce had died.

Shara had lost her faith in the police when they'd arrested her for Bruce's murder and the police had claimed Jules's warning had been Shara's way to set up the crime and place blame elsewhere. It was true that Shara had fired the bullets that killed her husband, but there were supposed to have been blanks in the gun. When the law found out Bruce had left his entire estate to her, the tabloids had had a field day. Law enforcement, who were supposed to look at the facts, failed to consider that she'd been a wealthy woman and hadn't needed her spouse's millions. They'd also refused to consider that she'd loved Bruce with all her heart. Worst of all, the homicide detectives had never figured out who on the movie set had switched the blanks for bullets.

Life became a living horror film, with months of being hounded by the press during a prolonged trial. A few weeks after her acquittal, Shara had run away to Jules's to lick her wounds.

Eventually, three long years later, a costume designer

from their last film had committed suicide and left a note, claiming she'd killed Bruce because he'd turned down her advances. The confession had cleared Shara's name, and at long last she'd begun to heal. While the pain of the tragedy would always be with her, so would her distrust of the police.

Recently, Shara had ventured back to California for business, staying out of the limelight, traveling in disguise and meeting privately with clients to discuss their scripts and which parts would help their careers advance the most. She'd even chartered a private yacht to sail through the Tahitian Islands, but she didn't want to be drawn that far back into the real world. And now, she most certainly didn't want the responsibility of stopping . . . Cade. Just the thought of going up against his kind of determination made her tremble.

She listened to the tape again. And again. And finally she concluded the best thing to do was to pretend to help Cade—until she figured out how to stop him. Or even if she should.

Carefully, she rewound the tape, placed it back in the case and into her closet. She should call Jules, just to see if she'd had any more of her visions.

A knock on her door interrupted Shara's thoughts. "Yes?"

Cade turned the knob, shoved open her door with his foot, a tray balanced in his hands. "I thought you could use something to eat."

Shara hadn't been hungry but she smelled eggs, toast, crisp bacon and her stomach unknotted. "You made breakfast foods for dinner?"

"Sorry. I'm unfamiliar with your ingredients and thought I should start with something simple."

She sniffed a combination of savory scents. "Did you fry up onions and put them in the eggs?"

"And I added cheese." He sounded totally satisfied and pleased with himself. "We don't have cheese on Rama. I found it quite good. Salty."

He'd brought one plate, one glass of juice. She raised an eyebrow. "You already ate?"

"I experimented and tasted a bit, before I cooked for you."

He hesitated, then admitted, as if he'd done something wrong, "I sprinkled extra salt on the food."

"I told you to eat what you liked." She took a bite of the fluffy eggs and a mix of delicate flavors melted in her mouth. "Delicious."

"Thanks." He seemed as pleased by her compliment as by her willingness to share her salt. Striding to her window, he took in the view. With the early evening storm long gone, the crescent moon had risen, and moonlight glinted through the opening. His voice, deep and dark and sinfully rich, soothed her ragged nerves. "It's difficult to imagine an entire ocean saturated with salt. Even though I knew before I came here, even though I almost drowned in it, so much salt boggles the mind."

"Are you a chef on Rama?"

"One of my brothers was the chef until—" His voice broke.

She paused her fork in midair and looked at him. From across the room, she could see the tension in his shoulders. "Until?"

"A salt shortage in the kitchen where he worked was blamed on him."

"He was fired?"

"His employer sent him for . . . reeducation." Cade's hands closed into fists, his tone turned raw and lowered into a furious hiss. "They wiped his memory clean."

"What do you mean?" Her throat closed and she put down her fork.

Cade's eyes bore into hers. "After reeducation, he had to relearn how to talk, how to walk. All his previous schooling, years of studying to become a chef were taken from him."

"I'm sorry."

"A week later, the new kitchen maid found the missing salt behind a jar of jelly."

"It was too late?" she guessed, her compassion engaged even as she told herself his entire story might be a lie to win her sympathy.

"It's been five years since my brother's reeducation and

he will never regain his memories. He doesn't remember playing with me as a child. He doesn't remember our deceased parents. He is just now learning to read again. During the years he couldn't work, he lost his home. His wife left him and took the children."

His story touched her but she was determined not to show it. According to Jules, she had to stop Cade and that would be easier if she kept him at an emotional distance. "We have many injustices here, too."

"You don't steal people's memories."

"No, but we lock them up for the rest of their lives, and some are innocent." She knew that well enough; it had almost happened to her. If not for her agent and manager and the money to buy an excellent defense attorney, she might have given up. After she'd lost Bruce, for a long while she hadn't cared what happened to her. No doubt she'd come a long way toward healing because for her, the system had worked, but she wasn't so naïve to think her life couldn't have turned out differently.

He pivoted to stare back at the sea. "The abundance of salt on your world will prevent many injustices on mine. But to send the salt back to Rama, I must first build the portal. I brought parts with me, but I'm not sure where to find them."

If he didn't have the necessary equipment to construct his portal, perhaps she wouldn't have to stop his mission after all. "You said your ship disintegrated. Were the parts aboard?"

"I ejected the cargo." He shook his head, dashing her hopes. "The parts would automatically break into several smaller pieces and descend to safe spots."

"Safe spots?"

"Uninhabited regions of your planet."

"Earth is a big place." She spread jam over her toast, then bit into the corner. "You could search for a lifetime and never find—"

"I'll build a locator device to pick up the signals. Any . . . hardware store . . . should have the requisite spare parts.

And we should leave Haven anyway, because Jamar will return."

She hadn't forgotten the shots Jamar had fired at them. That alone made his story very real. She didn't know a lot about the military, but the technology she'd seen so far seemed literally light-years ahead of what she'd seen in the news.

"If Jamar comes back to Haven while we're gone, will he destroy my island?"

Cade shrugged. "Your island is the easiest place to open a portal, but not the only viable location. He wants me first, my missing portal pieces second, and your island third."

3

Before going to bed, Shara phoned a local pilot who promised to fly to Haven and land his seaplane in her lagoon the following morning. She figured it was the fastest way to leave Haven and to head for Hawaii. Before she committed to stopping Cade, she needed to talk to Jules. Since Cade hadn't a preference for where to buy his hardware, she'd take him to Oahu where she could consult with her friend.

Earlier that morning, Cade had thrown one surprise after another at her. He'd slept in the guest room—at least, she thought he'd slept. When she'd padded down the stairs before dawn, he was already awake and she'd found coffee perking. He'd poured her a mug as if he were already at home in her kitchen. But his new apparel, not the coffee, startled her wide awake. His golden flight suit of yesterday was gone, replaced by a short-sleeved white shirt that revealed muscular forearms. He'd left the top two buttons at the neck unfastened to expose an appealing triangle of bronze chest. Faded jeans molded to his slim hips to complete an outfit she'd never seen before.

Since she hadn't pulled him from the ocean with a suitcase attached to his arm, and none could wash ashore on an outgoing tide, she was certain he hadn't brought excess clothing with him. And she didn't keep men's apparel on hand.

She narrowed her eyes over the brim of her coffee. "Where did you get the clothes?"

His tone, awake and at ease, didn't strain to find an answer. "My flight suit can alter to any color or shape. The fabric is nanotechnology."

"May I?" She reached out to touch the material of his shirt between her thumb and forefinger, recalling her certainty that when she'd pulled him from the water he'd worn long sleeves that ended in gloves, but later they'd been cut short at his biceps. "It feels like cotton."

"It is cotton." He grinned one of his charming grins at her.

No way was she allowing his grin to alter her suspicions. "Can you change the shirt color?"

"Sure."

Before her eyes, the white altered to solid crimson, then green stripes, then a yellow-and-blue pattern before he again changed it to white. "Satisfied?"

She swallowed hard. Yesterday, she'd asked him for proof that he was from Rama. Today he'd supplied it. She couldn't even use the excuse that he'd hidden a drug in her coffee and she was hallucinating. Drugs didn't work in such a selective fashion. What she'd seen was real.

Her mind veered from the fact that an alien was standing in her kitchen, serving her coffee. Or that Cade's mission was to build a portal between two worlds. Or that according to Jules, she was supposed to stop him. It was too much information to process, too much responsibility to bear.

Instead, she stuck to more day-to-day concerns. "You could make a fortune with that formula, although you'd put a lot of people out of work. How long will the material last?"

"A few days."

"And your arm is healed?"

He gently shrugged the shoulder. "Almost."

"You heal . . . fast."

Ignoring her observation, he dug into his pocket and pulled out a red, sparkling stone the size of her thumbnail and placed it in her palm. "I need to convert my gemstones to planetary currency in order to pay our expenses."

Shara lifted the stone to the light and her eyes widened. No jewel expert, she'd nevertheless worn her share of bling to the Academy Awards and to movie premieres. "Is that a ruby?"

"Yes."

"I've never seen one that red or that large." And he'd said 'gemstones.' He'd implied he had more of them stashed away in his pockets. "If this stone is a real ruby, it's worth a small fortune."

"Good. I need to make many purchases and arrange for banking credit."

He'd certainly come prepared and he handled the stone with no more care than if it were made of clay. She handed back the ruby and he pocketed it with a casual air that made her believe the gems might be quite common on his world.

His world. She'd started to accept his story. During the night she'd tossed and turned, wishing that Jules's prediction wasn't coming true—that Cade wasn't from Earth. But apparently, Jules was once again correct. Cade's story might sound incredulous, but he was for real.

She could no longer deny the truth—no matter how farfetched. His clothing technology was far more advanced than any fabric she'd ever seen. Even if he'd somehow hypnotized her to accept the color change, the material had to have come from somewhere. He hadn't found it on Haven. If she looked at the evidence, it came down in favor of his telling the truth. And yet, his story was so outrageous . . . she had difficulty believing him, probably because she was still praying Jules's vision was wrong.

Although the seaplane flight from Haven to Hawaii wasn't quick, it still wasn't long enough for Shara to come to terms with everything that had happened. Unsettled, she phoned Jules after they landed on Oahu to warn of their impending arrival. Then she'd rented a car, intending to drive straight to her friend's home, but Cade had other ideas.

"Where would be the best place to sell the gemstones?" he asked with a musing look.

"Define 'best'?" Shara pulled into traffic with the ease of a confident driver. She knew her way around Oahu and she'd always loved to drive. It was one of the few things she missed on Haven. There was something about sitting behind the wheel and watching the world flow by that relaxed her.

Driving in Oahu amid the dense traffic and the palms swaying in the breeze eased some of her worries. She felt safer, hidden among the masses of tourists and natives. Jamar was unlikely to find them here. And while she was a celebrity and tended to stick out in a crowd, hidden behind the tinted car windows, she looked like everyone else.

Beside her in the passenger seat, Cade wore his seat belt as if he'd ridden in cars all his life. He didn't seem overly curious about the people, the huge hotels, or Waikiki beach. Obviously all those TV shows had portrayed a genuine representation of Hawaii, so that he could take it all in with a casual perusal—Shara had a hard time picturing him watching *Hawaii Five-O*.

Cade ticked off points on his fingers with determined efficiency. "We need a place where I can convert the stones into currency immediately. A place where they won't ask too many questions. A place where I won't attract attention."

Hell, anywhere there were females was a place he'd attract attention. Now that his shoulder no longer seemed to be bothering him, his wan look had turned back to its original deep bronze. She wondered if he was aware of his attractive features, or if his people had different standards of beauty.

She turned the car toward the business district. The hot sun baking on the crowds slowed the pace of foot traffic. Streams of people along the sidewalks and streets moved at a steady but slow pace, the mood polite and casual.

"If you sell the stones to a legitimate jeweler, he will write a check, which you cash at a bank—but for that you'll need identification."

He plucked a driver's license and passport from his rear jeans pocket, held them up for her to see. "Will these do?"

"You certainly came prepared." His driver's license was from Florida, and his passport appeared to be a few years old and actually had stamps from European countries in it. "How long have you been planning your journey to Earth?"

"All my life." His eyes darkened with emotion.

"Since you were born?" She gave him a startled look, realizing how little she really knew about him. He'd told her his mission, but he had limited the personal information.

He leaned back and let out a soft chortle. "I was speaking in metaphorical terms. Our scientists verified that salt was plentiful on Earth over ten years ago. Since then, we planned in secret and with extreme care. Yet, obviously we had a leak since Jamar was waiting here for me to arrive."

Cade's admission surprised her. "I assumed he followed you from Rama."

"Jamar didn't make the journey with me. He was already here on Earth, scheming."

"You're sure?"

"Yes. If he'd left Rama during the time it took me to come here, my instruments would have spotted him."

"So it's possible Jamar isn't here alone?" she asked with a sinking feeling. It was bad enough that one alien wanted to kill Cade—and her, too, if she remained with him—but for all she knew, there could be an entire army of Ramans living among Earth's population.

"Jamar prefers to work alone."

"How do you know his name and his work habits?" The moment she asked the question, Cade grew still. Cautious. She sensed he was going through a long history between himself and the other man and filtering through his experiences to choose exactly what to say. She reminded herself that stopping him might be the most difficult thing she'd ever tried to do, especially since she didn't know why Jules had told her to do so.

"Before Jamar shot me down, my ship recognized his signature."

"His signature?"

"His ship's engine has identifiable markings."

"And you recognized *him* because . . . ?" she prodded.

She swung into an empty parking spot in the business section, yet wanting to hear his answer, she didn't turn off the engine that would stop the cool blast of air-conditioning and force them to leave the car. Unsnapping her seat belt, she turned to look at Cade. He stared straight ahead, but she suspected he didn't see the ice cream stand or the people streaming by on the sidewalk.

Cade appeared lost in thought, his expression pained. "Jamar is one of the chosen ones. He's always had all the salt his body requires and he's very powerful."

"You know him personally?"

"Yes." Cade's eyes flashed green fire. "Jamar is . . . my brother."

Her lower jaw dropped in shock and what must have been a most unbecoming expression. "Your *brother* is trying to kill you?"

He closed his eyes for a moment, as if desolation swept through him. "As a First, he believes that is his right."

"A First?"

"Firstborn." He spoke with so much hatred, his tone came out a low hiss.

Stunned, she tried and failed to keep the horror of brother hating brother from her tone. "Are you telling me that all firstborn children have the right—"

"To all the salt they need." Visibly, he collected himself, and finished explaining in a hard tone. "Because the rest of us are lacking the vital nutrient, we don't grow properly. Our brains don't mature correctly during childhood and we are . . . inferior."

She understood what Cade was telling her, but emotionally, she just couldn't accept that he was inferior in any way. In her eyes he was just about the most perfect specimen of masculinity she'd ever seen. But his words accounted for his modest attitude. She'd been around enough gorgeous men to learn that they'd been doted upon all their lives, first by their adoring mamas and grandmothers, then by legions of females. She'd known handsome men who'd grown up poor but who nevertheless held attitudes of entitlement. They expected women to worship them, because women always had. Cade didn't act that way and she found that side of his demeanor refreshingly attractive.

"Are you saying you have a lower intelligence than your brother?"

He nodded, eyes once again flashing anger. "A lower intelligence. Slower physical reactions. A weaker immune system. Poorer reflexes and muscle control. The list is long and boring."

"And since Jamar doesn't wish for you to change the status quo," she muttered, recalling Cade's earlier words, "he's willing to kill you?"

"He doesn't see me as a man." Cade's tone was low, tortured, bitter. "So he doesn't consider my death at his hand to be murder."

Slaves on Earth had once been considered inhuman. Yet, that time had been centuries ago and she had difficulty comprehending such narrow-minded viewpoints in a world so technologically advanced. Although humanity had its share of horrors, she'd never heard of a society where the firstborn could kill a sibling without it being a criminal act.

"How did you manage to travel to Earth?" she asked, confused that someone who was as low as a slave could manage such a feat. Getting here must have taken considerable resources, ingenuity, and much planning.

Cade shrugged. "I stole the spaceship along with the plans to build the portal with the help of some desperate friends," he admitted. "We may not be as perfect as my brother and the other Firsts, but we should have the right to work for ourselves, to own property, and to pass it down to all children, no matter their birth order." His big hands tensed against his thighs. "Many good people gave up their salt and weakened themselves, possibly giving up years of their own lives, so I would have the strength to accomplish my mission."

His society was almost incomprehensible to her. "So would your firstborn child become a First?"

Cade shook his head. "Only the firstborn of a First can become a First."

"But then wouldn't the First population diminish by half in every generation?"

"Male Firsts sire one firstborn with their wife and are allowed to sire another firstborn with anyone else they choose. That child is raised by the First wife and rarely knows its mother."

"The women *accept* this?"

"They have no choice, but many tears are shed."

Shara shuddered. She couldn't imagine the pain of bearing a baby and then having the child taken and raised by another—as a matter of course.

Cade must have seen the distaste in her expression. "Will you help me?"

His eyes found hers and the burning determination she saw there gave her pause. Deceiving him, stopping him, seemed wrong. Shara had to talk to Jules before she did anything.

"Come on. Let's go sell your rubies." She almost leaped out of the car, hoping he didn't notice that she'd never answered his question.

Cade followed Shara from the car, wondering if he should have shared the truth so freely. From his extensive research, Americans seemed open to new ideas and other cultures. When he'd told her about Raman society, he'd seen both sympathy and horror in her eyes. From watching television shows like *Entertainment Tonight,* he'd gathered that successful actresses tended to lead self-centered, pampered, and luxurious lives, much like the spoiled Firsts on Rama. He had to remind himself that besides good genetics, on Earth, talent and hard work could win status, whereas only the luck of birth order established rank on his world.

One fact he knew for certain. To win her over, she needed to know more about his world. So as they walked, he continued the conversation. "On Rama, one can never fall off the salt train. Birth order alone sets one up for life, giving Firsts superior minds and stronger bodies."

"Don't you have laws to protect—"

"Our justice system prevents anyone other than a First from inheriting wealth. Virtually all of them live off a combination of slave labor and their giant trust funds. Access to the justice system is denied to those who aren't eldest. So all Firsts are wealthy, due to the hard work of everyone else— and even if they are cruel, they remain wealthy."

She frowned at him. "Just because one has earned wealth on Earth, doesn't mean one will stay that way. And riches can be earned by all, or lost, for a variety of reasons varying from bad luck to stupidity."

"You have more equal opportunity here and that gives you hope that hard work will allow you to build a good life for yourself and loved ones. That's why I must build the portal and send salt to my people. All Ramans deserve to have hope for a better future."

"Your cause sounds like a good one," she said, but she didn't sound so certain.

He knew better than to push her about using her island, again. Cade would gamble that he could appeal to Shara's humanity. Strangely, movie stars on her world were well known for taking up the causes of others. He didn't understand what made those privileged few who'd reached the pinnacles of success on Earth declare their empathy for others when the Firsts on Rama did not. Perhaps movie stars took up the causes of the masses to retain their popularity and further their careers. Or perhaps they simply had different morals. But Cade was determined to use whatever differences he found and employ them for the good of his suffering people.

He'd glossed over much of his life, suspecting if Shara truly understood the deprived conditions from which he'd come, it would separate them so much that she would no longer feel any sympathy. He'd watched enough Terran movies to understand how easily humans felt sorry for a neglected dog, but thought nothing of building homes or roads that disturbed the homes of millions of insects—no doubt because an insect was so far beneath them they couldn't empathize with a bug.

He'd done his best, choosing his words with care to explain his situation to earn her understanding, but he'd still seen a wariness in her eyes that suggested he had more convincing to do. He hoped the more time he spent with Shara, the more opportunities he'd have to win her to his side. When it came down to the very basics, they were about the same age, could expect the same life spans. More important, they shared the bond of humanity.

And he needed her island. Without access to Haven's perfect location and live volcano, he might never be able to build the portal. One process at a time.

"What do you think of Hawaii?" she asked.

"The island is beautiful. And it should fit all my objectives."

They lapsed into silence and he hoped he'd said nothing wrong. He hadn't objected to her choice of destination. Hawaii, a large island settled by a variety of peoples, bustled with activity. The central city was large enough to conduct business.

"You speak our language so well and seem to understand a lot about us. How long did you spend studying us?"

"We have machines that dissected your television programs and then fed me English, and your culture, geography, and history while I slept. But before my journey began, for over a decade—ever since our scientists detected your salt-filled oceans—I'd wondered if I could feel at home here."

"And do you?"

"Every so often there's a language glitch, but I can usually figure out meaning from context. Surprisingly, it's not difficult for me to relax. But I cannot let down my guard."

"Why not?" She glanced sideways at him, her quick steps keeping up with his longer and slower strides.

They stopped at an intersection, waited for traffic to pass and they crossed the street, even with the light still red and a police officer on the corner. These Americans made their own rules and he liked their independent natures that showed up in ways both large and small.

He stopped observing to answer her question properly. "My friends and I tried to anticipate many contingencies, but never did we expect Jamar to learn of our plans. The First has a huge advantage in arriving on Earth before me."

"You seem to be adapting quite well. And your shoulder seems healed."

"Yes, thanks to your medical care, my shoulder is back to normal." But she didn't understand. "Jamar has no doubt already established a secure base of operations, infiltrated necessary computer systems, perhaps has paid snitches or hired mercenaries."

"How do you know?"

"That's how he operated when he took over a mine back on Rama. And his tactical advantage by scouting your world ahead of me is enormous."

As they strode down the sidewalk, he watched for Jamar's reflection in the store windows. A man his brother's size would stand head and chest above the average American. But he saw no sign of the First and finally when Shara stopped beside two double brass-plated doors, he was ready to duck inside, eager to do business.

Shara had to give her name through an intercom before the owner buzzed her inside the locked front doors. Inside, cool air-conditioning welcomed them. Several jewelry store clerks stood behind brightly lit displays and helped other customers make decisions. Glass cases were filled with many different colorful stones set in rings, bracelets, and necklaces, displaying fine craftsmanship.

A tiny man wearing glasses sat hunched over his work. He looked up, spied them, and placed his metalwork aside. "Shara!" The man hurried over, his smile wide and friendly. "Aloha. I hadn't heard you were back on the island."

Shara shook his hand and hugged him at the same time, a gesture reserved for good friends of the opposite sex. Her voice warm, she made introductions. "Ben Stillman, meet Cade Archer."

The men shook hands and the diminutive jeweler possessed a surprisingly strong grip and friendly eyes. "What brings you to my humble establishment, Mr. Archer?"

"Cade," he corrected and reached into his pocket. "I hoped you might be interested in purchasing these." He held the stones in his palm and they sparkled a deep reddish hue under the bright lights.

Ben's eyes narrowed. "May I have a look?"

"Sure." For years, Cade had worked long and hard on his language skills. He'd gone out of his way to pick up American slang expressions and idioms. He fully intended to get by as a native and, so far, that part of his plan seemed to have succeeded.

However, he had yet to find a way to win Shara's agreement about the use of her island. He understood why she might not wish to sell Haven. But what objection did she have to leasing him use of the volcano? She wouldn't even know he was there.

Cade may have studied Terrans for years, but he didn't understand Shara. From the spark of her eyes to the coolness of her voice she sent him contradictory signals. At times, he sensed she was interested in him as a man. At others, she seemed reserved, as if she'd retreated behind a shield.

As they strolled back to Ben's workbench, he caught Shara eyeing a tanzanite-and-diamond ring, a pensive expression in her exquisite eyes. Although she neither needed nor wore any jewelry to enhance her beauty, she could most certainly afford it.

"You like tanzanite and diamonds?" he asked, wondering why her admiration didn't turn into a purchase.

"I was admiring Ben's skill."

"That ring design is very popular. I'm having trouble keeping them in stock," Ben told her.

"Business is good?" she asked.

"Excellent."

Without prodding, she commented to both men. "Actually

I prefer opal with tanzanite. Diamonds are such a cold stone."

Cade looked at her. "You don't wear jewelry. Not even earrings."

At his mention of her lack of adornments, she fingered a pierced ear and sadness darkened her eyes. "All my jewelry is safely locked away. Swimming with bright metal objects can attract sharks."

Her rationale might have been sound, but he suspected there was much she hadn't said. Before reaching Earth, he'd caught a news blip about a memorial for an actor that mentioned Shara had been his life mate. Since it was customary for her people to gift lovers with jewels, it would make sense that she didn't wear her jewelry out of sadness. After all, if she was worried about sharks, she could remove the metal before swimming in the sea.

Out of respect, he did not ask, but he wondered what it would be like to love so deeply that the loss of a mate made one retreat from the world for years. His people didn't usually form permanent attachments and Cade had seen the wisdom of following their ways. What was the point of loving a woman when a First could claim her for his own? Or when a First could ruin a family by wiping a memory clean as had happened so unfairly to one of his brothers.

To avoid falling into such a situation, Cade preferred to take many casual and temporary partners. Since he'd always tried to give back as much, if not more, than he received, he rarely spent more than a night or two out of every cycle alone. Women enjoyed the extra attention he provided and he took pleasure in his lovemaking skills. Their hard lives permitted little time and few pleasures besides mating, and like most other youths, he'd often temporarily find relief from the misery of his life by seeking sensual experiences . . . sensual experiences he'd enjoy sharing with Shara.

The woman would have been a goddess on any world, with her large turquoise eyes, which tipped up at a sensual angle, her high cheekbones, and lush golden blond hair that curled around her face and emphasized her gorgeous skin. She had curves in the right places, too, plus long lean legs and toned arms, but her intelligent and practical nature combined with her innate sensuality attracted him and would have enticed, enchanted, and excited any man.

It was too damn bad for him that he would be leaving soon.

4

❄

Jamar couldn't believe his bad luck. The thunderstorm had knocked out his generator, preventing him from immediately refueling. By the time he'd flown back to Haven the following morning, Cade and the bitch were gone.

After two years of waiting and scheming, Jamar had hoped to take out his brother and the portal on the first surprise shot. But everything had gone wrong yesterday.

Jamar had known exactly where the underfirst's trajectory would place him over Haven, but not when he would arrive from Rama. Yesterday, Jamar's long wait had ended—but his brother's ejection was only the first of his problems. If only Jamar hadn't taken Ulani, the Polynesian woman he was training, with him. But no First could go so long without the basic amusements. So while Jamar had waited to see if Cade would reappear from the water so he could shoot him, he'd entertained himself with the Polynesian.

Ulani had shifted position beside him. Tired of staring at empty ocean and waiting to see if his brother was alive or dead, Jamar had taken out his displeasure on her. After all, that was her place—to serve him. "I told you to sit still."

"I'm sorry, master." Ulani trembled, but her tone wasn't subservient enough.

Obviously she required more training. He turned to her and her eyes darkened with fear. *Good.* Fear would make her more attentive to his next lesson.

But Cade and Shara in clear sight on the beach had set off his scope's alarm, drawing him back to the helm. With a quick pull of his joystick, Jamar skimmed over the island, while simultaneously reaching for his shooter that would shower Cade and his new friend with deadly laser fire.

Unexpectedly, Ulani bumped his hand, causing the laser to miss. And before he could react, she yanked on his fuel lever, dumping all but his emergency landing supply into the ocean.

With a roar of frustration, Jamar backhanded the interfering bitch. Her head slammed into the bulkhead and her neck snapped.

Disgusted, Jamar set the autopilot and kicked Ulani's dead body aside, furious that he'd killed her so quickly. After she'd ruined his aim and then forced him to abort his flight due to a fuel shortage, she'd deserved to suffer more. She'd died too quickly for him to take any enjoyment in her death.

Damn Cade. His underbrother had the proverbial seven lives of a *cataw.* Still alive, still tormenting him. Still keeping him on this backwater planet.

As he turned around and flew back to base to refuel, Jamar's gaze fell on Ulani's broken body. Who would have thought that with her training progressing so well that she would dare defy him? She'd clearly been terrified in his spacecraft but that hadn't stopped her rebellion. And once again his quarry had escaped. Jamar didn't have enough fuel for another run, then the storm had taken out his generator. By the time he'd returned, Cade had fled. He'd have to kill him another day.

Hours later, Jamar still fumed over Cade's luck and how the devious traitor had protected the missing portal parts. At least Jamar could take satisfaction in the fact that while he hadn't yet destroyed the portal, Cade still had to collect the parts. Jamar thought over his options. What should he do first? Make another attempt on their lives or wait for them to activate the locator beacon and go after the parts himself?

Luckily for Jamar, Cade and the slut, Shara Weston, had more limited options. With Cade's spaceship disintegrated, the underfirst would be forced to use the slow local transportation to retrieve the portal parts. And after Jamar checked the local airports in the vicinity, he'd learned a seaplane had landed on Haven at dawn. He must have missed them by only an hour. But it had been a simple matter to track their flight to Hawaii.

Since tailing his quarry was demeaning work, Jamar hired a private investigator to follow the underfirst and the woman. Besides, Jamar couldn't do everything, so he'd save his efforts for his powerful brain and the pleasure of the final kill.

If only his *Quait* powers of control weren't weakening, his task would already be done. Either the salt on this world was inferior, or the plenitude of salt in the air, ocean, and earth was upsetting the natural order. No matter how much salt Jamar ingested, his *Quait* diminished every month. And he'd been waiting for Cade to arrive on Earth for two long years.

And by now Cade was no doubt learning a secret that Firsts had kept for thousands of years—with increased salt intake, Cade's *Quait* would strengthen—how much, no one knew for certain.

Jamar's mission was critical. He must stop Cade from recovering the three portal parts—and destroy them to prevent anyone from sending salt home to Rama. And in addition, he would kill his brother, for causing trouble, for inconveniencing him, and for daring to disturb the natural hierarchy on Rama. As a First, Jamar couldn't imagine anything but success—nothing less was acceptable.

Meanwhile, he required a woman to replace the idiot Ulani. Hopefully, Hawaii would have better pickings.

"Jules," Shara squealed in delight as she flung herself into the arms of her good friend. After completing all Cade's errands, they'd finally arrived at Jules's by dinnertime. Tantalizing barbecue aromas from the grill outside teased her nostrils, but nothing was quite as welcoming as Jules's wide grin and sparkling eyes.

After a steady day full of Cade's charm combined with the information he'd shared about Rama, Shara felt as though she might cave and join his cause—or at least, do nothing to stop him.

One good reading and Jules would help set her straight.

As the two women embraced, Shara caught Cade's wide-eyed amazement as he looked around at the unusual architecture and eccentric decor that Jules had used to make the house she'd inherited from her grandmother her own. Psychic talent was a family trait that skipped every other generation—and created tension between Jules and her mother who lived in town—so she lived by the beach and decorated however she wished.

The house was open to the breezes in all four directions. Between the wind and the tiki roof that removed and dispersed the hot air, the house remained pleasantly cool and didn't require expensive air-conditioning. Potted lilies, honeysuckle, and hibiscus spilled outward into the yard and a goldfish-filled fountain bubbled from the patio into a pool in the living room under a decorative arched bridge. Visitors had to look closely to see exactly where the house stopped and the outdoors began—just the way Jules liked it. Chimes tinkled in the breeze. A cut-crystal dish glowed orange and perched next to a carved jade elephant on the ceramic dining table. Four chairs, none of them matching, but each lovingly hand-painted with Hawaiian symbols, sat under a string of vintage Japanese lanterns. The entire decor shouted bohemian, down to the macramé and string beads that draped the hallways leading deeper into the house.

Finally Jules released her. "I have so much to tell you."

"Me, too." Boy, did she ever. "But I've been rude. Jules, this is Cade Archer. He dropped in on Haven, right out of the blue sky, and landed in my lagoon."

"I can see why you fished him out." Jules's admiring tone

was light, but Shara could see that her friend was disturbed by his presence, yet she covered with gracious manners. "Please, come outside. I try never to miss a sunset and the soy burgers are almost done."

The outside patio, an extension of inside, was shaded by a trellis covered with vines. A hammock hung from two corner poles. Jules's cat, Kapuna, sat under the grill waiting for crumbs to fall. The setting sun dominated the view. With volcanic mountains behind them and the sun's orange ball plummeting on the horizon, clouds of luscious magenta and striking flamingo spanned the brilliant sky.

"This beachfront property has been in Jules's family for generations," Shara told Cade.

Jules picked up a spatula and flipped the burgers. "A good thing. I could never afford to live here otherwise. If the real-estate taxes weren't grandfathered in and prevented from rising a small percentage every year under a special tax provision, we'd have to sell." She shook her own special homemade barbecue sauce onto the grilling burgers. A drop spattered and Kapuna licked it off the patio.

For the first time since Cade's arrival, a measure of peace stole through Shara. After Haven, Jules's house was like a second home. Somehow, her friend would help her figure out what to do. She recalled one of Jules's sayings: "A burden shared is a burden eased." She certainly hoped so.

During a delicious dinner of perfectly barbecued burgers, a crisp salad, and corn on the cob, topped off with coffee, the conversation had remained light and unimportant. Jules didn't comment on the extraordinary amount of salt Cade had poured over his burger. Instead, they'd chatted about Jules's cat, her garden, and the tourist season. Oddly, Cade had fit right in, but he may have sensed she wanted some alone time with Jules. After coffee, he excused himself to walk on the beach.

With the breeze teasing his black hair, his silhouette outlined by the sunset, he exuded masculine grace, his long legs heading toward the high-tide mark. Shara had known the man only one day, but she'd found him kind, caring, and intriguing. He might be a stranger but she was beginning to read his moods, a darkening in his green eyes that signaled impatience or the intriguing glints that sparked with desire.

Jules's tone was serious. "Stop drooling."

"I wasn't," Shara protested.

Jules's eyes looked troubled, not teasing as Shara expected, and drilled her. "You brought him to me for confirmation. And the answer is . . . he's real and you must stop his mission."

Although she expected it, Jules's sudden pronouncements always amazed Shara. Despite that her friend had proven once too many times that her visions or flashes were genuine, Shara still found her abilities unnerving. But just as she couldn't deny that Jules had a gift, she also couldn't ignore the fact that her friend occasionally misinterpreted her visions.

"What makes you so positive?" Shara leaned forward to catch every nuance of Jules's expression, hating that Jules sounded this certain. But she saw no doubt in her friend, not in her sad gaze, nor the resolute set of her shoulders.

She kept hoping that Jules's vision could steer them differently, that free will would allow them to become Cade's ally, or at least not his enemy. But Jules's expression was so grim that she braced for bad news.

Sometimes her friend's gift came to her like dreams and required interpretation. Sometimes, the meaning wasn't obvious. But damn it, this time she sounded as if her vision was as clear as Orion's Belt in the heavens.

Jules shuddered, glanced around to make certain they were still alone, then lowered her tone to a husky whisper. "I . . . think . . . I've seen . . ."

"Yes?"

"Death."

"What?" Fear crawled down Shara's back and settled into her stomach. The last time Jules had made such a declaration, Bruce had died. He'd never made it to his thirtieth birthday because she hadn't listed to Jules. Shara wouldn't make that mistake again.

Jules pulled her chair closer to Shara until their knees almost touched. Nervously, she played with the end of her braid, curling it around her finger. "I'm seeing freaky things. Cataclysmic images. Boiling lava. Fires. Explosions."

"Is my volcano erupting?" Shara asked, thinking of Haven. Was Jules seeing the disintegration of her island? Did Jules's visions mean Jamar would destroy Haven?

"I don't know. However, the destruction and Cade are connected." Jules paused. "It's so strange that he could do such damage because I sense no evil in him."

"I like him," Shara admitted.

"Don't go there," Jules warned. "You cannot afford to be taken in by his good looks or his charm or his keen intelligence. It is your destiny to stop him."

Shara twisted her fingers together in her lap. "I'm not sure I can."

"You must."

"How?"

"I have no idea."

"He's a very strong and competent man. I may not be able to—"

"Many lives depend on what you do."

Perhaps there was another option. "Suppose I stay with you. Let him go on alone with his mission."

Jules shook her head. "Listen, girl, and listen good. Cade is one dangerous rebel. What he seeks . . . is wrong. He's on the wrong path."

"Don't go vague on me. I need specifics."

"I'm not sure I have them. My visions have been so strange lately—almost as if they are too . . ."

"Too *what*?"

"Too clear." Jules shook her head and her big hoop earrings jangled.

"I don't understand."

"You know how I see things in flashes? And have to piece them together?"

Shara nodded. She'd never seen Jules this intense or upset. Her friend tended to live life and enjoy. By nature she was the least political creature Shara knew. "Live and let live," described her free-spirited attitude.

"These flashes last longer," Jules continued, "and are more vivid and urgent. Yet, my balance is off."

"Balance?"

"I've always seen many paths. Think of a tree with one strong trunk. Life is rooted in the ground, comes together in the trunk with purpose, but can diversify again and again. Each choice leads one to a thinner branch, a more fragile route. But now my visions don't have a variety of offshoots. There is only one path—that you must stop Cade."

"He claims his people are no more than slaves. He's trying to help them."

"So he says and maybe he even believes it. Worse— maybe it's true. But helping his people will topple his society and start a war."

"Could your cataclysmic visions take place on Rama, his world, and not Earth?"

Jules sighed in disgust. "I don't know. But I see widespread panic. War. Devastation."

"You're certain the war and devastation are connected to Cade?"

Jules shrugged. "I also see another man who's been haunting me for months."

Haunting her? Could it be Jamar who Jules was seeing? Or was she talking about the supernatural? Jules couldn't contact the dead. She only saw the living. So Shara didn't understand. "You're being haunted—like by a ghost?"

"Perhaps 'haunting' was the wrong word. As far as I know he's still alive. His name is Lyle Donovan and he lives in Montana. And night after night, he comes to me in one fiery flash after another. I'm thinking about going to see him."

"To Montana?" Shara gazed at Jules in open surprise. She'd never seen her friend disturbed enough by a vision to seek out a stranger. And she rarely left Hawaii. To go to the mainland was a big deal for Jules, who didn't like the cold, or leaving her extensive family that included five brothers and sisters, numerous aunts and uncles, and more than twenty first cousins.

"In my visions, I always see Lyle's face with flames of fire overlaid. Not as if his flesh is burning or melting or anything gross. It's just that every time I see him, there's fire."

"Maybe he's a fireman," Shara joked.

Jules didn't even crack a smile. "He's a volcanologist." She paused to ensure Shara made the connection between the flames and the possible volcanic eruptions she'd seen in her visions and Haven. Jules stared off at the ocean. "I thought I should talk to him. But he never answers the phone or returns my calls."

"What do you expect to get from the conversation?" Shara asked.

"If I could talk to him in person, maybe I'd have a better idea how to interpret the catastrophic visions."

"The revelation is that urgent?" As far as Shara knew, Jules had never before envisioned anything so serious. Usually, she saw minor stuff, a fender bender, a blind date gone wrong, a pregnancy. Yes, she'd predicted the accident on the set that had killed Bruce, but her day-to-day revelations were usually more mundane.

"It's almost as if the volcanologist is calling to me." Jules frowned. "He would have to live practically in the damn Arctic Circle."

"Not quite."

"I keep hoping he's away on vacation and will return to answer my phone calls, but I checked with the university and he's working on a project and hasn't taken time off in months, maybe years."

Shara used to have friends who kept second homes in Montana and played at being ranchers. She suspected Jules would only consider traveling at all because she was worried about Shara, and Jules's concern made her realize what good friends they'd become over the years. "What's a volcanologist doing in Montana?"

"Yellowstone National Park sits atop the site of the largest volcanic eruption ever. When she blew, she probably set off an ice age." Jules's glum voice rattled Shara as much as the information.

Shara had come to Jules for guidance and friendship, but she always counted on her friend's optimistic attitude. Except right now, Jules would qualify for the pessimist-of-the-month club.

"You think your visions of Cade and Lyle are connected?" Shara asked.

"It's possible. Why?" Jules's gaze pierced her.

"Because one of Cade's enemies, Jamar, actually came to Earth *before* Cade did. He was waiting for Cade to arrive so he could shoot him out of the sky. After he failed, he tried to kill us both at my house. Cade says he may have a base and friends here. Could Lyle and Jamar be friends? Could Lyle be from Rama, too?"

"Oh . . . my . . . heaven." Jules's lower lip quivered. "You're suggesting the mother of all conspiracy theories. If there are a bunch of aliens living on Earth . . . about to start a war with one another. . . . You mention this to anyone but me and they'll lock you up for sure."

"Cade told me Jamar prefers to work alone, but if Lyle and Jamar are connected," Shara insisted, "if they are trying to stop Cade, then that would make Lyle and Jamar our allies. Yes?"

Jules's gaze narrowed in thought. "The enemy of my enemy is my friend?"

Why was life so complicated? Shara liked Cade and the idea of trying to stop his mission would be so much easier if she didn't. If she had to take a side, she'd prefer to take *his* side. Shara had never been overly political, either. After high school, she'd left home determined to become a film star. She'd spent years waitressing and taking acting lessons before her first break, a tiny part in a television commercial. A director had noticed that part and offered her the role of a lifetime.

Then she'd met Bruce and his contacts had opened up more doors. But she'd been so busy with her career, she'd never had time for politics or even charity work. After Bruce's death, she hadn't considered going home to the Midwest and parents who didn't approve of her lifestyle or dreams. Instead, Shara had withdrawn from the world for a few years, then an actress friend had sent her a script and asked Shara's opinion if she should take the part, Shara had read the script, been enthusiastic, and a new consulting business was born.

For the last two years, she'd worked a few days a week, but it wasn't like her to take up a cause. Or take sides in an argument. Now, she seemed to be in the middle of something way too important and critical for her to make any immediate decisions. But Jules was right, if she told anyone else, they'd think she was insane.

And if anyone but Jules had made these predictions, Shara would have ignored them. "Do you realize what you're saying? You want me to stop a man whose cause I admire. And help Jamar who has already tried to kill me?"

"Jamar only went after you because you were with Cade."

"So why do I feel as if I'm taking the wrong side in this conflict?" Shara muttered. She totally trusted Jules and her visions, but she hated to think she was such a bad judge of character, that Cade was lying to her and she couldn't see it.

"Maybe Lyle will have answers for both of us."

Jules sounded as if she'd made up her mind. She was heading to Montana. "So what will you say to Lyle when you see him? If you ask him outright if he's an alien . . ."

Jules remained silent a long time. "I wish I knew what to do."

Before Shara could ask another question, a car alarm started honking.

Cade returned from his walk to find the women gone from the patio and a loud, repetitive, and irritating noise, a car horn, blaring from the front yard. Fearful that Jamar had found them, Cade broke into a sprint, running around the house. Worry that his elder brother might hurt either of the women increased his speed. He'd seen Jamar backhand his own wife, terrify his daughters, and even threaten their mother. Not even their father would stand up to him. On Rama, Jamar was revered for his powerful mind and did as he pleased. Unfortunately, his intelligence only served to spur his ruthlessness.

Cade had spied many manicured lawns during their drive to Jules's home, but this yard resembled a rainforest, with tightly grown bamboo that blocked his progress at every turn. He should have run through the house instead of trying to fight his way around. Giant leaves slapped his face, roots tripped him, and when he finally broke through the growth, headlights blinded him.

Squinting, Cade saw a large man lunging clumsily forward, swinging a long pole at the women with menacing fury. Jules and Shara backed up. All three people were shouting, and he couldn't understand what any of them were saying.

As he closed the distance, relief washed over Cade that a stranger, not Jamar, had found them. Yet, he couldn't discount the danger. The intruder was a big man with a wide girth. Cade estimated he was double his own mass, and although the long pole wasn't thick, he swung it with anger and strength, keeping the women back.

"Let me turn off the horn!" Shara shouted.

"Stay back." The man slashed the pole as if it were a sword, threatening her and preventing her from advancing.

But suddenly Jules's car horn ceased blaring of its own accord. Cade used the moment to edge closer.

While Cade had no idea of the man's identity or what he was doing here, he was puzzled that the women didn't seem particularly frightened, only angry. He was about to try and circle around behind when the man spied him. With a shout, he pawed the ground with his foot and let out a roar. Face red with fury, he threw the rod at Cade.

He dodged. Caught in midstride, the sudden evasive maneuver unbalanced him. While he fought to remain on his feet, the stranger ducked his head, closed the distance with a speed that belied his weight and rammed Cade in the stomach. Powerful arms closed around him in a wrestling hold.

Taken by surprise, Cade reacted automatically, slamming his head into the other's face. His attacker grunted in pain and his arms relaxed, but Cade fell hard, the weight of his attacker landing on top of him, walloping a double blow, one from the ground, the other his opponent. Crushed, Cade gathered his muscles to shove the man off.

Hearing a woman's shout, he glanced up, surprised to find Shara and Jules, standing over the two men. Shara was kicking the strange man in the side, trying to shove him off Cade. "Get up, Lou."

Lou? So the women did know him.

Jules climbed onto Lou's back and pulled his hair. Lou yowled in pain and tried to twist out of her grip. Cade shoved at the man's chest and finally freed himself from beneath the other's massive body. His opponent may have appeared fat, but he was solid and muscular beneath the excess weight.

Rising to his feet, Cade caught sight of Jules slapping the man across the face with an open hand. "You idiot. How dare you show up at my home uninvited. I told you not to come back. Not ever."

The man cowered and covered his face. "You didn't mean it."

"What part of 'I never want to see you again' don't you understand?" Jules stood back, fisted her hands on her hips, and glared.

Shara picked up the pole and broke it over her knee. "Lou, leave before I call the cops."

Cade looked from one woman to the other. He'd never expected them to attempt to rescue him. *Damn.* Together, without a weapon, the two of them had taken on this Lou, not even hesitating to place themselves in danger.

Oh, Cade had studied American culture, seen the television shows and had most of the slang down cold. But like fairy tales and cartoon stories, he hadn't believed that females could be so independent. But Shara and Jules resembled the females he'd seen on cop shows—tales he'd thought were fictionalized nonsense.

Never had he seen women like these two. The women Firsts on Rama whined and complained to get their way. The seconds and thirds were subservient, as were the males.

To see two women fighting with feet and fists . . . to help him, rocked him back on his heels. And made him feel slightly foolish. He hadn't even thrown one punch.

Lou, who had seemed so dangerous only moments earlier, deflated with every angry word cast in his direction. "I miss you, Jules."

Jules spit at his feet. "You should have thought of that before you cheated on me with that *haole*."

Cade didn't comprehend the word, but sensed negative connotations.

Shara prodded the man's gut with the broken pole. "Go."

"I made a mistake," Lou pleaded.

"So did I," Jules's nostrils flared. "I trusted you, and you betrayed me. You didn't just cheat. Your brought her here to *my* home. To *my* bed."

Shara sucked in her breath, her expression for her friend sympathetic, but one glance at Lou and her eyes narrowed in harsh judgment. In obvious disgust, she tossed the snapped pole at Lou's feet. "I'm going to the house. If you aren't gone by the time I get there, I'm calling the police."

Cade's glance vacillated between the two furious women. All this fuss because the man had taken another woman for the night? He understood these people had different customs, that once they married they vowed to forsake all others—but from their TV shows, many people broke their promises. And Jules and Lou hadn't taken such vows. He didn't really comprehend the reasons for all this female anger.

Lou's double chin quivered. His eyes never left Jules's face. "I was drunk."

"Too bad." Jules turned her back on the man and followed Shara to the house.

Lou let out a sob and turned toward a beat-up truck. "Be careful, dude. Those are two unforgiving *wahines*."

Cade couldn't help but agree—although he had the good sense to keep that thought to himself. He needed Shara's help to use her island and he didn't wish to offend or anger her, but it bothered him that as much as he'd studied these Terrans, he didn't understand them.

Or was it simply women he didn't understand? When the women had come to his defense, he'd truly been shocked. And yet, he had seen their television shows. He should have realized there were very real differences between their peoples that had to be experienced to be truly understood.

Back on the island he'd flirted with Shara out of a genuine attraction to her. He liked her independent spirit and no one could doubt her fabulous looks. The woman could have been a film star on any world.

But now that he'd begun to get to know her, he wondered if that constituted a relationship. And if so, what kind of unspoken rules restrained him. At what point did these Terrans consider the relationship exclusive?

To confuse him even more, the television shows that he'd viewed seemed to have different ideas about exactly what kind of behavior was acceptable and when. In some respects Earth was very complicated compared to Rama. Yet, the differences fascinated him.

Cade wanted to get to know Shara much better and he hoped his words about his mission had drawn her to his cause—not just because he needed her help, but because he enjoyed her company. But he had to proceed with care.

Would she ever accept his arms around her? He recalled the many times she'd touched him to help him after his plunge into her lagoon. Each time, her skin reminded him of the softest luxury sponges.

However, she'd locked him out of the bedroom last night and would likely do so again tonight. He had no idea how quickly he could proceed and he supposed there was only one way to find out. Did he dare? A physical union would bind them and perhaps she'd be more inclined to allow him to use her island. But if she refused, he might be placing their working together in jeopardy.

The voyage from Rama had been long, lonely. Perhaps, he should find a way to encourage her to come to him.

5

✦

Shara took a shaking Jules into her arms. They'd had many long phone calls about Lou, but she hadn't realized until just then how badly his betrayal had hurt her friend. Jules appeared to have really loved the guy but had enough self-respect not to put up with his cheating ways. "Lou's gone now and I doubt he'll come back."

Jules sobbed harder. "If you hadn't been here when he said he missed me and looked at me with those puppy dog eyes, I might have given in."

Heart heavy, Shara glanced over Jules's shoulder at Cade. He seemed unusually interested in their conversation. Standing in the shadows, he remained still, as if fearing that if he drew notice to himself they'd send him away. But no matter how motionless he remained, no matter how far he blended into the shadows, Shara was too aware of him.

She told herself that awareness stemmed from her lack of understanding him more than anything he'd done wrong, or even Jules's warnings. Men born on this world were difficult enough to figure out, one from an alien world would be impossible. Especially a man as careful as Cade.

She watched him standing guard by the window, scanning for danger, and her heart rocketed up another notch, wondering if by coming here she'd brought more trouble to Jules. What was he thinking? Did he believe Jamar could track them, find them and her friend?

She smoothed Jules's hair and stepped directly to the bar and fixed her a gin and tonic. Just because Shara couldn't drink, didn't mean that Jules couldn't have some relief. "You said that you were better off with Lou out of your life."

"I did and I meant it." Jules blew her nose into a tissue, tossed it into the trash, then accepted the drink. "Thanks." She jiggled the ice and stared into the alcohol as if she could find an answer there. "The damn man is no good but that doesn't mean I can snap my fingers and be over him."

Hell, Shara certainly understood. She doubted she'd ever be over Bruce and the thought of joining her friend in a drink zinged her. Needing something to hold in her hand, something to swallow, she retreated to the bar and poured herself a cola. Recalling Cade's last reaction to liquor, the way a few sips had made him drunk, she didn't ask his preference, just poured him a soda, too.

"Thanks." He tasted the cola, grinned at the sweet taste and then downed the entire glass in one long swallow.

Shara loved watching the man drink and eat. He did so with such enthusiasm, but now was not the time for distractions. Jules needed her.

Besides Shara's longing to drown her sorrows and Jules's complete indifference to alcohol's ability to dull her pain, the major difference between the two women was that Shara didn't want to forget about her former lover and Jules did. Shara had loved Bruce with her whole heart. She missed him every day. If Bruce had ever cheated on her . . . she might even have forgiven him—she'd loved him that much. Perhaps Jules should give Lou another chance, especially if she missed him as much as he seemed to miss her.

Shara spoke softly. "Lou seemed so sorry, maybe you should consider—"

"Forgiving him?" Jules shrugged, sighed and collapsed back into her chair. Kapuna leaped into her lap and she petted him, setting aside the drink, untouched. "I made that mistake once already. Twice would mean *I'm* the idiot."

"Oh." Jules hadn't told her that before. But Shara wasn't so surprised. Her friend had a kind and forgiving nature and no doubt she hadn't mentioned Lou's cheating and her going back to him because she'd known Shara would have disapproved—although for Jules's sake, she would have tried to keep her opinions to herself. Just as she kept her yen for that drink tamped down to a dull roar.

Why was it that everyone who wasn't a raging alcoholic seemed to have no clue or no longing for even one tiny sip? While Shara would have liked nothing better than to pour the liquid straight into her soul, she would not go there.

She'd hit rock bottom and it hadn't been pretty. One sip was all it would take to start sliding down that slick slope of despair. She hadn't realized coming back into civilization would tempt her so. After all these years of abstinence she felt as though she should have been cured. But she couldn't seen to shake the craving for booze any more than she could stop her fascination with Cade.

Despite Jules's distress, Shara assessed every expression that crossed his too-handsome face. How his eyes glittered with intelligent interest. How his mouth quirked up with just the right combination of sympathy. How his gaze caught and held hers across the room in a glance that spoke volumes, that said he wanted to become more than friends.

Jules turned her head and glared at Cade. "Why does every man I find attractive turn out to be no damn good?"

"Perhaps you find the wrong traits attractive," Cade suggested, his tone gentle and slightly confused, as if he feared her hostility might be directed at him personally, instead of at all men in general.

Jules flopped her head back and closed her eyes. Her tone turned dreamy. "I want a man that's happy and loyal. One that has enough confidence in himself that he'll let me be me. What's so wrong with that?"

Cade didn't answer. His gaze lasered in on Shara. "What about you?"

"Me?" She arched a brow.

"What kind of man attracts you?"

Shara shook her head and folded her arms across her chest. "I'm no longer interested, so attraction's irrelevant."

Jules snorted and rolled her eyes at the ceiling. "That's so not true."

"I'm happy living alone," Shara insisted. "I've already loved once—and what Bruce and I had was so rare, I don't expect to ever have that again."

Jules shook her head. "Bruce was a fine man, but he wasn't a saint."

Shara wasn't ready to go there. Not now, maybe not ever. Her memories of Bruce were all she had left, and she kept them locked away in a private treasure chest to be taken out on those occasions when she needed a reminder of what she'd lost. "We were discussing Lou."

"I'm over him. He's history. Those are absolutely the last tears I'll ever shed over the no-good SOB."

A beeper at Cade's hip went off. He reached excitedly for the device and read the text message.

Earlier, after he'd sold his rubies and they'd left the bank—where Cade had set up a checking account, transferred most of his funds into it and taken some in cash—they'd stopped at two different electronic stores for supplies. While she'd driven the car to the far side of the island where Jules lived, he'd assembled his locator device and had explained that he would tap into Earth's satellite system to capture the signals.

"You found the portal piece?" Shara asked.

"The first of three." He turned off the beeper and pulled a global map up on his GPS. He pressed a few buttons and Shara found herself holding her breath. Before he'd ejected from his craft, he'd rocketed the three portal pieces into orbit. Apparently, each had its own cloaking device and was designed to land in unpopulated areas. Since 75 percent of the planet was water, she expected two of them to land in the ocean. If she was lucky, at least one of them would have splashed into an underwater rift so deep it would be irretrievable. Cade's mission would be over right here and now, and she wouldn't have to do one thing to stop him.

"I'm punching in latitude and longitude." Cade peered at his device. "The first portal piece appears to be on the other side of the world. In the Dead Sea."

Shara held back a groan. She didn't know if a visit to Israel was dangerous right now, but since there had been fighting in that part of the world for the last two thousand years, she expected it wasn't real safe. "What about the other pieces?"

"They won't beep until after I retrieve the first piece and send a code to the others. My people made the locators that way to prevent anyone else from going after one piece while I hunted down the other."

Shara tried to make her voice sound concerned, when in truth she hoped the other man beat them to it. "Are you saying Jamar is receiving the same GPS signal that you are?"

"It's possible. He knows how my equipment works." Cade slung a backpack with his gear over his shoulder. "Will you take me to the airport?"

"Now?" She gestured to Jules in an I-can't-leave-her-in-this-state gesture.

"I'm sorry. I cannot allow personal issues to delay me."

"Go." Jules waved her away. "I'll be okay."

Shara looked from her friend to Cade and back. Cade had asked her only to take him to the airport but to stop him, she needed to go to Israel with him. She'd have to come up with a good believable reason for Cade to allow her to accompany him, but she wouldn't abandon Jules. She turned to her friend. "There's no way I'm leaving you here alone. Come with us."

"Trevor, I want a story I can sink my teeth into." Ralph chewed his unlit cigar and glared at his top reporter, Trevor

Cantrell. Accustomed to Ralph's tirades, Trevor didn't even bother to remove his crossed ankles that he'd draped over the edge of Ralph's desk. The Oahu newspaper's chief editor had been on a rampage of late, but Trevor had written too many front-page stories to worry about keeping his job.

As the *Hawaiian Sun*'s only Pulitzer prize–winning reporter, he had certain privileges—one of them was dressing in a comfortable Hawaiian shirt and wearing khakis while at work. Leaning back on the rear legs of his chair, Trevor eyed his boss with amusement. "Nicotine's a tough habit to kick."

Ralph plucked the cigar from his mouth, eyed it, then tossed it into the trash. "Get me a story that the AP will pick up."

"I can't manufacture news."

"No, but you can dig up something interesting. What's going on with the hotel labor dispute?"

"They're at a stalemate."

"The sugarcane import tax?"

"Stalled in Congressional committee."

"I suppose you've heard the titillating rumor that Prince Charles and Camilla have leased the penthouse suite at the Hyatt?"

"That was last week's rumor. This week, they're going to Vegas to gamble away the crown jewels."

Trevor watched his boss's eyes narrow. Ralph's mouth tightened to a pinched look, and in another moment he was going to start complaining about circulation numbers and that corporate might can them all if they didn't come up with real news, leaving Ralph strapped to pay alimony to three ex-wives and an assortment of kids. Trevor was fairly certain Ralph was a workaholic because he hated going home to his latest wife. So he let his boss steam for another few minutes before presenting his idea.

"I heard about an unusual gem sale today."

Ralph's eyes brightened. "A movie star in town?"

"The guy had the looks *and* he arrived on the island with Shara Weston, but he's an unknown commodity."

"Shara Weston? She's kind of old news, but she takes a fabulous picture. Can you drum up a new angle?"

"The guy sold his gemstones for ten million. If he hadn't been in a hurry, he could have gotten more."

"So what? The interesting part is Shara Weston—not some gemstones."

"They were an assortment of rubies. The jeweler tells me he's never seen anything like them. Each ruby had the exact same weight and color and they were spectacular quality. It would have been rare to find one stone like that, but the matching set was remarkable." He saw Ralph's eyes start to glaze with disinterest. "Okay, here's where it gets fascinating."

"I'm listening."

"The guy, Cade Archer, has an American driver's license and a U.S. passport. But when I ran the identification numbers with my friends at Immigration, they couldn't find anything on the dude. He has a birth certificate, but the hospital had no record of his birth."

"His papers must be forged," Ralph said.

"His passport was perfect, his number *in the system*. Who could pull that off except Mossad or the CIA? And Cade Archer owns no property, went to no public school, and has held no job that I can find."

"Maybe he's not American but working with our government. So what?"

Trevor knew how to interest Ralph. "The jeweler says the rubies are real but they came from no mine he's ever heard of. Says the color and size and structure don't match anything he's ever seen before and the guy's an expert."

"So how does he explain it?"

"He thinks the rubies came from a meteorite."

Ralph snorted. "You call that news?"

"The dude drops out of nowhere and sells gemstones that come from a meteorite. I'd like to follow up."

"Have you got anything else?"

"I talked to a pilot. He was flying by Shara Weston's island two days ago and heard a sonic boom."

"So?"

Trevor had done his homework. "The U.S. Air Force has no record of any craft in the area that could make that kind of racket."

"The Russians?"

"Not even the Chinese. I checked with my source on the base."

"So what do you think this is, the return of Superman?"

Trevor shrugged. "We have a sonic boom over Shara Weston's island. Then she shows up with this guy who has ID, but no background that I can authenticate, and he sells rubies worth a small fortune that are like nothing seen on Earth." If he hadn't piqued Ralph's interest, he didn't know what else he could say.

"Where would you start?" Ralph asked.

"When Shara Weston visits the Big Island, she always stays with her friend the psychic. I can poke around, talk to her and the neighbors. And I want to do more digging on Cade Archer."

"All right."

"Thanks, boss." Trevor stopped talking. Once he had Ralph convinced, there was no point in wasting more words.

Jules had bought Shara enough time to try to formulate a believable lie to get Cade to take her with him to the Dead Sea. As if Jules had understood Shara's dilemma—needing to go with Cade but unwilling to leave her friend—she'd stood and headed toward the beaded strands that separated the living quarters from the back room. "I should head to Montana anyway. Give me a half hour to pack and I'll go with you."

Cade nodded and accepted the reasonable delay. "Please, hurry."

At least for now, the three of them could travel as far as L.A. together. Cade would likely think Shara was accompanying Jules, and between now and the time they landed,

Shara would think up a reason to go with him, instead. If she had to, she'd pretend she wanted to know him better and hope he bought her act. At least she had the training for that kind of role and could pull it off. She might not have acted the charmer in years, but she could slip into a role as easily as other women donned a robe.

Jules left them to pack and Kapuna followed her out of the room, leaving Cade and Shara alone. She refilled their colas. "Thank you for waiting."

"You're welcome." He paced, unable to sit still, but stopped to accept the drink. "What's the best way to travel to the Dead Sea?"

"You picked the farthest point from here. It's halfway around the world. But the best flights will be out of New York, so I'd say, first stop is California, then the Big Apple and on to catch a direct flight to Tel Aviv."

"How long will it take?"

"With great connections? At least twenty-four hours." She read impatience on his face. "It may even take longer. We could have up to eight-hour layovers."

"There's nothing faster?"

"Short of military aircraft or private jets, no."

He sipped his cola, savoring it this time. "Tell me about private jets."

"They are smaller, fast, and expensive." Shara had flown that way to make films in Europe. And as she thought about setting up a good reason for Cade to believe she wanted to go with him, an idea formed in her mind. "I worked on a film in Israel once and I've always wanted to go back."

He grinned, as if he'd been waiting for this opportunity. "Then come with me."

"Just like that?"

"I've studied your world but there are many things I don't understand. You can be my guide." His eyes said he'd like her to be much more than his guide. "And tell me more about these jets. Can I afford to hire one?"

"Sure. It'll set you back a few hundred thousand. Would

you like me to make the arrangements? I can have your bank wire the funds."

He didn't hesitate. "Please, yes."

She picked up the phone and called the airport. She hadn't used a private jet in years but recalled the luxury. Instead of going through security and baggage handlers, passengers simply drove onto the tarmac and boarded the plane, which took off when they wanted to leave, instead of on a predetermined schedule.

Private jet companies catered to the whims of the rich and powerful. The fully-fueled G350, with a pilot, copilot, and catering, would be ready to leave by the time they drove to the airport. She hung up the phone and headed toward the back bedroom, speaking to Cade over her shoulder. "We're all set. I'll go tell Jules and help her pack."

"Please, hurry." Cade repeated the same exact phrasing he'd used earlier. As she departed, he'd gone back to pacing.

Knowing the next few minutes might be the last that they had alone, Shara hurried down the hallway toward the master suite, which was decorated in Jules's funky chic style. There was a canopy bed draped with tie-dyed sheets, which formed a tented pavilion over the bed. Red-shaded lamps warmed the private suite with a campy glow and illuminated Jules's collection of vintage clothing, which she hung on the wall like art. Soothing cinnamon incense burned next to a flicking set of candles.

Shara walked in to find Jules tossing items onto her bed beside an empty case. "Need some help?"

"Sure. Start rolling the clothes." Jules dug into a closet and tossed a pair of heels and a pair of scuffed hiking boots onto the bed.

Kapuna curled up atop the pile of clothes that needed to be packed and when Shara shooed him away, he glared at her with how-dare-you-disturb-me attitude. "We're flying by private jet. If you want to take Kapuna with you, there's room and no regulations."

"Great. His carrier's in the garage." Jules tossed a pair of denim jeans dotted with rhinestones onto the bed, T-shirts, thick socks, and a Christmas stocking.

"What's with the stocking?" Shara frowned and sniffed. She smelled smoke. Had the stocking been placed too close to a fireplace?

"I need a hat."

Shara chucked it into a corner. "Buy a new one."

"Some of us aren't ex-movie stars with megabucks in the bank due to DVDs and cable reruns."

"A new hat will set you back maybe twenty bucks, and you can buy matching gloves, too."

"Why would I want the hat to match the gloves? I'm not even sure the gloves should match one another."

Shara laughed and breathed in more smoke. Turning her head, she sniffed again. "Jules, do you smell smoke?"

"It's my new candles."

"I don't think so."

"The incense?"

Shara blinked. Smoke poured into the open window from the direction of the patio. Had a spark from the grill caught? Her heart quickened. "The house is on fire."

As if her words had summoned the flames, a fiery inferno crackled over the walls, up the ceiling. Kapuna yowled and leapt into Jules's arms.

Surprised, Jules nevertheless caught him. In the reflected light of the flames, horror widened her eyes and she swore.

Cade sprinted into the room, his pack on his back, and pointed. "We've got to get out that window."

Jules took one step toward the exterior wall. Flames crackled over the opening in a blazing sheet of fire, forcing her back to the center of the room. "Let's go down the hall."

Smoke curled into the house and made breathing painful. Shara grabbed a stray shirt and placed it over her nose and mouth, trying to filter the air. Beside her Jules did the same, but coughed anyway.

Cade snagged Shara's wrist and she held on to Jules, forming a human chain. Together they hurried down the hallway, Cade slowed as they reached each room, glancing in to see if they could escape through a window. But the fire seemed to be hottest around the perimeter, as if it had been set to trap them inside.

Lungs aching, heart hammering, eyes tearing, Shara stumbled into Cade's back. He'd stopped, and with the smoke as thick as pea soup, she could barely see him or Jules.

Cade muttered. "The smoke's worse here."

"Go right," Shara ordered, hoping the spare bedroom where she'd stayed so often and the big bay window might offer them an escape route.

Cade found this door closed. He placed his palm on it to check for heat, then cautiously cracked it and stepped through the doorway. "Come on."

He pulled Shara inside and she in turn dragged in Jules and the cat. The air in the bedroom was almost breathable and she gulped huge breaths of air. The interior walls had yet to catch and Jules slammed the door shut behind them.

Cade didn't waste a moment. Picking up a chair, he flung it through the picture window. Shara grabbed an umbrella from a stand and knocked back the biggest glass pieces still stuck in the edges of the frame, but even as they worked in frantic haste to clear a path, the outside wall burst into flames, blocking the window opening.

"We can't go through that. We'll burn alive," Jules shouted.

Fire blazed across the ceiling and lit them up like center stage. Smoke curled under their feet as the old wood burst into rivers of fire. Burning ceiling tiles rained down. Sparks flew dangerously close.

Cade grabbed Shara's hand again. "We can't stay here, either."

Even as she reached for Jules, Shara knew they were going to die. There was no way to pass through that wall of fire and live.

Staying here they would burn. Fleeing they would burn.

Oh God. They weren't going to die an easy death of smoke inhalation.

She smelled fuel. Someone had set the fire, poured it around the perimeter. Trapped, they were going to roast alive.

6

Reporter's instincts on full alert, Trevor watched the fire trucks douse the flames at the psychic's home, wondering if there were bodies inside or if Jules Makana had set the fire to cover her trail and those of Shara Weston and her mystery friend. If those rubies had been stolen, perhaps all three people needed to disappear with the cash before the police were onto them.

Except Shara Weston was wealthy. Could someone be taking advantage of her? Had she been abducted? Trevor had no idea what had happened but he had to consider all possibilities.

The chief of police's second-in-command, Dan Brandon, recognized Trevor from other fires he'd covered and wandered over. Ex-military, Dan had settled on the island after serving his second tour of duty. Face smudged with smoke, his experienced eyes remaining on the crew hosing down the last sparks, he clapped Trevor on the back. "Didn't expect to see you this far out of the city."

"It's a slow week. How's the family?"

"Good, thanks."

Black smoke rose in thick plumes into the night sky. The firemen hosed down the dense foliage around the home to control the flames. Trevor spoke in a casual tone, coming at the topic he wanted to discuss in a roundabout technique that made his interviews less formal and more like speaking with a friend. "That home was over a hundred years old. Those old wooden beams must have gone up like straw."

"This fire burned hot and fast."

"Was it arson?" Trevor didn't ask about bodies. Any fool could see it was too soon to search through the smoldering embers.

"Someone poured a ring of accelerant around the perimeter."

The fire had been set. Whether it had been insurance fraud, murder, or to cover up another crime had yet to be determined.

Dan glanced at him and kept his tone low. "Of course that's not official until our investigator—"

"Understood." Trevor surveyed the crowd that congregated beyond the fire trucks. Most looked on with sadness, as if realizing the old home's historic value could never be replaced. But was one of those faces of sorrow a mask that hid an arsonist or a murderer? Had the person responsible for the blaze returned to the scene to see if his fire had trapped Jules Makana, Shara Weston, and Cade Archer inside?

Trevor suspected the arsonist had been after the movie actress and her male friend. It seemed too much of a coincidence that an enemy of Jules's could have burned down the home on the very same night her famous guest and the mystery man who'd sold the rubies had arrived. At the sounds of shouting, Trevor's gaze again turned to the crowd.

A native Hawaiian man in a torn shirt shoved past a throng of bystanders, ripping past the arms of an older female who tried to hold him back. She might as well have been trying to stop a whale. The guy was big, solid muscle, covered with extra layers of fat. Yet it wasn't his size, but his red eyes and the tears pouring down his face that held Trevor's attention.

Dan moved to intercept the Hawaiian before he could near the smoking blaze. "Sir, can I help you?"

"Jules." The man's voice broke in anguish. "Is she . . . was she . . . in there?"

"We don't know. You part of the family or a friend of hers?" Dan asked.

Trevor remained silent, observing. The Hawaiian's distress was clear but Trevor saw fear in his eyes and perhaps guilt, too. The man's shirt had two torn buttons and grass stains smeared across his chest and belly, as if he'd rolled in the dirt. A long, ugly, and recent scratch still oozed along his forearm. Perhaps most significantly, his breath reeked of stale beer.

"Jules and I . . . uh . . . I was just here. We fought. I left and when I came back . . ." He gestured to the fire. "I found . . ."

"Sir. What's your name?"

"Lou. Lou Smith."

"So Lou, what did you and Jules fight about?" Dan asked.

"I wanted to get back together. I would have convinced her, too." His face hardened, his meaty fingers closed into tight fists, and his voice deepened in frustration. "Except her friends were protecting her. In front of them, she couldn't forgive me."

"Why did she need to forgive you?" Dan pressed.

Lou rubbed his teary eyes on his torn shirtsleeve. "Doesn't matter. But she would have loved me again—if only they hadn't been around."

"Is that Jules's car?" Dan pointed to a charred white sedan.

"Yeah."

"Did Shara Weston and Cade Archer come in another vehicle?" Trevor asked.

Dan raised his eyebrows at Trevor's mention of Shara Weston. Apparently he hadn't known about Jules's famous house guest or the male friend.

Lou shrugged, his tone belligerent. "I don't remember how many cars were around. I'd had a few beers and I was focused on Jules."

"So you were angry with her?" Dan pressed.

"More like she was angry with me."

"How'd you get that cut on your arm?"

"In a fight."

The Hawaiian spoke freely, as if he had nothing to hide or lacked the intelligence to understand that he might be implicating himself in a crime.

"Who did you fight with? Jules?" Dan asked.

"No. Shara's friend. At first, I thought the guy was seeing Jules and I was jealous. I came back to apologize for being an idiot. And I found . . ."

"Is that your vehicle?"

Lou's swollen eyes rounded on Dan and, for the first time, revealed suspicion. "Yeah, I drive a fuel truck. Mostly I supply diesel to big machines, but I also carry a gasoline tank in the bed for our generators." His eyes narrowed as if he realized he was a suspect. "But hey, I couldn't have done it, the tank's full."

"Then you wouldn't mind coming down to the station with me to get to the bottom of this?" Dan asked.

"Sure. I want to know who would hurt Jules."

Dan nodded to one of his men. Trevor assumed they'd call over a police detective. Trevor had listened to Lou, but wasn't certain if he believed him. Lou did have the means, motive and opportunity to set the fire, but whenever he'd spoken of Jules, it had been with love.

Still, love caused men to do strange things. Maybe, the big guy had snapped.

And if he hadn't set the fire, who had?

"Sir," one of the firemen strode over to Dan. "There doesn't appear to be any evidence of bodies."

"Thank the Lord." Lou sagged to the ground, dropped his head into his hands, and cried tears of relief.

Unless he was the best actor in the world, Trevor now believed he was innocent—although he still could be wrong, he'd been so before. While it was possible that Jules herself could have set the fire, one thing was for certain: with an accelerant around the perimeter this fire was no accident.

To find answers, he needed to talk to Jules, Shara, and Cade, and he had no idea where they'd gone. A resourceful reporter, Trevor had his work cut out for him, but if he was lucky, someone would recognize Shara Weston and the gossip would eventually reach him. Meanwhile, Trevor would put out feelers across the island, tapping into his established network of sources.

They'd turn up. Sensing a big story, he would follow.

A few hours ago Shara had thought her life was over. The walls had caught fire and the blaze ripped across the plaster with astonishing speed. Above their heads, the ceiling had sizzled and popped. Sheets of flame had blocked the only escape out the broken window. Smoke, black as hell, had pummeled her lungs.

Jules had cried out, "We're going to burn."

Then the inexplicable occurred.

Cade yanked Shara and Jules close to him. Voice full of gravel and smoky low, he muttered in a language she couldn't understand, then switched to English. "Stay close. We can survive."

Yeah, right.

"Walk with me to the window," he instructed.

"What for?" Jules asked.

As if a wind current had blown in to clear out the flames, a pocket of air around them suddenly cleared. But the roar of flames and burning wood signaled the roof was caving. Shara ducked her head; however, nothing fell on Cade, her, Jules, or Kapuna, who Jules had tried to protect by wrapping him in a towel.

"Keep going," Cade urged them forward.

As they advanced through the flames, the burning wood on the floor in front of them hissed and oddly subsided.

Had Shara already died and gone to hell? Nothing made sense. The clear pocket of air. The burning ceiling falling down and missing them. The material under their feet that had ceased to burn or even feel warm.

Together, they moved toward the hellish wall of flame. But there was no heat. No stray sparks. No smoke.

Staying side-by-side, they climbed through the window, walked right through the fire, their skin unblistered as they passed the reeking stench of burning fuel. As if they were ghosts, not one spark caught on their clothes, the fire didn't touch them.

Mystified, elated, Shara glanced at Cade for answers but he'd turned gray. His entire body shook and his chest heaved with effort as sweat poured off him, convincing her he'd done something to save them.

"Are you all right?"

He grunted a "yes." At least she hoped it was a "yes."

They staggered from the fire toward the rental car. After breathing in the stench of fuel, she was certain someone had set that fire, intending to trap them inside. And she didn't plan to stick around so the arsonist could learn he'd failed.

Jules halted on the front lawn, uncovered her pet, who seemed no worse for his escape from death. She petted the cat and looked back at her burning house, tears making rivulets on her soot-smudged face.

"Don't stop walking," Shara ordered Jules, knowing her friend had to be devastated by the loss of her precious home. But now was not the time to grieve. First they had to be safe. And that wouldn't be until they'd disappeared.

They'd almost reached the rental vehicle, when Cade crumpled to the grass. Kapuna leapt from Jules's arms. Jules didn't seem to notice. She'd again turned to watch her house burn, her shocked eyes full of tears.

"Jules." Shara grabbed her shoulder and turned her from the ugly sight. "Help me drag Cade to the car."

Jules ignored Shara's request and asked, "How did we

walk through fire?"

"I don't know."

Jules glanced at Cade. "What happened to him?"

"I don't know that, either." Frustrated by the inexplicable, worried by his collapse, Shara knelt beside Cade. "Maybe he inhaled too much smoke." Leaning forward, she placed her cheek near his lips and felt him exhale a breath.

Jules frowned. "Is he going to die?"

"He's still breathing, and he's got a pulse. Help me get him to the car," she asked again.

Jules shook her head. "Maybe we should leave him."

"Didn't you smell the gasoline? Someone set your house on fire and they likely knew we were inside. They wanted us to die in that inferno and they may come back to make sure they succeeded. If they find us . . . they'll know they failed. Maybe they'll try again."

"What about stopping him from completing his mission?" Jules's words might have sounded cruel, but it cost her to say them. She shook, couldn't meet Shara's eyes.

"Cade just saved our lives. I'm not leaving him to die. And neither are you."

"Okay. Okay." Jules moved to Cade's other side. Each of them took an arm and they dragged him across the grass. Kapuna trailed after their feet.

Cade regained consciousness just in time to help them remove the pack from his back and slide him into the car's rear seat. But he kept mumbling in his native language. His head rolled to the side and his muscles twitched.

"You drive," Shara instructed.

"Keys?" Jules picked up Kapuna and placed him in the passenger seat.

Shara climbed into the backseat and eased Cade's head in her lap. With his big body scrunched up, Cade couldn't be comfortable but Shara didn't want to wait for an ambulance. "How long will it take to drive to the hospital?"

"Thirty minutes to an hour depending on traffic. I can't recall how many cruise ships are in town today." Jules backed out, hit the pavement, shifted into drive, and careened around a corner.

"No hospital," Cade groaned and opened his eyes.

Shara smoothed his soot streaked hair from his forehead. "You need medical attention."

"Need salt," he whispered, his voice choked with pain.

"What?" Shara bent over to hear him muttering.

"Salt."

She straightened and spoke to Jules. "He says he needs salt."

"He's half out of his mind." Jules sped down the road, throwing up a cloud of dust behind them.

"Maybe not." Shara recalled his strange reaction to alcohol and how he'd ingested large quantities of salt with every meal. Obviously his body chemistry was different from theirs. "Since he's been here, he's eaten an extraordinary amount of salt. Maybe his efforts to save us from the fire depleted his store of energy."

"Fine. We'll stop at the first fast-food joint up the road. But if salt doesn't work—"

"We go straight to the hospital," Shara agreed.

But the fast-food joint had closed for the night. "Now what?" Jules asked.

Cade had closed his eyes again. His breathing seemed as erratic as his pulse that throbbed in his neck. When she spied a rest stop up ahead with the lights on, she pointed. "Stop there."

"I doubt they have salt."

"Yeah, but they should have potato chips in the vending machines."

"No chips. Salt." Cade spoke without opening his eyes. At least he remained conscious but Shara could tell talking taxed his strength.

"Trust me. You'll love potato chips."

Jules parked. "My purse . . ." She wet her lip and started again. "I don't have any money, do you?"

Shara shook her head. Cade's hand dropped to his pack. "Here." She'd forgotten he had cash stashed in his pack.

Leaning down, she unzipped and handed Jules some money. "Buy every bag of chips in the machines and some bottled water to wash it all down."

A minute later, Jules returned with an armful of snacks. Shara opened a bag of plain chips and placed one between Cade's lips. "Eat."

Obediently he opened his mouth. She slipped the chip between his teeth and watched in satisfaction as he chewed and broke into a blissful smile. "Good. More, please."

She'd fed him chips until he'd revived enough to sit up and stuff huge handfuls into his mouth. Kapuna leapt into the backseat and mopped up the crumbs, but not even the cat could keep up.

Shara warned Cade. "Hey, if you don't slow down, you'll give yourself a stomachache."

He shook his head. "Do you have any idea how good these chips taste?"

She laughed in relief. "You keep eating like that and you'll get fat."

"On Rama, no one is fat."

"Are there food shortages?" Shara asked puzzled. She didn't understand how his people possessed the technology to undertake space travel but not have enough resources to feed their people.

"Salt is the catalyst that lets our bodies digest nutrients. We don't have enough to go around."

"What about the Firsts? None of them ever eat too much?"

"They burn up the calories with mental effort."

"What kind of mental effort?" When he'd described the Firsts' powerful minds before, they'd sounded pampered. Were they intellectuals? Shara desperately needed to grasp the basics of his culture. It would be so much easier to work against Cade if she better understood the Firsts whose cause she would be helping if she stopped his mission.

"Firsts control the rest of us with mental domination. We call their ability *Quait*."

"What?" She tried to keep revulsion from her tone, but

even with her acting skills, she failed to disguise her extreme distaste.

Cade's matter-of-fact tone only made his revelation more sickening. "Using *Quait,* they can make us do whatever they like."

"Anything?" She raised her brow in skepticism, horrified at even the idea of helping such monsters.

"Anything. Even murder." His tone grew serious but he kept eating the chips. The supply that she'd figured would last a week was almost gone.

"So if the Firsts are all powerful," Jules asked from the front seat, "how did you escape?"

"They can't read minds. We kept our plans a secret. What they didn't know about, they couldn't stop."

"So why doesn't Jamar just walk up to you, do his mental *Quait* thing and stop you?"

"I'm not sure. Our scientists theorized that the First's powers might be weaker on a world like Earth. Apparently your salty environment prevents Jamar from employing his full mental powers or I wouldn't stand a chance against him."

"Does his strength over you depend upon proximity to us?" Shara asked.

"Perhaps. I don't know. Ramans have never been here before."

"What about us?" Jules asked.

Cade frowned. "What about you?"

Jules's tone filled with revulsion. "Can Jamar control Terrans the way he controls people on Rama?"

"I don't have all the answers." Cade didn't seem particularly worried, but Shara caught Jules's expression in the rearview mirror. Her eyes were hard. Clearly, Jules believed that if Shara didn't stop Cade, Jamar would bring untold terror to Earth. With even partially working mental powers combined with his superior technology, he and his people might be able to enslave every man, woman, and child on the planet.

But if Shara stopped Cade from building his portal, Jamar would likely go home and abandon Earth. At least that was Jules's implication. But after seeing the rich salt deposits available on Earth, would Jamar really leave and never return?

Now that Cade was able to talk, Shara wanted more answers. Although she was very grateful that they were alive, she wanted to know how they had walked through flames that should have charred the flesh from their bones.

"Cade, does anyone besides your Firsts have mental powers?"

"Not on Rama." He stopped eating and stared out the window, avoiding her gaze. "My people believe, or *most* believe, that Firsts are special born and deserve the majority of the salt due to their abilities."

"So *you* have no special mental abilities?"

"No."

"Then how did you survive the crash into the ocean? You fell thousands of feet without a parachute and sustained no life-threatening injury, just a dislocated shoulder."

Cade's eyes narrowed. "There are people on your world who have survived such a fall, yes?"

"Yes, but those people didn't also walk through a wall of fire without so much as scorching their eyebrows."

At her words, Cade turned his head to look at her, his eyes clouded with confusion, or denial. "Are you suggesting, I . . . that I could have . . ."

"Saved yourself from the impact into the ocean and again saved us from the fire with some kind of mental ability." Surely, Cade had to be a little more conscious of his mental powers than he was admitting or he wouldn't have known how to save them? Unless the power was instinctive and didn't require conscious thought, because he sure didn't appear to be acting.

"But that's not possible. I'm not a First."

"Maybe all that salt you're eating is changing you into one of them," Jules suggested.

"Never." Revulsion and horror tightened his face. "I'd rather end my life than turn into a First."

"Whoa . . . let's slow down here," Shara suggested.

"You don't understand," Cade's voice filled with dread and disgust, "on Rama, Firsts take pleasure in cruelty. I have seen the Firsts compel men to rape. I've seen men and women coerced into killing their brothers and sisters and children—all for the Firsts' amusement." He closed his eyes but not before she read his agony. "I have seen little children . . . the children go hungry and live in constant fear of . . ."

"Stop it." Shara couldn't stand his emotional pain, which was even worse than watching him when he'd suffered from the lack of salt. "Just because you may be gaining some of their *Quait* powers doesn't mean you'll have their moral values."

"Power corrupts," Jules muttered. "Absolute power corrupts absolutely."

"Not necessarily," Shara argued.

"On Rama, it is true," Cade's tone turned sad, then determined. "Before I turn into a First, I shall end my life."

"I'll bet the rest of your people won't be so noble," Jules sneered. "If you build that portal, they'll come here. Enslave us."

"I will not let that happen," Cade told her.

Jules snorted and rolled her eyes at the car's ceiling.

Cade ignored her skepticism. "But in the meantime, the extra mental strength is a tool that I will use to fight Jamar. On Rama, Jamar would hold every advantage. On Earth, perhaps I can defeat my brother."

Jules's expression turned fierce and dark. "Are there any other Ramans on Earth besides you and Jamar?"

Jules must be thinking about the volcanologist. Shara held her breath, waiting for Cade's response.

"I thought I would be the only one from my world to come here. But if Jamar made it, it's possible there are others here, too, but not likely."

Jules accused him, "And when more of you Ramans do come to Earth—"

"That's not the plan."

"—you'll turn our world into a battle ground. You'll pull us into your confrontation. Destroy us all, rip us apart."

"That is not my intention."

"Your plans and intentions don't matter." Jules glared at Cade in the mirror. "Your actions speak for themselves."

7

✵

"**R**eport," Jamar ordered his private investigator, beckoning the lackey into his hotel suite.

"Good afternoon, sir." As Tom Grayson stepped through the office threshold, Jamar's latest whore made a gesture to pull together the tear in her blouse.

Jamar had been celebrating his victory over killing Cade by tormenting the female. His luck had changed for the better when Cade had activated the locator beacon before the fire had taken his life. Now Jamar could follow the signal to the Dead Sea, engage it to set off the next beacon, and then the next—before he headed home, his mission accomplished. With Cade reduced to ashes, Jamar was in no huge rush to go after the beacon until he finished tying up some loose ends here in Hawaii.

"I didn't give you permission to move," Jamar snapped at the woman.

As her eyes lowered in misery and she dropped her hands to her side, he gloated at her submission.

Jamar applied the pressure of his mind to force Grayson's eyes only on him—not because he gave a damn if the PI saw

the partially-naked twit, but because it amused him to prolong her embarrassment. Even though she was dumber than
a stick, even she had to realize that after he dismissed the PI,
he'd get an eyeful on his way out.

With Grayson's eyes forced front and center due to the
power of Jamar's mind, the PI's expression showed confusion over his limited mobility but nevertheless he stuck to
business. "I'm afraid the news isn't very good."

"Be precise." Jamar's confidence of success and the expec-
tation of going home to receive accolades from his cohorts
began to fade. He'd been certain his luck had changed, but
nothing on this infernal planet ever seemed to go as planned.

"I checked with the arson investigator. The house burned
to the ground."

"But?"

"There were no casualties."

"What!" Jamar roared. Since he'd only trusted the natives' competence so far and couldn't afford a mistake, Jamar had dirtied his own hands to pour the ring of gasoline, a
messy, smelly task. And his brother Cade should have
burned alive—the only thing that could account for Jamar's
failure would have been Cade's increased powers. Ingesting
the salt on this world must be strengthening the underfirst
more quickly than Jamar had assumed. "Are you certain?"

"The fire chief assured me personally that his crew found
no bones in the ashes."

"So what happened to the former occupants?"

"No one knows."

"Find out."

"There's the small matter of my expenses."

"I don't care what it costs. Just find them."

"Yes, sir."

"Well, what are you waiting for?" Jamar finally released
the man's muscles to his own control. "Get going."

"Yes, sir."

The private eye turned around. He caught sight of the twit
who had braced to endure her shame. But Jamar was no
longer in a mood to enjoy her humiliation.

If Cade wasn't dead, then the underfirst was on the way to the Dead Sea and had a head start. However, now that Cade had activated the beacon, Jamar knew exactly where he was heading. He could beat him to the stolen equipment and recover it himself, perhaps set an ambush. Cade might have ingested some salt and grown a bit stronger, but he was no match for Jamar's intelligence.

Cade no longer had his spaceship and would be forced to fly in inferior Earthly transportation. Jamar simply had to travel across this planet faster than his brother.

Cade tried and failed to sleep on the private jet during the flight from Hawaii to the mainland. Despite his exhaustion, the sudden appearance of his *Quait* powers had disturbed him too much to sleep. In all of Raman history, no underfirst had ever displayed any First abilities whatsoever. Although he had no idea if he was an aberration of nature, or if every underfirst who ingested enough salt would exhibit the same limited abilities he had, he couldn't stop his automatic self-loathing.

His newfound abilities had probably saved his life as well as those of Shara and Jules—yet every cell in him rebelled against the metamorphosis. During his entire thirty years of life, he'd loathed all Firsts on a level so basic that Cade didn't feel as if he could function until he came to terms with what was happening to him. Firsts were cruel, ruthless, and self-centered to the extreme. The idea that he would become like them, that he might lose sight of his goals, filled him with the deepest fear he'd ever faced.

His entire plan to send salt to his people, salt that would turn them all into Firsts, was flawed—unless they regulated their intake of salt. While he was certain that rationing could be accomplished with strict adherence to new laws, he couldn't take that option himself. He needed to gain as much *Quait* as possible to defeat Jamar, even if the idea sickened him.

Yet, perhaps the advantage had just shifted in his favor. If Cade adapted quickly, he might have a better shot at completing his mission. He'd seen the power of Firsts—all too often—and he didn't ever expect to approach their abilities. A First had total and full control of their powers all the time. Only the strongest of emotions activated Cade's own powers from dormancy. The rest of the time he remained his normal self and should be able to maintain his mental balance.

Shara distracted Cade's thoughts by opening her eyes and stretching her arms over her head. She arched her back and her breasts rose, causing the fabric to stretch and tighten across her chest. Before boarding the aircraft, the women had stopped at a souvenir stand and acquired clothing to replace their smoky shirts. Although Shara hadn't complained, hers was a tad too small. Disheveled and sleepy, she looked the perfect combination of sexy woman and sassy girl. And he couldn't help admiring the smooth skin of her flat stomach that teased just above the line of her jeans.

When she noticed the direction of his gaze, she tugged down her shirt, but the fabric wouldn't close the enticing gap, leaving a taunting inch of bare skin and saucy navel. Cade realized that this world might not have the technology that had produced the flight suit that would clothe him for another day or so, but it did have advantages . . . like a beautiful, intelligent woman.

Pressing a button in the arm of her seat, Shara spoke directly to the pilot, in a voice loud enough for Cade to hear but low enough not to awaken the sleeping Jules. "How long until we land in L.A.?"

The answer came back from the cockpit over the intercom. "Another half hour."

"Have you taken care of a limo?" Shara asked, her ability to make arrangements very useful.

"Everything's all set."

"Thanks."

"Why do you wish to stop on the coast?" Cade asked from the comfort of his leather seat. The private jet offered many luxuries: plumbing, a shower, food and drink, and the plush leather seats even reclined into beds. Since the plane possessed a range of three thousand miles, it was too soon to land. "Do we require fuel?"

"I need to see someone in L.A." Face tender, Shara tucked a blanket under Jules's chin. Her friend slept, her pet cradled in her arms, and she didn't waken as Shara covered her. Although Cade admired loyalty, he looked forward to the time when he and Shara would once again be alone and he could regain the closeness they'd shared on the island.

He, too, kept his tone low and reminded her, "It's imperative that we reach the signal as soon as possible."

"I understand. But I'd like to find out what happened at Jules's house."

Cade frowned. "I explained as best I could."

Shara's voice turned hard and determined, but the businesslike effect was spoiled as her T-shirt rose up over her belly again. "I'm not talking about *Quait*. I want to find out who burned down Jules's house."

"We don't have time. I will pay for the damage," he offered.

"Look." She crossed her arms over her chest. "It's not about money—although I'm sure Jules will appreciate the offer; insurance never covers everything."

"I don't understand."

"It's possible that someone else besides Jamar might have burned down Jules's house."

"It doesn't matter who burned down the house." He tried to control his impatience. She could go after the culprit later. He didn't have time for justice *or* retribution. Besides, he was certain the fire had been Jamar's doing. He didn't know how his brother had tracked him to Hawaii and Jules's house, but he was a resourceful First. Cade feared it wouldn't take Jamar long to find them again or figure out where they were headed and why. If Jamar used his spaceship instead of local planes, it might be impossible to stay ahead of him, but Cade was determined to travel as quickly as possible.

"Of course it matters who tried to kill us. It's possible the fire didn't have anything to do with your brother. Maybe someone is after me. Or Jules. It was her home."

"Why would anyone want to kill you?"

"During my life, I've been stalked twice. I've had death threats. My former profession . . . often drew out the nut-cases." He suspected that period in her life had been painful. Clearly, from the shortness of her breathing, the memories still bothered her. Then, as if regaining control, she squared her shoulders. "That was over for me five years ago, but some fans obsess and have long memories."

He changed the subject slightly. "And why would some-one be after Jules?"

"She's a psychic. Maybe one of her clients didn't like her reading. Maybe they think they can alter the future by taking out the messenger. Maybe they think she'll sell the family land if the house is gone. Or maybe they are just crazy. My point is that we need to know if we have more than just Ja-mar after us."

"How will stopping in L.A. give us this knowledge?"

"When I lived here, I hired a security company to protect me. They have many resources and I intend to hire them to investigate."

"This must be done in person?"

"Maybe not. But I also need to arrange for false identifica-tion and a disguise. For that, we must stop. Otherwise, we'll attract too much attention and make it too easy for Jamar to find us."

" 'Us'? He's not looking for you."

"If he's the one who burned down Jules's home, then he knows we're together. I can't have our every movement doc-umented in the press."

She was thinking ahead, making plans, but not including him in the process—as if she didn't trust him. "There's something else you aren't telling me."

Her mouth twisted in a small smile of acknowledgment. "My investigator, Teresa Alverez, might be able to find and track Jamar. It's possible Teresa and her team might stop Ja-mar for us."

"Jamar is too dangerous for your people to encounter di-rectly."

"Wouldn't it would help you to know more about Jamar?" Her eyes challenged his and he enjoyed seeing the sparkle back. Clearly taking the initiative agreed with her disposition. "Teresa's a good investigator. She can search for his base of operations, his whereabouts now, discover his contacts. Even finding out how long he's been here might be helpful."

"Perhaps," he agreed, but would the delay be worth the knowledge they might gain? Cade moved into the seat next to Shara. She had all their arrangements thought out. And when he'd accused her of hiding information from him, she hadn't hesitated to reveal her concern about Jamar. He'd also liked the way she kept saying "us"—as if she had a stake in the successful outcome of his mission. But he couldn't help feeling as if they hadn't quite regained the closeness they'd shared on Haven. Perhaps her realization of the dangers Jamar represented had made her pull away. Or did his *Quait* make her as uneasy as it did him?

How could a woman as famous as Shara Weston vanish on an island as small as Oahu? None of Trevor's snitches had caught sight of her. No rumors surfaced. Certain that she'd turn up soon—unless she was dead—Trevor shifted his attention to investigating Shara's past.

He hadn't needed to go farther than his computer and a Google search to find her meteoric rise documented in headlines from *Newsweek* to *People* to *The National Enquirer*. At age sixteen, Shara had ditched her rural small-town roots for the fame and glamour of Hollywood. Like most high-school dropouts, she didn't become an overnight star. She'd struggled in the usual jobs, waitressing and temping—but she managed her limited funds with the thrift of an accountant. Most girls blew their money on clothes, wheels, and men. Shara spent her hard-earned money on acting classes and it had paid off.

Shara and Bruce, already A-list celebs, became superstars and she'd spoken openly about her former alcoholism and how Bruce was the rock that made a sober lifestyle a full and happy one. Bruce had been a man of large gestures. On her twenty-first birthday, he'd given her a private jet.

Trevor scanned dozens of photographs of Shara and Bruce in Casablanca, Tibet, Tokyo, and Milan—departing the jet, climbing into limos, heading off to party in seaside mansions, skiing in exclusive resorts, or sunning on tropical islands with other stars like Brad Pitt and Julia Roberts. He read a tiny article about Shara earning her GED, of buying her folks a new home.

She might not have had a classic education but Shara had proved her intelligence in publicity, in choosing the right agent, manager, and husband. Film was one of the most competitive industries in the world and she had been the queen—until the terrible accident that had taken Bruce's life.

Then Shara had sold the jet, retreated to Haven and become a recluse, giving up her acting career, her lifestyle and her friends. He'd heard she now had an exclusive client list of actors who consulted her about which parts they should accept. Trevor wondered if she'd returned to Haven.

Trevor's cell phone rang. He checked caller ID and his eyebrows raised. His boss didn't usually work this late. "What's up?"

"Your pal at the fire department just faxed a report on the fire."

"And?"

"A chemical test on the accelerant has proven the octane that started the fire at Jules Makana's home matched the fuel in the ex-boyfriend's truck—however, the gas additive was different."

"Was the additive another accelerant?"

"Apparently not. Just an engine cleaner. The arson specialist doesn't think the boyfriend did it."

"Thanks." Trevor shut down the computer, picked up his jacket and headed out the door.

If Shara had taken Jules and Cade back to Haven, he'd drop his investigation. But if they hadn't returned to her private island, he wanted to know what she was up to. Between her coming out of seclusion, the fire, the rubies, and the mysterious Cade Archer, Trevor suspected far more was going on. But before he put the pieces together, he had to find Shara.

While Trevor drove to the private airport, he checked with the charter companies who offered flights throughout the South Pacific. No one admitted flying Shara Weston to Haven. But halfway through his list, he turned over a clue. Someone had hired a jet with only two hours' notice. The girl on the phone of Charter Air Island wouldn't give him specifics, but she'd been breathless with secrecy, suggesting someone important had chartered a recent flight.

Trevor hung up and drove to Charter Air Island's main hangar. Pretending to be the brother of one of the pilots, he learned that the fuel crews and mechanics hung out in the Sugar Cane Bar after their shifts. A short drive later, he parked at the ramshackle bar that blared pop music.

At this time of the early morning, the bartender appeared half asleep. The regulars nursed their beers and no one gave Trevor a second glance. It was the kind of place where the clientele minded their own business and ignored strangers. After he bought a few rounds, tongues loosened and he'd learned that Shara Weston, another woman, and a big man matching Cade's description had taken off and headed to the U.S. mainland.

He would have booked a flight right then but no one knew where they'd landed. Apparently the flight had had enough fuel to go halfway around the world. So Trevor intended to drill deeper, check the pilot's filed flight plan. His reporter's instincts jangled every nerve, certain there was a story here—especially since Shara had not returned to Haven. All he had to do was to keep digging and he'd find . . . another Pulitzer.

Teresa Alverez's office, one block off Rodeo Drive in Beverly Hills, possessed the kind of quiet, yet elegant appearance that inspired confidence. The double steel doors with polished silver handles opened on well-oiled hinges and

Teresa's efficient assistant ushered them into the study. Burning logs in the fireplace, a sumptuous leather couch with clean Italian lines, and custom cherry shelves lined with leather-bound books made the room almost homey.

Shara knew from previous visits that a scrambler and a jammer prevented eavesdropping. Teresa's efficient assistant carried a weapon, and security cameras manned by the best surveillance people money could buy kept the premises secure. Teresa had a reputation for hiring ex-FBI and CIA agents and Shara had been pleased with her previous work.

Dressed in impeccably tailored black slacks, a long-sleeved, V-neck white blouse, and a black pearl necklace, Teresa Alverez joined them. She'd pulled her hair back into a tight knot that emphasized her intelligent chocolate-brown eyes. Her assistant made certain everyone had coffee, tea, or water and then withdrew. Shara made introductions and told Teresa everything—from Cade's alien status to Jamar's mission to stop him, leaving out only one critical piece of information, Jules's prediction that if Shara didn't stop Cade from building the portal, disaster would occur.

Teresa's gaze rested on Cade. "What exactly do you want me to do for you?"

Cade returned her look, his expression neutral. "Shara said you could find Jamar or his base of operations."

"That's not going to be easy. Do you know what name he's using? Which country he's operating from?"

Cade shook his head.

"Do you have his picture?" Teresa asked. "A last known address? Or the name of places he frequents, people he knows or has hired?"

Cade shook his head and reached for a pad of paper and a pen on the table. "Would a sketch be helpful?"

Teresa shrugged and turned to Shara. "I'd like to help but you haven't given me anything to go on. Jamar's alien status means he has no history. No parents from Earth. No schools. Associations. Hobbies."

Shara refused to give up. "You found my stalker and we didn't have much then, either."

"But in that case we protected you until the stalker came out of hiding." Teresa drummed her fingers on the arm of her chair. "Why not let me protect you this time?"

"Because we have to move fast to locate the portal pieces and security measures will slow us down," Cade answered.

"Not necessarily," Teresa countered.

"And additional people will draw more attention to us. Shara and I can easily pretend to be a couple on vacation. A group will be noticed."

Shara noted how Cade had taken charge of the meeting. He wielded authority with an obvious poise that made it easy for her to leave the decision making to him. But she had her own reasons for not wanting a large contingent of people around. If she had to stop Cade, she figured it would be easier for him to relax and let down his guard with less eyes watching their every movement.

She hadn't come to Teresa for more than background help. Any intelligence her firm could dig up on Jamar might be helpful to stopping Cade's mission. At the moment, she only had Cade's side of the story and Jules's warning . . . a warning she'd taken to heart. A warning that made her sick every time she thought about how to stop such a determined man. If not for Jules's track record, Shara would have gone back to Haven.

So far Jules had said nothing since their arrival and Shara hoped that meant she had no feelings one way or another about Teresa's involvement. Jules's talents were always unpredictable and when they eluded her, she didn't pretend otherwise. However, her presence soothed Shara, who found her return to civilization jarring.

Shara had forgotten the temptations here, the pressure, the hurried pace. And everywhere they went, liquor stalked her. The jet plane had had a fully stocked bar. So had the limo. Her gaze flickered longingly to the cut-crystal liquor decanters on the sideboard filled with an expensive variety of alcohol. Not that she needed expensive to entice her—right now a cheap beer would take off the edge.

Interrupting Shara's cravings, Cade thrust his completed drawing at Teresa. "What do you think?"

The detailed picture depicted a handsome man a few years older than Cade. He wore his hair shorter and his mouth and eyes possessed the same shape as Cade's. If Shara had seen the two men side by side, she had no doubt that she'd have noticed the family resemblance. But where Cade's eyes were warm, Jamar's had the icy glare of a fanatic and his mouth twisted in a cruel smile.

"Are you an artist?" Shara asked. In just a few minutes, Cade had captured his brother's essence as well as his features, portraying a skill she hadn't known he possessed. She couldn't help wondering what else she didn't know about Cade. He didn't speak often about himself and she had no idea what kind of work he'd done on Rama.

Teresa studied the sketch and then raised her warm brown eyes to Cade. "Does this man share your skin coloring?"

"Yes."

"One of my people is a whiz at Photoshop. How about we take your picture and let her alter your features to match this sketch and see how close she can get?"

"Fine," Cade agreed. "Just keep in mind that Jamar must be observed from a distance and cannot know your people are watching him. He won't hesitate to kill."

Teresa didn't call in an assistant and Shara suspected that the moment Cade had agreed, Teresa had the artist snap the picture from a camera already hidden in the room. But ever since Teresa had saved her life from the stalker, Shara had trusted her, as well as the discretion of her employees.

"What else can you tell me about Jamar?" Teresa asked.

Cade didn't hesitate. "Jamar's intelligent. A fine athlete. And he abides by no rules. Think of a sociopath with super-human strength and keen intelligence." Cade went on to describe *Quait* and Jamar's abilities to use mind control.

Teresa crossed her legs and leaned forward, her expression intent. "But finding this man without more to go on than a description is like looking for one superstar among all the aspiring actresses on Hollywood Boulevard. Unless we get lucky, I don't have much hope of finding him from just a picture—especially if he's altered his appearance since you saw him last."

"That's unlikely," Cade said. "He's too arrogant to bother hiding his features since he believes we can't stop him."

"Teresa, you'll do your best?" Shara asked.

"Of course. But why don't we try to flush him out of hiding?"

Shara liked the way Teresa thought. She much preferred to take action than to flee without knowing where and when Jamar would attack again. "What do you have in mind?"

"I've brought in people to disguise your identity. But before they go to work—why don't we let the paparazzi find you?"

"Why?" Shara asked, not liking that idea at all. One of the boons of living on Haven was that the paparazzi were no longer part of her life. Inviting them back sounded almost sacrilegious.

"We'll use the press and then observe who comes looking for you. Maybe Jamar will show up and then we can tail him."

Cade frowned. "Your plan sounds dangerous. Jamar will be looking for a trap and advertising our whereabouts will make it easier for him to find us."

"Hear me out," Teresa said.

Shara looked at Jules to see if she had any psychic feelings one way of another, but her friend merely shrugged and petted her cat. "What do you propose?"

"I'll leak your whereabouts to the press. By the six o'clock news, I'll have planted a rumor that you're in town to attend Spielberg's premiere."

"We can't stay that long," Cade protested.

"I don't expect you to stay." Teresa grinned. "After the paparazzi spot Shara, you switch hotels, change your appearance and fly out of town. My people will video the crowd at the premiere's runway tomorrow night and see if we can find anyone who looks like your brother. But if we do spot him, we keep our distance and follow."

"Sounds like a plan. I like it." Shara stood and shook Teresa's hand, refusing to look at the liquor decanters that would fortify her for the encounter with the press. "Let the paparazzi know we'll check into the Beverly Hills Hotel within the hour."

8

"**W**hy are we stopping?" Cade frowned as Shara asked their limo driver to pull up in front of a store. He'd assumed they'd drive straight to the hotel.

"We need to shop. You need a suit. I need a facial, a manicure, a pedicure, and to have my hair cut and styled. If my face is going to be splashed across the world, I intend to look good."

Jules grinned and her eyes lit with teasing. "Not even you can get ready in an hour."

Cade refrained from rolling his eyes at the ceiling, a gesture he'd learned Terrans often used when frustrated, but he couldn't contain his sigh at yet another delay. He hadn't seen the vain movie star part of her before, and he certainly didn't approve. His mission was critical to millions of peoples' lives and she wanted to stop to do her nails?

He considered going on without her, then reminded himself that retrieving the portal parts without her island and volcano would do him no good. He trailed behind the woman as they entered the Spa, a place that smelled of unusual and exotic spices.

A fountain of water gurgled in the Spa's lobby. Polished marble floors, decorated wooden beams on the ceilings, and the soft music gave the area a luxurious and exclusive feel. A man dressed in a black suit with a light blue shirt and a yellow tie looked up, caught sight of Shara and sashayed over. Cade couldn't help but stare. Dressed like a man, he nevertheless moved with a feminine grace and his squeal of delight sounded absolutely girlish.

The man squeezed Shara in a quick embrace. "Sweetie, Shara. Where have you been hiding yourself? By that exquisite tan, I see you're still living on that savage island."

"George. Good to see you—and Haven's a wonderful place."

"If you say so." George made it very clear he didn't believe her. "But my God, what have you done to your hair?"

"Nothing." Shara laughed. "And I'm only giving you one hour to work your magic on me and my friends."

Cade shook his head. "I don't need any work."

George's interested gaze gave him a thorough going-over from head to toe and then he nodded approvingly. "Shara, where did you find him? He's absolute perfection."

Clearly George didn't expect an answer. He strode to his desk and called in his assistants—six of them—who ushered them into a back room. Within minutes, George was cutting Shara's hair. Others worked on her hands and feet and face, while still more people did the same to Jules, a gift from Shara.

Cade was offered a comfortable chair, a newspaper, a drink, and little cookies that he could pop into his mouth without taking a bite. Someone came by and measured him for clothes, but they otherwise left him alone.

These people looked as if they considered it an honor to speak with Shara. Cade could see the admiration, excitement, and respect in the workers' eyes, and it startled him. On Rama those who served did so because they must to survive. But here, it was clearly different. From the look of adoration on the manicurist's face, he suspected she'd be telling her friends and family about her encounter with a star for many years.

That Shara garnered so much respect for her work made him all the more curious why she lived on Haven. Yes, he'd read about the tragedy, but why did she choose to punish herself for an accident? Why did she take herself away from her own kind and a work that garnered so much adoration?

While Shara and George conversed, a bevy of young and beautiful people brought out clothing items and Shara shopped for shoes, slacks, shirts, coats, belts, jewelry, purses, hats, and sleep clothes as well as underclothing for all of them. Cade was most amused by her underclothing of filmy lace, and as he imagined Shara's body wrapped in one provocative item after another his discomfort grew, reminding him that never in his adult life had he gone so long without a woman.

To hide his arousal, he crossed his legs and set the newspaper over his lap. But his gaze returned to Shara again and again. Although Jules sat beside her, undergoing much the same treatment, she didn't glow like Shara. Before his eyes, Shara transformed from a beautiful woman . . . to a gorgeous work of art.

Her haircut, the styling, the makeup, and finally a change into a simple delicious black outfit, the bodice wrapping across her chest, had altered her into a goddess. And the dress looked as if it would slip off her shoulders at any moment, since the tiny shoulder straps barely kept it on. Shara had morphed into a creature so stunning, he stared in amazement.

What the hell was wrong with him? Cade couldn't ever recall a woman's beauty fascinating him the way Shara's did. When he contrasted this sophisticated beauty to the dripping wet one who'd fished him out of the sea, he couldn't say which image of her he preferred more. But Cade couldn't deny she intrigued, compelled, and captivated every soul in the room—even the effeminate man who had looked at Cade with hungry eyes.

When Shara's gaze found Cade's, she must have seen the approval there, or perhaps his simple lust, because her eyes brightened to match the dusting of sparkles that now graced her shoulders. He had to fight to keep his eyes focused on her face instead of her chest, where every man in sight must be imagining her skimpy shirt falling off to reveal . . . more.

Jules went to change her clothing. The assistants and George vanished and Shara walked over to him. Cade's mouth went dry. He couldn't take his gaze off her, because something had changed besides the hair and makeup and clothing. It was if Shara had slipped into a role of pure glamour.

As she neared, he breathed in her scent, a scandalous mix of spices and a salty tang that he found irresistible. She knew she looked fantastic. She knew how she affected him. He read the confidence in the angle of her head, in the set of her jaw, in the poise of her stance and the sexy sway of her hips.

"You've transformed into someone I barely recognize."

She arched one delectable eyebrow. "You sound as if you don't entirely approve."

Cade's voice came out deep and sincere. "There's not a man anywhere that wouldn't approve." He shot her his most charming grin and offered his arm to escort her from the premises.

She hesitated. "It's a role I play."

"And you do it very well." He let her hear his genuine admiration. At the same time he wondered if he'd ever really know this woman. Such a fabulous actress could hide behind a thousand masks. Was she the suspicious and practical woman he'd met on the island? The courageous woman who'd been terrified in the fire but who'd still kept her head while facing death? Or the superbly confident superstar actress on his arm?

Had she shown him different facets of the real Shara or were they all roles she'd played? And why did he believe she was keeping secrets from him? Important secrets?

Cade had lived in a world where his instincts had kept him alive and away from the wrath of the Firsts. He'd honed his perceptive instincts to observe the tiniest details and realized that Shara Weston was a master of her craft. With her by his side, he believed he could accomplish anything.

* * *

"Damn it, Shara, you like him." Jules had cornered Shara in the Spa's ladies' room.

"You have to admit, there's a lot to like," Shara quipped, but when she noted Jules's fierce expression her smile ebbed. "He saved our lives in that fire."

"You can't let your feelings stop you." Jules's troubled eyes brimmed with tears. "What I saw this time . . . my vision was too strong to be a false path."

She'd had another vision and Shara's gut plummeted. "When did you—"

"On the airplane. I wasn't sleeping. But I was drawn in so deep that I couldn't break out." Jules shuddered and grabbed her arm, her fingers gripping so tightly, Shara winced. "You must believe me."

"Of course, I believe you. But even you have told me we can change what you see by altering our actions."

"That's why I'm praying you can stop him. Because if you can't . . ."

"What exactly did you see?"

Shara had often seen Jules upset. Her friend usually wore her emotions on her expressive face for all to read. Those emotions helped convey her visions. But Shara had never seen her so wild-eyed and yet determined.

"Everything was red. Red blood. Red flames. Red lava. Red explosions and dust clouds covering the sky. It was like a vision of hell . . ."

"Maybe it was—and has nothing to do with us."

"No." Jules swallowed hard.

"What do you mean, 'no'?"

"You and Cade were there, too."

"On Haven?"

Jules closed her eyes and spoke in a low whisper. "You and Cade were both covered in blood."

Shara's mouth went dry. "Jamar?"

Jules shook her head.

"What about you?"

Again Jules shook her head. Her face paled.

"What aren't you telling me?"

"I was watching the vision . . . from the ground. I wasn't moving, wasn't looking at you. It looked as if I was dead."

"Jules," Shara took her friend into her arms. Jules released a sob and shook. Shara held her tight. "Maybe you just had a nightmare."

"Don't p-patronize me. I know what I saw."

"Okay, okay. But how do we know what you saw is the result of me failing to stop Cade?"

"Huh?" Jules sniffled, reached for a paper towel and dabbed at her running mascara. "Damn. When George sees what I've done to his makeup artist's work, he's going to kill me."

"Jules, maybe I'm supposed to help Cade."

"No. I saw Cade toss a shiny ball of metal into the volcano and it set off ground-shaking explosions. I'm not sure, but I am certain that you were horrified. Cade's eyes were full of sorrow. Cade's shoulders were bloody. Fire and lava exploded around him and you. And I looked . . . dead."

"Oh . . . God. I won't be responsible for your death."

"Thanks. I'm never sure how to interpret my visions. You know that. But this one was powerful. As clear as any I've ever seen. Worse than the one of Bruce. When I saw your husband die, I saw a gun, but I didn't know it was you who would pull the trigger or that he was the man who would die. It's not just my own death that worries me. Yours, too."

Jules's reminder shook Shara all over again. If she'd listened to Jules, if she hadn't tried to make that last film, Bruce would still be alive. And now here she was, doubting her friend all over again, simply because she didn't want to stop Cade—wasn't certain if she *could* stop him—even if their lives depended on it.

"Can you tell me anything else?"

"I saw a ring of fire . . . and the Pacific Rim is a volcanic ring. It's almost as if Cade's going to set off a chain reaction through every volcano in the Pacific."

Shara winced. If Jules was right, that meant those who

survived the volcanic eruptions would suffer from tidal waves, earthquakes, and flooding.

"Call my cell if you have another vision," Shara instructed, knowing they would have to separate soon. She and Cade would go to the hotel and allow the paparazzi to "surprise" them. Jules would take a taxi back to the plane and fly to Montana in the middle of the night, and George had volunteered to watch Jules's cat.

Hopefully, when the press discovered Shara was gone, they'd assume she'd continued on the same charter jet as Jules.

But she and Cade would leave much sooner.

Shara had forgotten how much she'd hated the multitude of camera flashes and microphones thrust into her face. But she pasted on her best diva look and gave the press a regal nod. When a reporter planted himself between Cade and the hotel's front door and snapped his photo, she had to give Cade credit for keeping his cool.

Another reporter in a red suit, black blouse, and running shoes jammed a microphone in Cade's face. "Are you the reason Shara Weston has come out of retirement?"

"You'll have to ask her." Cade's tone remained polite but his muscles tensed.

"Have you popped the question?"

"What question?" Cade raised an intimidating eyebrow and Shara realized that as good as his English was, there were idioms and expressions he didn't understand.

"Shara, are you pregnant?"

"When's the baby due?"

"Ms. Weston, are you playing the Scarlet O'Hara role in the remake of *Gone with the Wind*?"

"Is Cade your next leading man?"

Cade chuckled at that one, but he looked the part in the designer dark suit they'd bought, tailored to show off his towering height and the breadth of his shoulders. At the last reporter's comment, Shara shook her head and kept walking, glad that he could keep his sense of humor through the photoflash attack. Already her head ached and her eyes throbbed.

Tomorrow's papers would have her married, pregnant, and fat with triplets, or anorexic and on her deathbed, broke or starting her comeback—whatever headline the editor thought would sell the most "news." But however much she disliked the questions, a small part of her took pride that in a world where one was only as good as one's last picture, after five years, Shara Weston had not been forgotten.

When the hotel's bellman opened the door to the lobby, a reporter for one of the sleazy rags stepped into their path. Cade tried to sidestep him, but the reporter shifted and blocked their way.

Cade spoke softly, but any fool would have heard the edge in his tone. "Please move. Shara would like to check in."

Apparently the reporter had less sense than the average fool. He winked and tried to look down Shara's shirt. "Will that be one room or two?"

Shara kept her haughty diva look and murmured to Cade, "Ignore him."

Cade bristled. "How? He's in our way."

Sensing neither man was about to yield, she snapped open her cell phone. "This is harassment. I'm calling the police."

The reporter didn't budge. Her threat failed.

Cade released her elbow and placed his hands on the reporter's waist. Then he lifted the man until his feet dangled above the sidewalk, before he set him to one side, gently lowering him back to his feet. At the tremendous display of strength, flashbulbs popped, and Shara laughed as if the incident were a joke, pretending the situation couldn't possibly explode into a fistfight.

The reporter smirked. "That's assault. I'll sue you for this."

"Go right ahead and sue," Cade spoke clearly over his shoulder as they finally entered the hotel, "I don't have any assets."

At his bluff and the reporter's glare, she figured it was a good thing the reporter didn't know about the cash in Cade's backpack or his hefty bank account. Shara's headache pounded and she welcomed the cool air from the lobby. Right now, she'd love a drink. Second best, she'd like to be back on Haven. As if knowing how tight her neck muscles had clenched, Cade placed his hand on her shoulder and gently kneaded as they entered the lobby.

She leaned against his solid side, grateful that hotel security prevented the paparazzi from following into the lobby. Still, mindful that a guest could snap a photo and sell it to the rags, she kept smiling.

The efficient staff checked them into the penthouse suite—five rooms with a flat-screen television and fresh flowers in every one, plus a soaking tub in the bathroom large enough for two. The plan was to order up dinner, change into their disguises, flee out the back exit and vanish before the paparazzi camping out front discovered they'd left the premises.

The moment after the bellman delivered Shara's purchases from the Spa and left them in privacy, Cade turned to her. "What's wrong?"

"Nothing."

"Do you need salt?" he persisted.

"Salt?"

"You look . . . depleted."

"Damn. My first pubic appearance in five years and I look depleted? You sure know how to dish out a compliment."

Concern darkened his eyes. "You look beautiful on the outside. But inside . . . you are in pain, yes?" He pulled out a plush chair for her. "Sit."

She sank, grateful for the pampering, surprised he'd seen through the glamorous facade to her discomfort. Either her acting skills were slipping, or he possessed an extremely fine-tuned sense of observation. And she'd received many compliments in her day, but none as casual as his off the cuff, "You look beautiful" remark that started a nice warm buzz, almost as good as a shot of whiskey.

"I'm fine really. Flashbulbs give me a headache."

"And salt won't help?"

"No, but scotch would."

"Scotch?"

Her gaze automatically went to the stocked bar. She licked her bottom lip and resisted temptation once again with a sigh of frustration. On Haven she'd settled into a routine that didn't cause so many cravings. With one unpleasant situation after another to deal with, her need for the soothing balm of alcoholic numbness escalated.

"Water and an aspirin will have to suffice."

Cade brought her bottled water and a glass, then fetched an aspirin from her purse. Without asking permission, he stood behind her chair and began to knead out the knots between her shoulder blades. "Why do you not drink the scotch when you obviously want it?"

If his hands hadn't kept kneading her shoulders, she might have leaped out of her seat. "I don't want to talk about it."

"All right. Can we talk about my problem then?"

"Your need for salt?" She leaned into the pressure of his hands. Between the aspirin and the magic of his clever fingers, her headache was receding. It had been much too long since a man had touched her, caressed her, held her in protective arms. Under Cade's attention her skin absorbed his touch like cracked leather soaked up baby oil. Each stroke of his warm hands ricocheted through her system, jolting needs she'd thought long dead.

And if Cade could excite her with such seductive strokes to just her shoulders, what could his marvelous hands make the rest of her feel?

"My need is for a woman. I am not accustomed to holding back and your nearness is affecting my judgment."

"Really?" So she hadn't been wrong about his eyes flaring with interest, and a thrill of excitement made her aware that the two of them were alone for the first time since they'd left Haven and in a hotel with a plush king-size bed.

"It's difficult for me to remember my mission when all I can think about is making love to you." He admitted his desires in a sexy baritone that zinged through her system.

Instead of coming up with a nefarious scheme to stop him

from building the portal, perhaps she could do something more to her liking. Perhaps a delay would give Jamar the extra time to find and destroy the scattered portal parts. Surely she still possessed enough sexual magnetism to detain Cade from his goal for a few hours? Shoving aside the twinge of guilt, Shara took the perfect opening he'd just given her.

Since Cade's compliments coincided with her sexual reawakening, she saw no reason not to yield to her desires. Once she made up her mind to have him, every yearning she'd kept pent up for five years crashed over her in an exhilarating wave that made her tremble with anticipation.

Cade caressed her neck and she dipped her head and nipped the side of his index finger, enjoying the slight tangy taste of salt as much as his clean male scent. And still she challenged him, understanding he knew her well enough to become suspicious if she gave in too easily. "Are you saying any woman will do? Or do you specifically want me?"

"That depends."

"Depends on what?"

After his up-front declaration, she hadn't expected him to qualify his response. She might have been married to Bruce for five years but that didn't mean men hadn't tried every line in the book to get her into bed. She didn't think there was a compliment she hadn't heard. So Cade's response intrigued her, especially since most men would have been trying to take her clothes off by now.

Just once, she wished he was like most men. She didn't want to talk. She wanted him to sweep her away in passion so she could forget that she was using the excuse of causing a delay to make love. Deep down, she recognized she didn't want to have time to think too hard or she might not let herself have what she so much wanted . . . Cade.

She wanted to make love to him and the strength of that desire scared her. But she didn't want to go there, either.

"What exactly do you want from me beyond our making love?" he asked. He kept his finger on the pulse of her neck, surely he must have felt it leap beneath his fingertip, and yet he seemed in no rush to move lower.

But his stroking had changed tempo and pressure. What had begun as a means to assuage her tight muscles had altered to teasing caresses that made her blood roar and made thinking beyond his touch a distraction. It was so much easier not to talk. Not to think too much.

"I haven't thought beyond making love," she admitted, at least not beyond making him too late to finish his mission.

"You should."

Wrong. She tilted back her head and looked up at him, noting the strength of his neck and the serious curve of his mouth. A tiny shiver of excitement played over her flesh, as if an artist painted on her skin with brush strokes of crimson heat.

From somewhere almost forgotten, she recalled how to flirt. "Are you worried you won't meet my expectations?"

He caught her earlobes between his thumb and index fingers and as he rubbed a zone she hadn't even known was erotic, her last question seemed ridiculous. She doubted there was one sensation this man couldn't create. Already she longed to fling off her clothes, and they had yet to share so much as a kiss.

"On Rama, lovemaking is more casual. We consider the experience to have no more significance than the sharing of pleasure."

"Sharing pleasure sounds good to me." She practically purred, her tone low and needy.

"On Rama, only Firsts are free to make real commitments. Underfirsts sometimes marry, but they shouldn't. It causes too many problems."

"But you are no longer on Rama." She would have stood, turned, and moved into his arms, but he placed his hands on her shoulders, keeping her in the chair. "On Earth, we can do whatever we want."

She didn't want to talk anymore. She didn't require a Ph.D. in alien psychology to realize that Cade's concept of a relationship was very different from hers. Refusing to bridge their ideological differences seemed ridiculous when all she wanted was to enjoy him and delay his mission.

He released her shoulders, clasped her arms and urged her to her feet, waited until she faced him before he spoke. "Right now, at this moment, I very much wish to make love to you. Is that also your wish?"

The formality of his question seemed to caress her entire body, wrapping her in a flame of need, compelling her to answer in a voice that didn't sound like her own, but one of a woman much more sure of herself. "Yes, I want to make love. Now, please. Shut up and kiss me."

She'd waited long enough for a real kiss. A kiss where she was aware of every delicious nuance. Tilting back her head, she flung her arms around his muscular neck, closed her eyes, and raised up on her toes, offering her mouth. With a quiet chuckle, he lowered his head. Her anticipation swelled. Would his mouth be hard and demanding or gentle and teasing? Would he taste of salt?

Her lips tingled in anticipation but he stopped without kissing her. She opened her eyes to find his mouth still a frustrating half inch from hers. Already on her toes, she stretched, leaned into him, her breasts tipped against his chest. Threading her fingers into his thick hair, she attempted to tug his mouth closer.

"Kiss me. Damn you. Kiss me."

9

Cade's mouth angled down over hers with a fierce supremacy that matched her full-bodied craving for him. Intense, overwhelming need to be skin-to-skin flared through her. But she couldn't bear to break his smoldering kiss that made her blood simmer and her bones go liquid—not even to tear off his clothing. Although her every nerve ending suddenly thirsted for his immediate attention, she couldn't gather her reeling wits to do more than breathe in his tantalizing aroma of rain on a blustery spring day, taste his deep heady maleness of salted hickory, and feel the solid thud of his heart against her chest.

What the hell was wrong with her?

She could do desire.

She could do lust.

But this was insane. She might not have made love for five long years, but her reaction was much more than her deprived body making up for lost time. Her hormones were raging out of control as if Cade had dialed directly into every needy cell in her body and had them all screaming at once.

Urgency she'd never known before drove her. Her emotions had shifted gears so fast she couldn't catch her breath. Her thoughts revved and her heart turned over, pumping her yearnings into overdrive.

Cade's fiery hot kiss boldly raked her emotions raw. She should slam on the brakes. Figure out what the hell was going on here. But the urge to have him touch her, hold her, take her, couldn't be delayed.

She needed him. Now. Right now.

But their searing kiss seemed to keep him fully occupied.

So rip off his shirt.

Unzip his pants.

Tell him what you need.

Her brain fired demands, but her body didn't obey the commands. Somehow she'd lost all control. Oh, she could tighten her hold on his head to increase the pressure of his mouth on hers. She could rub her breasts against his chest.

It was if his will had usurped hers. Despite her desire to do so much more, he wanted to continue kissing and all she was able to do—was comply. Her lips moved under his. Her tongue danced and shimmied, but she couldn't exert her desire.

At the realization that something bizarre, something otherworldly was going on, alarm bells pealed. Adrenaline surged. Apparently, the mental and physical compulsion that allowed her to kiss him—but nothing more—was his doing.

If she'd wanted to stop, she couldn't have done so any more than she could urge him to go faster. Talk about total control. Utter domination.

She had no free will.

Only scorching desire.

A need so hot she burned.

And when he finally broke their kiss, she gasped for air.

"You taste delicious. Salty." He gave her that one breath and then before she'd gathered her wits to say a word, he swept her into his arms. She kicked off her shoes, tossed her hair from her eyes and snuggled closer. Desperate to smooth her palms along his bare flesh, she regained enough control of her greedy fingers to unbutton his shirt. Rewarded with a broad expanse of bronze flesh over corded muscles, she practically purred in satisfaction.

He carried her into the master suite. Set her on the bed. Now, they were getting somewhere.

She slipped his powerful shoulders free of his shirt, let it fall to the floor and feasted on him with her eyes. She didn't know what she wanted to do first. Look her fill. Skim her hands over his skin. Or use her mouth.

"Come here," she demanded. Positioned on the mattress, on the foot of the bed, on her knees, she waited for his next move while he stood, towering above her. With his height, she would have had to tip back her head to see his face. His chest and stomach were at her eye level, his slacks within easy reach.

She tried to raise her hand toward him, but couldn't.

Yet, she still retained power of her vocal cords and could speak. "Let me take off your pants."

"It's my turn."

His turn?

He cupped her chin, angled her head until their gazes locked. His heat poured into her. "I want to watch your eyes."

"You'd better do a damn lot more than just look into my eyes."

At her comment, his lips quirked into a charming grin. She couldn't have broken his gaze, not even for all the liquor in the suite. His gaze compelled, overshadowing her need to do more than hold her breath in anticipation of what he would do next.

"I will do whatever I wish," he promised. "Touch you wherever I like."

"Good."

"Whenever I like."

It occurred to her that she couldn't have said no—even if she'd wanted to. As her knees sank into the mattress, she realized her thoughts were her own—yet her freedom was limited by . . . something she couldn't explain. Even as desire raged through her so hot she felt as if she were about to go up in flames, she understood that somewhere along the line she'd lost the option of choice. Her will was gone, taken over by a riveting force she couldn't name in English, never mind understand.

While she could now speak, she clearly recalled when she couldn't. Sensing the inconsistency was a clue, but one she couldn't fathom at the moment, she put aside the puzzle. Although she might not have a choice—there was no place she'd rather be. Not even back on Haven.

Waiting for Cade to touch her, unable to move, knowing he would give her pleasure was a good place to be. She had no guilt in the wanting.

Compelled to lock gazes, she searched his eyes. The ferocity of his lust precipitated a corresponding rise in her own. It was if they'd connected in a way she didn't understand. While her thoughts were hers, she couldn't be certain of her emotions. Was he spiking the lust in her with a sixth sense she hadn't known she possessed?

He placed his fingers on the side of her neck, just below her jaw. Jolted by a sudden electric excitement, she let out a soft moan. Holding her gaze, he ever so slowly teased his fingers down her neck, taunted his way to her collarbone, eased his fingertips under her bra.

She sucked in air and her breast lifted into his fingers. Her nipple hardened and his thumb raked over the sensitive tip. At the same time, his eyes darkened to twin green pools of pleasure. Keeping his hand inside her bodice and under her bra, Cade continued to graze her breast while his other hand began a similar journey. Along the way, he must have unzipped her dress because she felt the sides flutter open, exposing her stomach.

Despite her own need to glance down at his hands, she couldn't break his gaze. And, as if knowing he was in complete control, he smiled in warm delight.

And when his other hand cupped her breast and grazed her nipple, the blissful sensations rocked her to the core. Tense, expectant with slick yearning creaming between her thighs, she ached for more. And yet what he was doing to her breasts felt so good, she didn't want him to stop.

She'd wanted a man before, but never like she did right now. And it wasn't because she had deep feelings for Cade. It wasn't because he was more skilled than her other lovers.

At that moment, she had to have him—no matter the consequences. She had to have him—even if it meant she'd never again be the same.

She wasn't drugged. Or hypnotized.

While she couldn't account for the extraordinary sensations, she understood they were something alien. She should have been frightened.

She wasn't.

She should have asked what was going on with his *Quait*. She couldn't.

She should have told him to hurry up.

She didn't.

She should be trying to understand why she was going with the flow, instead of asserting her will. But Shara would figure out what had happened later. Right now, she'd live for this moment.

Cade's hands on her breasts, the heat in his eyes, the intensity of his expression had turned her on. She hadn't ever felt this glorious—not even with Bruce, the greatest love of her life.

Cade snapped open her bra, swept it aside along with her dress, leaving her as deliciously bare as he was from the waist up. He slid his hand up to her chin, gently made certain that she watched him lower his eyes to rake over her breasts. She hadn't thought her nipples could tighten any further, but they had. His bold stare returned to meet her eyes, and the intimacy sent a shockwave of heat lacing through her.

With a suggestive gesture, she shimmied her hips to remind him that he had more undressing to do. "Don't you want to take these off?"

"Yes . . . ," he kissed her brow, "but . . . ," he kissed her cheek, "not . . . ," he kissed her neck, "quite . . . ," he kissed her collarbone, "yet."

When he gently sucked the tip of her breast into his mouth, his tongue licked and the corresponding jolt of pleasure caused her to arch into him. She grabbed his shoulders to maintain her balance, but nothing could steady her thumping pulse. She'd always suspected Cade was a very sensual man. But what he could do with his tongue shouldn't be legal. And after five years of sensory deprivation in the making-love department, she greedily enjoyed his lavishing her with such attention.

She was so ready to pounce on him. And yet, even as her brain instructed her muscles to tug him onto the bed, they failed to work. Oh, she could hold on to him to keep herself upright. But the tugging-him-where-she-wanted-him movements were denied her.

Quait hadn't made sense when he'd explained it to her. It wasn't as if she were paralyzed. She could skim her fingers over his shoulders and back and his supple skin stretched tightly over corded muscles pleased her. She could arch her back, lifting her breasts into his mouth. She could release soft moans.

But she couldn't reach below his waist to unfasten his pants. Her muscles simply wouldn't follow her mental command. It was as if he were a director who'd choreographed a scenario and she couldn't escape his preset parameters.

She could only react within the limits he'd determined. If she hadn't been enjoying herself, she might have been more concerned.

His tongue circled her breast, then wickedly he moved to the other. Cade was clearly determined to make sure she had a very good time.

"Cade."

"Mmm?"

"Let me take off your pants."

"All right."

She reached for him and this time she had no difficulty with the task—beyond normal fumbling due to her trembling fingers. But within moments, she sent his slacks and boxers to the floor and he kicked them off.

And just when she thought she might climax from his attention to her breasts alone, he pulled his mouth back and helped her to stand on the bed. She was taller than him now. But as she watched him undo her own pants, hook his thumbs into her panties, and toss them aside, a wicked gleam entered his eyes.

His gaze had fixed at the triangle of hair between her legs. He licked his lips as if eager for a snack and then urged her to part her legs.

Shivering with need, wanting his mouth on her, she stood on the bed, placed her hands on his shoulders and waited for his mouth to claim her. And when he did, she released a cry of delight. Tender, yet forceful, he seemed to know exactly what she liked.

And when she thought that if he took one more lick of pleasure that she'd collapse in a heap, he finally allowed her to sag onto the bed, bringing him down along with her. She landed on her back, with him atop her, his hips centered firmly against hers.

Sensing he was about to enter her, she tried to reverse their positions. She wanted to be on top. She wanted to ride him long and hard. She wanted to watch his eyes darken with excitement and cloud with passion.

But she also had no intention of accidentally making the paparazzi's headlines predicting her pregnancy become a reality. "Birth control?"

"I took a pill before I left that prevents me from becoming a father."

"What about disease?"

"We don't have those kinds of problems on Rama."

"Great." So she flexed her hips to roll them. And she might as well have tried to rock a tiger.

He raised an inquisitive eyebrow. "Is there something you want?"

"You. On your back. Under me."

He shot her a wolfish grin. And complied with her request.

Delighted, she took him into her, inch by inch. Watched

moisture glisten on his forehead. Watched the pulse at his neck throb. Watched his nipples tighten. But most of all she enjoyed the curve of his mouth that let her know he was enjoying himself as much as she was.

Oh . . . my. The man was totally yummy. And right now he was all hers.

And when she finally took him all the way into her, his fullness stretched her wide and caressed all the right places. After a subtle tilt of her hips, every stroke of his sex aroused her. Long, slow, strokes heated her. And when his hands again closed over her breasts and tweaked her nipples, she exploded in a spasm that broke long and hard and left her breathless.

Gasping for air, she opened her eyes to find him watching her. She tightened her muscles to find him still hard inside her. Learning that he'd outlasted her and remained good to go, she chuckled at her good fortune. "Wow."

"You're a very passionate woman."

"Yes. I am." She grinned, wriggled her hips and began to move again. This time she pumped her hips faster. Took him deeper. Already so sensitive, her tension gathered once more, swirling, cresting. As if he understood that she was ready to climax again, he reached between her parted thighs, found her sweet spot and she shattered. Aftershocks kept her sizzling.

And still he remained hard.

She couldn't help but feel flattered and challenged and concerned. Obviously he was enjoying himself or he wouldn't still be erect. But if he didn't find her exciting enough to orgasm then she wasn't giving him what he wanted. And he'd pleased her so much, she wanted to do the same for him.

"What do you want?" She asked him the same question he'd asked her.

"To be on top."

She laughed as he answered her the same way she had him. "All right."

She expected to change positions and remain face-to-face.

But instead, he gathered up every pillow on the bed, stacked them in a pile and bent her over them. Her backside was in the air. He parted her legs.

She held her breath, waiting for him to enter her. But he placed his mouth between her legs and blew air over her, into her. Her fingers clutched the sheets as her flesh plumped and slicked at the new sensations. She would have squirmed but his hands on her hips held her right where he wanted her. She couldn't close her legs, not with him kneeling between her knees. She could do nothing but take whatever he wanted to give. Between his breath and his lips and his hands holding her hips, she exploded again.

Creamy moisture seeped between her legs and he smoothed it over her bottom, massaging her cheeks, then nipping her, he reached forward to tweak her nipples. She could no more escape the tiny bites and his fingers tight on her nipples than she could anything else.

But she was suddenly frantic to have him again, wild with need. She lifted her hips higher, waved her bottom from side to side but he kept nipping and licking and stroking, his hands on her breasts keeping her bent over.

Moans of pleasure ripped from her throat. She couldn't believe she'd already come three times and was again desperate for release. She practically sobbed his name. "Cade." Her voice broke, muffled into the mattress. "Cade. Now. I must have you now."

At her words, he thrust into her, hard and deep. And then his hips rode her, stoking a wildness that she didn't recognize. The tension gathered, united into a tight ball of fire, expanded, then ruptured in a torrent that arched from the top of her head to the tips of her toes.

A hoarse scream ripped from her throat, matching a primal grunt of pleasure pouring from his. And this time, he spurted with her, his fingers finding her center, wringing every ounce of pleasure from the moment.

And oh what a moment. She couldn't move. Couldn't speak. Couldn't think. Pure bliss engulfed her, wrapped around her and swept her away.

Every muscle in her body had melted down. She hadn't known a body could be this relaxed without being asleep or drugged. Moving seemed too much trouble, but as if being with her another second caused him pain, Cade practically leaped from the bed.

She opened her eyes to watch his magnificent body pad into the oversized bathroom. Shara expected him to be as relaxed as she was. But his jaw clenched with fury, his big hands closed into fists and even muscles on his back twitched.

"Cade?"

"Later." He snapped the word like a whip. But that one word conveyed a load of self-loathing.

Rolling onto her side, she wound the sheet around her and began to follow him, confused over what had gone wrong. As her thoughts cleared, she wondered if it might be a better decision to let him cool off.

Because as incredible as the lovemaking had been, there were too many times where he'd taken control with his *Quait*. And she'd been totally helpless. She recalled a moment when he hadn't allowed her to speak. Many others when she hadn't been able to move. Talk about domination.

Sitting up, she dropped her face into her hands.

Think.

Making love to Cade had been the most wondrous sexual experience of her life. Every time she'd thought they'd reached a plateau he'd urged her up another peak. And the glorious ascent couldn't compare to the leap off the summit.

Shara had known women who enjoyed a man's domination. She'd known women who enjoyed all kinds of sexual games. But she wasn't one of them. She wasn't into kink or perversions. Shara was a farm girl who didn't think her tastes were much different from middle America, where she'd been born.

So she found Cade's ability . . . strange . . . disturbing.

And she would have to think long and hard before encouraging him to make love to her again.

Glancing at the clock, she saw that she'd delayed them even longer than she'd planned. And they still had to eat.

Picking up the phone, she ordered room service, then delayed their flight another two hours.

Taking a deep breath, she followed Cade into the bathroom, wondering what kind of reaction she'd receive. The way he'd peeled out of that bed, she wasn't even certain he'd welcome her presence.

Too damn bad.

The man had just made love to her. If he had issues, he'd have to deal with them.

Cade stood in the shower, the hot water sluicing over him. He'd scrub his skin to the bone if it could rid him of what he was becoming. Unfortunately, soap and water wouldn't solve his problems. He could think of only one way to stop the transformation into a First and that was to stop ingesting so much salt. But if he did, he would never be a match for Jamar's full-powered strength. How ironic that unless he accepted the evil he was becoming, he couldn't stop the evil from preying on his people.

"Cade?"

Ashamed, he couldn't bear to look at her. Perhaps if he didn't answer, if he pretended not to hear, she'd go away and leave him in his misery.

"Cade? Are you all right?"

"No."

Clearly concerned, she dropped the sheet and stepped into the shower—but that was only because she didn't understand what was happening to him. "Do you need more salt?"

At the incongruity of her words, he snorted. "More salt will likely make me stronger." He lifted his head and drilled her with a stare. "You should leave."

"Why? I thought you needed my help and my island."

"Give me Haven and go away before I hurt you."

"You won't."

"Of course I will. The salt is inducing *Quait*. Terrans don't have a translation for the Raman term."

"I thought *Quait* was mind control."

"It is. The best translation I can give you is: the power to dominate others." And he'd used it on her. Disgust and self-loathing washed over him and by the horror he saw in her eyes, she was clearly sickened by his actions.

"Why did you use it on me?"

"*Quait* is the power of the Firsts. They have this power all the time. Mine is more sporadic. Right now, I seem to only use it when experiencing extreme emotions. And it taxes my strength. But that too shall pass. Remember after the fire, I was too weak to stand until after I ingested more salt?"

"You don't look weak right now."

He nodded. "This time I'm shaking, but I can still walk. As my body adjusts to the new salt intakes, I suspect I'll grow even stronger."

She picked up the soap and worked it into a lather. "So when you used the *Quait* on me . . ."

"I'm turning into a monster. I can't control—"

"Let's not get dramatic." She shrugged. "You could eat less salt."

He shuddered. "If Jamar wasn't trying to stop me, I'd gladly follow your suggestion. But when Jamar catches up with me, I'll need all the *Quait* powers to defeat him."

"Maybe Jamar won't find us."

"You don't fully comprehend what a First is. On Rama, Jamar can make any underfirst do whatever he wishes."

"So there's no hope?"

His eyes narrowed. "Not necessarily. While my powers are strengthening, his must be weakening."

"I don't understand. How do you know?"

"When I entered your atmosphere, my spaceship tested the salt. Based on a chemical analysis, my computer indicated that your salt is slightly different than what we have on Rama. The difference is enough that the First and I are adapting to the salinity of your world in different ways. Earth salt is enough to strengthen me, but it's weakening him. Although he must have brought a pure supply from Rama, he's breathing your air, eating your food. Your environment is likely changing his body chemistry, although he may still be much stronger than me."

She placed her soapy hands on his upper chest and began to massage his shoulders. "Can you learn to control this *Quait*?"

He eyed her curiously. "What do you mean?"

"Just because you have a power doesn't mean you have to use it."

"When you open your eyes, can you stop yourself from seeing? When you put food in your mouth, can you stop yourself from tasting? When I speak, can you stop yourself from hearing? *Quait* is another sense. Not using it—isn't an option."

"But after you complete your mission, if you eat less salt, won't you go back to normal?"

"My body chemistry will have changed. If a First doesn't have enough salt, they don't weaken like I do—they die. This metamorphosis is permanent."

Her eyes widened and her fingers trembled, but she didn't stop kneading his shoulders. "Then I can think of only one other solution."

He hissed on an indrawn breath, reached up to capture her hands between his, letting her see he was serious. "You will kill me after I complete my mission."

She shook her head. "We cannot make love again."

And so she set the terms of their bargain. He would not touch her again, and after he completed his mission, she would kill him. At this soulless solution, he jerked away from her touch, grabbed a towel and stalked from the shower. "The water's all yours."

10

⚙

Trevor hadn't expected to Google Shara Weston and learn she'd returned to L.A. But after finding numerous photographs of the glamorous woman who always carried herself like American royalty, complete with shadowed secrets in her eyes and a tall, handsome escort by her side, Trevor's suspicions increased with the ease that he'd discovered her plans to attend a premiere. He booked a flight to the mainland. Press credentials would get him into the premiere, where he hoped to secure an interview or at least have a few questions answered by the former star.

"This could be a wild-goose chase," Trevor had warned his boss.

Ralph chewed on his cigar, glaring at him over the webcam that connected their offices. "With half the paparazzi snapping her picture, we're certain she's in California, right?"

"She's there all right. But it doesn't make sense. If she's on the run because someone set that fire, why would Shara make such a public appearance anywhere, but especially in

L.A.? It's almost as if she's daring the arsonist to come after her."

"Maybe she thinks she's safe and that she's left the arsonist back in Hawaii. Maybe she's desperate for publicity and/or work. Or maybe she thinks the fire was an accident and she's not concerned about—"

"Someone poured a gasoline ring around the house. It was no accident. She'd have to be an idiot to believe otherwise and Shara's no bubble brain. She's had the good sense to align herself with the best management team in one of the most competitive businesses in the world. And her investments in real estate are solid."

"What about Cade?" Ralph asked. "You turn up any more information on the dude?"

"Nothing." Frustrated by the lack of information on the mystery man, Trevor suspected Cade was the key. If he could discover the man's real identity, he might unlock the rest of the puzzle. "Either he's using an alias or . . ."

"Or?"

Trevor shrugged. "Even my friends at the CIA have no clue who Cade really is."

"The world is a big place."

"Not so big that a man who sells millions of dollars in rubies should be a complete unknown." Trevor had dug deep. "No one in the mining world or the gem world has ever heard of Cade."

"Maybe he's a thief."

"No thefts of stones that large or of such high quality have been reported. And I have feelers out from Bangkok to São Paulo."

"Maybe he's one of those guys who searches for ancient treasure."

"No country has a record of him ever using his passport." Trevor checked the notes on his computer screen. "And the psychic, Jules, is another puzzle."

"What do you mean?"

Trevor knew the facts on Jules by heart, but he kept hoping he'd missed a piece of useful data and rechecked his screen. But the facts remained: same old, same old. "During her lifetime, she's left Hawaii only once—the day Bruce Langston died, Jules flew to Shara's side. Obviously, the women are close, but why the sudden trip now? You'd think she'd have a million details to clear up after her house burned. But instead of contacting her insurance company and talking to contractors about clearing the rubble so she can rebuild, she takes off for the mainland with Shara."

"It does seem odd—unless she's scared."

"Then why didn't she go to the police? And why is Shara advertising her presence in front of the paparazzi? Nothing makes sense."

Ralph stabbed his cigar at the screen. "So how much is it going to cost me to find out what's going on?"

Trevor's lips twisted into what he hoped was a confident grin. "That depends on how soon I catch up with Shara Weston."

When the satellite phone in the seat next to her on the plane rang, Jules jumped. Hesitantly, she picked it up, well aware that the expensive charges could top twenty-five dollars a minute. "Hello."

"Did I wake you?" Shara asked, her voice beaming from Los Angeles into the plane with the same clarity as a landline.

"I'm awake." Jules's worry escalated. "Where are you? Is anything wrong?"

"I'm still at the hotel. We got delayed."

"By the paparazzi?"

"They're still camping outside the lobby, but we haven't left the hotel suite."

Shara had probably tried to keep the sexy satisfaction from her tone, and she was a great actress, but Jules knew her too well not to notice the humming vibrations in her voice that told Jules all she needed to know about what had happened in the hotel after her departure.

Jules didn't need her psychic talents to guess. "You let him jump your bones, didn't you?"

"Yes, but—"

"Are you out of your mind? Sleeping with Cade is a complication you don't need."

Sleeping with Cade would only make Shara's task more difficult for her to carry out. Shara was one of those rare people—once she befriended you, she remained loyal, no matter what. And it would tear her apart to betray . . . a lover.

Shara's voice lowered to a whisper. "Jules . . . something strange happened."

"If you tell me you've fallen in love and weren't just working off some overripe lust, I'll order the pilot to turn around."

"Please. Pay attention. Remember when Cade saved us during the fire?"

Jules knew she owed the man her life, but when she weighed his actions against the cataclysmic visions, she remained firm in her resolve to urge Shara to stop him from building the portal. Although Jules knew Shara believed her as much as anyone who didn't see her visions could, Shara's feelings toward Cade were clouding her judgment. So Jules sought to give her reasons not to trust the man so that she could see for herself.

"Shara, have you considered that he arranged to set the fire so he could save us?"

Shara came quickly to Cade's defense. "Why would he do that?"

"So we'd trust him."

"Actually . . . that hadn't crossed my mind. And it doesn't fit what he told me about himself—"

"Unless he's lying."

"When we made love . . . he did things."

"Shara, that's really none of my business." Jules and Shara were close, but they weren't the kind of friends who shared intimate details.

"He used *Quait* on me."

"You okay?"

"I'm fine. But how can I stop a man who has the power of *Quait*?"

"Tell me exactly what he did to you." Jules had spoken to people who claimed all sorts of skills—astral projection, telekinesis, telepathy. The worst were the psychic predators, ones who had no powers but pretended they did as they happily lightened the wallets of the marks they scammed, giving all of those with real talent a bad name.

"At times, Cade stopped me from speaking."

"What? He like . . . gagged you?"

"Pay attention. He used his mental power to prevent my mind from connecting with my muscles. At times I couldn't use my vocal cords or move my hand where I wanted it to go."

"That's not . . . are you sure?" Jules frowned.

"He thinks what he did was so despicable that he actually asked me to kill him after his mission is over."

Empathy with poor Cade's plight oozed from Shara's tone. Clearly, he'd won her sympathy with stories they had no way of verifying. But Shara was one smart lady. Mind control should terrify her—except Cade had convinced her he didn't like his growing powers.

"This is so bizarre, even for me." Jules's thoughts raced. Bizarre or not, Shara had reached out to her and she wasn't being much help. "Be careful, girlfriend. Everything the man says and does might be calculated to win your sympathy."

"If he's that good an actor, he should win an Academy Award."

"Maybe he's not that good. Maybe he's playing with your mind, altering your thoughts and feelings along with your movements."

"I don't think so. When he stopped me from speaking, I was damn well aware of it."

"Yeah, but you had a good time in the sack. I can hear it in your voice and now you're defending a man who can and did control you—without asking I assume?"

"He didn't expect to be able to—"

"Why not? He knew exactly what he'd done to save us

from the fire. He knows what the Firsts on his world can do. He should have been able to extrapolate what else he could do from the facts he had."

"Good point," Shara conceded. "So how am I going to stop him?"

"Does he have the power all the time?"

"He claims that it only works when his emotions are strong."

"Then maybe you can surprise him. You're going to have to be very, very careful. Don't do anything until you have a great plan."

"If you see a scheme in your vision—or if you think up anything I can do—"

"I'll let you know."

"Thanks."

"This conversation must be costing you a fortune, but I'm glad you called. Shara, don't trust him. Sleep with him if you must. Get it out of your system—but the visions are so real, so strong. Every time I close my eyes, they repeat. The colors are more vivid than ever and—"

"Any new details?"

"I'm afraid not." Jules wished she had more control over her talent but she always got flashes, like three seconds of a movie, never the entire film. Interpretation was usually the key. However, she'd seen Cade and the portal and Shara in a maelstrom of fiery darkness followed by horrible volcanic explosions overlaid with the Montana volcanologist's face.

Shara interrupted her gloomy thoughts. "Room service just arrived."

"Then I'll say good-bye."

"Okay. But stay in touch. And Jules . . . you be careful. Montana's a long way from Hawaii."

"Don't you worry about me. I've got my winter coat and mittens." Despite the warmth in the perfectly temperature-controlled airplane, Jules shivered, pulled her jacket up to her neck and tried not to miss her cat, left behind with George. "I'll be fine."

*   *   *

Shara had tested her disguise by walking out the hotel's service entrance and crossing the street in front of the lobby.
The paparazzi had shown no interest in the overweight
woman who wore a maid's uniform, ugly white shoes with
thick soles, and an ill-fitting tweed jacket and granny
glasses. Shara kept her gray-wigged head tilted sideways,
causing her back to hump slightly, and she walked slowly,
with a slight limp, as if she had arthritic knees. Between her
sallow skin, her slow gait, and her dowdy looks, none of the
paparazzi seemed to even notice her.

Cade's height and the breadth of his shoulders were impossible to hide, so he'd slipped from a low balcony onto
the hotel grounds and had met up with her on the next
block. They'd taken a taxi to a store that specialized in outdoor camping equipment. While he went inside to make
purchases, she spied a grocery store and took the opportunity to stock up on salt. She bought more chips, pretzels,
and cookies and, remembering how Cade had poured salt
onto his food, she purchased several large containers of
pure salt.

She returned to find Cade had filled the trunk with assorted backpacks, a tent, sleeping bags, a cookstove, outdoor
clothing for both of them, as well as walkie-talkies and a
grill. She gave him a frown. The only camping she liked to
do was in the penthouse suite at the Ritz.

"Will we be camping in Israel?"

"We're going to the desert. I'm not sure what kind of ac-
commodations we'll find and I like to be prepared." He gestured to the gear. "I'm pretty good at surviving off the land
but I thought you might like the comforts."

He called a sleeping bag a comfort?

Determined to make reservations in the best hotel near the
desert and commute—by private chopper if necessary—
Shara didn't say anything more. But she made a mental note
to make all their travel arrangements and reservations from
now on.

After shopping, they had the taxi driver take them straight
to the private airport. No sooner had they settled into an-

other private plane and taken off for the long flight to Israel than a phone rang. Automatically, she reached for the satellite phone she'd bought to make and receive worldwide calls, sure that Jules had had another vision, but her new phone wasn't ringing.

"It's this one." Cade picked up the plane's phone and handed it to her.

Hastily, she reached for it, confused about who would have this number, since no one was supposed to know they were on the plane. Vowing to hang up before revealing their secret getaway plans to anyone whose voice she didn't immediately recognize, she spoke in a flat, noncommittal tone. "Yes?"

"Teresa Alverez here." Shara had forgotten her private investigator would have this number, but Teresa *had* made all the arrangements. "My people are covering the premiere. So far no one who looks likes Jamar has shown up."

Shara sighed. "We always knew it was a long shot. Cade thinks Jamar will follow the locator beacon and go directly to the Dead Sea." Knowing Cade was listening to her end of the conversation, she spoke as if she wanted to reach the portal pieces before Jamar when the opposite was true.

"My people did discover a Mr. Trevor Cantrell, a reporter out of Oahu, asking a lot of questions about you."

"What kind of questions?" Shara wasn't unduly alarmed. Asking a bunch of nosy questions was a reporter's job. And even if she returned to seclusion immediately, the press would hound her former friends and business associates in the film industry for weeks.

"He asked your old friends a lot of the usual questions. Like, why weren't you at the premiere? What project would you take on next? Are you pregnant and did you come back to have an abortion or a face-lift?"

Shara sensed Teresa wanted to keep her informed without alarming her. In this case full knowledge was essential— maybe to staying alive. "What else?"

"Trevor flew from Oahu to L.A. today and one of my people thought it odd."

"Why?"

"Don't the Hawaiian papers usually pick up the entertainment stories from the AP or UPI?" Teresa asked.

"Usually." Shara should have thought of that herself. But, because she couldn't think of everything, she'd always tried to surround herself with a good team. Even major newspapers didn't have the funds to fly halfway across the Pacific Ocean to track down stories for the gossip column.

"Trevor Cantrell also asked about Cade."

Cade? Alarmed, Shara's neck prickled. If a reporter got wind that Cade was an alien, it would make headlines around the world.

Don't panic.

"Any man in my life creates public interest." Shara wasn't bragging. Her words were a simple, annoying fact of life that every celebrity had to deal with and the realization calmed her immediately. It had been so long since she'd had to deal with the press on a daily basis she'd forgotten how unnerving their incessant need for details about film stars and their lovers could be.

Lovers?

She and Cade had made love—but if they didn't do so again then they were . . . what? Friends? But she couldn't risk any more lovemaking since passion caused Cade's *Quait* to kick in. She should avoid all lovemaking since it gave Cade such power over her. The man really was a gifted lover—totally creative, an intoxicating mix of raw strength and gentle understanding—but his control issues and the *Quait* unnerved her.

And if she betrayed him and he discovered it, he'd be furious. His *Quait* would take over and dominate her every action, preventing her from trying again.

Teresa brought Shara's thoughts back to the present. "But the same reporter also put out several feelers about Cade being in the jewelry business."

Damn. The reporter must have found out about the rubies Cade had sold in Oahu. The sale of the valuable stones, perhaps even the fire at Jules's home combined with Shara's disappearance must have triggered the reporter's interest, and he'd followed them from Hawaii. He must have caught the next flight to L.A. to make the premiere—but it could be done, which indicated a very determined man. "Teresa. I want you to trail this reporter for a while. If he follows us, let me know immediately."

"I'm on it."

"Have you found anything on Jamar?" Shara asked, noting Cade's interest in her phone conversation pick up when she mentioned his brother's name. Cade had been silent since making love—as if he was having difficulty coming to terms with his transformation. Well, he wasn't the only one having a hard time with the idea—his mind control that had overpowered her will was freaking weird.

"We're still looking for Jamar."

"All right. Thanks."

Shara hung up the phone and conveyed the information about Trevor. Cade stared out the window but there was little to see. Since they'd left the populated West Coast, the land below them was as dark as the heavens. With his eyes narrowed, his lips pursed, he was clearly brooding. And when he finally turned to look at her, his demeanor remained serious. "The reporter isn't the problem."

"Really?"

"The delay in L.A. may stop me from getting to the portal pieces first. Jamar might have left immediately and headed straight to Israel, and it's possible he flew on his spaceship, which would cut his travel time even more."

Shara used all her acting ability to withhold her satisfaction from showing in her demeanor or on her face. "Let's not assume the worst until—"

"With Jamar one must always assume the worst." Cade's tone wasn't simply cold, it was chilling. Deadly. "I learned that the hard way."

"Are you talking about his attempt to kill us on Haven?"

Cade shook his head, his back stiff, his shoulders squared. "After spending my life around Jamar, I learned there are things much worse than dying."

Shara didn't know whether she wanted to hear more. Was Cade about to feed her some horrible lie in order to win her to his cause? Jules would think so. And yet, Cade didn't know that she and Jules weren't on his side. So he had no reason to lie that she could see. However, for all she knew, it was Raman custom to lie to everyone.

There existed no way to check his facts or to verify whatever he told her about his past. Yet, if he was lying, it would be difficult for him to keep his story cohesive if she drew enough details out of him. Besides, she wanted to know more about his life.

She fixed them both a soft drink, handed Cade a bag of pretzels, and settled into her seat. "You've never told me what you do in your work."

"From the day underfirsts leave the creche, Firsts assign them to designated tasks. Most of us don't specialize. The labor is usually hard, dangerous, and menial. Our position on Rama is much like the one your slaves suffered on Earth—except rebellion is next to impossible."

"Because of the mind control?"

He nodded. "My journey to Earth was due to the sacrifice of many people. The Firsts have the salt requirements needed for life down to an exact science. When I worked in the salt mines, if the overseers caught anyone pilfering even so much as a few extra grains of salt, that criminal was forced to kill, one by one, all his friends and family, even the creche babies. And the deaths were not . . . swift."

Her stomach heaved. The conditions on his world sounded barbaric and yet Ramans had the technology to travel across the stars. She'd never been a huge science-fiction fan, but she knew that most writers in the field speculated, and many scientists extrapolated, that in order to develop advanced engineering and science, an alien race would have to work together. She'd have thought a race as technologically advanced as his would have been more civilized, that they'd have found a way to solve health issues, war, and starvation. Instead, their Firsts took advantage of others with a cruelty that made her stomach turn.

She forced the words from her mouth, needing to make sure she had the facts straight. "Your people were forced to torture their loved ones as punishment for stealing salt?"

"With consequences so severe, not too many people risk it."

"But yet, you said you were given extra salt portions."

She wanted clarity on that point. Jules might accuse him of stealing the salt from others, but if her friend could have seen the loathing in his eyes, she would know Cade spoke the truth, at least about this subject.

"Many people scrimped, causing great harm to their own health, to given me extra." Cade's voice turned steely. "Some of the elders gave up years of their lives so I would be strong enough to make this journey. A few of the women didn't know they were pregnant and the lack of salt damaged their children."

She winced and didn't know what to say. Terrible guilt must weigh on him. And that guilt could be a powerful motivator. The necessity to succeed at any cost must be enormous. And yet she had to balance what he told her against Jules's vision.

As much as her heart went out to Cade, she tried not to allow her sympathy to override caution. "Tell me about the portal."

He pulled himself together and his troubled tone eased. "It's in three pieces. Once I recover the parts, I'll have to assemble the device, tap into the volcano and the ocean. The portal will automatically withdraw the salt from your seawater and then I can send the salt back home."

"How does it work?"

He shrugged. "I have no idea. Our scientists have assured me the portal taps into gravitational forces and folds in space. The salt will arrive almost instantly."

"What do you mean your scientists have assured you?" She frowned. "Are you saying they haven't tested the portal?"

"They can't."

"Why not?" she challenged, wondering whether the volcanic explosion Jules had seen could be a terrible accident, a miscalculation on the Raman scientists' parts.

"Once the portal is activated, it draws upon the volcano's heat and pressure, converting the energy into electromagnetic waves. If we'd tested the device on Rama, our Firsts would recognize the energy, follow it back to its source, and destroy the machinery as well as everyone who'd worked on the project. We had to keep the work on the portal wrapped in secrecy. My being on Earth is the culmination of the work of many for entire generations."

"So the portal has never been tested?" She tried and failed to keep the horror from her tone.

"It will work. The portal has three pieces, three brains, any one of which is capable of opening the portal by itself. But in triplicate, there is little room for error."

Little room? She shivered. If his portal failed, it wasn't his island that would be destroyed, not his home at risk. "How do you know that the portal won't cause all of Haven to erupt?"

"Scientists have assured me—"

"You're scaring me."

"They've checked and rechecked their calculations. The portal will work," he repeated and gave her an odd look. "Why would you even think that the portal could cause a volcano to erupt?"

Because Jules had seen it! Shara couldn't tell Cade that. "When you tap into a volcano to open up folds in space, you're talking about tremendous forces. What's to stop things from getting out of hand?"

"You'd be better off worrying how to stop Jamar. He's the real danger."

"To Earth?"

"To whoever gets in his way. I once saw an underfirst trip and spill wine on Jamar's favorite robe. Jamar lined up his entire family. Aunts, uncles, second and third cousins from four generations. And then he used *Quait,* forcing the servant to shoot his brothers and sisters and nieces and nephews until the gun grew so hot, the metal burned off his hands."

Sickened, she set down her glass before she spilled the rest of her drink. "He's a monster."

Cade nodded, his face tight. "And I'm becoming just like him. You should sell me your island. Walk away while you still can."

11

Jamar hadn't had much difficulty tracking Cade and Shara to the private investigator's establishment. Humans tended to be creatures of routine. He'd staked out Shara's former agent, manager, accountant, and private investigator.

And now he would learn everything Teresa Alverez knew. He let himself into her office, pleased when Teresa looked up from her desk, her eyes widening in shock as she clearly recognized him. Immediately, she tried to recover, demanding, "Who are you? What are you doing here?"

"I have need of your services." Jamar slipped smoothly into the seat before her desk.

"We're closed."

"I can pay you well. Perhaps twice what Cade and Shara offered."

"I have no idea who you're talking about." Teresa raised her eyebrows. She slipped her hand into her desk drawer— no doubt in search of a weapon. Jamar grinned. He always appreciated watching the fall of the I-can't-be-bribed types.

This detour, which had began as an annoyance, might turn out to provide some well-earned entertainment. He folded his hands in his lap. "You're going to tell me everything you know about Cade and Shara."

Teresa aimed the gun at his chest, her hand steady, her gaze direct. "Get out of my office. Now."

"Ah. You really are a delicious piece of work." Jamar shook his finger at her. "Since you're being so naughty, I'll have to punish you."

"I don't know what kind of game you're playing, but I'm not interested."

"Surely you'd rather dance with me—than shoot me?"

"You are not the kind of dance partner I would ever choose."

"Fine. You dance. I'll watch." With a mental shove of *Quait,* Teresa's hips undulated. Astonished, her jaw dropped and he burst into a snort of derision. "Really, Ms. Alverez. Your dancing would be much sexier if you weren't wearing so many clothes."

With satisfaction Jamar forced the woman to take off her shirt and bra and slacks until she stood before him naked from the waist up, except for her panties and heels. Confused, humiliated, and furious, she remained silent since he wasn't allowing her to speak.

He snapped his fingers. "I told you to dance." With no music, her movements not of her own will, she nevertheless gyrated her hips and spun and twisted into the most pornographic combinations he could think of. And after her body broke a sweat and she stood panting, he forced her to bend over her desk, her forehead down so she couldn't see him.

Only thin panties separated her quivering ass from his view. His mouth watered as he imagined her terror at her helplessness. Perhaps if he was lucky, she would cry and beg before she began to scream.

"Ah, Ms. Alverez." He snapped the waistband of her panties. She gasped and he let out a laugh of satisfaction. "Do I have your complete attention?"

Over the years, he'd found the combination of humiliation, plus the fear of what he would do next, a potent combination that made the most stubborn woman eager to tell him

what he wished to know. However, sensing Teresa had yet to
break, he removed a belt made of thin, supple leather that
he'd worn especially for this occasion. He snapped the
leather in the air, appreciating the whistle, enjoying the
flinch of her buttocks beneath the thin cotton panties.

He had no doubt she'd tell him everything he wanted to
know. But he didn't want her to give up the information too
soon—that would spoil his fun.

One moment Cade sat next to Shara on the plane, his mind
focused on his mission and whether Jamar would reach Israel before them, the next second—out of nowhere—danger
flashed at him. Not just a hint of danger. Deadly danger.

Quait had fully kicked in, and suddenly, he knew—as
clearly as if he'd seen his brother fire the missile—that Jamar had targeted this aircraft and was about to shoot them
out of the sky. Cade didn't have time to think, barely had
enough time to react, still he wondered how Jamar had
found him.

Moving faster than he'd ever done in his life, he grabbed
Shara into his arms. She'd just turned her shocked gaze on
him, when the plane exploded.

Tucking her head against his chest, Cade erected a force
field around them, similar to the one he'd used during the
fire. Giant pressure ripped apart the plane, shredding and
whipping at their flesh, but his shield held. Metal burst,
charred, and twisted around them, and then they plunged
downward with the debris, tumbling end over end toward the
Earth below.

Shara clutched him and screamed, "We're going to die!"

Cade closed his eyes, already grieving that he couldn't
protect the pilots, yet desperate to save Shara and himself.
He'd automatically created a bubblelike force field around
them, but their rate of descent was too fast.

But suppose he altered the shield's shape? What if he
could change the shield to catch air the same way a parachute did? Falling, spinning, holding Shara close, he summoned his new powers and widened and flattened the force

field above their heads. His efforts did enough to keep their feet pointed toward the ground, but air still rushed by so fast, that if they hit the dirt at this speed neither of them would survive.

Shara's extra weight might get him killed. For the sake of the mission and all those who'd sacrificed to send him here, he should release her from the bubble's protection. Saving himself was the rational decision. Sometimes in war, troops had to be sacrificed, but Shara was an innocent civilian who didn't deserve to die.

Cade couldn't shove her away—not even if it meant failure. He'd always suspected he wasn't ruthless enough, or strong enough to complete his task . . . and now he knew. He'd failed.

At least he would never turn into a monster like Jamar. He wouldn't live long enough.

"Damn it, Cade. Slow us some more."

Cade dug deeper. Perhaps, he *could* spread the force field wider, thinner. Every inch he gained increased the drag tenfold, keeping them together, but taking a terrible toll on his *Quait*. With complete darkness below, he couldn't be certain how much longer he must fight the tremendous forces.

"You're doing it," Shara encouraged. "We're slowing."

Her words came to him as if from a great distance. He could no longer feel her in his arms, hear the air roaring by. Expending huge stores of mental energy and salt, he focused his every thought on holding the shield around them, over them, under them, spreading the force field of wings so far and wide that it might disintegrate at any second. Only the idea of Shara's death, of her smashing into the ground and breaking every bone in her body kept him focused.

As if knowing his strength was ebbing, Shara pleaded, "Hold on a little longer. I see the ground."

He grunted, all he could manage, but the wind tore the sound from his throat.

"We're coming in too fast. Too fast."

Cade redoubled his efforts. Sweat poured from him. His feet touched. His knees buckled and then he must have passed out. Because the next thing he noticed was Shara's lips on his and the wondrous taste of salt.

Ah, her lips were feeding him life-giving salt. Her skin was not only flavored with the precious substance but fed him just enough strength for him to pry open his eyelids.

He couldn't see much in the darkness—not even Shara's face. Her silhouette hovered over him, but he'd recognize her musical voice on the other side of hell. "Cade. Are you all right? Are you in pain? Talk to me."

Speaking was an effort. He'd never been so drained, so exhausted in all his life. "Salt."

Her voice filled with sadness. "The plane is gone. Our supplies are gone. I think we're in the desert somewhere in Arizona, New Mexico, or Utah. And I don't see any lights. Haven't heard any cars. But you saved me, Cade, and once the sun comes up, maybe I can find salt in the plane's wreckage. Next time we go to a store, I'm going to buy some string and tie a packet of salt around your neck."

As he dipped in and out of consciousness, she talked to him. He couldn't always follow her words, but at one point she'd drawn his head into her lap. She smoothed back his hair and the next time he came to, she was still there, her eyes worried. Dawn was just breaking over the horizon—a good thing since she was shivering with the morning dew.

The ground beneath his body was cold, chilling. She was shivering but he wasn't—not a good sign. With his depletion of salt, hypothermia had begun to set in. But with the rising sun, the temperature climbed and chased away the chill much faster than he'd expected. The current problem was no longer cold, but the air was so dry, it was already sucking the moisture out of his mouth, making him crave both water and salt.

Weak, so weak, he couldn't raise his head. They needed salt, water, and shade in that order. Somewhat of an expert in survival, Cade wanted to tell her what to do but he couldn't force the words out of his throat.

The next time he wakened, she was dribbling water onto his lips. He opened his eyes and she tipped back his head. "I found some water in the plane's wreckage. But no salt. Be careful. The container's edges are sharp."

She raised his head and lifted a piece of curved plastic to his mouth. Gratefully, he swallowed the water, which barely soothed his parched throat, never mind curbed his craving thirst. Still, the liquid lifted his spirits.

"Thanks."

The sun had risen, almost directly overhead. While it wasn't hot, the air was so dry, the moisture was evaporating from his flesh. He could have drunk ten times what she'd brought him, but appreciated the wet mouthful.

She'd tied a bit of cloth around his head, leaving a brim to shade his face. When her head blocked the sun from his eyes, he could see her lips were cracked. Dirt and dried blood from several assorted scrapes marred her perfect skin that was already reddening from the strong sunlight.

She peered at him, her beautiful blue eyes filled with worry. "The plane's wreckage spilled over a wide area. So far, I haven't found any salt. This afternoon, I'll walk in the other direction and search."

She shouldn't be walking in the heat of the day. The effort would sap her energy. Yet, if she waited for dark, she couldn't see well enough to find anything. And he didn't know this region of her planet well enough to know if wild animals could be a danger.

"Stay." At least he could keep her with him through the hottest part of the day. Wishing he could explain, knowing he didn't have the strength to speak, he clasped her hand. But he must have drifted off again, because when he wakened once more, she was pouring more water between his lips.

She looked like hell but she'd scavenged scraps of material to wind around her head to shield her face from the sun. "Look what I found." She waved an unopened bag of chips in his face. "This was sitting all by itself, right in the shade of a rock, as if waiting for me to find it."

She opened the bag and placed a chip between his lips. As soon as the salt touched his tongue, he felt an immediate zing of reviving energy coursing through him. During the fire, he'd depleted what little salt he'd had in his system. And he'd done so again to protect them from the fall from the airplane. But this time, he was reviving more quickly. His body seemed to require less salt to recover.

His *Quait* had increased in power and he tried not to dwell on what he would become. Recovering more quickly than he'd expected was a boon that would aid in their survival. And he allowed her to feed him half the bag of chips before sitting up.

She closed the bag, carefully folding down the top. "We should save these. I don't know if we can find more."

"Agreed." Despite the cloth around her head, her skin looked dry and cracked. He would insist that she drink immediately. "Is there more water?"

"The little I found was in a broken piece of plastic that may have once been part of the plane's tank. You needed it more than I did."

She'd given him every drop of water. Her generosity stunned him and made him even more determined to save her. But now was not the time to let his emotions sidetrack his focus. If he intended to save her, he must assess their situation. "Communications?"

She shook her head and her tone reflected sadness. "I searched but I didn't find the satellite phone. Or any sign of the pilots."

He nodded and buried his guilt. He could do nothing for the dead pilots' families if he and Shara didn't survive. So as much as he wanted to express sorrow for their deaths, he shoved aside the inclination. The next decision he made might be the difference between living and dying. Dehydration was already setting in and when the sun went down tonight, the cold would lower their resistance to hypothermia. It might be warm enough now, but in the thin air of this desert, the night could be brutal.

So they needed water and fire. He shoved to his feet and slowly turned all the way around. Contrary to city dwellers' opinions, the desert was not flat. Ridges and gullies, cactus and dry grasses, and layered and loose rocks made up his view. As far as his eyes could see in every direction, he saw swatches of reds and patches of browns. And the scent of burned metal and dust permeated the dryness of every breath.

"What are you looking for?" Shara stood beside him, focused on him instead of the bleak landscape. A woman accustomed to luxury, of buying whatever struck her fancy, she appeared to be holding up remarkably well. She'd foraged and found him salt, fed him their only precious water, and had yet to voice one complaint. He couldn't have asked for a better companion—even if she had no knowledge of the desert, she possessed extraordinary common sense and a generosity of spirit in abundance.

He so badly wanted to give her encouragement. His gaze flickered to a dark smudge of gray-green on the horizon. "Is that a stand of trees?"

She squinted. "Maybe. Why?"

"Trees need water. And so do we."

"I planned to forage in that direction next. From what I can tell, we seem to have landed in the center of the plane's wreckage." She raised a hand to shade her eyes and searched the sky. "I don't understand why no one is looking for us."

He turned to her, puzzled. "Who would come and why?"

"Every pilot files a flight plan before leaving. And there's a black box on the plane—"

"Black box?"

"A locator device that tells the authorities, among other things, where the plane went down."

"Jamar would have sent out an electromagnetic burst to jam the signal. Your authorities won't know we went down until the plane doesn't show up in New York where we planned to refuel in a few hours."

"Then they won't send out a rescue party until morning and by then we'll be dead." She said the words with a calm that told him she had little energy left, that the lack of water was already sapping her will. Under normal circumstances a human could go three to four days without water, but in the desert the end would come more quickly.

"Listen to me." He placed his hands on her shoulders and locked gazes with her. "We are not going to die."

She snorted, pulled away and shoved a lock of hair out of her eyes. "Yeah, right."

"We can live off this land. I have survived in worse places." Hope brightened her eyes but before she asked more questions, he demanded, "Tell me what you've seen so far and where." Before they expended any more of their critical energy, he needed to assess all the data.

"That way"—she pointed north, responding like a soldier—"was the tail section of the plane. That's where our baggage was stored, but it appears that the fuselage cracked open and spilled the contents across the desert." She didn't mention seeing any of the camping equipment he'd purchased that would have helped them to survive. Instead, she pointed east. "And over there were pieces of the wings—I think. There were flaps and one charred, flat three-foot-by-five section. I found nothing useful except the bag of chips and the piece from the water tank."

"You did great." He knew they shouldn't waste more energy speaking. Just parting his lips dried out his tongue and the lining of his mouth and throat, but the walk to those trees would be difficult and long. He needed to give her all the encouragement he could to help sustain her will. She'd already expended a lot of stamina in foraging and taking care of him. Now it was his turn to help her.

Unfortunately, he doubted he was strong enough to carry her. He gathered her into his arms, tucked her head under his chin and rubbed her back. "We need to walk to those trees. It's our best chance to find water."

"This is a desert. There is no water in a desert."

"Sure there is." He pointed to a gully. "See those ridges? Water made them." He pointed to tracks in the sand, made by a large mammal that he hoped wouldn't attack people. "Whatever animal left that track has found a supply of water nearby to keep it alive. Water is here. And we will find it."

"Okay." She pulled back. "What about Jamar? Is he waiting to attack us again?"

It amazed him she was thinking beyond her immediate need for water. Shara had an unexpected depth to her that made his admiration soar. "Most likely Jamar's already left for the Dead Sea to recover the portal."

"I'm sorry."

"My mission isn't over yet."

"But even if we get out of here alive, Jamar will surely get to the Dead Sea first."

"Don't forget he'll have to set off the beacon to locate the second part. Perhaps we'll make it out of here in time to ambush him. Or perhaps I'll let him find all three parts and then steal them back."

"Suppose he destroys them?"

"He can't. Not until he finds all three." He held out his hand to her. "Come on. We're wasting sunlight."

They walked for a little over four hours, the pace slow. The terrain underfoot was rocky and they had to choose each step with care. Turning an ankle could be a death sentence. Lethal snakes curled on rocks in the sun and rattled their tails when they approached too closely, forcing them to take wide detours. Shara recognized the rattlesnakes and told Cade they had deadly venom.

He also avoided spiderwebs, knowing the tiny creatures' bites could be poisonous, too. And he kept a wary eye out for the large four-legged animal he couldn't identify from its tracks, pleased that its footprints seemed parallel to their path toward the far stand of trees, since it might indicate the animal was on its way toward water. But by far the most dangerous element couldn't be avoided—the sun. Without a cloud in the sky, the merciless dry air continued to draw moisture from their skin.

Shara's breath grew labored. Occasionally she stumbled from exhaustion, but she didn't ask to stop, displaying remarkable stamina. Cade had seen men in better shape than she fail to display her kind of quiet determination, and his admiration for her grew.

Along the slow journey, Cade saw parts of the airplane strewn across the desert, but he didn't dare stop to forage. Water had to be his top priority, their only priority. And as the sun began to set, they finally reached the trees.

"Hear that?" His voice was cracked.

Wearily, Shara shook her head.

"Listen." Cade heard the trickle of moving water and his heart lightened. They would not die of dehydration—at least not in the next twenty-four hours.

Shara leaned against a tree. Spent, she remained swaying on her feet as if knowing that once she sat, she wouldn't find the strength to shove to her feet again. Her hair dirty and matted with dust, her face smudged with dirt and dried blood, her lips cracked, she'd never looked more beautiful.

He hadn't expected her to walk all afternoon without complaint. And he marveled at her strength of will— because only mental toughness had kept her going.

"Come on. There's water. I can smell it." Taking her hand, he tugged. And like a puppet on a string, she staggered forward by his side.

They rounded a few trees to find the wonderful sight of water gurgling through the rocks. Together they stumbled, advancing to the edge of a clear pool that trickled and tumbled through a series of rocky ledges under the stand of trees. Dropping onto the warm rocks, they leaned over the pool. And side-by-side, they drank; to Cade those first mouthfuls sweet and cold and tasting better than candy from the Universal God. He had to force himself to take only a few sips and stop. Beside him, Shara guzzled and he pulled her back.

"I'm still thirsty."

"I know. But take only a few sips at a time or the fluid won't stay down. And heaving will dehydrate you even more than you already are."

"Okay." After removing the cloth she'd wound around her head, she splashed water onto her face then used the cloth to wipe it dry, smearing the blood and splashing her clothes in her eagerness to wash.

"Let me do that." Gently, he took the cloth from her hand,

dampened it, and then carefully rubbed away the dirt and dried blood, pleased that her scrapes didn't appear to be festering, the skin around them no redder than the sunburned parts of her flesh.

"When the sun sets, it's going to get chilly." He pointed to high grasses. "Can you pull up some grass for us to sleep on tonight? It will help keep us warm."

"Sure." She gazed longingly at the water. "Can I drink some more?"

"As much as you want. But only a little at a time. And don't get your clothes wet."

She sipped a few more careful mouthfuls as did he before standing. They'd found water, now he needed to keep them warm. "I'll try to start a fire."

"You have matches?" Her voice rose with happiness.

He chuckled. "I'll have to do it the prehistoric way."

He'd expected Shara to laugh with him or marvel that he could build a fire without the modern conveniences. Instead, she stared past his shoulder, her eyes wide with terror.

"Look out!"

Cade spun around and caught sight of the feral eyes of a pack of six wild beasts, the largest one charging straight at them. In an instant, he tried to put up his shield. Failed. Realizing he was too salt-depleted from the walk to protect them, he stepped forward and yelled at Shara. "Run. Climb a tree."

"Dr. Lyle Donovan?" Jules strode through an office door with the volcanologist's name beside it. She recognized him immediately from her visions. Tired gray eyes behind stylish glasses stared at a book tilted to catch the late Montana afternoon sunlight. He wore his thick brown hair tied back in a sexy hippie look that seemed at odds with his crisp white lab coat.

"I'm busy." His warm baritone caused her stomach to clench. Must be excitement over finally tracking him down. Her reaction certainly couldn't be from his expression, the scientist had yet to look up from his book, never mind smile.

Jules rested her hands on her hips. "You're always busy. You don't open your mail." Her gaze swept his perfectly neat desk to the huge stack of unopened mail that included magazines, letters, and packages that tumbled from a shelf onto the floor in a corner. His message machine blinked, waiting for him to answer the calls. "You don't answer your phone. Or knocks on the door—so I let myself in."

"I'm still busy."

Jules had had enough of the scientist's nonsense. She'd traveled across half an ocean and half a continent and might likely freeze to death before he deigned to notice her. So Jules, who didn't consider herself particularly rude or aggressive, had no intention of leaving. She was worried because Shara hadn't answered her satellite calls and her plane was late. Jules wanted answers about her visions and the infuriating scientist could at least deign to act as though she existed.

Stepping forward, she plucked the book from his hands.

"Hey." He glanced at her but instead of the annoyance she'd expected, his mouth widened into a charming smile that shot an electric jolt into her system. "What took you so long to find me?"

She tossed the book out of his reach, then folded her arms across her chest and leaned against his desk. "First you ignore me and now you're feeding me lines?" She grinned to show him she wasn't angry. "And people think psychics are crazy. But it's *really* scientists like *you* who are insane."

He leaned back with a laugh and his eyes crinkled pleasantly at the corners. For a scientist, he had a warm mouth, a sexy jaw, and very tan skin. Clapping, he applauded her with clear—not mocking—enjoyment. "You do know how to capture a man's attention."

"I've flown a very long way to talk to you."

"How about dinner?"

Was he asking her on a date? His sexy smile said he was interested, flirting. The way he was coming on to her after he'd totally ignored her for months had her totally off balance. She gaped at him. "Dinner?"

"We can talk over dinner."

"About volcanoes?"

"About anything you want." His eyes said that he was hoping she wanted him.

The oddest thing was . . . she did—right up until the moment the volcanologist removed his coat from a hook and she caught sight of a picture hanging on the wall. In the photograph, Lyle stood in front of a volcano, right next to Jamar.

12

⬡

When Trevor didn't see any sign of Shara and Cade at the movie premiere, he covered the event anyway and filed his story. Then he stopped by the hotel to see if they'd already checked out. For a C-note, a maid had let him into the now empty penthouse suite, verifying his premonition that they'd once again disappeared in the middle of the night. He'd checked the airport to learn their charter flight had taken off the evening before with a scheduled stop in Montana.

Trevor returned to his hotel room, discouraged, but more certain than ever that something very newsworthy was going on. After booking a flight to Montana, he researched Shara Weston's life in Los Angeles, learning the name of her business manager, her agent, and her attorney. And while reading an article about a former stalker, he came across the name of a bodyguard she'd once hired to protect her.

On a hunch that she was again in trouble and might require the services of the same bodyguard, he phoned the man, who picked up on the first ring. "Foster, here."

"My name is Trevor Cantrell, Mr. Foster. I'm wondering if you could tell me—"

"I don't give out information about particular jobs or clients."

"Are you working right now?"

"Actually, I'm free this week. What kind of protection are you looking for?"

"The kind you did for Shara Weston. I read in the newspaper that she'd hired you to protect her from a stalker. You think she'd give you a good reference?"

"Shara Weston doesn't give references and she didn't hire me. Her private investigator did. You can contact Teresa Alverez at . . ." The bodyguard reeled off a phone number that Trevor wrote down.

He dialed the number on a hunch that a PI might answer the phone 24-7, even this early in the day. It was busy. Trevor checked his watch. Already close to dawn, he had just enough time to stop by Ms. Alverez's office before leaving for the airport and Montana.

Trevor surveyed the outside of the classy building with a sense of foreboding. One car was parked in the lot, next to a sign that said in metallic script TERESA ALVEREZ. A light in the third-floor office burned brightly. The rest of the building remained dark.

His reporter instincts on alert, he let himself through the unlocked front door into the lobby, questions seething in his head. Why was the security system turned off? Why were the doors unlocked? And why was Teresa Alverez working this late, all alone?

Not wanting to advertise his presence, Trevor took the stairs, quietly opened the door, and strode through the building. Teresa's door was closed, but the light shined brightly, leading him to her office.

Heart pounding, Trevor placed his ear against the door. He heard nothing. Not the shuffle of paper turning. Not the beep of a fax. Not the sound of music. Perhaps she'd fallen asleep at her desk, but every instinct told him something was wrong.

Breathing lightly, he picked up a faint coppery odor. The polite thing to do was to knock. And yet he sensed something ominous behind the door, something unpleasant.

So instead of knocking, he slowly turned the knob. The door opened soundlessly on well-oiled hinges.

At the sight of so much blood on the walls, he almost missed the bloodied heap of flesh on the floor.

Trevor vomited. And then dialed 911.

The boarlike animal with a large head, flattened ears, long snout, and thick coat of gray bristly hair charged straight at Cade's legs, jaws wide as if intending to bite. With Cade's order to run and climb a tree urging Shara forward, she headed toward a mesquite tree to hide, uncertain the thin branches could hold her weight if she attempted to climb.

Heart hammering, she peeked over her shoulder, horrified to see Cade kicking the speedy and agile creature away—just as the rest of the pack gathered to attack. Adrenaline surged and she searched for a weapon, but unlike in the movies where a perfectly shaped branch the shape of a baseball bat lay at her feet, there was nothing at hand except dirt and rock.

Rocks.

Stooping she picked up several and hurled the missiles, praying she didn't hit Cade. Her aim was poor and she missed the boars. Worse she didn't have the arm to do any damage from this distance—not even enough to scare them away.

Cade picked up one of the boars as if it weighed no more than a basketball and tossed the heavy body into two other animals. The three tumbled, a spinning mass of outraged grunts and squealing snouts.

Determined to do something to help, Shara scooped up more rocks and advanced closer before hurling them, each time screaming as loud as she could. "Go! Get away! Leave us alone!"

One rock bounced off the side of the largest pig. He shrieked, shook his head, twitched his ears and stared at her as if preparing to charge.

Uh-oh.

Cade slammed the knife-edge of his hand against a boar's thick neck. The animal shuddered. The boar behind him, knocked into him and two more went down. But when none appeared injured badly enough to stay down or break off the attack, frustration ripped through Shara.

She was bending to gather more rocks, when out of the corner of her eye she saw a boar knock Cade to his knees. Cursing, angry, she heaved another rock . . . and missed. As if sensing Cade's weakness on his knees, the animals regrouped and looked as though about to charge as one.

Terrified, but determined to do something, Shara faced the beasts. She could no more stand back and let the beasts tear into him than she could refuse to give him life-giving salt. Shara knew what it was to take a life, to live every day knowing that the other would never see another sunrise, never laugh, never love. She simply didn't have it in her to kill Cade, or to stand by and watch him die—not even if it meant risking her own life.

Screaming as loud as she could, she ran straight at the boars, unloading rock after rock into their midst. A lucky shot landed on the leader's snout and left a bloody mark. Roaring in pain, the animal changed direction in midstride and stampeded straight at Shara.

Cade stuck out a foot. The boar tripped and fell, upended, almost doing a headstand before keeling over. Frightened at the sight of their leader going down, the other boars nudged him with their long snouts and feet. Slowly the beast lumbered to his feet.

Shara reached for another rock—but none was nearby. Yelling and waving her arms like a crazy woman, she ran straight at the boar. She locked eyes with the beast and fear lurched up her throat. Perhaps it had taken enough punishment, perhaps it feared the shouting woman charging toward him like a maniac, but with a final shake of its snout, it turned tail and lumbered away, the herd joining their leader to disappear through the mesquite.

Unsure if they'd return, Shara reached for another rock and held her breath, waiting to see what they'd do next. But the footfalls grew softer and lighter until she couldn't hear them at all. And she finally remembered to breathe.

Letting the rock drop from her numb fingers, she rejoined Cade, breathless and worried. "Are you all right?"

"Yes. You?" He rubbed the joint and calf muscle just above his foot and winced.

She nodded. "Did you twist an ankle?"

He gave her an I-told-you-to-climb-a-tree-and-you-didn't-listen look, but said nothing about her failure to obey his order, perhaps realizing he might have been boar food if she hadn't helped. "My foot's a bit sore from kicking the beast but otherwise, I'm fine. Too bad we didn't have the means to kill one of them—meat would have tasted good after we roasted it over a cooking fire."

"What fire?" she teased, and handed him the bag of chips.

He opened the bag and offered her a chip. She shook her head. "You need the salt more than I need calories."

He gestured to a spot on the dirt beside him, then popped a chip into his mouth. "We can share."

"I'm not a martyr but if you grow too weak to fight off the boars, what chance do I have?"

"You did your full part by chasing away those creatures. Your screams certainly scared me," he teased.

"A blood-curdling scream is necessary if an actress wants certain parts . . ." Her stomach rumbled and she walked past him and the tempting chips to drink. To lose weight for a role, she'd learned that hunger pangs could sometimes be alleviated by filling the stomach with enough liquid. And drinking was no hardship. The air remained dry and she never seemed to have enough fluids in her system, but she also worried how they would find their way out of this desert, because now that they'd wandered so far from the crash site, rescuers would have a hard time finding them.

Leaving what might be the only source of water for miles around could prove foolhardy—but if they stayed here, they'd starve. The choices depressed her or perhaps it was the simple fact that now that her adrenaline surge had ebbed, exhaustion was setting in along with the chill of night.

She drank deeply. When she lifted her head to the scurrying sounds of an animal's noises, she jerked upright, fearful the piglike creatures had returned. Obviously, many desert animals would come to this spring to drink, so perhaps camping here made them a target and wasn't the best site after all.

The sounds of scampering little feet seemed to come from the pool of water below the one where she drank. Something small, a squirrel or mouse scampered into the leaves, but a flat stone with smooth edges caught her eye. After a day in the desert, she'd learned little out here was straight or smooth. Curious, she investigated the flat, chalky-colored stone, wondering why the wild animal had been drawn to it.

Shara bent to pick up the stone but it didn't budge. And when her fingers pulled away, a residue clung to her flesh. First sniffing at the tangy scent, then licking the rock, she grinned. Salt. She'd found a salt lick.

Excitement washed away her exhaustion and she found a small sharp stone to chip off several salt nuggets. When she returned to Cade, she'd seen he'd also been busy. He was stripping bark from the mesquite branch and collecting the soft underside for tinder. He'd made a flat board with a hole at the bottom and had set aside a bowed branch where he'd tied his shoelace to the two ends to pull it into the shape of a bow.

Carefully, she opened her hand and held it out. "Look what I found."

He stopped and peered into her palm. "A rock?"

She grinned and lifted her hand higher, urging him to take the *rock*. "Taste it."

"I'm not hungry enough to eat rocks."

"Taste it."

"Fine." Gingerly he picked up the piece and licked it. "Salt? Where did you—"

"Ever hear of a salt lick?" When he didn't say anything, just popped the piece into his mouth and sucked happily, she explained. "Water often has salt in it and when it passes over rock and dries, it can leave salt deposits behind. I saw tiny creatures on this rock and investigated. You can have all the salt you need."

"Shara, you are truly a marvel. Thank you. And with all this extra salt, I'll have the energy to expend to make us a fire."

While he returned to working on his fire, she plucked more high grass for bedding and gathered firewood. Tired from the exhausting day, the work seemed to take forever, but eventually, she figured she'd collected a pile thick enough to spread under them both and enough wood to keep the fire fed through the night—if Cade really could start a fire.

After the sun set, she suspected the air temperature might drop enough to make staying outside a long and uncomfortable night without a fire. Lying on the ground with only jeans and light jackets wasn't enough to keep off the chill and she didn't want to think about those beasts returning to attack in the dark.

But with the heat from a fire, they would be comfortable. Already she had begun to shiver, using calories she didn't have to spare. "You think it will help to stuff some of this grass into my jacket for insulation?"

"Go ahead." One corner of his mouth pulled into a slight smile as if he was pleased by the difficult task now facing him. Cade picked up the bow, twisted the shoelace around a spindle, placed the spindle into the hole in a board and began to saw back and forth. "This may take a while."

"I'm not going anywhere."

He laughed, his grin widened and she found him irresistibly devastating. How many men could laugh in the face of their daunting circumstances? If she had to be stranded in the desert, she couldn't think of anyone she'd rather be with.

Relaxed, yet focused, Cade kept his eyes on the bow. Knowing she wouldn't be caught staring at him, she assessed him in a way she hadn't before. Those strong hands that had saved her from the boars, that were making the fire to keep her warm, had also given her pleasure. Although his mind had taken control of her will, she didn't find the notion as frightening or alien as she once had. Cade had saved her life so many times that her wariness of his alien differences was easing.

Shara wondered if another conversation with Jules would change her perception of Cade, but as he worked with a smooth precision that suggested he'd attempted this process before, she admired his skill and his determination. The repeated back-and-forth movements had to be tiring. And yet, he kept his rhythm strong, and as the sun set and the light cast reddish orange hues across the land, nothing was more beautiful to her than the sight of his patient persistence.

"Have you camped on Rama?" she asked, always curious to hear more about his home, about him.

"Underfirsts often run away by attempting to survive in the wild. The first time I tried I was only five. I didn't think to pack food or supplies, I had to return or starve."

"Were you punished for running away?"

"Of course." His tone was so matter of fact, it chilled her. "But the lure of freedom is a strong one." He spoke with the conviction of a man who'd never be satisfied with only a dream of autonomy. "So I read a few books on how to survive, and the next time I ran away, I survived for several months."

She imagined his world as full of cities and technology, not a planet where one needed survival skills. "How old were you then?"

"Ten."

At ten she was playing with dolls and the hardest task she'd had to perform was helping her father muck out the horse stalls in their barn. "And you lived on your own for months?"

"Finding food and drink was the easy part." He spaced his words evenly, and she suspected he was making light of all the hardships he'd suffered, as if speaking of what he'd endured was too horrible to repeat.

But she had to ask, had to know what drove a man to leave his world and everyone he knew on a mission that would likely fail. "What was the hard part?"

"Loneliness."

She lived alone on her island, but she was an adult, with all the comforts money could buy. He'd only been a kid and the self-reliance he'd learned hadn't seemed to have hardened him as it had her. In fact, until this very moment, she hadn't realized that she'd been lonely on Haven.

At first pain had forced her to build a shell. But sometime during those years she'd healed—only she hadn't known it. And she'd been so anxious to block the pain, she hadn't let herself feel anything—not even loneliness.

Even now, she didn't want to think about if she'd changed since meeting Cade, since leaving Haven. Sensing her question had stirred up memories in him that caused deep pain, she placed a comforting hand on his shoulder.

Despite the power of his muscles as he sawed back and forth on the bow, she noted his jerk at her touch. "Sorry, I didn't mean to mess with your rhythm."

"Do not forget who I am." He spoke mildly, but the edge of warning in his tone told her he'd forgotten nothing.

"You'll never be a First."

He snorted. "Now you sound like my brother."

She took a perverse pleasure in keeping her hand on his shoulder. He was so solid and warm. The repetitious motion took much energy and created a heat that radiated off him and she wished she could wrap her arms around him and sink into his warmth.

"I meant that your background and personality will always set you apart. Just because you have a power doesn't mean you'll use it cruelly."

"I shouldn't use it at all," he spat, his hands increasing the speed of the bow.

She breathed in and smelled . . . smoke. Kneeling down, she blew softly on the spot where a tiny stream of smoke curled into the air. "Keep going," she whispered in encouragement.

A tiny spark flared and quickly expired. But the smoke kept rising and she fed the tiniest, softest bits of bark into the thick part of the smoke and again blew lightly. The smoke thickened.

And burst into fire.

Cade stopped sawing and removed his bow from the flames. He placed dried leaves and twigs into the fire, then slowly added thicker pieces of wood, careful not to smother the tiny fire. A minute or two later, the fire crackled and popped and she held out her cold hands to the flames, delighted with the fire, but wishing she could warm her hands on Cade.

"You did it." Shara didn't have to force enthusiasm into her tone. Thirty minutes of patient friction had paid off, and she would benefit from his hard work with the comfort of heat. As Cade ringed the fire with rocks, she tried to recall all the reasons she should remain suspicious of him, but right now, in the middle of the desert, none of them seemed to matter.

As night descended quickly, the cheerful fire not only warmed her, she felt safer. She seemed able to focus her thoughts more clearly than any time since they'd make love. Shara had been alone for so long, hiding from the world on Haven, that she hadn't even known how much she missed the company of people. Of friends. Of a man. When Cade had admitted to his loneliness, a window had cracked open, letting her see that there was more to life than healing.

First she'd used alcohol to escape. Then she'd used Haven. Would she ever be strong enough to live without crutches?

How did Cade do it? He'd admitted to his childhood loneliness with an ease that told her he was comfortable in his own skin, accepted his need for others in a way that she never could. Certain that he'd been punished for returning to his people, she didn't ask more questions, just stared into the fire wondering if she would ever choose to meet life head-on—especially if she knew her actions would cause her more pain.

Trevor missed his flight to Montana. Instead, he'd waited at the hospital. Twenty-four hours after the doctors had given Teresa Alvarez a massive blood transfusion and sewed up her wounds, she recovered consciousness.

"How are you feeling?" Trevor asked as he pulled up a chair beside her bed so she wouldn't have to crane her neck to look up at him.

"I'm alive." Her eyes flashed between the bandages. "Thanks for getting me help. After a little plastic surgery, I should be back to . . . myself."

She didn't say back to normal. But Trevor suspected after going through that kind of ordeal, she might never be the same again. "I'm worried about Shara Weston. She's disappeared."

Teresa spoke quietly and with restrained dignity. "I owe you for saving my life, but I don't give out client information to reporters."

"So Shara did hire you," Trevor murmured, certain that much more was going on than he understood. And Teresa knew some of the answers. He could see it in her worried eyes. "Can you at least tell me her real destination so I can check to see if she arrived?"

"I already had someone check." Teresa hesitated as if debating how much to say and finally spoke again. "She's missing—and if you report that, it might cost Shara her life."

"I'm not a monster. And I can withhold my story until Shara is safe. Work with me." Trevor noted she hadn't told him where Shara had gone and placed his card on the night-stand. "Check me out and you'll find I'm reputable."

"If you weren't, I wouldn't be talking to you." Teresa's voice had an edge, an edge that might have been sharper without the pain medicine.

In pain, still drugged, she'd already done her homework from her hospital bed. Impressive.

But why did she look so guilty?

Trevor had been a reporter long enough to know when to push, and when to remain silent. This was one of those times he remained quiet. Teresa glared at him, clearly worried, and he suspected she wanted to reveal more than she had.

"There's no proof about what I'm going to tell you, but Ja-mar, the man who attacked me . . . he used some kind of hypnotic suggestion, maybe brainwashing—except that takes more time than he spent."

Trevor filed away the name "Jamar" for future research. "Could you have been drugged?"

"He gave me nothing. And my mind was clear." Her voice lowered in horror. "I *clearly* recall telling him everything."

So that's why Teresa felt guilty, but Shara couldn't blame her for talking. No one could have withstood that kind of pain. "He tortured you. You can't blame—"

"You don't understand." Teresa's voice broke. "He made me talk first."

This Jamar had hurt her for no reason at all. Trevor's fury flared that Jamar had put her through hell for nothing.

When Trevor didn't say anything—because he didn't trust himself to speak past his anger—she lifted her chin. "This is where you're going to think I'm crazy. I told my mouth not to move, but I spoke. I told my hand to clamp over my mouth, but my hand wouldn't move. Somehow, Jamar took over my mind, took everything from me, down to my fine motor control."

"Maybe you panicked. The mind does weird things under extreme stress."

"Perhaps. The guy was a monster. After he made me tell him everything, then . . . he hurt me—for the pleasure of it."

Trevor didn't know what to think. Teresa seemed so strong, too strong to break. "How is Jamar connected to Shara and Cade?"

"He wants them dead." Teresa closed her eyes.

His interview was over. He hadn't gotten much, but he now had a name: Jamar. And he'd heard a very disturbing story to go along with the one about the matching set of rubies that still couldn't be explained.

Could Teresa's claim of mind control be true? And what was the psychic's role in the story? Were Jules, Cade, and Jamar trying to pull some kind of elaborate con on Shara Weston?

13

⚙

The picture of Jamar and Lyle triggered one of Jules's visions. She saw Shara falling and flinched. Jerked, as metal fragments exploded. Trembled as tendrils of fire arched through a dark and cloudy sky. A sensation of uncontrolled descent, one so strong she heard the air rushing by her ears, her stomach plummeting. And then Shara's scream pierced her—a scream as strong as if she'd been standing next to her. Horrified, Jules watched Shara and Cade plunging toward the earth and spinning out of control in a sickening, spinning death spiral.

The next thing Jules knew, she'd collapsed against Lyle's supportive chest and arms, her legs shaking, her mouth gulping for air while she fought for equilibrium. She must have gasped or shouted because her throat was raw—or maybe that was due to fear for Shara. Ignoring the pain in her shoulder where she'd slammed against the door, Jules tried to think through the vision.

Had Shara's plane crashed?

"Jules?" Lyle spoke quietly. "Do you have epilepsy?"

God. The man thought she'd had a seizure. She almost blurted out she'd had a psychic vision when she remembered he was a scientist. He'd want explanations, proof. And she didn't have time—not until she found out whether Shara was okay. Tearing free of his arms, she dug into her purse.

"Do you need medicine?"

"My phone. Where's my damn phone?" Jules finally plucked it out, turned it on and dialed Shara. It rang. And rang. And rang. "Come on. Come on. Answer, damn you." But Shara didn't pick up and Jules didn't bother to leave a message. "She's likely dead."

"Excuse me?"

"My best friend's plane exploded. . . . Or maybe it's about to . . . I should warn her—but she won't answer her phone."

Lyle folded his arms across his chest, peered at her though his glasses and eyed her warily. "And you know the plane exploded because . . . ?"

"I'm psychic. And before you tell me there's no such thing, and that I'm some kind of fruitcake, let me tell you I see things every day that happen. That's why I came to this freezing place to find you."

"Because . . . I'm your fantasy man?"

"My best friend may have just died and you're making jokes?" Jules's anger rose up to choke her. All her life she'd known the outside world didn't believe in her abilities, but it had been enough that her family and friends respected her talent. They understood that her visions weren't perfect, but that didn't make them less valid. She didn't care how many years this man had spent studying science. She didn't care that he'd attended MIT, was a Rhodes scholar and had a Ph.D. from Stanford University. Right now, he could take all his science and shove it down the toilet. Because she knew as clearly as she could see the shock in his eyes that Shara was in trouble.

His tone was gentle, as if he feared saying anything to send her off the deep end. "I'm sorry. I shouldn't have assumed—"

"Damn right, you shouldn't." Ignoring him, she called Teresa Alverez. "Maybe Shara's PI can tell me what happened."

But Teresa didn't answer, either, and that disturbed Jules even more. She wasn't certain what time Shara's plane had left L.A. or which route they'd chosen. Sometimes her visions happened during the actual event. But often she didn't receive the vision until hours, days, or even weeks later. And sometimes she saw the future . . . perhaps Shara was still safe.

So Shara's plane could have exploded on takeoff, on landing, or anytime between. Or she might still be fine and the explosion Jules had seen might occur next year or in . . . She groaned. Dialed Shara again. Got the same recording. This time Jules left a message. "Shara, call me ASAP."

Jules put away her phone and looked up to see Lyle offering her a bottle of water from his office refrigerator. "Thanks." She twisted off the top and drank, enjoying the fact that he wasn't bombarding her with questions.

But he looked deeply disturbed and, for a few moments, he hesitated as if debating whether to say anything at all. Finally, he offered, "My mother was always thirsty after one of her *encounters,* too."

"Encounters?"

"Visualizations. Dreams. The second sight."

"Your mother is—"

"Was. She died a few years ago."

"She was a psychic?"

"So she claimed."

"You sound skeptical."

"I'm a scientist . . . and yet . . . she was right too many times to discount the possibility of . . ." Clearly he didn't want to admit that some people had a gift that science couldn't explain. "I thought my mother was unusually sensitive to her environment. That she unconsciously picked up signals that allowed her to guess the future more accurately than most people. She was atypically intuitive. She was so accurate, people traveled from other states to consult her. And her fortune-telling put me through college."

"So you don't think I'm crazy?"

He chuckled. "I didn't say that, but I figured a colleague found out about my mother and decided to play a joke."

"I came here because I keep seeing you in my visions." And she'd thought he might be another alien, an ally of Jamar's. But Lyle had too many documents on his walls, photographs that went back years. Of course, they all could have been altered in Photoshop and his tale a complete lie, but his tone while he'd told the story about his mother had sounded so genuine, she was inclined to believe he was human, born on Earth.

He shifted from foot to foot and stared at her. Most people, when hearing that she possessed psychic abilities, would ask far more questions than she could answer. Lyle didn't ask *any* questions. She could see he didn't want to know what had brought her all the way from Hawaii to Montana—and him.

His eyes darkened and he stepped back from the door of his office and her. "I think you should leave now."

"That won't make the vision go away."

His tone was flat, resigned. "Yeah, but I can't worry about what I don't know."

"You intend to remain ignorant so you can pretend that you're safe?"

"Sounds like a plan."

"A stupid plan. Every time I see your face—"

"I don't want—"

"I don't care what you want. Your face is always surrounded by—"

Lyle shoved her out the door and slammed it behind her. She'd always known he might not help but she'd never imagined he'd refuse to hear her out and her fury escalated. He didn't want to listen to her—not because he thought she was a kook, but because he feared her visions were genuine.

She pounded on the door. When he didn't open it, she

yelled at him: "Your face is always surrounded by an exploding volcano." He didn't say a word but he had to have heard her through the door. "Did you hear me?"

"Everyone in the entire building must have heard you."

"One of your volcanoes is live."

She expected him to shout. Instead after a short pause, she heard him laughing, deep belly laughs. Now she was the one who thought him crazy. She'd expected him to be unfamiliar with psychics and skeptical. She'd thought he might be angry. Upset. Instead he found her dire prediction . . . funny.

"How dare you refuse to take me seriously?"

"I take you very seriously." At her words he laughed even harder and reopened the door.

"Then why are you laughing?"

"Because Yellowstone's volcano is *always* live."

Jules frowned at him. "You've got to be kidding."

Lyle slipped into his coat and placed his hand in hers. "Come on. I'll show you."

Even with the fire blazing, the desert night on planet Earth was cooler than anywhere on Rama. Cade's homeworld possessed a more temperate climate and less variation in animal life. Even in darkness he could hear animal footfalls, tiny ones rustling in the brush, birds flapping overhead, insects humming and buzzing. He slept lightly, wakened several times to feed the fire, but he couldn't sleep much when he ached to gather Shara into his arms.

No matter how often he told himself she was off limits, his body didn't listen. After making love in the hotel, he knew how good it could be between them. Her soft skin, her enthusiasm, her genuine sensuality called to him. He must not listen. Unable to control his *Quait,* he'd agreed not to touch her again. He'd been shocked she wanted anything to do with him. And after saving his life, she deserved more than total domination.

After Cade fed the fire for the third time, he returned to his spot in the long grasses beside Shara. The fabric at her throat parted and he saw the hollow of her neck fill with soft shadows. Her slim waist flared into agilely rounded hips and the sun had burned color into her high cheekbones. Loose tendrils of hair tumbled carelessly over her shoulders and softened her face, giving her a delicate and ethereal quality in the flickering firelight.

Yet, today Shara Weston had shown him she was no fragile desert flower but a strong and competent woman. She'd found him salt. She'd thrown rocks at boarlike creatures, she'd pulled up grass for their bed. And he owed it to her to protect her . . . even from himself.

Cade built the fire high and fell asleep. And he'd awakened with her back pressed against his chest, his sex hard, his hand under her shirt cupping her breast. Despite his determination to stay away from her during the night, he'd gathered her into his arms, or she'd snuggled against him for warmth—he wasn't sure who had moved closer to whom. Automatically, he folded her against him, willing to share his heat, unwilling to share his growing arousal. Gritting his teeth, he tried to think of anything but this luscious woman in his arms.

But while he controlled his waking thoughts, he couldn't steer his dreams. Half asleep, he yearned to kiss her neck, her lips, her collarbone, and sometime between sleeping and waking, his dreams turned into a reality. Half asleep, he must have used *Quait* to remove their clothes so they could be skin to skin.

When she snuggled against him, her skin as soft as gossamer, her hair so silky, he could think only of having her again. Unaccustomed to holding a woman and denying himself, his body demanded release.

And *Quait* kicked in, stronger than last time, taking over his conscience until he set aside his scruples. He wanted her. He could have her. What could be more simple?

He could no more stop his hands from holding her than he could stop the stars overhead from shining. No more stop his lips from settling into the recess of her neck than he could stop the fresh water from bubbling in the spring. No more stop his body from seeking hers than he could stop the gravitational pull between the Earth and the moon. Fighting *Quait* was like halting the most powerful and elemental forces of nature—impossible.

"Mmm." She turned, groaned deep in her throat, a sexy soft moan that shimmied straight through him.

He kissed her long and hard and deep, taking what she offered, then demanding more. So giving, so responsive, Shara Weston teased him, taunted him, tantalized him, tormented him, with her luscious lips and her tempting hands and her sensuous legs that wound around his. And when she arched her spine, pressed her breasts against his chest and her nipples tightened, he lost himself in the smoothness of her skin, the softness of her curves, the pounding of her heart against his.

Perhaps it was the lack of civilization, perhaps it was the knowledge that they could have died earlier that day and might yet die tomorrow, but living in this moment had enhanced, brightened, and intensified each of his senses. Making love to Shara became the most important thing on Earth, the only thing on Earth.

For heart-pounding minutes that extended into the night, she became the focus of his every yearning desire. The powerful and potent need to dominate her, to subject her to his will erupted with the force of a supernova—inexorable, unstoppable, irresistible.

"Take me." She opened her eyes wide, wound her hands around his neck and attempted to roll to her back, trying to pull him with her.

But he denied her wish. He denied her movement. Instead, he kept her on her side, tilted her chin up so he could watch her eyes, and reached for her breasts. "You're so soft."

He cupped her breasts and ever so slowly circled his thumbs around her nipples, never quite touching the deliciously hardened tips. "You're so sensitive."

She released a soft moan of need. Her eyes dilated with yearning. A muscle twitched in her jaw. But she couldn't move.

He didn't allow it. And he enjoyed making her wait to see what he'd do next.

"You're so very beautiful," he murmured, sinking his teeth into her shoulder and nipping her flesh.

He pulled back his head to watch her expression in the firelight as he roughly flicked her nipples with his thumbs. After the tender caresses, her eyes widened further with surprise and need. Darkened even further with desire.

He needed to hear her speak. And he lessened his *Quait* enough to let her talk. But she didn't seem to realize her new freedom.

He grinned wickedly and pinched her nipples. She gasped at the pain and pleasure he'd just given her. And when he dipped his head to suck away the sting, he urged her knee to bend, allowing his fingers access between her legs.

"Tell me you want me," he demanded.

"I want you." When she didn't hesitate to respond, a predatory ruthlessness washed over him. He wanted to make her frantic for him. He wanted her wild with need. He had to have her out of her head with desire.

"Tell me you trust me," he ordered.

She started to speak but must have caught a gleam of his wildness. "I . . . I . . ."

He chuckled at her vacillation. "Ah . . . Shara, Shara, my beautiful Shara. You and I . . . we're going to have a very good time."

"Yes."

"And I'm not going to take you . . . until I melt all resistance from your soul."

"What resistance?" Her fingers clutched his shoulders. "I want you. Don't you know that?"

For answer, he leaned over and bit first one nipple, then again sucked away the tingle of pain he'd created, swirling away her ache with his tongue before he gave her other breast the same devotion. Before he'd finished with her breasts, she was panting, her breaths irregular between tiny coos of pleasure that broke from her throat.

Cade slid to his back. "Straddle me."

Without hesitation, she climbed over him and placed her knees to either side of his hips, eager to take him inside her. She tried to lower her hips.

He kept her on her knees. "Not yet."

He wriggled a bit, turning her to directly face the fire. With the light flickering over her flat belly and pert breasts, her hair tumbling over her shoulders, her eyes wild, she resembled a magnificent goddess.

When she realized that he'd frozen her muscles so that she couldn't lower herself onto him, frustration clouded her eyes. Her lips quivered.

"I like looking at you." He ran his fingers over her jaw. "I like touching you wherever I want. Whenever I want." He lifted her breasts, testing their weight, watched her try to restrain a soft groan. "And now your legs are open, parted, waiting for my touch. You want me to touch you, don't you?"

"Yes."

"But I'd rather keep you waiting."

"Noooo." She sounded so disappointed and he grinned, flicked her nipples, and as she tensed, more gulps of delight came from her throat. "Ah. Oh . . . Oh . . . Arghh."

Her eyes grew wild as he held her still, waiting for him to decide what he would do next. Firelight bathed her. Her nostrils flared. Her breath grew ragged.

Her tone was proud, throaty with longing. "Let me take you inside me."

"Not yet." He removed his hands from her breasts and placed them on her bottom.

At his touch she quivered but he still didn't allow her to move. Then he slid lower, until he'd positioned his mouth between her open thighs.

When he blew warm air on her most delicate lips, she gasped, sputtered, shook. He slid his fingers from her bottom to part her woman flesh, opening her wide. And then, at the same time he raised his head and his mouth found her center, he squeezed her cheeks.

She yelped at the combination of sensations and sweetly shuddered into his mouth. "Oh . . . my . . . oh . . . Cade . . . oh, oh, oh."

He savored every single incomprehensible syllable that she uttered. And as she orgasmed and broke over him in wave after wave, he kept his tongue swirling in her slick, tasty heat, kept his hands clasping her buttocks, keeping her orgasm alive, and burning, hotter, higher, harder.

She shook with her shattering and screamed, a tight howl of pure lust. And as her shudders eventually began to subside, he rubbed the sting from her bottom with his fingers and palms and gently licked her cream.

"I can't . . . can't . . . oh . . . my God. You were so fantastic . . . I . . . Cade." Her tone changed from wild and throaty to feminine curiosity. "Let me have you."

"I don't think so."

Frustration and wonder threaded her tone. "What the hell are you doing?"

He gave her a few seconds to recover from his mouth. "I thought we should find out how many times you can have your woman's pleasure."

"You're going to kill me."

He chuckled. He flicked his tongue over her center. "I don't think so."

"I suppose—oh . . . ooooh." She laughed, her tone low and husky, clearly eager for more. "I suppose there are worse ways to die."

Four orgasms ago, Shara's concern over Cade's unusual ability had disappeared. Three orgasms ago, she'd lost her ability to think past what he was doing to her. Two orgasms ago, her self control vanished. One orgasm ago, she'd begged.

At his complete mercy, he'd wrung her dry. If he hadn't controlled her muscles with *Quait,* she would have pooled into melted bliss. But he had more than enough stamina and determination for them both. She hadn't known her body could take such pleasure without frying her brain cells.

Well, maybe they were fried. She couldn't think beyond the last mind-blowing orgasm. Her body had grown super-sensitive. The slightest caresses caused her to tremble, but surely he was about to short circuit every exhilarated nerve ending.

Finally, finally, finally, he grasped her hips and lowered her onto his delicious hardness. And she craved his fullness, tensing to ride him.

But he let her do nothing. He lifted her with his hands, thrust into her with his hips, making sure that each long stroke caressed her where he'd create the best friction. "Faster. Please."

He gave her exactly what she asked for. And the ferocity of his movements matched her burning desire to have him deeper. Harder. And right now.

Her thoughts spun. Her mouth gasped. Her throat tightened. Beneath her hips, his bronzed flesh, slick with sweat, glistened in the firelight and showed off his burnished physique. But it was the intensity on his face that drove her. Never had she seen such naked passion.

He took her over the top with him. This time, he gathered her close against his chest, held her as pure sensual heat poured through her system. He held her for a long time, until their rapidly beating hearts slowed, and her ragged breath ebbed to normal.

"We shouldn't have done that," he growled as he rolled out from under her.

"Hey, it was *your* idea." Being dumped into the cool grass after being pillowed by his warm flesh set her teeth on edge. So did his insinuation that she'd had any say-so. She'd been asleep and wakened to pure seduction. He'd never given her brain a chance to catch up to her body and she'd simply gone with the flow. She couldn't imagine a woman who would have done otherwise.

"*Quait* kicked in. Having you again was a mistake."

"Great excuse," she muttered, the idea of putting clothes back on her sweaty body was as totally unappealing as staying by the fire to argue with him. Gathering up her clothes, she stalked to the stream, determined to wash as best she could before dressing.

How dare he make love to her so thoroughly and then tell her it had been a mistake? Damn him. They'd agreed not to do this and yet she couldn't put all the blame on him. She'd wanted him and, if she was truthful, it had been more than lust.

Every muscle in her legs still trembled from the amazing experience. She was certain she'd walk bowlegged for a week—that is, if she could find the strength to walk at all. But she hadn't once considered telling him to back off. Obviously his *Quait* didn't bother her enough to turn her off.

Hobbling to the pool, she drank deeply and splashed water on her face. The icy water took her breath away, which was probably just as well because she had absolutely nothing less than R-rated words to say to Cade—calling their lovemaking a mistake really irked her.

As much as she hated the idea of donning her clothes without a bath, she didn't much like the notion of freezing to death, either. She'd started to slip into her bra when she heard splashing.

Turning around she saw he'd already thrown more wood onto the fire, stoking up the heat. And naked, Cade was using two sticks to pluck stones out of the fire and toss them into the small pool.

"What are you doing?"

"How about a bath? At least one at lukewarm temperature?"

He was throwing hot rocks from the fire pit into the pool to heat the water. Such a simple idea, yet brilliant. And one she'd never have thought of.

When he finished throwing, she bent to test the water temperature. The springs flowed in a series of rock pools and he'd wisely chosen a small and shallow one off to the side where the current wouldn't quickly sap the heat.

"It's tepid." She stepped into the water and found cool spots as well as warm spots. Knowing the temperature would chill fast, they made the most of the heat, washing quickly, then using the bits of cloth they'd wound about their heads to protect their flesh from the sun to dry them before dressing in their dirty clothes and hurrying back to the fire.

Perhaps they could wash their clothes in the daytime.

After returning to the fire, Cade sat on the opposite side from her, feeding more wood into the flames and then again making a pit of rocks along the perimeter. Stiff, brooding, he wore a closed, stoic look and his eyes, sad and slightly hostile, didn't invite her to start a discussion.

So she shivered by the fire and watched the sun rise and felt very much alone. She had no idea which desert they'd landed in or how far away it might be to civilization. There was only her and Cade. And his hot lovemaking followed by his declaration that sex had been a mistake made him seem darker, stranger, more alien, than he had since they'd met.

Perhaps his pulling back was a good thing, reminding her that beneath his civilized exterior was a man she didn't know very well. Jules had warned her not to trust Cade and her friend was always on Shara's side. And right about now Jules had to be worried sick about her.

Jules would have tried to call Shara. And when Shara didn't answer, she would assume something had gone wrong. Of course she wouldn't panic immediately. Even satellite phones could go dead. But eventually Jules would kick up a fuss. Send out search parties.

Would anyone know where to begin to look? And would they still be alive by the time a rescue party found them?

Perhaps they should consider trying to walk out of the desert. But she had no idea which direction to go, hated to give up their water supply, yet staying here likely meant starvation. And the sooner they began their journey, the more strength they would have.

Cade had so much more survival experience, she wanted to ask his thoughts on the matter. But after another look into the clear hostility in his expression, she maintained her silence.

Clearly, he didn't like that he'd been unable to resist making love. And Shara really didn't want to think about it, either.

14

❂

"Yellowstone Volcano Observatory is a partnership between the United States Geological Survey, Yellowstone National Park, and the University of Utah," Lyle lectured Jules in a tone that told her he'd repeated the statement many times as he led her out of the office building toward his four-wheel drive Jeep. "We closely monitor volcanic activity at Yellowstone."

Although it was early fall, snow flurries obscured the distant mountains. In the thin air, Jules shivered, tried to put aside her worry over Shara's failure to answer the phone, as well as her vision of Shara's plane exploding to pay attention to what Lyle was telling her.

But how could she think when it was cold enough to see her breath in the air? When all she wanted was to go home to lush palm trees, warm Hawaiian breezes, and white sand beaches?

Lyle opened the door for her. "It's my job to monitor real-time data for earthquakes, ground deformation, stream flow, and selected stream temperatures."

His explanation went in one ear and out the other without

leaving much of an impression in her brain. She already knew Lyle was smart or he wouldn't be a scientist, but she finally knew why she was here and what she wanted from Lyle. If Shara couldn't stop Cade from building his portal, Jules needed Lyle to go to Haven and use his expertise to convince Cade that the portal would cause a catastrophic explosion.

She'd already told Lyle she was a psychic and while that had gone over better than she could have hoped, she knew she couldn't come right out and tell him more. She could just imagine his expression if she explained that an alien wanted to build a portal to another planet and her vision predicted it would cause a series of volcanic eruptions across the Pacific Rim. Yeah, it was so scientific and sane that no doubt he'd do just what she wanted—leave his job and book the next flight to the South Pacific.

Jules didn't like lies, or scheming, and she dreaded the idea of driving over the icy road. She hated the cold. Snow seemed bizarre to her Hawaiian genes. She didn't think she'd been thinking clearly or had been warm since her plane had landed. And concentrating on Lyle's job or what to do next wasn't even uppermost on her mind. She wanted to know about that picture of Cade's brother on Lyle's wall.

So after he walked around the vehicle and slid behind the wheel, she tried not to think about the cold leather seat. "Tell me how you know Jamar."

"Dr. Jamar?" Lyle started the engine. Frosty air blasted from the heater. "In addition to monitoring the site, I collaborate with scientists from around the world to study the Yellowstone volcano."

Lyle shifted and smoothly pulled into the snow-tire tracks of other vehicles. She casually braced her hand on the dash and ignored her churning stomach. "So Dr. Jamar also specializes in Yellowstone?"

"Actually, he wanted me to analyze the difference between volcanic action here and on Haven, a tiny island in the South Pacific." Lyle glanced at her. "Is it a coincidence that that island is in your region of the ocean?"

Jules ignored his perceptive question. "How long ago was this?"

"About two years."

Wow. Jamar had arrived way before Cade. Jules wasn't sure how this fact was significant and filed it away to think about later.

"Was Jamar fearful the island might erupt?" she asked, cautious, yet curious.

"The science of forecasting a volcanic eruption may have advanced significantly over the past twenty-five years but not on an island as tiny as Haven."

"I don't understand." The back rear tire slipped and she restrained a gasp of fear. Lyle didn't even seem to notice the skid.

"We now believe that we can measure signs of volcanic activity in advance of a catastrophic eruption."

The man had to have balls of steel to drive to work every day over roads that resembled an ice-skating rink. With all the slush, snow, and ice, she could barely make out where the road was. "What kind of signs?"

"Strong earthquake swarms and rapid ground deformations typically take place weeks before a major explosion."

The Jeep hit a rut and her teeth gnashed. When they reached a smooth stretch of road and she could speak without fear of biting her tongue, she asked, "So wouldn't those same signs happen on Haven?"

"The island might be too small to show land deformations. In addition quakes under an island are hard to pinpoint, especially an island way out in the middle of the Pacific Ocean."

"Hold on a sec. I want to try and reach my friend again." Jules tried Shara on her cell phone, but again, no one answered. She also tried Teresa Alverez and got the same result. Resigned to being out of touch for now, Jules stuffed her phone back in her bag, determined to call every hour until she reached them. Beside her, Lyle drove with easy familiarity and she focused on him, rather than the chilling outdoors. "What did you mean when you said that you're always around active volcanoes?"

"Yellowstone possesses many geysers, hot springs, steam vents, and mud pots and all are evidence of active geologic forces." Lyle spoke with the ease of a college professor, his tone deep, enthusiastic and . . . masculine. His eyes sparkled behind his glasses as he warmed up to his subject. "Earthquakes around here are common, with one thousand to three thousand annually."

"That's a lot of earthquakes."

"So when you tell me you've seen me around an active volcano, well . . . we're driving over one of the biggest active volcanoes in the world."

"You're serious?" *Damn. Damn. Damn.* She recalled the image in her vision of his earnest face and the volcanic eruption spewing lava. Now, he told her they were driving over a land that averaged three earthquakes each day.

He must have seen the look of horror in her eyes. " 'Active' doesn't mean it's going to explode. In fact, the probability of a major explosion here has been calculated to be as probable as a one kilometer asteroid hitting Earth."

"Thanks. I feel so much better now." She peered out the darkening window, almost grateful she couldn't see more of this frozen land.

When he stopped, she feared they were stuck. He checked his watch as casually as if he were about to catch a bus. "We should just be able to make it."

"What?"

"I thought you'd like to see Old Faithful."

He sounded so enthusiastic, but the idea of stepping out of a perfectly warm vehicle into the snow and cold had about as much appeal as ice fishing at the North Pole. She tried to sound disappointed. "It's too dark to see anything."

"We have night lights for special showings." He sounded proud, enthusiastic.

Great. Jules swallowed hard, pulled up her scarf to cover her chin and neck and forced her voice to sound cheerful. "That sounds awesome."

The moment she opened the door, frigid air blew down her neck. Her feet slid on the ice, snow drizzled into her shoes.

Lyle took her arm. "Let me help you. The walk can be slippery."

No kidding. "Thanks." Jules pasted a smile on her face and prayed Shara would call her soon, because if she didn't hear from her by morning, she was contacting whomever she must to begin a search and rescue.

Like any First, Jamar detested physical labor and while it would have been easy enough for him to mentally enslave enough of the Israeli people into obeying his will, if he used them to uncover the first portal piece, they'd remember what he'd made them do. And since he had to work in secret, using them and letting them live wasn't a good option. And killing them would have caused an incident that might have set the authorities against him . . . so he'd decided that doing the nasty work himself was the correct choice.

But with every shovelful of muck he dug under the hot sun, he cursed Cade. The slime worm would pay for every blister, every drop of perspiration, every second of back-breaking labor on this empty stretch of land along the muddy bank of the Dead Sea.

One of the lowest places on this barbaric planet, the smelly water sat in the middle of a desert. It was beyond him why anyone would want this worthless land, never mind fight over it for three thousand years.

Shoving the blade into the soft muck with his foot, then extracting each sucking load caused his lungs to heave. Making slow progress, he sought to work faster before the mud seeped back into the hole he'd just dug. According to his instruments, the portal piece was only another two feet down, but the mud filled in almost as fast as he could dig.

Using determination and super-Raman effort, Jamar finally struck something hard. Dropping to his hands and knees, he scooped out the muck, eager to recover the first portal piece and turn on the signal to see where the second one had fallen.

After Jamar matched the GPS signal to a map, he swore. "Salt's blood."

The portal was supposed to land in unpopulated areas. Yet the damned thing had landed in the northeastern part of the United States in a state called New York.

Interrupting his cursing, Jamar's cell phone rang. "Yes?"

"We've picked up a report of two people, a man and a woman who seemed to have survived a plane crash, near the coordinates you asked for us to monitor."

Damn Cade. Once again, he'd managed to survive.

Jamar's communicator beeped. Receiving a message from Rama was rare enough to startle him. "Hold on, I have another call."

He set down the cell phone and hurried to read the response to his last missive home, where he'd informed the Council of Firsts that Cade had arrived on Earth and that his *Quait* had grown strong enough to walk through fire. He read the message twice, sweating and cursing their stupidity.

The Council had ordered Jamar to keep Cade alive long enough to test the underfirst's new abilities. Didn't they understand that Cade was dangerous?

The underfirst had eluded death too often for Jamar not to be wary and he had no way to judge his growing powers. Cade had survived everything Jamar had thrown at him—the shooting of his spaceship, the island laser-burst attack, the fire, and the plane crash. And damn Cade to everlasting hell, he'd apparently survived the rigors of the desert, too.

Of course, it might be the pilot or copilot and the woman who'd lived, but Jamar couldn't count on luck. He picked up the cell phone and gave his orders. "There's been a change in plans."

Watching the geyser gush had been an experience that Jules would have enjoyed more if she hadn't been so cold or so concerned about Shara. The spectacular fountain of water bursting into the air had served to remind her that mother nature's powerful forces shouldn't be messed with without taking the utmost precautions.

Afterward, Lyle had driven them to a restaurant for dinner. She'd periodically attempted to reach both Shara and

Teresa all evening but surprisingly her concern didn't stop her from enjoyment of the meal . . . or Lyle's company. After dinner, he'd escorted her to her hotel room and joined her for a few glasses of wine in the bar. Sparks darted between them, and Lyle had kissed her good night in the doorway of her room.

Talk about sizzling connections. Damn, the scientist sure knew how to turn her on.

With the way her nerves were jumping and her pulse was racing, the evening might have proceeded in a romantic vein—except her phone rang. Light-headed from the kiss, Jules fumbled with the phone, checked the caller ID and frowned at the number she didn't recognize.

"Hello?"

"It's Teresa Alverez. Have you heard from Shara?"

Fear spiked down Jules's back. "I was hoping you had. But I had a vision of her plane exploding over a desert."

"Most of Israel is a desert—I think." To Jules's horror, Teresa told her that she was in the hospital after suffering a brutal attack from Jamar.

She hung up the phone, numb.

"What's wrong?" Lyle asked.

Jules felt as if she'd been punched in the gut so hard she was about to vomit. Jamar had tortured Teresa. The man was brutal. And according to her vision, Cade was even more dangerous. Now her best friend in the world—if she was still alive—was alone with Cade, trying to stop him.

Jules's eyes brimmed with tears. Where was Shara? What was happening to her?

"If you don't tell me, I can't help." Lyle took her into his arms and held her.

Jules appreciated his calm strength. At the turn of events, he'd turned passion into compassion and she appreciated his giving her time to come to grips with what she'd just learned.

Finally she spoke, choosing her words with care. "The private investigator that Shara hired was tortured. Teresa was forced to reveal Shara's flight plan. I'm afraid that's why her plane didn't arrive in Israel. I have to notify the FAA and the FBI to begin a search and rescue."

Shara awakened to beeping. Although she hadn't risen to the sound of an alarm clock in years, half asleep, she automatically reached to turn off the irritating noise and her hand landed on something hard, a muscular shoulder to be exact.

Snuggled against one another to share body heat, they'd fallen asleep beside the fire. The sun was rising and Shara had no idea what was causing the electronic beeping.

She shook his shoulder. "Cade?"

He muttered something but didn't otherwise move.

"Cade." She shook him harder, then stood, hoping the sound of civilization meant rescue. But the desert remained empty, except for a few tiny creatures scurrying by the salt lick.

Cade blinked sleepily and opened only one eye, as if deciding whether waking was a good idea. Unwilling to allow him to slip back into sleep, Shara kneeled beside him. "Is that beeping coming from you?"

Cade sat up so fast, she jumped backward in surprise and toppled to her bottom. "What's wrong?"

He stood, dug into his back pocket and removed the device he'd made out of RadioShack parts back in Hawaii. She peered at it warily. "Is that the locator beacon alarm?"

"Yes." He frowned and switched off the beeper. "Jamar's found the first portal piece."

"But he can't destroy it, right?" She was fuzzy about the portal pieces' engineering.

"Correct. If he destroys the first sphere, the beacon won't activate the two other pieces."

"Why would Jamar care? If he destroys the first piece of equipment, won't he have succeeded in stopping you?" And Shara wouldn't have to do so herself.

"Not necessarily. While three pieces are optimum to tap the volcano, in theory one piece might suffice."

Might? Shara didn't like the sound of that and wondered if the lack of a piece could lead to the cataclysmic explosions of Jules's visions. "So Jamar needs to find all three pieces to make sure he stops you?"

"The beeping woke us after he found the first piece and it activated the second beacon."

"Where is it?"

"Upstate New York, which gives us a chance to arrive there first. He's still in Israel. We're closer."

"Uh—have you forgotten that we're stranded in the middle of the freaking desert?" Standing, she dusted off her backside. Her stomach growled. She hadn't slept well after their lovemaking and subsequent argument.

She would have killed for a hot cup of coffee with scrambled eggs, wheat toast, and strawberry preserves. Or flaky croissants slathered with honey butter. Or pancakes with blueberries and whipped cream. But as hungry as she was, she'd have traded all the breakfast food for a good shot of whiskey and the satisfying burn that would spread through her system and bring on a fuzzy warm glow.

At first she thought the buzzing in her ears was simply due to weakness from lack of food. But then she saw Cade peering between the trees toward the sky, his hand raised to his forehead. "It's a plane."

He raced for the open desert and she peeled off after him. A plane meant rescue from the heat of the day, the cold of the night, and the gnawing hunger. Rescue meant a hot shower, communication with the world, and a call to Jules.

Heart pounding, Shara sprinted after Cade, ready to wave her arms and guide in their rescuers. But the plane flew into the sunrise and the eastern sky, clearly unable to spot them and she skidded to a halt. Despair and exhaustion struck her and she wanted to throw a temper tantrum, stomp her foot and scream at fate—but she couldn't find the energy.

"More planes will come and we must be ready." Cade's words interrupted her pity party.

"How do you know more will come?"

"The plane appears to be flying a search pattern." He pointed to the sky. "See. It's turning."

"But it's not coming back this way. Maybe it's simply changing course."

"Maybe. But how long must you be out of touch before Jules will know something is wrong and call in help?" Cade took her hand and led her back toward their camp. "If you gather enough branches, we can move the fire into this clear spot and create a lot of smoke the next time a plane flies our way."

His words made her feel better. Whether he believed them or not, she didn't know, but his determination awed her. "What makes you so strong?"

"The salt you found for me." He answered simply and squeezed her hand.

"I'm not talking about physical strength, I'm talking about how you manage to stay positive. How you don't give up—no matter what."

"What other choice do we have?" He frowned as if he didn't understand her question.

Shara might founder, but Cade kept going. He solved problems and looked for solutions. It was as if he put all his energy toward the goal, leaving no room for doubts or despair or the what-if-no-one-finds-us question. His special kind of mental fortitude awed her. He did it without alcohol, without family, without any of his people to help him. He did it alone.

And this was a man who hated his mental control? If anyone could use absolute power for the good of his people, she would bet on Cade. She'd heard the saying "Power corrupts and absolute power corrupts absolutely," but she'd never met anyone so strong-minded, so determined to succeed.

To stop him, she'd need to be just as determined. She'd have to pick her moment with the utmost care, because if she revealed her strategy too soon, he'd own her.

"Come on." Cade interrupted her thoughts. "We can move the fire after breakfast."

"Breakfast?" At the memory of the locator device in his pocket, she wondered what else he had stashed away. "Have you been holding out on me?"

Together they strolled back toward the stand of trees

around the spring. Cade glanced sideways at her, his expression puzzled. "What do you mean?"

Her voice rose in anticipation and her mouth salivated at just the idea of food. "I'd forgotten about the locator device and thought perhaps you might pull a granola bar from your pocket, too."

"There's food all around us." He gestured to the desert and she considered whether he was hallucinating. All she saw was dirt, rock, and cactus.

"Yeah, right. Just beyond the next rise, there's a gourmet feast just waiting for us to eat."

He chuckled at her sarcasm, and pointed to a hole in the dirt. "That's a burrow."

"Looks like a hole to me."

"It's a hole made by an animal."

"And?"

"If we catch it, we can eat it."

"You're assuming the animal is still around. Maybe it made the burrow last winter."

He kneeled down, parted the grass and pointed to a tiny indentation in the sand. "That track is fresh."

"How can you tell?" Sometimes Cade's knowledge amazed her. He'd just arrived on Earth but he knew how to survive here better than she did.

"The edges are sharp and clear."

As hungry as Shara was, she didn't want to think about what kind of animal lived there. Or about killing and eating it. "I'll gather more wood," she volunteered, leaving the hunting for food to Cade—a task that made her squeamish.

She'd grown up on a farm and if he caught food, she would eat it. So she certainly wouldn't condemn him for hunting. She just preferred to avoid the unpleasant task. She soothed her conscience with the knowledge that he was much more qualified to hunt than she was. In fact, she had no idea how to go about it.

"Choose the branches with lots of leaves. They'll make the most smoke." Cade snapped a stick and knelt beside the burrow.

During her trips from the stand of tree where she gathered branches, she watched his progress. Cade found a large flat rock that he propped up with the stick. He baited the trap with a potato chip. Clearly, he hoped that as the animal went for the chip, the rock would fall. Primitive, but efficient.

Dragging the wood in the hot sun required frequent rest and she drank often at the spring. After one trip, she dumped armfuls of branches and rested near the fire. "Are we moving camp?"

"I'd rather stay by the trees, because it's a bit warmer there at night, but keeping two fires going takes too much effort."

"All right. I'll move our bedding grasses next."

"Here." Cade thrust a flat green piece of cactus at her.

Gingerly she took it. Cade had smashed the edges, knocked off the spines and peeled one thick side away. "What is it?"

"Food. I ate a piece last night. It didn't make me sick. Go ahead. It's not meat, but it doesn't taste bad and helps fill the belly."

"Thanks." He'd tested the cactus himself to see if it was harmful. However, she wasn't certain they shared the same biology, since she didn't require anywhere near the vast amounts of salt he consumed.

She licked the pasty substance and then began to eat in earnest. "What made you think that cactus might be edible?"

"We have similar plants on Rama. Our worlds are different but the similarities are endless."

"Really?"

"We have insects and fish, birds and mammals, too. The variety here is much greater, perhaps because your world isn't as ancient."

"Do any other species on your world use *Quait*?" she asked.

"*Quait* is what separates Ramans from animals. That is why underfirsts aren't considered human. But even if my people knew they could develop *Quait* by ingesting enough salt, the Firsts would never allow it. They need our labor to survive."

Shara tore apart the cactus innards with her teeth, determined to ingest every morsel. "So what will happen to the Firsts if you succeed in building the portal and sending salt back to your world?"

"They will either learn to work like the rest of us or . . ."

"Or?"

"They will die."

She peered into his eyes and tried to keep her own devilish smile under control. "And how will the underfirsts adjust to their new powers of *Quait?*"

"They'll adjust. They have no choice."

She closed the verbal trap that she'd baited and hooked. "So they won't think they are becoming monsters—like you do?"

15

❂

The drone of an aircraft prevented Cade from having to respond. Instead of answering Shara's question, he sprinted to the signal fire. After tossing handfuls of kindling on top to build the blaze quickly, he placed leafy branches over the flames, careful to smother the fire just enough to cause clouds of smoke, without choking it of all oxygen.

Beside him, Shara picked up and waved a leafy branch, trying to enlarge the smoke signal. Cade didn't look up. Busy feeding the fire, he focused on the task, refusing to let his hopes soar, knowing they might be forced to use this technique several times before a plane spotted them.

"It's turning. The plane is turning," Shara shouted and began waving the branches wildly.

Cade looked up. The small aircraft seemed to be flying directly toward them. He ceased working on the fire and began waving branches, too. The plane circled overhead, dipped its wings. "He sees us."

"No. He's leaving." Beside him, Shara collapsed onto the ground as the plane flew away.

"He saw us. He dipped his wings. He'll radio others for help. He can't land here without an airstrip."

"Oh." Shara nodded, her shoulders sagging, her head down so that he couldn't see her expression. She played with a rock, absently digging in the dirt. "You think they'll send a chopper?"

"Maybe." Cade had no idea why one moment she'd been so excited, the next, almost despondent. Before the plane's appearance she'd asked him a pointed question about his people, and he sensed she had concerns she had yet to voice.

He came up behind her and kneaded her shoulders, unsurprised to find knots of tension. "You okay?"

"Yes."

"Aren't you happy that we can get out of here?"

"Of course."

She didn't sound happy. "So what's wrong?"

"Tell me how the portal works."

Her request took him by surprise. "I don't understand the science behind it but—"

"I'm not talking about the physical mechanism. Is it like a door? Can people from Earth go through it to your world?"

"They could, but they wouldn't want to go to Rama. The Firsts would abuse them just like the underfirsts."

"But your Firsts and underfirsts could come here?"

He understood her concern. She feared the portal would open her world to an invasion by his. "Firsts will not like it on Earth. While my powers of *Quait* are increasing, due to the increase in salt, the reverse is true for them since the salt here isn't exactly the same as on Rama, plus so much salt in the environment weakens them."

"You've mentioned the environment before, but I really don't understand."

"It's about balance. Suppose you have an illness and you require a drug to keep you healthy. The doctors give you enough to keep you well, but too much of the drug would be an overdose and cause you to become very sick. So while I need more of the drug to make me strong, too much is weakening Jamar."

"Okay. I get it. But what of the underfirsts? If they came

here, they would be stronger than people from Earth. They could enslave us like the Firsts have done to you."

"The plan is to send back salt. Not to bring my people here."

"But if any of them come, it could throw Earth into chaos."

"Our plan is to colonize another world in our own solar system."

"Plans can change. Your people might use the portal to come here."

"I will make sure that doesn't happen." Cade had no wish to enslave her people, take over her world or do to others what had so cruelly been done to him.

"How?" She turned and stood. "Once you build that portal, everything will change."

"Since my people will not wish to turn into Firsts, we will regulate and monitor our salt intake. But in case anyone's tempted to ignore the new laws we must enact, I will configure the portal to allow nothing besides salt to go through."

"What is the upside for Earth? Seems to me we're taking all the risk with nothing to gain."

Cade frowned, wondering if, now that she'd experienced his growing *Quait,* she feared him. Last night, he'd tried to be gentle. He'd tried to give her pleasure. But she'd had no choice in their lovemaking. From experience, he understood that the lack of freedom upset how one thought of oneself and the world. "I can't give you a guarantee."

Shara rubbed her brow. "Could we send a large shipment of salt through the portal, then close it forever?"

"Perhaps." He understood her fears. On Rama nothing was more precious than salt, for without salt, one couldn't live in full health. One couldn't grow properly. Not physically. Not mentally. Salt was nourishing, life-giving. Without salt, happiness and freedom were no more than impossible ideals. "Closing the portal might cause the volcano to erupt."

At his words, her face paled. She tightened her lips. Then her eyes shifted to the west. "Is that a helicopter?" She broke into a wide smile. "I can so taste a crisp grilled chicken salad drizzled with balsamic vinaigrette. And feel a hot shower with scented shampoo and a bed with clean-scented sheets."

He grinned at her enthusiasm and focused on the black dot in the sky. His sharper vision picked out rotating blades. "We'll be out of here in a few minutes." He expected her to comment on the chopper, on the luxuries she missed so much. But she remained quiet, pensive. "Since we won't need to take life to survive, let's dismantle my traps."

"Okay." She placed her hand in his. "By the way, I don't think it's possible for you to turn into a monster like Jamar."

Confused, he eyed her. First she questioned him about his people wanting to invade her world. Then she told him he couldn't become like a First. And the two sentiments seemed contradictory. "Why not?"

"After a First no longer needed to eat, would he worry if his traps killed an animal?"

"Of course not."

"And does Jamar ever concern himself with pleasing his partners?"

"The concept would be foreign to him." Cade understood that she was trying to tell him that he would never become like the Firsts—no matter how much power the salt gave him. He wished he could be so certain.

But he also wondered if the underfirsts were ready to cope with even limited powers of *Quait*. It was ironic that the salt they needed to make them strong enough to escape their captivity possessed the ability to turn them into monsters like their captors.

In all the discussions he'd had, none of the underfirsts had considered the possibilities or the ethical problems. They'd believed the salt would give them only physical strength. They'd all believed *Quait* was inherited by Firsts alone. So none of them had realized that salt could give them the power of *Quait*.

Cade had many doubts about what might happen to his people after he sent back the salt, but he didn't even consider abandoning his mission. Until one had lived under the absolute control of a First and had suffered from the abject agony of living or dying solely on the whim of another, one couldn't understand that taking almost any risk offered a better life than the misery in which his people now existed.

Shara's questions deserved answers. Answers he couldn't yet give her. Cade knew he needed to elude Jamar, build the portal and come up with a plan to protect both his people and Shara's. He hoped he'd covered the major contingencies.

Apparently, the helicopter couldn't land safely in the uneven terrain. Instead, their rescuers lowered a line and a harness. After they strapped into the harness and the line reeled them up toward the helicopter, he looked down at the desert below.

Shara squeezed his hand. "The stand of trees and the spring appear to be the only source of water within miles."

"We were lucky." He said a short prayer for the pilots who apparently had not survived.

Her eyes shined with grateful tears. "You saved us when the plane exploded and you knew where to look for water. That's not luck."

When they reached the helicopter, Cade helped Shara into the craft. Then he climbed inside, shut the hatch behind him, and turned to thank their rescuers.

One of them held a gun to Shara's head. Her eyes wide with confusion and horror, she stared at Cade, looking for answers.

He had none.

Worse, he could do nothing to help her. Not when her captor's finger tensed on the trigger. Not when a second man aimed another weapon at Cade's chest.

Cade had no idea of these strangers' identities, but every bone in his body told him that Jamar paid and controlled them. Which meant they wouldn't be subject to bribery or any display of compassion. If Jamar followed his normal working procedure, the First had either threatened these men's families or might even be holding their relatives hostage.

One man shouted orders at him, his voice carrying above

the noise of the chopper. "Place your hands behind your head and turn around."

With Shara's life in danger, Cade had no choice. He did as ordered and within a moment, his captor snapped metal handcuffs over his wrists.

This was by no means the first time Cade had worn chains. But he'd never become accustomed to the helplessness and frustration of failure. Ever since he'd arrived, Jamar had taken the initiative, outsmarting him. Cade was tired of always trying to catch up.

As his anger simmered, he tested the handcuffs' strength and found them surprisingly sturdy. When he caught sight of Shara, her gaze dropped to her captor's pocket, where keys dangled.

Possibilities of escape entered his mind—none of them feasible at the moment. Cade raised his voice to be heard over the engines. "Where are you taking us?"

"To Jamar. He said to tell you that he wants the pleasure of watching you die."

Jules heard a rescue plane had spotted two people in the Arizona desert and she was certain it had to be Shara and Cade. However, when the helicopter returned to the designated location, another unidentified helicopter had carried them away . . . to an unknown destination.

The authorities had no idea who had made the flight. While Teresa's team tried to track down every charter helicopter and crew in Arizona and three of its neighbors—Nevada, New Mexico, and Utah—Jules fumed. She didn't need a psychic vision to know that Shara and Cade were in danger. Again.

While Jules wanted to stop Cade from building his portal, she most certainly didn't want Shara killed in the process. From her hospital bed, Teresa Alverez promised Jules she would find Shara and Cade, so while Jules continued to worry, she also knew that she could best help Shara by staying on task. However, guilt rode her because spending time with Lyle was an unusually pleasant job.

Over a late lunch, she wondered what would appeal to

Lyle enough to encourage him to leave Montana for Haven. Washing down the last of her clam chowder with a swallow of tart lemonade, she eyed him over the dining table of the cabin he'd turned into a home.

The log cabin possessed an A-frame roof, and although a massive stone fireplace bisected a wall of floor-to-ceiling windows, the rock chimney only enhanced the snow-covered mountain view. A worn leather couch, a scuffed coffee table with a stack of science magazines splayed across the pitted surface, and a plasma television over the mantel revealed he often camped out in the living area. With the blue sky and pristine light shining in through the windows, she had to remind herself that the distances here were as deceiving as the charming volcanologist.

Although he'd solicitously ramped up the fire to a roar and placed an afghan over her shoulders, she wondered if he'd told her the truth about Jamar. And while she tried to think of a casual way to bring the conversation around to the subject, she wiped up the condensation her glass had left on the wooden dining table with her napkin.

"So what would you like to do this afternoon?" Lyle asked.

She dragged her gaze back to him and leaned forward, appreciative of the hot soup in her belly, the roaring fire, and that Lyle seemed willing to take time off from work to spend it with her. Leisurely, he stretched his long legs under the table and waited for her reply.

"What are the choices?"

"Snowmobiling, cross-country skiing, a Jeep ride through the park."

She shivered with cold just thinking about the low temperatures. "What about indoor activities?"

He grinned wickedly and touched his forehead lightly in a mock salute. "And what are the choices?"

Jules couldn't help but smile back at him, pleased by his flirting. "If we made love today, you'd get the wrong impression."

"That you're not interested in me?" Lyle removed his

glasses, shoved back from the table, and raised a sexy eyebrow.

"You know I'm interested."

"But you're not interested in seeing my bedroom?"

"I might be convinced . . ." She let her words trail off. "But . . ." Again she let her words dangle.

"But?"

"I don't usually move so fast."

"Me, neither." He rubbed his brow. "According to my ex-wife, I'm not good at . . . paying attention to women."

"Maybe your ex was wrong."

He shook his head. "I should have tried harder to make her happy."

"No one can *make* someone else happy."

He shrugged and his eyes twinkled. Lyle really did have kind eyes and whether he focused inwardly or on her, she liked the intelligent and thoughtful glimmer in his expression. "She was lonely and I worked long hours. In the end, she met a tourist passing through who had lots more to give her than I did."

"You miss her?"

He winced, but his tone remained honest and direct. "I should, shouldn't I? We were married three years and she left six months ago. But often . . . I forget that she's gone. I find myself hurrying home because I'm late and then I remember there's no one waiting for me." He sipped his coffee. "What about you? Anyone waiting for you at home?"

"Not even an empty house." She shook her head, missing her cat and hoping George was taking good care of Kapuna.

"Have you ever been married?" Lyle asked.

"I'm not the marrying type."

His eyes widened in surprise and curiosity, but no condemnation entered his tone. "What does that mean?"

"Oh, I like men—don't get me wrong. It's just that I see no need for a piece of paper from a civil servant to validate any relationship I might have."

Lyle leaned farther forward and took one of her hands between his. Heat penetrated her skin, but his words burned into her soul. "So tell me, what are you doing here?"

She tried an impish smile. "I told you that I came to see you because of my vision."

"Why is it that I don't think you came all this way because you envisioned us making love in front of my fireplace?" he teased, but she heard the bite to his question.

"I could use a romantic fling in my life right now." At her words, his eyes hardened as if she were lying. "Really. But you're right," she added quickly, knowing if she antagonized him, he'd never go along with her plan, "a vacation is not why I came. But I'm not sure I'm ready to tell you the details of my vision."

She might have told him she'd seen his face and an exploding volcano but she hadn't told him about Cade, about Rama, that aliens were already on Earth and wanted to open a portal back to their world, a portal that would cause the volcanic explosion.

"Why won't you tell me the details?"

"You'll think . . . I'm crazy."

He actually looked intrigued. "Yours wouldn't be the first crazy story I've heard."

"Yeah, but I want you to believe mine. And if I rush and tell you, you won't get to know me well enough to know that for a psychic, I'm a solid citizen. I pay my taxes. I don't commune with the dead."

"And you haven't been abducted by little green men?"

"Not exactly."

After all Jamar's hard digging in the muck on the banks of the Dead Sea, his primitive vehicle got stuck in the sand. Alone in the desert he cursed his rotten luck.

With no slave labor to coerce, he'd have to dig out the truck. Already sore and blistered from digging the first portal part free, he should be rushing to New York to retrieve the second piece. Instead, he was stuck in the muck. He swore by every grain of salt in his body that Cade would pay for his pain. If the underfirst hadn't come to Earth, if he hadn't ejected the portal pieces before Jamar had disintegrated his spaceship, if Cade had died, Jamar would be on a flight back home to Rama, not stranded on this hellhole of a planet, the sun beating down on him as he dug in the sand and sweated salt like a primitive.

When his satellite phone rang again, Jamar swore, tossed the shovel aside, and pressed the "talk" button. "What do you want?"

"You said to report." The muffled words came through the phone along with the whir of helicopter blades.

"Then report."

"We have Cade and the woman."

Satisfaction poured through Jamar. "Good."

He ended the call, his sense of urgency ebbing. With Cade and the woman in the clutches of mercenaries, Jamar needn't rush. He could take the time to find someone else to do his dirty work.

As a Jeep pulled up beside him and a young couple approached, he smiled at his changing luck. A muscular young man with curly black hair and dark eyes removed a shovel from the back of his vehicle. "Need some help?"

"Would you like some cold water?" A pleasant looking female, with hips a bit too wide for his taste offered him a canteen.

"Thanks." Jamar didn't have to use much *Quait*. The couple already wanted to help. When they finished digging him out, they offered to take him to their home at a kibbutz. Apparently, they lived with many other like-minded people, collectively working for the greater good. Idiots.

Jamar was about to apply more *Quait* to take further advantage of the woman's hospitality, when a convoy of soldiers passed by. Deciding he could find a better-looking female in the city to tend to his needs, he waved good-bye to the stupid Samaritans and headed for Jerusalem.

Jamar took over the penthouse suite of the city's finest hotel. He spent an hour on the phone making arrangements. While using his cloaked spaceship to travel around the planet would have been more convenient, he had to uncloak to land and he didn't want its unique design to attract notice—that ship was his ticket back to Rama and was safely hidden. And finally he called the hotel concierge and told him he wanted a dozen professional women. Jamar was in no mood to taunt an innocent who would likely faint if he revealed the violence seething in him requiring release.

Only ten women showed and Jamar demanded that they all strip—except for their high heels—and stand like statues for his inspection. Four he dismissed with five hundred shekels each for their trouble. He left his thick wallet in plain sight. The remaining six whores gloated, pleased with his generosity to the others, believing they would be well paid for their evening.

Good. The greedy bitches would take more pain before complaining—exactly as he wanted.

But first, the naked women could bathe him, massage him with oils, and pamper him. Ah, he deserved a little indulgence. His hands still stung from blisters. And his reddened skin burned from too much sun.

But Jamar had the first portal piece and he had located the second. More important, he had captured Cade. He would have rubbed his hands together, but the women had maneuvered him onto a padded table. Two women massaged his hands, two his thighs and calves and feet, while one rubbed his head, neck, and shoulders and the other kneaded his back and buttocks.

One bitch carelessly didn't use enough oil and popped open a blister on his palm. He picked up his belt.

16

After Trevor's brief talk with Teresa Alverez, the reporter went to work. Teresa had told him nothing about Shara, but Trevor had learned that her plane had gone down in Arizona, that a search-and-rescue plane spotted them, and how the rescue helicopter's pilot reported that a different chopper had picked them up first. From there, the trail had gone cold. Even Teresa's government contacts couldn't help her locate the chopper.

Unfortunately a missing retired movie star wasn't important enough to request time on spy satellites. Trevor had to decide what to do next. Since Jamar was after Shara, he figured if he found Jamar, he might also find the movie actress.

A man as cruel as Jamar might leave a trail of other victims—more brutalized women—behind. If Trevor could find those women, his legwork might eventually lead him to Jamar. Trevor hit his computer, grateful for the Internet. Research that might have taken weeks could now be done in hours, especially since Trevor was a master at reading between the lines of newspaper stories.

He set up his search engines to look for stories about

women brutalized by strangers. Although he combed databases of newspapers throughout the U.S. and South Pacific, surprisingly, there weren't as many as he'd feared. Most women suffered battery and abuse from fathers, lovers, and husbands. Once he eliminated all crimes by anyone except a stranger, he had less than a hundred cases. And when he again narrowed the stories down to only the most brutal and cross-checked to see which women had survived their ordeals, he had merely a handful.

If necessary, he would ask questions of the investigating police officers of the dead women, but Trevor preferred to speak to those who had lived. Meanwhile, he added one other country to his search: Israel. Shara had been heading there. It made sense to include that country's news, but since he required translations, the search there was slow.

Meanwhile, he called the first victim. She refused to speak to him. The second didn't answer the phone. The third hung up on him. Trevor kept dialing. Although Trevor would have preferred to visit the women in person, he didn't have the time or the expense account.

The fourth victim, Donna Finneran, now lived in Georgia. A former airline stewardess, she'd met a man on a flight between Tahiti and Moorea. According to the story, Donna would have bled to death if a maid hadn't found her in the penthouse suite of a four-star hotel.

"Hello." Donna picked up the phone on the first ring, her southern accent clear and vibrant.

"Donna, my name is Trevor Cantrell, I work for a newspaper in Hawaii. The reason I'm calling is that I believe the man who hurt you is hurting other women. I'd like your help to try to find him." Trevor knew some reporters would have whitewashed the truth and tried to win Donna's confidence before revealing what they wanted. And sometimes he himself operated in that fashion to make his job easier—but he only did so to secure information that was relatively unimportant. In this case, Donna had been through enough deceit and trauma. He would not lie to a woman who'd been so badly beaten.

She spoke slowly, carefully, and without emotion, as if

still in shock, as if she still lived the nightmare but refused to let it touch her more than it already had. "I'm not sure I can help you. I don't remember much about that night."

"Actually, I'm more interested in what happened *before* he hurt you. Can you tell me how you met the man?"

"He called himself Jamar." When she spoke the unusual name, Trevor figured he had the right man. "I'm not certain how we met."

"What do you mean?"

"He claimed we met on one of my flights, but the airline had no record of his purchasing a ticket. And I don't remember seeing him on the plane."

"Where is your first recollection of meeting him?"

"At the hotel. I was napping by the pool and opened my eyes to find he'd taken the chair beside me."

"And Jamar acted as if you'd already met?"

"Yes. And I didn't want to admit I didn't remember him. So I pretended that I did."

"That's understandable. I'd imagine most women would have done the same thing." He wrote furiously as she spoke, taking exact notes. "What happened next?"

"He bought me a drink."

"And?"

"I don't drink. I'm allergic to alcohol. I have weird body chemistry—it makes me sick." Donna stopped talking.

"And?"

"I've never told anyone else what happened. You'll think my mind is unhinged because of what that bastard did to me. But . . ."

The hair on the back of Trevor's neck prickled. "I've heard many inexplicable things about Jamar. Please, tell me."

"I didn't want that drink—and I'm not a recovering alcoholic. Yet, somehow despite my abhorrence of alcohol, I was picking up the glass, raising it to my mouth, swallowing the vile stuff. Did I mention alcohol smells terrible to me? Well anyway, I drank the entire glass—against my will."

"You were afraid if you didn't drink it that he would hurt you?"

"No. It was as if he took away my will. No, my will was strong. I didn't want the drink, period. But Jamar . . . somehow he made me pick up the glass and drink."

"Did he hypnotize you?"

"I don't know. I can't explain what he did. I was fully aware that I didn't want to drink. I actually tried to toss the liquid in his face. But it was as if some other power controlled my body."

"I'm so sorry." Trevor's thoughts raced. What exactly had he stumbled across? He had a jeweler who'd never seen gemstones like the ones Cade had sold. He had a pilot who claimed he'd seen Cade's ship explode out of the sky. Teresa Alverez had told him Jamar had usurped her will and now this woman claimed Jamar used some kind of mind control over her. Two sources were all he needed to verify a story. "Do you recall how long it was before you'd last eaten or drank before Jamar approached?"

"Hours. I don't think I was drugged."

"Do you have any clue at all, why he picked you?"

"After he tied me up, the bastard told me."

"I'm sorry to cause you this pain."

"Don't worry about it. It's not like I ever forget. He haunts me. I want him caught. I want him dead."

"So why did he pick you?"

"Because many flight attendants would have been happy to flirt and party and sleep with a wealthy, handsome, single man."

"Are you saying he picked you because you *weren't* interested?"

"Yes. I was about to be married. I was happy. Jamar got off on my resistance. He doesn't just enjoy creating physical pain. He sucks up *mental* pain. Embarrassment and humiliation are his way of warming up for what comes later."

"Donna, did Jamar use any unusual devices?"

"He likes to use his belt. Whips. Chains. A scalpel. Or a razor. He actually made me scar my own cheeks with a razor."

Trevor shuddered. "Actually, I meant did you see any kind of a device that would account for his ability to use mind control?"

"Sorry, no."

"What about any unusual habits?"

"You mean besides cruelty?"

"I want to find him. I'm not asking you these questions because—"

"You have a job to do. The man seemed normal—right down to his penchant for margaritas—without the salt on the rim."

"I promise you. If I find him, I'm turning him over to the authorities."

"If you find him, you'll have to kill him," she warned. "A man like Jamar won't be taken alive."

Hands cuffed behind her back, Shara inched closer to Cade. With the noise of the helicopter, they could talk freely without fear of their captors, who both sat up front, overhearing the conversation.

"Why aren't you doing something?" she asked Cade, not bothering to keep the fear from her voice. After crashing in the desert, hoping for rescue, only to be taken by their enemy, her roller-coaster emotions were too close to the surface to bother attempting to keep frustration from her tone.

Cade raised an eyebrow. "Exactly what would you like me to do?"

"Why not use your *Quait* and force them to release us and set us down next to a four-star hotel?" Then she could empty her bladder, eat a hot meal, take a shower, and sleep in a bed with comfy three-hundred-thread-count sheets.

Cade shook his head. "Even if I was a First, *Quait* doesn't work that way. Whoever dominates a mind first usually maintains control until the First releases them."

"Usually? There are exceptions?"

"If a First is distracted or ill or injured, there can be momentary lapses—the lapses only last mere seconds and are difficult to pinpoint, never mind take advantage of."

Disappointed, Shara wasn't about to give up. "What about going for the handcuff keys?"

Although the guard had moved to the copilot's seat, the

keys still bulged temptingly in his pocket. A quick snatch, a lucky kick to the head, and they could free themselves and force the pilot to land.

"Even if I could take out the guard before he shot me, the pilot has another weapon. And we can't hurt him. We need him to fly this helicopter."

"There must be something we can do." Shara braced her back against a seat and wearily closed her eyes, trying not to think about a bathroom, food, a hot shower, safety.

"It's not all bad."

"Really?" She opened her eyes to take in Cade's handsome face. Even with his ragged dark hair and his torn clothes, there was no trace of defeat in his posture. Head high, eyes alert, and intelligent, he maintained an air of poised calm that helped her fight her rising panic.

"They are taking us exactly where we need to go. Jamar has the portal pieces."

"Jamar intends to kill us."

"Our capture may be the opportunity we needed. The First thinks we're helpless."

"We are."

Cade's voice deepened. "Jamar can't know how much the salt has changed me."

The pain in his eyes reminded her that he saw *Quait* as a necessary evil. She supposed now was as good a time as ever to set him straight. "On our world my people have endlessly debated whether weapons are good or evil. But a gun is a hunk of metal, an object that has no soul, no morals, no inherent will until someone chooses whether or not to use it."

Cade's eyes flared. "*Quait* is not like an object one can decide to ignore. With *Quait* I have no choice. Can you eat food without tasting it?"

"Of course not. But I can decide which foods I taste and how much I put in my mouth and when I eat. And so far I haven't once seen you use *Quait* for evil or wrongdoing. Seems to me you do have freedom of will—"

"Wrong." He shuddered as if in agony but held her gaze. "You know better."

She had no clue. "What are you talking about?"

"When we made love. I forced you."

She shook her head and locked gazes with him, hoping her eyes flashed annoyance. "I was willing."

"I forced my will on you."

"You didn't do one thing I didn't want you to do. You didn't do anything I didn't enjoy. If I'd asked you to stop, you would have done so."

He looked away. "I'm glad you think so."

Clearly he didn't believe he had that much control, but she knew better and, although her heart ached for him, she'd had enough of his stubbornness. He'd shown her repeatedly that he was a caring man with a good heart. "You hate all Firsts and their abilities so much that you can't appreciate your new talent."

"You see in me what you wish to see," he countered.

"I see what is there. Without your help I wouldn't have survived the desert."

"Without me, you wouldn't have been in the desert."

"Oh, puh-leeze. Your pity party is really getting old. Have you tortured or raped or killed anyone? So we had a little kinky sex—get over it. Focus on all you have accomplished. Did you ever in your life think you might have a shot to fight Jamar on an equal footing?"

"I'm not an idiot, but don't kid yourself. No way do I have his strength—even here on Earth. But I do comprehend the opportunity I've been given."

"I don't think you do. Not down deep. You haven't accepted how you are now is the same man you were before. You think the *Quait* will change your principles. I believe *Quait* is a tool that will allow you to stand up and fight for those principles. Hell, you might even win. You don't really know how weak Jamar has become."

She could see doubts in the shadows of his eyes and knew she hadn't gotten through to him. And yet, perhaps debate would start him thinking in the right direction. Never before had she wanted to shake some sense into him. For Cade to retrieve the portal pieces—so she could at-

tempt to destroy them—he would have to muster all his resources. He couldn't debate or hesitate. He couldn't hold
back.

She wanted him to focus solely on winning—not question
the morality of using *Quait*. Perhaps that was shortsighted.
But Shara really needed Cade to recover those pieces from
Jamar to give her a shot at stopping him. Too bad she still
didn't know how she could accomplish her goal. Stealing the
pieces herself wasn't a viable option—not when a locator
beacon would lead the men right to her. She had to think of
something. And although frustration swelled in her chest,
she'd never felt more alive, more challenged.

For a long time after Bruce had died, she'd wished she'd
died right beside him. But while the pain of losing him
would always hurt, the open wounds had healed, leaving
scars she'd learned to live with. She'd once again begun to
think of a future, dared to dream of one with Cade. But there
was no way she could have a life with him—not if she
stopped him. If she succeeded, he would never forgive her,
and if she failed they all might die. Never had she faced such
terrible choices and it tore at her.

Even if she lived, she had no idea what to do with her life.
Returning to acting hadn't appealed to Shara for a long time
and she'd kept busy by reading scripts and advising A-list
actors which parts to take. But she'd had nothing new to replace her old dreams. If not for Jules's visions, she would
take Cade's side and help his people. She would have liked
to have been around when Earth's leaders learned that they
were no longer the only intelligent life in the universe. She
would have liked to have been a part of that future, would
have liked to dare to love again.

Fear had held her back for a long time. It wasn't easy to
open up to the idea of loving someone, especially when she
knew how badly it hurt to lose a lover. And yet, remaining in
her shell, taking no risks at all, had been almost like dying.

But there was no use wishing for the courage to fight for
them as a couple—not when he would see any act against his
mission as a betrayal. And her conscience wouldn't allow

her to do nothing, not when doing so allowed Cade to set off volcanic explosions. If only she could think of a way out of this predicament. She might be in handcuffs, the chopper might be taking them to Jamar, but Shara had struggled against bad odds before. She'd worked hard to make it as an actress. She'd fought the booze even harder. And now she would fight for life—with Cade or without him—she wanted to live.

"Cade?"

"Yes."

"We're going to find those portal pieces. I don't know how, but we aren't giving up."

"Agreed." Approval shined from his eyes, warming her straight down to her bones.

The chopper veered, the altitude descending, and she supposed she shouldn't be thinking about the future right now. But any thoughts that took her away from the ache in her wrists, the numbness in her hands or the uncertainty of living even another few hours bolstered her courage.

They were about to land.

The diversity of this planet never ceased to surprise Cade. From lush tropical islands to red-hued deserts to mountainous areas dusted with snow, each region possessed its own uniqueness and beauty.

After the helicopter landed, their captors had allowed them bathroom privileges before escorting them to a waiting vehicle. While Shara tried to convince their captors to feed them, Cade took the opportunity to survey upstate New York. Intellectually he realized that Manhattan was only a tiny part of the state, but he didn't expect the Albany area to possess tree-covered hills and a relatively sparse population. He thought of New York as crowded, filled with buildings, business, and traffic, but this part of the state was two-story suburbia, steeply pitched roofs on houses set on large tracts of land, and children riding sleds in an early fall snow.

Their captors made no efforts to hide their route and when they pulled the van into a store named Stewarts and filled the vehicle with fuel, the driver returned with coffee, sand-wiches, and a treat called Little Debbies. Cade and Shara couldn't eat with their hands cuffed behind their backs but the smell of the food made their stomachs grumble.

"Come on, guys. How about a few bites?" Shara asked.

One of the men threw a paper-covered sandwich into the back.

Cade turned sideways in his rear seat, grabbed the prize behind him, and unwrapped it. He held up the bread and meat as best he could for Shara. "Go on. Eat."

She had to shift her knees to the floor in order for her mouth to reach the sandwich. "Thanks."

Shara ate half the sandwich quickly, then regained her seat and took the other half from his hands. "Your turn. And the ham has lots of salt."

"Good." Cade didn't know when he'd next have another opportunity to ingest more salt, but he planned to conserve his *Quait,* keep his ability a secret for as long as possible. However, unlike Shara, he wasn't counting on his newfound ability to defeat Jamar. He knew better. Although his strength had grown, he knew too well how Firsts wielded their powers, and he was nowhere near their level. Even ac-counting for Jamar's weakened state due to the planetary in-fluences, the First's powers would be far superior to his.

Instead, as usual, Cade planned to rely on muscle and guile. The unknown factor here was Jamar. Ever since Cade had arrived, Jamar had been trying to kill him. Why hadn't the First ordered his men to shoot them on sight? Why had the First let them live? What had changed? Was it possible that after all the trouble Cade had caused, the First would want to personally oversee their torture and death? At the idea of Jamar hurting Shara, Cade's pulse raced. His every protective feeling for her rose up to choke him. He hadn't in-tended to allow his feelings to grow so strong. This was the exact reason that back on Rama he'd never stayed with one woman long enough to know her. But Shara was Shara—irresistible, intelligent, compassionate.

He would do his best to protect her, but he feared his best

might not be enough. Cade ate quickly, then snuggled against Shara, placing his mouth close to her ear, certain the drivers couldn't hear him above the loud music playing from the speakers. "It would be best if Jamar believes you mean nothing to me."

Shara turned, favoring him with a tiny smile. "Your statement implies that you do have feelings for me."

Cade picked up that Shara's thoughts had become serious, but he didn't understand why. "After all the time we've spent together, how could I not have feelings for you?"

"Ah . . . Cade. For a smart man, you can be as dense as any man born on Earth."

At her clear annoyance with him, Cade wished he had a hint of what she was talking about. "You do know that I can't read your mind?"

"Trust me. Right now that's a good thing—for you."

"I have no idea why you're irritated with me."

"That's why I'm irritated."

He narrowed his eyes. "You aren't making sense. And we don't have time for a personal discussion."

"Agreed." She immediately turned reasonable, and yet he sensed something significant had happened. In some way he'd come up short and it bothered him that he didn't know why. Her failure to explain also rankled. Shara had proven herself to be reasonable. Perhaps the stress was getting to her.

He lowered his voice even further. "Once we arrive at our destination, we should make a move to get free."

"What do you have in mind?" Her tone remained cool, almost professional.

"Can you distract the men?"

She raised her head and shot him a queenly stare. Despite her hands behind her back, she straightened her shoulders, then slightly angled her chin. "It would be better if my hands were free, but I can still act."

"Good."

He sat back, glad Shara seemed back to normal. He watched the terrain change from rolling hills to a more mountainous area, and saw towns go by like Latham and

Schenectady. They turned off the highway at exit twenty-two, at a town named Lake George and he glimpsed a stunning dark blue lake with numerous mountain homes dotting the rocky banks.

"So what's the plan?" Shara asked.

"Huh?" He pulled his focus from the awesome lake to Shara. "I explained everything to you."

"You explained nothing," she hissed.

"You distract them. I take them out. It's simple."

"It's moronic."

"Did you just insult me?"

"You don't know how to plan. What you're suggesting is muddled chaos," she sputtered, clearly outraged that he hadn't given her more details.

He chuckled, but how could he say more when he had no idea what they would face? However, he was enjoying her outrage, enough to push her further. "So you have a better idea?"

"How can I have an idea when we don't know where we're going to stop?"

"Exactly," he agreed.

She swore under her breath. "Do you have to make your point in such an annoying fashion?"

"At least I made mine." They drove through the charming town of Bolton and turned toward the lake and a private drive. "I still don't know what you were in a snit about—"

She tilted her nose in the air. "I was not in a snit."

"Excuse me. You were in a funk."

"I was not."

The van pulled down a long, winding private road and halted before a charming two-story home with a steep-pitched roof, a smoking stone chimney, and a two-car garage. Interesting. Cade expected armed men to exit the house, but no one poked a head out the door or looked at them through a window. Their driver pressed a remote control button that opened the garage door and the van drove inside.

As the door closed behind the van, Cade used the cover of

the noise to pop his handcuffs apart. But he kept his wrists pressed together and awkwardly got out of the van, then nudged Shara.

She immediately began her distraction. She stepped right into the arms of one of their captors. "Please, let me go. You do recognize me, don't you? I'm Shara Weston, the actress. I'm a wealthy woman and I can pay you a million dollars."

"Sorry." The man stepped back.

Shara edged right up against him. "All right. Two million. You'd both be rich."

While she distracted the men, Cade moved closer, as if interested in listening to what she had to say. With both men armed, he'd have to move fast and be lucky not only to avoid getting shot, but to avoid the sound of gunfire that would draw the wrong kind of attention.

"Lady, our boss would kill us and we can't spend your money if we're dead."

Cade tensed, gathered his muscles and kicked the gun from the first guard's hand. Then all hell broke loose.

17

✦

Shara tried to keep track of Cade out of the corner of her eye, but when the guard she was trying to distract reached for his weapon, she lost sight of Cade. Stumbling into her guard, she released an erotic moan that could have won an Academy Award. The astonished man suddenly found her chest pressed against his, her thigh in his crotch, and her mouth against his neck.

Over the guard's shoulder, Shara glimpsed Cade kicking the second man's hand in a move that caused the gun to tumble and spin across the garage floor. Cade moved in fast but, with a glint in his eye, his attacker pulled a blade from his sleeve and Shara's throat tightened in fear. When Cade's opponent didn't try to stab but sliced back and forth—a technique she'd seen stuntmen use in the movies that indicated the guy knew how to handle a weapon—her pulse rocketed up another notch.

Unarmed, Cade circled warily.

Shara knew within seconds the second guard's confusion would end and he'd shove her aside, draw his gun, and shoot either Cade, her, or both of them. Heart hammering, she could think of only one way to stop him. She pulled back from their semi-embrace, then slammed her body into his. Surprised, off balance, he clutched at her and toppled backward.

She fell right on top of him. The air whooshed out of his chest with a soft "oof." He landed on the concrete floor and softened her spill as she descended on top of him. His head thunked on concrete and his eyes glazed over.

She didn't wait for him to come to, immediately ramming her knee into his groin. An odd screech squeaked from his throat. His pupils rolled back into his head. She slid off him, her thoughts wild. Should she go for the handcuff keys or his weapon? Reason took over and settled her nerves. Unable to shoot a gun with her hands cuffed behind her back, she awkwardly hunted for the keys.

Meanwhile, Cade's opponent slashed the knife at his throat. Cade shifted and the blade narrowly missed his neck, instead catching his upper arm. He hissed in pain and blood welled through the tear in his shirt.

The guard laughed. "Come on, tough guy."

Cade circled warily, ignoring the wound.

Mouth dry, Shara jammed one hand into the downed guard's pocket and retrieved the keys. However, inserting the key into the lock with her hands behind her back proved more difficult than she'd imagined. Hands sweaty, pulse pounding, she had difficulty placing the key into the hole.

Cade attacked, feinted right, swept his foot upward in a hooking motion. But he tripped over an old crate filled with ice-fishing gear and tumbled, just as the other man lunged.

"Look out!" she yelled and dropped the keys.

Cade grabbed the wrist of his opponent's knife hand and the two men rolled across the floor, struggling for control of the weapon. Telling herself not to look, that she could only help Cade by freeing her hands, she picked up the fallen keys and once again tried to open the lock.

Sick with fear, palms so damp that the keys seemed to

jump in her hands, she finally inserted the handcuff key into the hole and twisted. But it wouldn't turn.

The other way, stupid.

Shara tried again and this time the lock popped. With another flick of her hands she was free. Quickly, she bent and retrieved the guard's gun. The moment she picked up the weapon her entire body began to shake. Her stomach rolled. Despite the danger, despite her worry over dying, she couldn't stop her reaction to holding a gun. The last time she'd held a weapon, she'd shot and killed Bruce.

Tears welled in her eyes and angrily she blinked them away. Last time she hadn't known the gun was loaded. Last time no one had been trying to kill her. Bruce's death had been an accident. And this was life or death.

Her thoughts reeled.

Get a grip.

She forced her thoughts to focus on what was going on around her. One guard still appeared to be out cold but she took no chances. She'd seen too many bad movies where the bad guy was assumed to be down and out only to have him "surprise" everyone by recovering. Shara slammed the gun into the guy's temple for good measure, then forced her thumb to flick off the safety and aimed at the two men.

Her hand shook so badly she didn't know if she could hit the side of a building. The men were rolling across the floor, struggling for the knife. Between her shaking hands and their wrestling, if she risked a shot, she could kill Cade by accident.

At the thought, her leg bones seemed to turn to water. Icy sparks shimmied down her spine. No way could she pull the trigger.

Perhaps she could help Cade by hitting his opponent over the head with the gun. Shara tightened her hands on the gun, determined not to drop it.

She approached cautiously. Between the twisting bodies and twirling arms and legs, she could easily trip, squeeze the trigger, kill another man. *Oh, God.* She wiped the sweat from her forehead and waited for the right moment to advance and strike, determined to help Cade.

Cade jammed his elbow into the man's neck. The guy reciprocated by butting his head into Cade's nose. Cade likely jerked his head back in time to avoid a broken bone, but blood dripped from one nostril and his lip swelled.

Cade twisted his opponent's wrist and the man shrieked and dropped the knife. The sound of a bone snapping sickened Shara and yet, contradictorily, she was also glad. The injured man scrambled away from Cade, holding his broken wrist, but she still didn't have a clear shot. Cade was between her and the other guy and he was fumbling on the floor for his lost weapon.

"Cade"—she pointed—"the gun."

"I see it."

Cade lunged forward, so did the other guy. Cade muttered, "Don't even think about it."

Despite his injury, the guard taunted, "You're a dead man, Cade."

If Cade's attacker retrieved the weapon, she'd have to risk a shot. Shara's mouth went dry. Her chest tightened. Her lungs burned as she forgot to draw in air. For a second, she had a clear shot. She raised the weapon, but her hands shook so hard she hesitated and then she lost the opportunity as the men were once again wrestling. Cade pummeled the man and the guard turned onto his stomach to avoid the the punishing blows to his face. Cade slipped an arm around his throat. His free hand gripped his head and with a sudden twist, Cade broke the man's neck.

At the snapping sound, Shara thought she might be sick. The guy's bladder voided and the reek of his emptying bowels hit her hard. This wasn't an arranged fight in a movie scene where the actors would all get up and clap one another on the back and go off together for a drink. The stench of death rocked her.

Wearily, Cade shoved to his feet. "You okay?"

She flicked the safety on, slumped against the van, waiting for her body to stop trembling. "I need air."

"Hold on a minute." Cade retrieved the second gun, stuffed it into the waistband of his jeans, then bent over the unconscious man that she'd taken out.

"What are you doing?" she asked.

"I have to kill him."

She stiffened. "No."

"No?" Cade shot her a troubled look.

"Jamar made him abduct us. He had no choice."

"If I don't kill him, Jamar will. And I assure you, Jamar will torture him for his failure. At least I'll be merciful." Cade placed his hand on the man's head, clearly he meant to break his neck.

"If you kill him, you'll be no better than Jamar."

"I *am* no better than Jamar."

His words hit her like bullets, but he dropped his hands to his sides. The cold glare in Cade's eyes indicated a man in a very different emotional place than the one who'd made love to her so tenderly, the one who risked his life to help his people.

But she'd taken one life and it weighed on her soul, every hour of every day. She couldn't abide killing a helpless man who'd had no control over his actions—no matter how murderous.

She tossed the handcuffs at Cade. "Lock him up. Put him in the van. We'll take him with us when we leave and drop him off by a fire station where he'll get medical care. If he escapes Jamar now, at least he'll have a chance."

"Fine." Cade didn't look happy but at least he'd agreed. He rolled the guy over, handcuffed him, and lifted him into the van.

She took the keys and freed the broken cuffs from Cade's wrists. "How's your arm?"

"It's just a scratch."

Clearly way more than a scratch, blood stained his entire shoulder, yet the wound no longer seeped blood over his skin. A man from her world would have required stitches, but his blood was already starting to congeal, reminding her once again of the differences between them.

Cade had looked at her with suspicion when she'd convinced him not to kill the man. Did he suspect she wasn't behind his mission one hundred percent?

Fearing the moment would soon arrive when she had to betray Cade, she closed off her emotions behind a wall. Betraying Cade seemed so wrong . . . and yet, how could she not, when the lives of everyone on Earth might be at stake if she let him set off his device?

She swallowed hard. "Now what?"

He headed toward a door that led from the garage into the house. "Now we search the premises for the portal pieces."

She prayed the house would be empty. No one else needed to die today, especially not them. "What does a portal piece look like?" Even as she waited for an answer, she almost hoped the portal wouldn't be there—then she wouldn't have to betray Cade, an action that scared her more than anything in her entire life, even dying.

Cade lowered his voice. "Each piece is a shiny silver spherical ball about the size of an orange. They are extremely heavy. You might not be able to lift it."

Cade raised his fingers to his lips and motioned for her to hide behind him. He waited for her to move, then reached for the knob.

After a thorough search, they learned no one else was in the house. The rental home yielded no clues about Jamar. He'd left no personal items in the building, not even a toothbrush, amid the Adirondack furnishings that suited a home in this region.

Cade removed his locator device from his pocket and turned it on. Immediately three blinking lights appeared on a tiny screen and coordinates popped up.

Shara leaned over his shoulder. "Has Jamar found all the pieces?"

"Nope. But he's activated the third beacon, which means he now has his hands on the second piece. From the GPS locators, one piece is here, he's found the other on the lake, and the third one's in the Caribbean."

She frowned at the blinking lights. "The two portal pieces aren't together?"

"Apparently not. He must have hidden one here while he searched for the second piece. We're practically standing on top of the one he hid. The other on the lake is heading this way."

"Why would he leave one piece behind?"

"They are very heavy. He may not trust anyone else and toting it around is inconvenient. Jamar hates to be inconvenienced."

"Jamar's found the second one—or he couldn't have turned on the third locator beacon, right?" she asked, wondering exactly how heavy the pieces were. If she couldn't even lift it, stealing it from Cade was going to be a major problem.

"I'm guessing Jamar's heading back here to recover the hidden piece. After he deals with us, he'll retrieve piece number three."

"So we need to find the hidden sphere before he arrives, right?"

"Yeah, but it's not that easy. The coordinates tell us one sphere is nearby but the GPS system is crude."

"What do you mean? I've heard our systems can find and read the date of a coin on pavement from space."

"Your military purposely scrambles civilian signals."

"Why would they do that?"

"To prevent terrorism attacks. Your Department of Homeland Security doesn't want to make it easy to target the Oval Office at the White House, for instance."

"So how close can you get?"

"It's within fifteen feet of the front door."

She restrained a groan and looked around the living room with its stone fireplace and view of the lake filtered through massive oak trees. High wooden beams above their heads might support the massive weight of a sphere. Or Jamar could have hidden it below them in the basement. Or outside in the fork of a tree branch.

Shara dropped to her hands and knees and looked under the

brown leather couch. Nothing but dustballs. "Can that device tell you how far away Jamar is and how soon he'll arrive?"

"You don't want to know."

Her pulse leaped and she shoved to her feet. "How long?"

"If he maintains his current direction and speed, maybe twenty to thirty minutes. We should see his boat appear long before he arrives."

"That doesn't make me feel better." She shivered, stepped into the kitchen and started to open the upper cabinets. Scotch, vodka, whiskey lined up and called to her. Her mouth watered and her hands shook. She'd give ten years of her life to bolster her courage with a drink. She imagined the taste, the burn of it going down, her body suffused with blessed heat. After surviving the rigors of the desert, a capture, and fighting hand-to-hand for freedom, surely she could handle one blessed sip.

"No." She slammed the cabinet door.

"What?"

"Nothing here."

"Search only the lower ones," Cade instructed and headed for the hall closet. "The sphere is heavy. Maybe forty or fifty of your pounds."

Ten minutes later they were no closer to finding the shiny sphere than earlier. Cade stared at the screen. "It's here."

"You said within fifteen feet of the front door, right?"

"So?"

"Maybe he hid it outside."

Cade nodded. "Great idea."

Shara followed him outdoors, wondering if she should have remained silent. If they found the sphere, she intended to study it in the hopes of finding a way to destroy it. She already knew water wouldn't hurt it. Neither Jamar or Cade had worried that it might fall into the ocean.

She wasn't accustomed to thinking like a damn double agent. She wasn't comfortable with her untrustworthy role. And she certainly wasn't a scientist who could do a chemical analysis of the sphere. If only she could call the authorities for help, but she knew they wouldn't believe her. At the moment, her best option seemed to be to wait, let Cade recover the spheres, and continue to look for an opportunity.

Cade studied his screen. "I think you were right. The light on the screen seems a bit brighter out here."

"It's probably your imagination," she grumbled.

"Okay, so where would he hide it?"

"The best place is right out in the open where it won't be noticed." She checked the mailbox, the firewood stack, and behind the bushes planted by the front door. Her shoes weren't standing up well to the cold and she shivered as snow melted into her socks.

Cade headed for the garage. She hurried to catch up, fearing he might change his mind and kill the man they'd left in the van. "Where are you going?"

"To the garage. Wasn't there a snow shovel leaning in the corner?"

They found two. Cade handed her one. "Come on. If Jamar shoveled the driveway to clear the snow, maybe the sphere's just sitting a few inches out of sight."

His enthusiasm was contagious and they returned to the driveway and began to dig. It was hard, heavy work. The snow had crusted over and the shoveling caused her to sweat, even as her toes turned numb with the cold.

"If we find this part of the portal, what do we do about the piece in Jamar's hands?" she asked.

Cade tossed shovelfuls of snow over his shoulder, working with the smooth precision of a machine who didn't tire. For a long time he didn't answer and she returned to digging on her side of the driveway. "We'll have to steal that other piece from Jamar."

"And if we can't?"

"Let's not get ahead of ourselves."

But she knew. He'd told her each piece could open the portal by itself, but all three would be safer. Damn it. To stop him she needed all three pieces.

Even then she didn't know what she'd do with them. She needed more facts and prayed that Jules would have them.

Jules.

Shara knew Jules would be worried about her. As soon as they left the area, she would call her friend.

The roaring sound of an outboard engine pulled her from her thoughts and she gazed past the house to the lake. A speedboat was racing their way.

"Jamar's coming."

"Keep digging."

"But—"

"It's here in the snow. I can sense it."

She squinted against the sun. "There are five men in Jamar's boat. We should leave."

"Not yet."

She heard a clink of metal on metal. Cade tossed his shovel aside, knelt and dug with his hands.

Shara looked up and saw the boat was almost to the shore. "Hurry."

"I'm digging as fast as I can."

"Did you seduce me so I'd fly to the South Pacific to examine your friend's volcano?" Lyle pulled the sheet up to his chest, put his glasses on, and stared at Jules, suspicion clouding his intelligent eyes.

Jules turned onto her side and didn't bother to pull up the sheet to cover her breasts. Hell, he'd already seen everything and it wouldn't hurt to remind him that he'd enjoyed himself. "Is that what your genius IQ is telling you? That I flew halfway across the world to seduce you?"

"But that's exactly what you did."

"Only because I like you. Obviously, if you believe I'm capable of acting so coldly, so deviously, you don't have half the brains I thought you did. Perhaps you were the one thinking with your hormones—not me. And now that I've cleaned your pipes—"

"Cleaned my pipes?" he sputtered, his expression one of outrage and denial.

"—you're claiming that I'm using you so you can justify getting rid of me." Jules's blood pressure pumped, until her ears roared. How dare he accuse her of manipulating him with her body. She might not be a volcanologist with a Ph.D. but she didn't think so little of herself. "Look, Dr. Donovan, there are other volcanologists in the world and—"

"Are you going to seduce them, too?"

"What is it with you? Don't you think a girl could like you without having an ulterior motive?"

"No."

His answer almost shocked Jules into silence. "No? What do you mean no?"

"I have little else to offer."

She let her hand trail from his chest to his belly and lower and grinned. "Trust me. You have a lot to offer."

"Don't toy with me." Lyle turned away from her reach. "I'm not made of stone."

"If you were, I wouldn't have made love to you."

Lyle turned back, questions in his eyes. "My ex claimed I was cold as granite."

Jules giggled, now that she understood Lyle had been testing her. "I assure you, she was wrong. Just as you were wrong to accuse me of using my body—"

"Sorry. It's just that you're a beautiful woman."

She arched an eyebrow. "And a beautiful woman can't want you unless she has another reason?"

"I'm not sure why any woman would want me, never mind one like you."

"You'd think with all those brain cells, one of them might have a little confidence."

"When it comes to my work—"

"You're world class."

"When it comes to women, I'm a nerd."

"Your ex sure did a number on you."

Lyle threaded his hands through his hair, refusing to meet her eyes, clearly uncomfortable with the conversation. "I guess she convinced me that I'm not perfect."

"No one's perfect. Not me. Not you. Certainly not your ex. The trick is to see if our imperfections match up in a way that makes us happier together than when we are with someone else or when we are alone."

"If I'd known you were so smart," he said as he reached for her, "I'd have been too intimidated to kiss you."

"Don't worry, sweetie. You had no choice. I would have kissed you and"—she gestured to the bed and smiled—"the rest would have been history."

He nuzzled her neck. "They say history repeats itself."

"Mmm. As much as I like that theory, I really need to know if you can predict a volcanic eruption." Jules was getting closer to telling him about Cade and the portal, but she still intended to ease in slowly. At the moment, Lyle thought she was concerned about Haven's volcano erupting, but he didn't yet know she feared the portal might cause the explosion.

"The kind of eruptions that shoot lava into the sky are the easiest to predict but it's by no means an exact science. Often a giant bubble grows on the side of the cone, indicating pressure is building under the earth. Increased gases, smoke, and earthquake activity help us predict when the increased pressures will cause the eruption."

"So if there's no sign of a bubble forming on Haven's cone, we don't need to worry?"

"Not necessarily." He shook his head. "There are other kinds of volcanos. Here at Yellowstone, the eruption six hundred thousand years ago was so great, we think the cone blew off. Or the cone collapsed into the magma below and created a caldera. If Yellowstone were to erupt, the first sign might be a pyroclastic flow—"

"Speak English please."

"It's a fluidized mass of turbulent gas and rock fragments at temperatures of a hundred degrees Celsius or more. These surges are difficult to predict."

"And they're dangerous?"

"Very. Pyroclastic explosions are enormously destructive because they release massive amounts of kinetic energy and lethally hot gas. One breath can vaporize all internal organs."

"And how far-reaching are the effects?"

"If Yellowstone erupts like it did before, it will send up

enough ash so no one in the continental U.S. will see the sun. We'd have massive crop failures and since we feed over half the world, we'd see massive starvation. But many people would die long before they starved. An eruption that large could set off tidal waves. Or other massive earthquakes. An explosion of this magnitude would be like setting off over a thousand atomic bombs."

She shuddered, wondering if the cataclysmic eruptions would end all life on Earth. And she wondered why she hadn't heard from Shara and if she'd managed to stop Cade from finding the portal. "Is there any way to prevent an explosion?"

Lyle eyed her curiously. "There are theories."

"Like what?"

"Releasing the pressure before it builds high enough to cause the explosion."

"But?" She sensed his reluctance to say more.

"Other scientists believe that tampering with forces we don't understand might actually set off the explosion. Even computer models disagree. We simply don't know enough. Instead of making one more Hollywood movie about volcanoes, if we could have those funds to study them, we might know a whole lot more."

She heard the frustration in his voice and wondered if she could use it to convince him to come to Haven. While she hoped Shara could stop Cade, her visions were too strong not to do everything she could in case Shara failed. "Wouldn't it be a good opportunity for you to visit Haven?"

"The likelihood of it exploding soon is very improbable. And from your description of the island, it's tiny, if you're right and it did explode, getting away might be impossible."

"You can't be afraid. You live atop the largest active volcano—"

"My work is here."

"How long since you've taken a vacation?" She shoved the sheet to the floor and let out a low, sexy chuckle. "And in case you're wondering, I'm now attempting to seduce you."

His eyes sparkled with male interest. "You don't play fair."

"I also have some more surprises for you."

"Sounds interesting."

"Oh, I'm better than interesting," she promised, deciding that she would tell him the entire story as soon as she heard from Shara. Meanwhile, Jules intended to enjoy this opportunity. Who would have thought a staid scientist could be so deliciously inventive?

18

When Jamar's boat was about a quarter mile from his rental home's snow-covered Lake George dock, Cade and Shara ducked behind the garage, remaining out of sight and peeking occasionally at the lake. Shara didn't know whether to pull her gun, yank Cade away from the snow, or help him dig. However, Jamar couldn't see them from the lake and she couldn't shoot him from here, and Cade wasn't likely to budge until he found the portal piece, so she dropped to her knees beside Cade and shoveled snow with her hands.

Too bad the ice around the dock wasn't frozen enough to stop the boat from unloading. "Cade."

"What?"

She dug away more snow. "Can Jamar use his *Quait* on me?"

"Yes. Why?"

"But suppose you use *Quait* on me before he does. Wouldn't that protect me from his control?"

Cade stiffened but he kept digging. And his silence told her that her assumption was correct.

"Look, I'd rather be under your *Quait* than Jamar's. And it might be our only advantage."

"If Jamar controls me, he can make me use you however he wants." Cade's tone was muffled by the snowbank, but he didn't sound certain.

"Are you sure?"

Cade grunted and pulled backward, his hands holding a shiny metal ball about the size of a cantaloupe. His arms strained with the weight, but he staggered to his feet, his eyes brightening. "We got it. Let's go."

She'd feared he would want to stay, try to surprise Jamar and steal the second one back, too. As Cade hurried to the vehicle, she used the shovel, placing snow back over the spot where they'd dug. Close scrutiny would reveal they'd found the portal piece but her deception might buy them getaway time.

While Shara remained uncertain how to stop Cade, she most definitely didn't want to tangle with Jamar. Sprinting for the garage, she ducked under the automatic door that Cade had triggered to open and slid into the passenger seat of the van. Hands freezing from her short stint at digging, she flicked the heater to high.

Cade had taken the driver's seat before she remembered that she'd never seen him drive. He'd started the van and shifted into forward with a jerk. "Maybe I should drive."

He grunted, his face set in concentration.

She snapped on her seat belt. "If you get us killed in a car wreck, you'll never build your portal."

"We have similar vehicles on our world."

"Ones with tires that slip and slide in ice and snow?"

"We don't have snow. Or tires on our vehicles. Our skimmers are like your hovercraft and don't touch the ground."

"So why don't you let me—"

He floored the gas, the force pressing her back into the seat before he let off. "There we go." He adjusted his speed and smoothly steered down the drive.

She remembered to use the remote to close the garage door behind them. "If we have two portal pieces—"

"We only have one."

"But you have a locator beam on the second one and hopefully we'll beat Jamar to it. So if we have two of the three pieces and you open the portal—"

"The chances of success go down, but only by about ten percent."

"And the chance of a volcanic explosion?"

"Go up." Cade frowned. "I wish I could be more specific. But I can't figure the odds until we tap the volcano's power—maybe not even then."

"What do you mean, 'maybe not even then'?"

He turned and headed north, then stopped the van by a busy intersection. "We can't go to the fire station—not with Jamar so close on our heels."

She jumped out of the van and together they removed the injured man from the back. Cade propped him up against a rock where he would be spotted easily from the road and then they got back in the van. Shara felt guilty leaving him there and dialed 911. She gave his location and condition to the woman who answered and who reassured her that help was only minutes away before hanging up.

"Sorry. Jamar might be able to trace my call but we'll be long gone and I couldn't leave him there to bleed to death."

"I understand." Cade's tone sounded neutral, as if he still believed it would have been better to kill the man but didn't want to argue. And he obviously hadn't forgotten her question about the portal causing a volcanic eruption. "I'm not a scientist. I can only estimate the volcanic consequences after I sink my instruments into the magma flows beneath your island."

"Jules confided in me that she's had visions of devastating volcanic explosions."

He glanced from the road to her, his eyebrows raised. "Volcanic explosions on Haven?"

"Yes."

"How accurate are her predictions?" Cade sounded more curious than argumentative and she wondered if she might be able to talk him out of his mission.

"She told me not to make the film that caused Bruce's death. I didn't listen and he died."

"Do people on your world usually heed the advice of psychics?"

"Sometimes."

"I got the impression their prophecies were considered less than meaningful."

"Jules has proven herself to me."

"She's always correct?" Cade eyed her curiously, but she noted that he kept scanning his rearview mirror for signs of pursuit. Remarkably coordinated—after his initial testing of brake and gas pedals—Cade drove the van like a pro. When the back tires slid on a patch of ice, he refrained from hitting the brake and turned into the spin with a skill that surprised her.

"Her visions are erratic. We believe what she sees is always accurate, but the trick is interpreting the visions. For example the volcanic eruption she saw on Haven might happen tomorrow or in another century—except she saw our faces combined with the explosions." She sighed as he pulled onto the interstate, heading toward Albany and the airport.

"What else?"

"Then there's the matter of free will. Jules and I believe that if we act correctly upon her vision, then we can alter her vision of the future."

"Are you saying if she's sees a fire break out—say due to a gas leak—if you prevent the gas leak then there will be no fire?"

"Exactly. So her vision was correct at the time she made it but then we altered the present and changed the future."

"Tell me more about Jules's vision for Haven."

"She claims the eruption is cataclysmic. That it might destroy all of us by setting off the chain of volcanos around the Pacific Rim."

"Define 'all of us.' "

"Everyone who lives on this planet."

"So that's the real reason why you came with me."

"Huh?"

"You want me to be careful when I open the portal?"

Shara pressed her teeth together to prevent a groan and lied. "Yes. I want you to be careful." She wanted him to abandon his plan but couldn't come right out and say it. By now she knew his work was too important to him for her to dissuade him with words. "And I'd like you to consult an expert Jules has been talking to."

"Sure. No problem."

Shara eyed him, wondering if his concession had been too easy. And why she felt guilty for lying to him as well as for failing to find a way to follow Jules's advice. But she'd had no opportunity to stop Cade—short of killing him—and she simply didn't have that in her. Whatever she did seemed wrong. And at the moment, if she'd had a beer in hand, she would have surely downed it in one long swallow.

Thankfully Cade changed the subject. "I need to call the bank." She dialed and handed him the phone. He arranged for checks, cash, a duplicate ID, and a private plane to take them to the Caribbean. Cade's cash had blown up during the airplane crash but he'd deposited most of his funds in Hawaii and had plenty left to cover their needs. But while he made the financial arrangements she wondered again how she could stop him. She would only get one opportunity and she had to make it count. Because once he learned her plan, he would likely be furious, his *Quait* would kick in, and he could totally control her every move.

Jamar hadn't been able to contain his anger that Cade had escaped due to his stupid orders to keep him alive. And he raged at the theft of the portal piece. Although he'd known the incompetent guard in his garage was already dead, he'd nevertheless emptied a full clip of bullets into his head and chest before hurling the gun at a window. He'd sweated precious salt to retrieve that portal piece from the Dead Sea. And once again Cade and his bitch had ruined his plans.

Oh yeah, the bitch had been at the lake with Cade. Jamar had smelled her female scent in the house. And if he'd gotten his hands on the second guard, his death would have been long and difficult.

If Jamar wasn't always surrounded by the unfit and the stupid, he'd be long gone, on his way back to Rama. Instead, he had to travel to another part of this primitive world.

Furious, Jamar had packed the sphere he'd retrieved from the Dead Sea, cursing his lot, once again forced to make new plans. He couldn't afford even one portal piece to remain in Cade's hands. The system was made in triplicate with safety redundancies but any one piece could open a portal back to Rama. If Cade retrieved the sphere in the Caribbean, he'd have two.

Cade didn't have much of a head start. Jamar could catch him, but he was so very tired of doing all the work.

Trevor's reporter instincts told him that he was onto a big story, maybe the biggest of the century. Between the mind control, gemstones not from Earth, the pilot's version of an exploding ship, and Shara Weston's disappearance, something unusual was happening. If only he had all the pieces, he might tie them together. As it was, Trevor had several theories—none of which he could prove without hard evidence.

The trail had gone cold. While his computer's search engines had found several women brutalized in Israel, Trevor had no proof that Jamar had attacked them. The description they'd given to authorities conflicted with one another's and could have matched Jamar or a thousand other swarthy-skinned and dark-haired men of Mediterranean descent.

Trevor had tried calling Jules but she never answered her cell. The private investigator in L.A. also had no news—or was keeping her findings to herself. And his boss was beginning to complain about not only the cost of research, but that he now wanted a story to justify Trevor's travel expenses—night after night even at inexpensive hotels like this one added up.

Perhaps he should go home. Give up.

He had so little to go on. A name. No nationality. No base

of operations. He knew Jamar spoke English, possessed a penchant for whips and chains that could be bought anonymously on many Internet sites. Finding Jamar was like tracing a phantom. And Trevor didn't understand how a woman of Shara Weston's celebrity could disappear, unless she wore a disguise.

His cell phone rang. "Trevor Cantrell here."

"Trevor, this is Shara Weston. I understand you've been looking for me."

At the sound of her sultry voice, Trevor's pulse escalated. Under most circumstances his first thought was that the movie star was trying to stage a comeback and after a publicity angle. But he could look past the obvious. Too many puzzle pieces didn't fit. And Shara Weston had the reputation as a classy lady. In all likelihood she was hiding from Jamar, not seeking publicity to restart her fabulous acting career.

"You've spoken to Teresa Alverez?" Trevor asked.

"She checked you out. She says you're a man of your word. A man who understands discretion."

"I like to think so."

"She also said you took her to the hospital and saved her life before she bled out."

"I'm searching for Jamar, the man who hurt her, and I've cause to believe that same man is after you."

"He is."

Trevor had expected Shara to deny that information. He raised his eyebrows. She obviously wanted something from him or she wouldn't have called. "Is that why you left Haven? And did Jamar burn down Jules Makana's house in Hawaii?"

"Yes. You have been busy." Shara hesitated.

Trevor knew that despite her PI's investigation, Shara wanted to make up her own mind whether he was trustworthy. "Let me guess why you called. You want my help, but you don't want me to print the story."

"Oh, you can have your story, I just want you to delay printing it until. . . ."

"Until?"

"I give you the go ahead."

She'd tweaked his curiosity. "And in return for your giving me an exclusive, what do you want?" Trevor asked.

"Impeccable reporting."

"Excuse me?"

"I want my story documented, photographed, witnessed. Because the world isn't going to believe us—not unless you can deliver with integrity."

"My reputation is—"

"Brilliant. Otherwise we wouldn't be having this discussion."

"It's a deal, Ms. Weston."

"If we're to work together, call me Shara. I want you on the next flight to St. Thomas."

"I'll be there." Trevor hung up the phone, his heart pounding crazily. He recalled seeing Teresa's bloody body, remembered the story of Jamar's brutality, and wondered what kind of danger he might be facing. Although he'd never carried a weapon, he'd never gone up against anyone capable of mind control, either. If Jamar was after Shara, Trevor wondered whether he might need a few self-defense items in addition to an extra digital camera, and decided to pick them up before he left the country and headed to the Caribbean.

Turning Shara down had never crossed his mind. If Jamar was part of some religious cult that practiced mind control and brutalized women, the story would be huge. However, Trevor couldn't forget about the gemstones that hadn't seemed to come from Earth.

Sensing Shara's story might be the biggest of his life, he called his boss, made arrangements, and headed for St. Thomas.

Shara called Jules on her new satellite cell phone. "Jules?"

"Oh, lord. Are you all right? Where have you been? Why haven't you called me until now?"

"It's complicated. But I'm okay." Shara sat on the bed of her hotel room in St. Thomas, avoiding the mirror that would reflect the poor quality of her wig—the best disguise they could come up with during their quick New York departure and ensuing flight to the Caribbean. Now she was hiding at the hotel while Cade had gone off to hire a boat and scuba divers to retrieve the third portal piece. Since this was the first time she'd been separated from Cade, it might be her only chance to talk to Jules. For the moment, it was so good to hear Jules's voice, to allow her warmth and caring to soak in. "Where are you?"

"Still in Montana with Lyle."

Oh, yes. The scientist who studied volcanoes. It seemed so long since they'd seen one another. Shara quickly summarized being shot down over the desert, Jamar's men picking them up, and the status of the portal pieces. "Cade expects to find this last piece today and then we're heading to Haven."

"Whoa. What about—"

Shara took a deep breath and prayed for a reprieve. "Look, I know your visions are strong. But his cause is so noble. Jamar is the monster, not Cade."

"I heard Jamar tried to kill Teresa," Jules admitted.

"He's hurt others, too." Shara refrained from talking about the women Trevor had told her about or the trail of dead bodies she and Cade had left behind, the pilots over the desert, the guard in the garage. "I'm not certain we should be on the same side as a man like Jamar."

"We have to do what's best for Earth. If Cade's portal causes a volcanic explosion—"

"I understand, Jules." Shara sighed, knowing the moment she had to act had almost arrived. "Can you bring Lyle to Haven with you?"

"I'm working on him." She lowered her voice. "I haven't told him everything yet."

Shara heard a note of satisfaction enter Jules's tone. "What *have* you been doing?"

"Besides worrying over you? I've been doing everything I've always dreamed. Even in the cold, Lyle keeps me warm."

"Maybe that why you envisioned Lyle's face with flames. He's hot?" Shara teased her friend, glad that she'd found some happiness. After Lou's cheating and then her house burning down, she deserved to meet someone special.

"What about you and Cade?" Jules changed the subject with the abruptness of friends who were almost always on the same page. Their conversations often jumped from topic to topic, both women easily making the switch.

"He's a good guy."

"Good in the sack?" Jules always did get straight to the point.

"He takes control," Shara admitted.

"I didn't think you were into the dominance and submission games."

Shara sighed. "Cade's upped salt intake has given him mind-control abilities."

"What?"

"Remember how he saved us in the fire?"

"Like I could forget."

"He can do other things and he thinks it'll turn him into some kind of savage."

Jules must have heard the doubt in Shara's tone. "You disagree?"

She'd seen Cade kill a man, but she'd also experienced his gentleness firsthand. Although he used his *Quait* to take control during their lovemaking, he'd given her nothing but pleasure, and he'd give his life to help his people. How could she work against a man like him? But she must.

Shara has lapsed into silence and finally spoke. "If it wasn't for your vision, I could be happy with Cade."

Jules swore. "You love him, don't you?"

"I've chosen not to fall in love."

"Don't give me that shit. You're talking to me. And you can't choose to fall in love any more than you can choose your parents. It just happens."

"So"—This time *Shara* changed the subject—"After we find this portal piece, Cade plans for us to return to Haven.

He says there are enough redundancies in two pieces for the portal to work with only a ten percent chance of failure."

"But having three pieces would be safer?"

"Yes."

"Do you believe him? Do you think a ten percent chance of blowing up the entire planet is work risking?"

"That's why I want you to bring Lyle with you. He's an expert on volcanoes."

"He knows nothing about the portal technology."

"Cade will fill him in."

"Suppose Lyle says it's not safe and Cade thinks it's okay to go ahead. What then?" Jules asked.

"I don't know." Shara's heart twisted. It was a choice she'd hoped never to have to make.

"You should stop him now. You're taking too many chances by waiting."

"So exactly how do I stop him?"

"You could call in the authorities."

"Sure. And they'd look up my history and find out I shot Bruce and have been a recluse. Plus I'm an ex-movie star—not a real credible background. They'd probably lock me up."

"You could . . ."

"I'm not killing him. I can't."

"Okay. Okay. What if you destroy the spheres?"

"I'd have to wait until we have both of them. But I'm not sure how to destroy them, and even if I could, if Cade discovers what I'm doing—"

"He's going to be furious."

"And extreme emotions bring out his *Quait*." Shara sighed. "If he catches me—"

"Don't get caught."

"You didn't have a vision that might tell me how?"

"Sorry."

Shara and Jules lapsed into silence. Finally, Shara's thoughts turned from betraying Cade to more practical matters. "Oh, I almost forgot to tell you there's a Pulitzer prize–winning reporter coming with us. In exchange for an exclusive and holding the story until we decide what to do about the portal, Trevor Cantrell's going to tell the world about Rama, that we are no longer alone. People may not believe me, but *he* has a sterling reputation."

"Are you sure that's wise?"

"I'm not sure of anything. But if Jamar and Cade made it here, others may follow. Earth's leaders need to be prepared."

"Why go public?" Jules asked.

"I don't want this to turn into another government cover-up like Roswell."

"It's your call, but the publicity will be a nightmare."

Shara sighed. She had a love-hate relationship with reporters. As a celebrity, publicity could make or break a career. And yet she hated a camera flash in her face as much as the next person, never mind the invasion of privacy. "When it gets to be too much, we can hide on Haven."

"Yeah, if Cade doesn't blow up the island or, for that matter, planet Earth. It really would be better if you stopped him. Perhaps you'll think of something. You usually do."

Despite Jules's dire words, her friend's tone had an upbeat lilt that made Shara smile. "You sound happy."

"Lyle and I are good together."

"Glad to hear it. Does that mean you can convince him to help us?"

"I'll work on it." Jules chuckled. "Work has never been so much fun."

"Or so dangerous."

Jules's voice immediately turned serious. "You've had problems since Jamar shot you down in the desert?"

"Jamar is evil and determined. He's not going to quit coming after us." Shara worried that her friend could lose more than the home she'd already lost.

"I hear you."

"Be careful, Jules. Jamar doesn't play by our rules. He can make a person do things with his mind that they don't want to do. And he has a cruel streak." Shara had spoken to Teresa, then called her banker and asked him to wire enough funds to cover Teresa's hospital bills and the plastic surgery. But no amount of money could make up for what had happened to her. "I wouldn't ask you to come to Haven if I didn't need you."

"I'm fine. We'll stop in California and pick up Kapuna. I'll have to feed that cat tuna fish for a week to get him to forgive me for leaving him for so long."

"I sent you a gift." Shara hesitated. Jules was proud and fiercely independent and while her home had been insured, insurance never covered everything.

"It's not my birthday."

"It's my contribution to your new home. And don't you dare refuse. It burned because I went to you for help. You could have died—"

"But I didn't." Jules's tone was firm.

"Still, you lost everything and although Jamar set the flames, I led him straight to you."

"Enough of the guilt trip. Sheesh. You're talking as if you don't expect to meet us at Haven in a day or two."

Shara's throat tightened. She hoped to come up with a plan to stop Cade before then. If she failed, this might be the last time she ever talked to Jules. "If I don't make it there, Haven is yours."

"Maybe you shouldn't try anything. Maybe Lyle can talk Cade out of—"

"Cade's determined. He's promised to listen to reason but unless Lyle has proof, there's no changing his mind." Shara saw no way out. She had to discover how to stop Cade and she needed to do it soon. "I'm trying to think ahead. I'm okay, really."

"And you'd better stay that way."

"You, too." Shara knew that Jules didn't always share her visions, especially if she had difficulty with the interpretations. "Any pertinent visions?"

"Define 'pertinent.' "

"Anything that includes you, me, Cade, Lyle, Jamar, or volcanic eruptions."

Jules's voice thickened with fear. "I had another vision of Lyle. He was lying injured on the ground, in the dark. Frantic. And then lava erupts."

Jules likely hadn't mentioned this earlier since the information couldn't help Shara and would only cause more worry, but she couldn't let it drop. "Was Lyle on Haven during the vision?"

"I don't know. I wish I had more." Jules sounded resigned. "Forcing my visions never works."

"Hey, you're giving us a warning. That's better than nothing."

"Is it?"

"Of course. Because of you, we're taking precautions, consulting experts, documenting our story with Trevor. And Cade trusts me. I'll think of a way to stop him."

"For what it's worth, I'm sorry."

Shara ran her hand through her hair. "So far, I haven't seen any opportunities to stop Cade . . . so I'll have to create one."

"You have an idea?"

"Maybe. I've got to go." Shara's gaze focused on the rolling suitcase where Cade had left one sphere. She needed to examine it, figure out a way to destroy the portal piece, so she'd be ready to act when Cade brought back the second one.

19

❂

Cade marveled at the sea life on this fabulous world. Luckily the cut in his arm had scabbed over and, with a bandage firmly in place, he could enjoy a swim in the Caribbean Sea. While he didn't have the expertise to dive down to the sunken portal piece, he'd hired a dive crew to do that for him. Shara had stayed on the island called St. Thomas to make phone calls and deal with the reporter, and Cade had free time on his hands, so he'd talked one of the divers into lending him scuba gear. He'd promised to stay right near the surface of the turquoise water, so he wouldn't have to deal with decompression issues. But the air tank, mask, and fins allowed him to become one with the reef.

The variety of sea life ran the gamut from round, white-and-gray brain coral to violet fans, to spiny sea urchins to an assortment of neon-colored fish that spanned the rainbow from yellow to purple. He spied a ray skimming along the bottom, a giant sea turtle and even a dark green moray eel lurking in the depths. And while he took the opportunity to sightsee, he kept an eye on the diving operation.

With his locator, they'd easily found the exact vicinity of

the third portal piece, but retrieval in over two hundred feet of ocean wasn't so easy. The boat captain had explained that the divers needed a different mix of air to breathe at those depths, and it would take time for them to go up and down since their lungs had to adjust to the air mix and pressure during the descent and corresponding ascent.

To make matters more difficult, the portal piece had fallen into soft sand. Between the tide and normal wave action, digging would be necessary to uncover the sphere. While Cade couldn't see down to where the men used a machine to blow the sand from the ocean floor, he could see the activity of men lowering the equipment. Appreciating the skill and the dedication of the divers, he caught glimpses of them as they worked quickly and efficiently.

Knowing Jamar could arrive and muck up the operation, Cade had placed the entire team under light mind control. Although reluctant to use his powers on others as Firsts had used them on him, he recalled Shara's preference that she'd rather be under his dominion than Jamar's. To prevent Jamar from swooping down and disrupting the mission by taking over the divers' minds and possibly stealing this sphere for himself, Cade had applied his own *Quait*. He'd used only enough force to prevent Jamar from taking away control. And he'd hired armed guards to stand watch on deck.

Still, using *Quait* was risky. Cade didn't want Jamar to learn how strong his new abilities had become. And yet, he felt obligated to protect the men who were risking their lives for him and the good of the mission.

Having all three pieces would have been better. But with two spheres and duplicate systems, Cade felt confident he could tap Haven's volcano for power, open a portal to Rama, and send home the precious salt.

Unless Jamar stopped him. The First would be furious over the loss of one sphere. Surely he was on his way here now. But Cade and Shara had beaten him to the Caribbean and hopefully they could recover the last sphere and return to Haven before Jamar could do any damage.

Since the probability of Jamar showing up at these ocean

coordinates was high, Cade had sought to protect Shara. He'd encouraged her to remain behind on the island with the other sphere. Around a First, a single beautiful woman was always a target.

Cade had also hired bodyguards to protect Shara, placing them under a light *Quait* force, too, hoping to prevent Jamar from turning his own people against him. Would Cade's precautions be enough? Should he have kept Shara with him?

Most strangely, all day his thoughts kept returning to her. After his arrival on Earth, they'd constantly been together, and he should have been ready to move on to another woman. In the past, one casual relationship led to the next. But the more Cade knew about Shara, the more she intrigued him. Although he'd learned to appreciate her strengths and her intellect and her lovemaking, it was her friendship he valued most. Unlike the women of his world who expected little and didn't judge, Shara expected a lot—perhaps more than he could give.

But he found himself enjoying the challenge of living up to her expectations. Instead of chafing at their closeness, instead of wanting to move on to the next relationship, he found his thoughts dwelling on her. He imagined her sitting by the pool, her skin carefully shaded by a straw hat and lots of sunscreen, her beautiful neck and shoulders tempting whoever set his gaze on her.

She'd really needed some down time to decompress from the stress being with him had put her under. And he feared that returning to Haven, tapping her volcano, and opening the portal might be more that he should ask of her. Perhaps recounting their story to the reporter would help her come to terms with his mission. She didn't have to tell Cade that she had doubts about his technology for him to know she was very worried.

He could see the concerns in her eyes whenever they discussed using the volcano to power the portal. Although the technology was unfamiliar to her, he didn't understand why she didn't trust his technology more.

Cade swam through the warm water, occasionally allowing the salty sea to seep onto his tongue. So much precious salt. Just a tiny portion could make such an enormous difference, literally freeing his people from mind control.

But Cade was also well aware of the problems: too much salt could create others as ruthless as the Firsts. Shara's people had to be protected as much as his people needed to be protected from themselves.

Opening the portal would solve many problems, but he had to think ahead. He didn't want his legacy to be one that ruined Shara's world. There was so much beauty here, not just underwater, but the people themselves.

Cade turned around and swam back toward the boat. Underwater, the dive team seemed to be slowly making their way to the surface. One of them kicked his flippers more rigorously to remain with the others and in his hands he held something round, something shiny.

The last sphere. *Yes!* They'd retrieved it.

Pleasure and satisfaction washed through Cade. Between this sphere and the one back at the hotel with Shara, he could accomplish his mission. The operation had gone so smoothly, it almost seemed too easy.

During the boat ride back to port, Cade had difficulty enjoying the balmy breeze, the hot sun, the rippling turquoise water. He kept looking over his shoulder, expecting Jamar to attack from out of the sky or across the sea. But the day stayed clear, sunny, and bright—and he spied no danger. When Cade reached St. Thomas, he paid the captain and crew, tipped them well, and flagged down a taxi to take him to the hotel, the precious sphere in a backpack.

During the ride, his concern over Shara mounted and he second-guessed whether leaving her alone had been the right thing to do. He'd expected trouble on the water or during the recovery, and when none appeared, he feared he'd made a huge mistake.

Had Jamar gone after Shara instead of him?

The taxi driver pulled up to the hotel and he tossed several bills his way, then headed for his room. He had the strongest feeling something was wrong. That Shara was in trouble.

He opened the hotel room door, his nerves taut. But when he heard Shara singing in the shower, tension drained from Cade. Had life been going wrong for so long that he couldn't accept a good day?

Eager to tell her about his success as well as the creatures he'd seen on the reef, he locked the door and stored the backpack in the closet, kicked off his shoes, shucked his shirt and shorts, and headed for the bathroom.

Cade called out to avoid startling her. "Shara. I'm back."

"How'd it go?"

"We found it."

"Any trouble?"

"None." He didn't want to think about Jamar's where-abouts when he had so much more pleasant things on his mind.

Her skin glowed a golden tan from the sun, water sluiced over her toned curves. She'd already washed her hair and the scent of citrus teased his nostrils. He couldn't resist taking her into his arms, holding her against his chest. His groin pulsed and the urge to kiss her roughened his tone. "I missed you."

She snuggled against him, letting the water pour down his back. "You sound like a man who wants to make love."

"That I do," he agreed. "But I want to do it with you."

"Mmm. Sounds good." She lathered her hands with soap and smoothed it over his back. Her fingertips lingered, exploring the muscles, the ridges, the hollows, enticing him to return the favor.

But he had a lot on his mind. "You aren't listening."

"What?" She stepped back, her eyes searching his.

He loved that about her. She seemed to comprehend that he needed to talk and she was willing to delay her pleasure and make an effort to understand.

"All day, I kept thinking about you."

"How much you wanted to make love?" She lathered her hands with soap and smoothed it over his shoulders, chest, and arms.

"Of course." He grinned, enjoying her touch that was full

of taunting caresses. "But," he chose his words carefully, wanting her to comprehend, "I don't only want lots of hot sex. I want to have it with *you.*"

At his emphasis, her eyes widened and a smile played at the corners of her mouth. She trailed her hands over his hips, his buttocks. "Are you trying to say that you have *feelings* for me?"

"Yes." He didn't hesitate to admit the truth and with the enticing direction her hands were taking, he spoke quickly, determined to force out the words. "I've never thought about another woman as much as you. We've never talked about the future, but I'm hopeful."

"After your mission, will we be able to spend more time together?" Her eyes held his, her chest expanded as she inhaled. Her hands dipped between his thighs, then moved lower to his knees, ignoring the part he wished she'd touch most.

Even if she stopped her caresses, he owed her his honesty. "I have to go home. My people need me."

"I know. But . . . suppose I went with you?"

Her words startled him. On Earth, she was wealthy, a celebrity, idolized by the masses. She had everything. But she was down on one knee, washing his calves, gazing up at him as if she feared his response might not be favorable.

She'd startled him. The idea of her accompanying him had never occurred to him. At first, he'd thought her company pleasant and he'd needed her island. But his feelings had grown to the point where he didn't want to say good-bye and obviously she felt the same, which heated his blood even more. That she might be willing to go back with him, stay with him, excited him, thrilled him, scared him. Suppose after she got to Rama, he decided that the kind of commitment she expected was too much for him—he'd feel guilty for taking her from her world. Trapped. And yet, the idea of waking up beside her every morning, spending the day together, or simply having every night with her appealed to him on a level so deep he didn't understand his own longings.

His heart might tempt him to throw caution to the stars,

but his head prevailed. "Why would you want to come to Rama?"

She finished washing his feet and stood. "You said that after you send the salt to Rama that your people hoped to settle on another world."

"They can't come here. I'm going to program the portal so that nothing living can pass through. There will be no accidental biological contamination. And it's possible the portal would make it too easy for unscrupulous underfirsts to attempt to do to your people what the Firsts have done to us. I want my legacy to be one of freeing my people—but not at the cost of setting up another world to be taken over."

Hope brightened her eyes. "You can do that?"

"Yes. The spheres are programmable. I've already altered them."

"I'd like to be part of settling a new world, building a home . . . starting a family." She finally closed her hand over his sex. "We don't have to decide our entire future right now, but I would ask one thing of you."

"Okay." His heart thumped. She wanted to settle a new world? She wanted to build a home with him? Bear his children? He hadn't dared to think that far ahead. He'd always known that completing his mission was a long shot. His chances of survival and success had been so low, but now that he possessed two spheres, he could actually hope that he had a real future to offer. And he owed Shara. Whatever she asked of him, if it was in his power, he would try to give it to her.

Pain flickered in her eyes. "If you wish to make love to another . . . you must tell me before you act on the urge."

He could see that making such a request distressed her, that just saying the words had been an act of courage. And while the custom on his world was simply to move on without making a big deal of such behavior, he was aware her expectations were different. Cade suspected that the conventions of his people would change once they controlled their own lives and they might not be so different from Terrans after all.

If Shara was willing to give up her home, her friends and her entire world for him, surely he could make such a promise. "Agreed."

Tipping his head back, he rinsed the salt water from his hair. Too eager to make love to her, he planned to shampoo later. But before he could open the shower door, Shara had closed her hands around his sex, placed her lips over the tip, circled her tongue around the head.

"Ah . . . you feel . . . wonderful," he murmured, purring almost like Jules's cat.

He reached down and dipped his fingers through her hair. The woman had sorcery on her tongue. Holding still, letting her have her way, had him tense, tight. On fire. Her hands and mouth and lips all served to please him. If she continued, he might spill his seed before he could give her pleasure. But she paid no attention to his gentle urging to free him. Thinking became difficult as all his blood seemed to rush between his legs for her attention.

Aching, tight, blood roaring, he ached for more. More pressure. More friction. More of Shara.

Closing his eyes, he leaned back against the cool tile, turned off the water. Her tongue teased, taunted, toyed, drawing him tight, the pressure increasing.

He prided himself on holding back. Sweat beaded on his brow. His breath came in bursts. And despite his effort to hang on, he was losing control. "Are you . . . trying . . . to destroy me?"

"Mm."

Shara's mouth eased and he restrained a groan. Her fingers found his balls and tickled, tweaked, tugged.

Her sassy torment made it almost impossible to hold still. Every cell in his body demanded he move, thrust, take, satisfy his need. Her willingness upped the thrill of being with her. His *Quait* escalated. Tendrils of mental force reached out to Shara but he herded them back, determined not to interfere. He wanted making love to be give and take—not submission and domination.

So he curbed the *Quait*.

But waiting increased the pleasure. And the pleasure was a beauteous soaring, floating wonder. Yet each time he thought he was going to explode, Shara changed the tempo, her touch, the pressure, driving him insane with longing.

She seemed to know exactly where and how to give maximum pleasure. And yet as giving as she was, she held back the ultimate blessing, keeping him on a raw edge, poised between excruciating need and lusty explosion.

Fearing he might take control with his *Quait* when he shouldn't, Cade steered the strengthening force upward, away from Shara. He was pleased with his success, but as if *Quait* had a will of its own, the force circled, snapped back at him, at her—forcing her to release him so he could have her exactly the way he wished.

And she immediately knew that he'd taken total control. She lifted her head, her gaze catching his, her pupils dilated with passion, her voice throaty with longing. "Damn you."

"Sorry, sweetheart. I couldn't wait." He helped her stand, led her from the shower, wrapped her in a towel, and carried her to the bed, all the while his sex throbbing, pulsing, demanding that he plunge into her heat. His blood roared in a frenzy. His head reeled with only the thought of having her.

"Do you mind terribly if I take over?" he asked, knowing he had no choice.

She licked her lips, her expression sassy. "I suppose that depends on your intentions."

"I can be . . . quite creative." Indeed now that he'd regained a bit of control over his lower half, he was determined to drive her into a wild place, the same reckless place she'd taken him.

After setting her down on her back on the sheets, he nudged her legs apart. "Seems to me that I've been neglecting you."

She laughed. "That's me, terribly neglected." She lifted her head and peered at him as he got comfy between her thighs. "I should be annoyed."

"You aren't."

"I'll let you make it up to me."

"Deal." He licked a water droplet from the inside of her knee.

"Ah . . . that tickles. You're in the wrong spot."

"Am I?"

"You're too low."

He licked a trail up the inside of her lean leg to her thigh. And stopped, tauntingly just short of her center. With every word he blew a heated breath over her sensitive area, fanning her with puffs of air. "You want me to go higher?"

"Yes."

He leaned forward, brushed her hair lightly with his lips, then planted a kiss below her navel. "There?"

"Lower."

He nipped the inside of her upper thigh.

"Tease."

He blew on her lips, then lightly caressed her, enjoying her quiver of excitement that caused her to cream. He breathed in, reveling in her female scent. "I like you like this."

"Define this."

"Naked. Ready. Sexed up for me."

She tossed a pillow at his head. "Stop talking."

"All right." He bent her knees, placed her hands on her shins, and had her hold herself open to him. "That's good. Now close your eyes."

"Why?"

"Because I want you thinking about where I'm going to touch you first."

"I already am."

"And I don't want you distracted."

"Like that's going to happen." Despite her words, she closed her eyes. Her muscles tensed and he grinned and scooped up her cocoa butter from the nightstand. Without making a sound, he unscrewed the lid, dipped his fingers into the rich ointment.

"What are you doing?" her voice rose half in complaint, half in anticipation.

"I'm deciding where to bite you."

"What?" She attempted to look at him. He used his *Quait*

to stop her from opening her lids. Shara let out a tiny groan, but she didn't release her legs, keeping herself open to him.

He knew she expected him to start slowly, perhaps tweak her breasts, or nip her neck. Instead, he dipped one finger that he'd covered with cocoa butter between her parted thighs, straight into her heat. She would have jerked, but he used *Quait* to hold her still.

Ever so slowly, he curled his finger and used the tip to tease her deep inside. At the same time, he placed his mouth directly over her sweet spot, his tongue beat gently, circled lightly.

With his free hand, he spread the ointment over her tipped-up bottom. At first, every time he touched her crease, she jerked, but gradually she began to accept his slippery fingers until he had two fingers inside her, stroking from two angles, and his mouth firmly in charge of her core.

"Oh . . . my . . . oh." Tiny grunts of pleasure encouraged him to increase the pressure, to plunge deeper. She would have been pumping her hips, rocking, but he allowed her no movement, no sense of sight. He wanted every one of her thoughts focused on his fingers plunging and thrusting while his tongue played over her clit.

He sensed she was tossing her head from side to side, felt her spasm sweetly into his mouth, heard her gurgle of pleasure, but he didn't give her even a moment to recover. Instead he changed his angles of pressure, racheting her up yet another notch.

"You're . . . going . . . to . . . ohhhh." She panted. "Wait. Oh, my. I . . . need . . . rest."

"Uh-uh."

"But . . . I'm ssoooo sensitive. I . . . ah . . . ohh." Again she exploded, this time her entire body shaking.

He eased back a bit, sensing she truly needed a few seconds to recover. But he couldn't resist leaning forward, taking her nipple between his lips and sucking hard, enjoying the feel of her nipple hardening right inside his mouth.

At the same time he slid his sex against her slick, open female folds. Her heat taunted him, but instead of entering her, he slowly slid against her clit, still tugging on her nipples with his mouth and fingers.

"I need you inside me. Now. Right now."

The idea of her wanting him so badly turned him on. Her need was escalating his own, making him feel desired in a way he'd never felt before. At her sweet demands, his blood fired. His heart hammered. He ached to hold back and give her a few more orgasms, but he couldn't wait.

He kept his mouth on her breast, placed his finger on her clit and slowly circled the soft bud. At the same time, he ever-so slowly lowered his hips, allowed himself to enter her heat. He hissed in delight. Her soft, slick heat surrounded him, warmed him.

"Move. Damn you. Move." Her tone was fierce, her voice impatient.

He flicked his finger faster, harder on her clit. She spasmed again and he actually felt heat flash through her skin, radiating outward. And he could no longer hold back.

She was too delicious. Too responsive. Too female. He succumbed to her, pumping deep, hard, fast. But as instinct took over, as primal urges forged, he knew this bonding was not one he would ever take lightly.

With every thrust, he kept thinking: *Mine. Mine. Mine.*

And when he exploded and she came with him once again, the pleasure of knowing she wanted him made the explosion all the more powerful. More intense. More personal.

They no longer seemed like two people giving one another mutual enjoyment. Their union possessed a unique joy, a special contentment, a deep thrill of coming together that he'd never known.

Even as the orgasm took him, his arms wrapped around her, pulling her close. He kissed her mouth, unwilling to settle for less than touching every part of her with every part of himself.

Long moments later, when his ragged breath had settled, when he could think clearly, he realized that for the first time in his life, he was . . . happy.

An hour later, Cade sat on the hotel balcony and Shara handed him a frosted glass with green iced liquid, the rim covered in salt. "What's this?"

"Tequila, lime juice, and Cointreau for you. My margarita's a virgin, mostly lemonade. We're celebrating." She licked the rim of her glass, her eyes sad for someone who was rejoicing. Shara clinked her glass with his, an Earth ritual he'd seen during his studies. "I thought you'd enjoy the salty drink."

20

✦

Shara didn't have to wait long for the alcohol to knock Cade out. Two sips and he was sloshed. Six and he was out cold. Trying to stem her guilt, she'd left him outside on the balcony and slipped into the hotel room. She couldn't hurt Cade.

She would have preferred to have all three spheres in her possession, but she had to make do. If Jamar had one sphere and she could destroy these two, Cade's mission would be over. And so would their relationship. Her gut knotted. But what choice did she have? She couldn't let Cade go on when he might kill everyone on the planet.

Arms straining, she carried one heavy sphere at a time into the bathroom, then lowered them into the tub. After placing a mask over her eyes, nose and mouth to avoid breathing the fumes, she stoppered the drain and removed from the closet the hydrochloric acid she'd had delivered earlier. Careful not to splash the powerful acid onto her skin, she slowly filled the tub and covered the metal spheres.

Chest tight, heart hammering as she betrayed Cade, she waited for the acid to do its work. The man at the chemical laboratory had assured her the acid would eat through most metal in record time. *Come on. Come on. Come on.*

Shara had no idea how long Cade would stay semiconscious. But the metal balls looked as shiny and unpitted as they had before she'd poured acid over them. Either the metal from Rama was especially dense and it would take longer to destroy than metal from Earth—or it wouldn't work at all.

Shara leaned over the acid, searching for a hint that her plan might work. She'd known water wouldn't destroy the sphere—the one taken out of Lake George had suffered no damage. And since Cade intended to place the sphere inside a volcano, she'd surmised heat wouldn't bother it, either. So she'd tried the acid.

But damn it, nothing was happening. Nothing.

And Cade would rouse soon. Pulse skittering, mouth dry, she hurried to the balcony to check on him. His eyelids had begun to flutter. He was coming around.

Shara cursed and ran back to the bathroom. The spheres remained bright and shiny, unpitted. She'd failed. But if Cade didn't know she failed, perhaps she could think up another plan. Praying she could put everything back before Cade awakened, she opened the drain and the tub slowly emptied, Hurrying, Shara opened all the windows and turned on the ceiling fans to let out the fumes. She dumped the acid containers in the outside trash and when she returned, the tub had completely drained. She turned on the shower to rinse the remaining acid from the spheres, her palms sweaty as she wondered if she might get away with Cade never learning what she'd done.

She turned off the water and reached for a towel to dry the spheres. The towel wouldn't come free. Shara looked up to see Cade gripping the towel, his eyes glazed with confusion as the last of the alcohol haze burned away, his brows narrowed. "What are you doing?"

Her heart jammed up her throat. "I . . . I thought the salt might damage the spheres so I washed them."

"What stinks? Why are you wearing a mask?"

"I didn't like the smell of the soap so I . . ." Even to her, the excuse sounded lame.

Cade released the towel and folded his arms over his chest. He shot her the most forbidding, scorching glare she'd ever seen. Whether his anger had caused the alcohol to disperse through his system or his head had cleared due to his body chemistry, he was clearly suspicious as hell.

She swallowed hard. And didn't say anything.

"What's that smell?" he asked, his tone harsh.

She pulled off the mask. The reek of acid fumes hit her immediately. "There must be a gas leak in the building."

"You're lying. That's not gas. It's . . . acid." His eyes narrowed. Clearly he was putting the evidence before him together and coming up with what had really happened. And as he realized what she had done, his expression raked her with fury and disdain. "You tried to ruin the spheres, didn't you?"

She squared her shoulders and lifted her chin. "I couldn't allow you to destroy my world without trying to . . ."

Glowering, taut with anger, he pointed to the bed. His voice cracked with contempt and pain. "So everything we did in there, everything you said to me was a lie?"

"No." She sputtered, struggling to control her shaking. She'd ruined everything. She'd lost her one opportunity to stop him. She'd failed. Utterly and completely failed, but she wanted to explain. If she couldn't have him, at least she would have his understanding. "What was between us was real. But I couldn't put my own feelings ahead of everyone else's lives. Your spheres can destroy Earth."

His curt voice lashed her. "You don't know that. Our best scientists concur—"

"Jules has seen utter destruction." Shara slumped against the tub, sick at heart, hands shaking. The pain on his face hurt as badly as her failure. "If you activate the portal, the volcano will erupt."

"She's wrong." Anger still ticking in a muscle in his jaw, nevertheless, Cade held out his hand to her, a gesture of truce. "And I'll prove it."

She ignored his hand and shook her head. "You're going to kill us all."

Trevor used a tape recorder to interview Shara Weston during the plane trip back to Hawaii. It took three hours for her to fill him in, and Trevor realized he had the story of a lifetime, but no proof. Shara had even told him how she'd attempted to stop Cade, taking all the blame for her failure and Trevor had seen the pain in her eyes, understood she'd fallen in love with the alien. Shara hadn't given him any evidence that her story was true. However, if Cade opened a portal to Rama, that would be all he required to verify her tale.

While Cade had allowed him to examine and take photographs of the spheres, the shiny substance didn't look otherworldly in the pictures. Only the portal pieces' tremendous weight would convince the world—and they intended to drop them down into the volcano.

Trevor wanted to speak to Cade, but the man had taken the spheres to the rear compartment and hadn't once come forward to their part of the plane—not even to eat. Trevor used the time to digest what Shara had told him. *My God, a real live alien on Earth—two of them, brothers fighting a war here that would affect their home world.*

"If Cade programs the portal so no life can go through and if his spaceship blew up—"

"Jamar shot him down."

"Then how does he plan to go home?"

Shara shrugged. "I'm not sure. We haven't discussed what happens after he builds the portal. Jamar keeps attacking, and we've been off balance. We're lucky to be alive."

"So where do you think Jamar is now?"

Shara shivered. "I don't know. But after hearing what he did to Teresa, plus Cade's stories about his behavior on Rama and the brutality you've pinned on him, I'd prefer not to meet him. But he's out there. He's going to try to stop Cade. And heaven help me I don't know if I want him to succeed or not."

"How do you defeat a man with his power of *Quait*?" Trevor asked.

"With another man who has that same power."

Trevor cocked his head and looked at her. "And what about Jules's vision?"

Shara Weston's beautiful eyes held his. "Perhaps I simply can't face the enormity of my failure. But I'm hoping that Jules had that vision so we could prevent a disaster. Perhaps by recovering the second sphere we've already changed what she saw in her vision."

"And if you're wrong?"

"Then you won't be able to file your story. There won't be anyone left on Earth to read it."

After partially recovering from jet lag, Shara was finally back on Haven. Cade wasn't talking to her. Clearly her betrayal had hurt him badly. She still felt sick every time she recalled the hurt in his eyes when he'd realized what she'd tried to do. And while he seemed to understand that from her point of view she'd had no choice, he most certainly hadn't forgiven her.

They'd stopped briefly in California and met up with Jules, her cat, and Lyle, the volcanologist she'd seen in her visions. They visited Teresa Alverez, who'd finally left the hospital and was expected to make a full recovery, before flying on to Hawaii and then chartering a seaplane to take them to Haven.

Never had her island hosted so many guests since she'd purchased it. Cade slept on the living room sofa. Jules and Lyle had moved into the guest bedroom and Trevor camped out on a futon on the back patio. After breakfast, Jules and Shara had left the men to confer about their work and had taken a walk along the beach.

Jules's cat appeared unwilling to let his owner out of his sight after their separation. Kapuna trailed behind them, playing with the waves, careful not to get his feet wet. The women had been friends so long that they didn't always fill the empty spaces with conversation.

Shara allowed the tropical sunlight to filter into her bones, gave the lapping waves a chance to calm her overwrought nerves, and dug her toes into the damp sand as they walked just above the high-tide mark. Palm trees rustled, a dolphin in the bay swam into the warmer waters to sun and play. For a moment it was easy to believe everything was right in the world—that she and Cade were still on speaking terms, that he wasn't about to set off the volcano, that the portal's opening wouldn't cause the end of the world.

Jules waited until they'd walked far enough from the house and the men couldn't possibly overhear. Although she appeared calm, her voice caught, snagged on the words. "I had another vision."

Shara's heart skipped a beat. "It was bad?"

"I saw the Earth from the viewpoint of space."

"Has that ever happened before?"

Jules shook her head. "Haven erupted but not like you'd expect."

"What do you mean?" Shara stopped and dug her toes into the sand.

Jules stopped, too. She gazed at the cone that towered above them at the far end of the island. Greenery covered the volcano's lower half as grasses and bushes slowly spread over the cone. "If Haven did erupt, I'd expect it to smoke, then for lava to run, and the top to burst."

"That's not what you saw?"

Jules shook her head. "It was so strange. The volcano erupted . . . sideways. The Earth looked like an egg that cracked, the fractures filling with lava, but the splits, the eruptions spread across the Earth's crust—not upwards."

The hair on the back of Shara's neck prickled. "What did Lyle say?"

"He said that my vision is scientifically impossible."

Jules wouldn't have mentioned her vision unless she believed what she'd seen was important. As usual, the interpretation of the vision was difficult, but who better than a leading volcanologist to determine what Jules's vision could mean? Obviously, her lover's words and extensive knowledge hadn't soothed Jules's concerns.

"What do you think?" Shara asked.

Jules refused to meet her eyes. She stared out to sea at the spot where the horizon met the sky, as if it could reveal something new. "Let me tell you the rest of my vision."

"It gets worse?" Shara guessed, her heart thudding. What could be worse than lava spreading like rivers over the planet's crust?

"All the continents turned to lava. The oceans boiled away. Then the lava collapsed on itself and the entire planet exploded." Jules shuddered. "I don't know what to think."

"You think that the portal could cause that kind of massive destruction?"

"Let's be clear. I saw total annihilation of the planet. Total extinction. Every human being, every animal, every plant down to the very last cell died." Tears ran down Jules's face and she angrily brushed them away with the back of her wrist. "If we can't stop Jamar—"

"Jamar!" Shara's heart skipped a beat. "I thought it was Cade we had to stop. Jamar's not the man conspiring with Lyle in my kitchen to tap into the power of the volcano. Jamar isn't trying to use the portal to send salt to another world. Jamar isn't bent on using alien technology to save his own people despite the consequences here."

"True. But Jamar wants to stop Cade. He flew here in a spaceship and likely plans to use it to fly home."

"So?"

"So suppose that spaceship has weapons aboard it. Planet-busting-size weapons. Weapons that could cause what I saw in my vision. Maybe that's why we haven't seen or heard from Jamar. He's going to shoot a bomb at us from space and then fly home."

"But if Jamar's intention was to shoot a bomb from space and to kill every man, woman, and child on Earth, then why would he have pursued Cade and me? Why did Jamar search for the spheres?"

"Who knows how that crazy son of a bitch thinks? Maybe his primary mission was to stop Cade, but when he failed he decided to take drastic measures." Jules peered at her. "Have you asked Cade about Jamar's ship and what kind of weapons he might have?"

Shara shook her head. "We were so busy staying alive and then involved with recovering the spheres that I hadn't even considered the possibility until you just told me your vision."

"I know you prefer the scenario of Jamar ruining Earth better than Cade blowing us up. To be safe, perhaps we have to stop them both."

Shara fisted her hands on her hips. "How? Despite his anger at me, even if I could bring myself to accept that Cade must die, I couldn't kill him. I couldn't even pull the trigger on a bad guy. Just *touching* guns makes me sick."

"Who says we have to kill him?" Jules rubbed her brow. "All we have to do is steal the spheres."

"And then what? Cade has a locator beacon. He can find them anywhere. Besides, since he caught me with the acid, he hasn't let the spheres out of his sight."

"Suppose we hiked up to the volcano and threw them in?"

"I think that's what Cade's going to do to make them work. They won't melt in the lava. They're made out of some alien metal."

Jules sighed. "Maybe Lyle will have an idea."

"Or Trevor."

"I'm not sure bringing the reporter in was a good idea." Jules began walking back toward Shara's house. "I like him and he seems honest . . . but—"

"The story's too important for us to keep quiet." Shara followed, knowing they all needed to discuss the problem. And yet she wanted to run the other way—to swim on her reef, go for a sail, or hike through her coconut palms. With so many unanswered questions, with so much at stake, she wanted to call in every expert—and leave it all to them. But she knew no one would take her seriously. Or arrive in time. "Perhaps we should let Trevor break his story now?"

"Are you insane? He'd set off a worldwide panic."

"We need help. We aren't experts—"

"Lyle is."

"Not even Cade knows how the alien technology really works. I—" Shara peered at her house. "Do you hear that?"

"What?"

"It sounded like a shout."

Jules frowned and narrowed her eyes. "I didn't hear anything."

Shara took Jules's hand and led her off the beach and into the cover of the trees. "Let's check it out carefully and not go running in."

They strode up to the house carefully, silently, listening for sign of trouble. But by the time they reached her home, Shara had heard nothing more than the lilting breeze, the rustle of palm fronds, and the lapping of waves on the beach. Heart thumping, she shoved open the door, half expecting to be greeted by blood, fallen bodies, or Jamar with a weapon pointed at her.

Quietly, they moved from room to room.

"No one's here." Jules pointed out the obvious. Cade, Lyle, and Trevor had vanished.

Lyle wanted to discuss the science behind using the portal to set off the volcano. Trevor had asked about the social and political implications of opening the portal. Cade didn't have time for debate. He needed to get the job done before another Terran decided to try to stop him.

As soon as the women headed up the beach, he'd placed both spheres into the backpack, strapped the heavy load onto his shoulders and, with Lyle and Trevor on his heels, headed out the back door. The trek to the volcano was about a mile. At first they traversed level ground and about ten minutes later reached the bottom of the cone.

Lyle tipped a bottle of water to his lips and then handed it to Cade. "Jules asked me to come here to offer my expertise."

"I appreciate that." Cade accepted the water, took a swig and handed back the bottle to Lyle. With the extra weight of the spheres he didn't need more weight to carry. "But I'm not a scientist. I can't tell you how the spheres work any better than the average American can explain how a television works."

"Surely you know the general principles," Lyle insisted. "And Shara told me that you altered the program so only salt can go through."

"What I did is as easy as flipping the TV channel. It doesn't mean I understand it."

Trevor eyed Cade. "Why don't we wait for the women to join us?"

"I'm expecting trouble." Cade spoke the truth. "They'll be safer if they aren't near us."

"No one's going to be safe if Haven's volcano explodes," Trevor argued. "Jules said she envisioned the entire island exploding, setting off a chain reaction in the earth's crust—"

"That's not possible." Cade shook his head and started the uphill climb. On this part of the cone, the trees and shrubs had claimed a foothold. As the cone steepened, as they climbed higher, the plant life would yield to hardened lava. "The spheres will descend into the volcano and encourage the gas pressure to build. When enough forces gather, the energy will fuel the portal. The energy can't spread outward."

"So you say," Lyle muttered.

"What kind of trouble are you expecting then?" Trevor asked.

Cade noted he always kept his voice recorder turned on and tried to speak carefully, fully aware that whatever he said might be read by millions in just a few days. He should have been just as careful around Shara. But he'd trusted her and she'd betrayed him. If that acid had ruined the spheres, she would have stopped his mission. That she'd caused no harm didn't make up for the fact that she'd set herself against him.

He might *understand* her fear, but he *trusted* Raman scientists. "As you know, Jamar followed me from Rama to Earth. He's here to prevent the portal from opening."

Lyle sighed. "Maybe I should talk to him. Seems it would be fair to hear both sides."

"Jamar has tortured and killed several women." In Trevor,

Cade found an ally, at least on this one point. The reporter recapped some of his research then added, "I have no interest in hearing anything Jamar has to say. According to the women who survived his butchery, he's a sick, sadistic sociopath."

Cade shifted the straps on his pack. As the grade steepened, the load changed and the straps dug into his flesh. He might have asked one of his companions for help, but although they appeared in good shape, they hadn't his Raman strength. "Did your research clue you in to where he might be based?"

"While his attacks were worldwide, the earliest ones were in the South Pacific."

"It's a big ocean with lots of islands. Can you be any more specific?" Cade asked.

Trevor shook his head. Sweat drizzled down his brow and sweat stains appeared under his arms. Lyle's breath came in great gasps and he stopped frequently. "Guess I'm not used to this heat."

Trevor stopped, removed his hat and sunglasses, wiped the perspiration from his face and stared at the volcano's rim. "How much farther?"

Cade set down his pack. "The distances are difficult to judge without any landmarks." They'd reached the uppermost and steepest part of the climb. The vegetation was no longer sparse—it was nonexistent. And the sun's heat reflected off the black crusty lava baking them.

Cade could feel the heat rising through his shoes. Beside the rim were several large pockmarked black boulders that would provide some shade. He searched the beaches below, wondering if the women had yet discovered their disappearance, but didn't see them. The island, about one hundred acres, wasn't that large, but the vegetation in some areas was thick and the walking tiresome in the heat. Even if the women thought to train Shara's telescope on the volcano and spied them, he doubted they'd follow.

After all, it was reasonable to think they'd come up here to do some research. But Cade wasn't waiting to convince anyone that he could safely open the portal. His conscience twinged over the fact that Shara had never given her permission to use her island—but his people were willing to trade with her in repayment. And once he opened the portal and she understood that the science really worked, he felt certain Shara would come to an agreement with his people—although he didn't know what would happen between them.

During the plane trip, Cade had been too angry to speak to her about his feelings. And they'd had no privacy since their arrival on the island. After he accomplished his mission, there should be ample time to sort things out before he left for Rama.

Cade planned to find out where Jamar had hidden his ship and use it to fly home. Jamar had shot Cade's ship out of the sky and he owed him. Of course, the First wouldn't see it that way. And one day the two would fight it out—of that Cade was certain. He just hoped to complete his mission first.

The last two hundred feet felt like a ninety-degree ascent. Gamely, Lyle and Trevor kept up, but they weren't carrying the tremendous weight on their backs. Cade's lungs strained and his calves cramped. They shared the last of the water before enduring the final surge to the top.

Physically spent, Cade reached the rim first, kneeled, plucked a sphere from his pack, and heaved it into the volcano. Lyle pulled himself up just in time to watch the silver sphere sink into the red-hot lava in the crater below. Cade placed his hand on the second sphere when a force grabbed him.

Immobilized him.

Cade swore under his breath. Although Cade could speak, he knew that Jamar had seized him in his *Quait*. Fighting back with his own *Quait* wasn't an option. Jamar might be weaker on Earth than on Rama, but he was still too strong for Cade to break his hold. And yet, he could manage tiny jerks.

Cade kicked out, deliberately knocked the reporter off balance. Trevor gasped and tumbled backward, rolling down the cone like an out-of-control skier. Hopefully, he'd plunge far enough to stay out of Jamar's reach, remain conscious, and get the women to safety.

Jamar stepped out from behind the large rocks, a sneer of triumph lighting his eyes.

Cade had grown considerably stronger since coming to Earth and ingesting salt. The First's hold on him didn't seem quite as powerful as it once had, but instead of feeling like a bug flattened by a freight train, he felt like an insect caught on flypaper. He could twitch feebly, but couldn't break free.

Cade focused on trying to nudge the backpack over the lip. The backpack would melt away in moments, and the second sphere would join the first, the automatic mechanisms taking over. Cade would certainly die at Jamar's hand, but his mission would succeed. The sophisticated machines would seek out one another in the lava flow, coordinate the explosion, control the volcanic energy, and open the portal. Once activated, the system was pretty much self-operating. Machines would dig through the volcanic rock and pump seawater into the portal where other machinery would extract the salt and send it to Rama. If Cade died, he was certain Shara and Trevor would prevent their government from stopping the flow of salt through the portal.

Cade nudged the pack with his foot, but to his horror, instead of going over the edge and falling into the crater, the pack slid the other way—down the cone—plunging and bouncing in Trevor's general direction.

"Fool. You stand no chance of success." Jamar sneered, lifted the one remaining steel ball that he'd saved—and he tossed it into the volcano.

Confused, Cade eyed Jamar. The First's actions made no sense. Cade would have thrown in all three pieces if he had them. So why would the First who wanted to stop Cade do such a thing? Cade didn't even consider that the man had had a change of heart. Jamar had no heart.

"What have you done?"

Jamar laughed in victory. "I reprogrammed my sphere."

"To stop the volcanic explosion?" Nausea and horror

curled in Cade's gut. Shara had warned him of Jules's vision. A vision where he failed his people and destroyed her world. He'd been too certain that the spheres would follow their program to take the psychic's warning seriously. But if Jamar had reprogrammed the second sphere to alter the tremendous forces of the volcanic eruption, anything was possible, including total destruction of Earth.

Fury burned through Cade. He'd almost succeeded. Almost. He struggled against Jamar's *Quait,* but he could only jerk and spasm.

"Oh, Haven is going to explode, but the second sphere will cause the forces to disperse laterally, along the Earth's crust. According to my calculations, the explosion here will spread horizontally. Eventually the planet will run red with lava—until it rips itself apart."

Instead of freeing his people, Cade had failed horribly. "You'd murder billions of innocent people to—"

"You should have thought of the consequences before you came here. Their deaths are on your head."

Lyle stared at the crater. Already the smoke had begun to increase. Hellish sparks burst into the air and bursts of ash flared into the crater then settled back into the lava. "How long before you destroy Earth?"

"Time enough for me to enjoy my reward."

"Reward?" Lyle asked.

Jamar kept his expression composed, but his tone threaded with evil. "By the time I'm done with Cade, he'll beg for death."

21

⚙

Shara shoved open the door to the back porch, but even before she and Jules had completed the search, Shara knew the men were gone. Had they deliberately chosen to leave while the women had been on the beach? Or was she paranoid and they'd simply gone off for a walk to explore the island?

Jules bit her bottom lip, her expression mystified. "This island is too small for them to just disappear. They must have gone to the volcano. Lyle wanted to explore it. He said something about taking heat and gas samples."

"If they headed to the volcano, Cade would take the spheres." Shara and Jules rushed to the closet where Cade had stashed the spheres. "The backpack and the spheres are gone."

"They went without us?" Jules frowned. "Lyle promised to take me with him when they opened the portal. Maybe if we hurry we can catch up. We were only gone for half an hour."

Shara's breath hitched. Cade intended to deploy the spheres. Why else would he go on a trek with such a heavy load?

Alarmed, Shara placed her own pack on her back, added several water bottles and PowerBars. She'd made the climb before, several times, and knew how draining it could be in the heat. "Put on sunscreen, sunglasses, and a hat. It's hot on that volcano and there's no shade."

Jules didn't budge. "Shara."

"What?" Shara paused to look at her friend. She knew that expression. It meant trouble.

"Something's wrong."

"Duh. The men went to the volcano without us."

"That's not what I meant." Shara expected Jules to tell her about one of her visions. Instead, Jules pointed out the second-story window. "Look."

From her bedroom Shara had a great view of the turquoise lagoon with its crescent sand beach and coconut palms, but she could also see the next protected harbor. Had Jules spotted the men? She peered at the vacant beach, but then she focused on a seaplane moored in the water. "Someone's here."

Jules handed Shara the binoculars she kept on her nightstand. "You recognize the plane?"

Shara focused the lenses quickly. "Never seen it before." And no one had called or used the radio to announce a visit. She scanned the beach next, looking for the unexpected visitor, her pulse escalating. Even if the pilot had flown in from the other direction, her house could easily be seen from the beach. Between the missing men and the missing pilot, Shara's fear escalated.

When she didn't see anyone, she focused on the volcano. "Is it my imagination, or is Haven's volcano sending ash into the sky?"

"Oh . . . my . . . God." Jules placed her hand on Shara's shoulder. "It's starting. Just like in my vision."

"We've got more trouble."

"Now what?"

Shara's blood turned cold as she focused the binoculars. "It's Jamar. I see him, Cade, and Lyle on the volcano."

"Here?" Jules voice rose an octave. "You see Jamar with them? What's going on?"

"I can't tell, but we have to assume Jamar's captured the men with his *Quait.*"

"Let's call for help." Jules turned to the radio, her expression turning to anger and horror as she spied pieces of smashed plastic and metal where the radio should have been. "Jamar must have broken both the radio and the satellite phone before going after the men."

Shara searched the volcano again. "I don't see Trevor."

"What are we going to do?"

"We take Jamar by surprise. Free the men."

Jules folded her hands across her chest. "If we go closer, he'll take us under his control, too."

"True. Look in the chest."

"For what?"

"Cade brought back the guns we confiscated from Jamar's guards at Lake George."

"*You're* going to shoot a gun?" Jules raised her brows up to her hairline.

"We can't get close to Jamar or he'll take us under his control, so maybe we can shoot him from a distance." Shara ignored the fear crawling down her spine and settling into her gut. She ignored the icy perspiration under her arms. She ignored the tremble in her hands.

Jamar had taken Cade and Lyle prisoner and he might have already hurt Trevor. If she didn't do something, Jamar would certainly kill them. The thought of Cade dying without him knowing that it was Jamar—not him—who would ruin her world, sickened her. And if she could save him and prevent the planet from exploding by using a weapon she despised, then she would find a way to do so.

More ash and hellish sparks burst sideways into the sky. They had to move fast, before the island exploded and set off a chain reaction to the other volcanoes in the Pacific Rim.

"Got them." Jules picked up the weapons, checked the clips and safety mechanisms, and handed one to Shara, her gaze a challenge.

Shara forced herself to take the gun and stuck it into the side pocket of her backpack, within easy reach. "Ready?"

"For what?"

"To go rescue the guys."

Jules stared at her. "You've changed."

"I have?" Shara headed down the stairs.

"A month ago, instead of taking on the worst bad guy in the galaxy, you'd have been telling me how badly you needed a drink."

"Trust me, I'd love a drink."

"But it wasn't your first thought, was it?"

As they headed back through the trees, she accepted that Jules was correct, her first thought had been about Cade, how much Jamar hated him and the danger they all were in. "I don't even want to think about what Jamar might be doing to the men." Shara increased their pace, ignored the heat, her burning gut, and the nagging fear that insisted she run the other way.

"Hey, slow down." Jules tugged on her shoulder.

"Come on. You've got to keep up."

"You aren't listening. It could be dangerous."

At Jules's insistent warning, Shara slowed her pace. "What's wrong?"

"I saw someone moving up ahead. A silhouette of . . . it's Trevor."

Shara and Jules ran to the reporter's side. Blood and dust had congealed on one side of his face. He had a black eye, possibly a broken nose, and he walked with a distinct limp. One hand cradled the other arm, his face grim, his eyes determined.

"You all right?" Jules asked.

"What happened?" Shara pulled her water bottle from the pack and offered Trevor a drink.

He took a long swig. "Cade threw one sphere into the volcano, then Jamar threw his in after."

Shara wondered if Trevor was delusional. No way would Jamar help Cade. "Why would Jamar do that?"

"Even part way down the mountain, I could hear Jamar boasting. Apparently, he's reprogrammed the damn thing to rip the planet apart. And Jamar's captured Cade and Lyle."

"We know. We're going to help."

"How? If you go up there, he'll take you captive and use you against the men to make them do whatever he wants."

"He can make them do whatever he wants anyway." Shara patted the compartment with the gun, as if she were confident, because in truth, she didn't know how far Jamar could extend his powers. "If we shoot him from a distance, we shouldn't come under control of his *Quait*."

"Have you ever fired a gun?" Trevor asked.

"Yes, you idiot," Jules answered for her, automatically protecting Shara.

"It's okay. Trevor's hurt. You can't expect him to know . . . about Bruce."

Shara must have turned white because despite his pain Trevor shook his head, apparently remembering that the last time she'd fired a gun, she'd killed her husband. "Sorry. But from a distance, shooting a man isn't that easy. Come back to the house with me. We'll use the radio. Call for help."

"Jamar destroyed the radio and the satellite phones. Unless you know how to fly a plane, we're on our own," Jules said.

"Did you check the radio in the plane?" Trevor asked.

"I didn't think of that. But Jamar probably did." Shara didn't want to waste time returning to check the plane. Cade needed her. She could feel it with every breath she took. But she tried to set aside her yearning to see him, tried to build a wall around her panic so she could function. "Jamar probably disabled the radio before he left the plane."

Trevor frowned. "I'd prefer to go back with you but I'd only slow you down. I think my arm's broken. But maybe I can get to the plane. If the radio doesn't work, I'll set off an emergency flare—unless Jamar took those, too."

"Okay. Thanks." Shara took a step toward the volcano.

"When you return, I expect you to fill me in on everything. I still want my story."

"You got it."

The women left Trevor. When they advanced far enough to be out of hearing range, Jules nudged her. "If he reaches the plane, and, if he can use the radio, and if anyone believes him, and if they send help—it will take hours."

"That's why it's up to us to save Cade and Lyle."

"Right."

"You wouldn't happen to have had a vision that might tell us the best way to go about taking out Jamar?" Shara asked.

"Don't have a clue." Jules sounded surprisingly cheerful.

"For a woman who's been worrying about the cataclysmic end of the world and who's lover is in life-threatening danger, you don't seem too concerned," Shara muttered.

"Fake bravado," Jules muttered. "But I think we can do this."

"Why?" Shara shot a look at her friend.

Jules trudged beside her, her face looking up at the mountain. "Because the alternative to surviving means we won't live through the week, maybe not the day."

Shara followed Jules's gaze to the volcano. Where before the ash was a drizzle, it now resembled a downpour. Ash fluttered around them and she raised the binoculars to see that Jamar, Cade, and Lyle had disappeared among the boulders. *Damn.* She'd planned to hide in the cover of the trees and shoot at Jamar's silhouette from a distance. With the men behind the rocks, the woman would have to move in closer and that would give Jamar a better chance to use his *Quait*.

Shara wished she knew more about how *Quait* worked. Would Jamar feel her presence before he saw her? How close could she approach before she had to worry about his overpowering her with his mind? And would it take a few seconds or would she have time to take a shot?

Lowering the binoculars, she hurried to catch up to Jules. "They've taken shelter from the ash on the other side of those rocks."

"That means we have to go up higher." Jules raised her shirt to cover her nose and mouth. "Breathing ash can't be good for the lungs."

Shara followed Jules's lead. "Once we get close, we have to be very quiet. And if either of us gets a shot at Jamar, we take it immediately."

"Got it." Jules took her gun from her pocket, flicked off the safety. "I'm ready."

They trudged up the last quarter of the volcanic cone, keeping their heads down to prevent the ash from coating their faces. The hot air made Shara's breath short and her pulse race. With no cover for them to hide in, Jamar would see them if he came out from behind the rocks and glanced in their direction—even through the falling ash.

However, the rumbling volcano was such a spectacular sight that it drew her gaze. She kept sneaking glances, wondering if it was about to explode. Shara wasn't a volcanologist but even she knew an eruption would increase the heat until it instantly incinerated them. She might never know she'd failed.

Walking through the gathering ash over the steep terrain was not only dangerous because she couldn't see loose rocks, it was slippery. A skid could send her sliding back down the cone. Her legs trembled with the effort. Beside her Jules stumbled over a loose rock and when Shara tried to steady her, they both almost plunged down.

Somehow, they maintained their precarious balance and made it to the rocks. Fearing that Jamar might kill Cade and Lyle at any moment, Shara allowed them to take only a few necessary seconds to rest. Not knowing what was going on added to her anxiety. Yet knowing Jamar would prolong the men's pain gave her hope they might yet be alive.

When a tortured scream filled her ears, followed by a rumble from the volcano, it was as if the mountain itself screeched in protest. Shara squeezed Jules's arm and gestured for her to circle around the opposite way. By splitting up, she prayed one of them could shoot Jamar before another horrible scream rent the air.

Jules had taken about five steps in the other direction when Shara realized she should have coordinated a simultaneous time to attack Jamar. She almost went after Jules, but at the sound of another torturous scream, she hurried forward.

Mere seconds might be the difference between saving a

life and Jamar killing either Cade or Lyle. Fear rushing up her throat, she worked her way around the rocks. The rumbling volcano hid her footsteps and she didn't worry about making noise. As much as she yearned to save Cade and Lyle, she also worried that if the volcano erupted it could set off a cataclysmic inferno that would kill everyone on Earth.

Balanced against the lives of billions, her own stupid fear of shooting Jamar shouldn't have counted for squat. And yet, just holding the gun caused her hand to shake. *Damn*. She would be no use to anyone if she couldn't control her nerves.

Shara scrambled over rocks, dodged a piece of flying debris. The heat had increased. Sweat poured from her skin, and her damp palm on the gun made keeping a grip difficult as she worked her way around the boulders.

She'd been to the rim several times, but had never explored this formation and hadn't realized navigating the perimeter would take so long. And she had no idea if she or Jules would arrive first, since she didn't know exactly where the men were.

The screams didn't seem to be getting louder. Perhaps the man was weakening. Or the wind was picking up. However, the increasing frequency of the howls had her heart pounding and her nerves popping like bacon grease in a hot frying pan.

Breathing the blistering air increased the pressure in her lungs. And the ash filtered through her shirt that she kept over her nose and mouth and caused a burning need for oxygen. She rounded a bend. Heard a shot go off—and then a man's roar of despair. A woman's scream.

Jules.

She had to get to her friend. Slipping and sliding over the steep and loose crust, Shara rounded the final bend. To her horror, Jules was on the ground, writhing in pain—but not bleeding from a gunshot wound. She wasn't so certain about Lyle. He was lying still and she couldn't discern if he was still breathing.

Cade didn't move and his eyes were full of anguish. Obviously, he had no control over his paralysis. Jamar had enslaved him in *Quait*.

Behind Cade, Jamar bellowed a mad laugh. "Go ahead, Shara. Shoot another lover. If you don't kill Cade, I'm going to put a laser burst in you."

This couldn't be happening. It was like a scene straight from hell. The volcano spit ash and coughed fire. Lava spilled over the far rim, the deadly red river burning everything in its path. The ground beneath them shook with tremors . . . or perhaps that was Shara's quivering knees.

Cade's face was calm, but his eyes burned. "Jamar has me in his *Quait*. Do as he says. Shoot me."

"What?" Horrified, she couldn't believe what Cade was saying. He wanted her to shoot him? Was he insane?

"Jamar won't let me live and a bullet is a better death than most."

22

❂

"I'm sorry." Cade's somber tone sounded as if he were trying to console her.

"How touching." Jamar chuckled and walked closer.

No way would she shoot Cade, not as long as Jamar offered himself as a target. Shara's hands shook, but she pivoted and raised her chin, straightened her shoulders. Her shirt slipped from her mouth and she held her breath, started to point her gun at Jamar.

She placed her finger on the trigger—but couldn't move. Jamar had immobilized her. She'd failed.

Jamar had her trapped in his *Quait*.

And now they were all at his mercy. No way could she raise the gun high enough to aim at Jamar and kill him. One thought was all it had taken for him to immobilize her.

"You stupid woman. How idiotic to think you could defeat a First." A gleeful look on his face, a triumphant light in his eyes, Jamar stroked her cheek lightly, like a lover. His touch sickened her, but she couldn't jerk away.

As if Shara needed another reminder of the enormity of her failure, the volcano shot a massive eruption of lava into the sky. In the reddish light, Jamar continued to caress her cheek and taunted Cade. "Perhaps I'll take Shara back to Rama with me and make her my personal slave."

Cade's eyes blazed with fury. "Take your vengeance out on me . . . not her."

Shara wondered if Cade got mad enough whether his own *Quait* would strengthen enough to break Jamar's grip. The idea took hold. She really had no other option but to prod Cade into anger. However, if her ploy failed, the bargain she was about to make would likely sentence her to a lifetime of pain, humiliation, and degradation. Right about now, a clean death seemed the better choice, and yet she owed it to all of humanity to try. Besides, Trevor had told her enough about Jamar to understand a little how the First thought and the best way to appeal to his sick mind. Jamar preferred to make his underfirsts do things against their will. When he used *Quait,* they didn't suffer enough.

Knowing she was bargaining with the devil, she still spoke up. Jamar would never release Cade, but she might be able to bargain for the lives of her friends. "If you allow Jules and Lyle to live, I will do whatever you ask of me, for as long as you want me."

"Of course you will."

"You won't have to use *Quait.*"

"Noooo!" Cade roared.

Jamar grinned and folded his arms across his chest, confident that he could stop her from harming him. "I accept. My first request is that you shoot Cade."

Horror crawled down her spine. "Wouldn't you rather keep him alive to watch what you do to me?"

"No. Shoot him."

"Don't you want Cade to suffer? You really want me to shoot him?"

"Only in the shoulder."

Oh . . . Cade . . . please forgive me. "I might miss. I'm not a very good shot."

"That's not what I heard." Jamar shoved her toward Cade.

She stumbled forward. "Place the gun right against his shoulder."

Her hands shook so hard, she had to brace the one holding the gun with the other. If she shot Cade, if he feared for his very life, would his *Quait* kick in? Would it be enough to break Jamar's monstrous hold?

Heart ramming up her throat, palms slick, lungs burning, she pressed the gun against Cade's shoulder.

Jamar rubbed his hands in glee. "Oh, this is going to be so much fun. Maybe even worth my trip to this barbaric planet."

Her betrayal, Cade's silent treatment fell by the wayside. They'd shared too much for her to escape her own deep feelings for him. Shara yearned with her entire being to miss. But if she went back on her word, she'd lose this opportunity. She had no doubts Jamar would use his *Quait* to prevent her from shooting him. And a miss would only delay the inevitable. Mouth dry as volcanic ash, she closed her eyes.

Angled the gun toward the fleshy part of Cade's arm, and pulled the trigger.

Cade roared in pain. Shaking, sick, Shara forced open her eyes. Blood streamed down his arm. Pain glazed his eyes and his mouth twisted tight. Nausea hit her hard.

"Now the other shoulder," Jamar ordered.

"What?"

"You want your friends to live? Then stop stalling. I expect immediate obedience."

How many bullets did the gun have? Shara didn't know. She only knew that she had to shoot Cade again. Tears fell down her cheeks. "I'm sorry."

"I know." Cade closed his eyes, obviously bracing against more pain.

What did Shara have to do for Cade's *Quait* to kick in? How many more bullets would it take? She swore at Cade. "Damn you. Don't just stand there."

"He's an underfirst, he can do nothing but obey." Jamar

strode over to Lyle and kicked him in the ribs. "The next kick is for Jules."

"Do it," Cade ordered. "Pull the trigger."

Shara shook with terror. If she wanted Jules and Lyle to live, she would have to shoot Cade again and again—empty the gun into him. She would have preferred to turn the gun on herself. But not only was that the coward's way out, Jamar wasn't giving her that option.

Again, she pulled the trigger. Cade swayed on his feet. His face turned ashen.

"Now his knee." Jamar gloated, enjoying her mental anguish as much as Cade's pain.

Come on Cade. Do something. When he'd fallen from the sky, he'd protected his body. Jamar had shot them down over the desert, and he'd saved her. Cade had kept Jules and Shara from being burned alive during the fire. Why wasn't his *Quait* kicking in?

The volcano rumbled and the ground directly beneath her feet shook, cracked. She stumbled. Cade toppled backward. Somehow, Jamar stayed on his feet. But the volcano fired rocks into the air and one struck Jamar's temple. Flailing his arms, he fought for balance.

And *Quait* grabbed Shara hard, forcing her to raise the gun. She closed her eyes as *Quait* forced her to aim. To pull the trigger.

She'd expected another shriek but heard nothing. Her eyes flew open, expecting to see more blood on Cade. Instead, she saw that she'd aimed at Jamar. A hole the size of her fist split Jamar's shirt. Blood had burst, staining the entire front of his shirt.

Slowly what had happened sank in. *Cade's Quait* had grabbed her, forced her to aim the gun and shoot Jamar. Whether the rock's blow to Jamar's temple or Cade's pain or a combination of both had set off Cade's *Quait,* she might never know. But together, they had defeated Jamar.

Stunned, trembling, knocked off her feet, Shara's thoughts reeled. Jamar's sightless eyes stared at the sky. She'd shot him.

Jules rushed over and embraced Shara but she couldn't feel her embrace. She was shaking too hard. And despite the heat of the volcano, her bones felt frozen.

Jules hugged her, rocked her. "You'll be okay."

Wrong. As Shara's gaze swept past Cade—who had risen to his feet despite his two bleeding shoulder wounds—to the steadily flowing lava, Shara didn't think she would ever be okay again. Haven had become an inferno.

The volcano was clearly about to erupt.

Lyle crawled over. His wounds weren't outwardly apparent and Shara wasn't certain if earlier Cade or Lyle had been roaring with pain, but she'd seen Lyle take a brutal kick to the ribs and he appeared dazed.

At least Jules was thinking clearly. She shredded Jamar's shirt and used it to bind Cade's wounds and stop the bleeding.

"How long until the volcano erupts?" Cade asked Lyle.

"They're always unpredictable. And I don't know how your technology affects the process."

Cade remained calm, his tone businesslike. "We need the third sphere. Do you and Jules think you can find it and bring it back here?"

Lyle frowned. "I don't understand."

"Instead of allowing the first sphere to open the portal, Jamar programmed the second sphere to alter the program. The volcano's forces need to be channeled in one direction. Think of computer systems in triplicate, if one goes out, the other two will take over. And if there are only two, the two systems fight for dominance. We have to use the third sphere to end the stalemate between the two opposing programs— programs that will rip Earth apart."

"I thought you didn't know how the sphere works?"

"I don't. It's like the difference between writing computer code and working inside a finished program."

His explanation made sense. She could write and send e-mail but she couldn't write a Netscape program. "Do you know where the third sphere went?" Shara asked.

Cade swayed on his feet. "I nudged it over the lip in the direction Trevor fell."

Lyle nodded. "We'll go look."

"I'll go with you," Shara offered, shoving to her feet, wondering if Cade would trust her enough to help. "The more of us searching, the better our chances of finding it."

"Are you sure you want to help?" Cade asked.

His words clawed her insides, shredded her emotions, ripped at her dignity. "Jules's vision finally revealed it was Jamar we were supposed to stop. Not you. I shouldn't have tried to stop you. I never meant . . . I'm so sorry."

"There's no time for this," Cade muttered.

Shara nodded and stumbled away. He hadn't forgiven her but she was determined to help.

And now that she'd had a few minutes to calm down, she knew that her plan to push Cade into *Quait* had worked. While every brain cell told her that this time she'd done the right thing, she couldn't stop reacting to the fact that she'd shot another man.

But she could deal with Jamar's death by her hand. If she'd been able, she'd have shot Jamar herself. The bastard deserved to die. She felt no sorrow over his death. No guilt over taking his life. And she certainly didn't blame Cade for helping her kill him.

It was shooting Cade that made her sick. First she'd betrayed him in the Caribbean. Now, she'd shot him. She'd been desperate, ruthless, and she'd fired a gun into the man she loved. Shot him twice.

What kind of person was she?

At least with Bruce, her actions had been an accident. But she'd deliberately shot Cade. And she didn't know how she'd live with herself.

As the volcano thundered and the ground shook so hard she fell to her knees, she thought living with herself might not be a problem. She might not live much longer at all.

Once the volcano exploded, Cade's third sphere couldn't stop the catastrophe. She had to put aside her personal life, concentrate on sliding down the cone and finding the third portal part. She prayed the backpack wasn't buried under the ash because that would make the task impossible.

Since Lyle seemed to know the direction where Trevor and the backpack had fallen, she followed him and Jules. The ash was floating down so thickly that opening her mouth to speak was nasty. She'd long since placed her shirt back over her nose and mouth and the cloth had clogged with ash so thick, drawing air through had become a problem.

Lyle motioned for them to spread out and begin searching. Head down, Shara slogged through the ash that now came up to her ankles in the low-lying hollows. Occasionally, lava seeped to the surface and she steered away from the cracks. One false step by any of them, they could combust, their flesh melt from their bones. Shuddering at the grisly thought, she brushed ash from her eyelashes. Gray ash. Gray sky. Gray thoughts.

Out of her peripheral vision, she spied a blue-tinged circular object that didn't belong. In the wilderness nothing was straight or so perfectly curved.

Hurrying, she trudged over, bent and found the backpack. She waved frantically to Lyle and Jules but they didn't see her and had moved much farther down the cone. She even risked a shout. "Over here!"

They didn't turn, couldn't hear her shouts. Discouraged, she spit out ash.

Shara tugged the pack from the ground. It was so heavy, she had no doubts the sphere remained inside. She struggled to lift the pack onto her back, but couldn't. So she sat, shrugged into the straps, and then stood. She didn't know how Cade had carried two of them up the volcano's cone. Gritting her teeth in determination, she turned, searched for the boulders and then took a step.

And almost toppled. The climb without the pack had been difficult. With the extra weight it would be murderous. But somehow she would make it. For every three steps forward, she slipped one backward. The ash was coming down so heavily, it was like a blizzard—only hotter than any day she could remember, and she'd lost sight of Jules and Lyle.

Steam hissed from fissures that opened and sometimes

she had to sidestep to avoid a lava flow. She put one foot in front of the other, focused on just a single step at a time.

Lungs straining to the max, heart thudding, she finally made it back to the boulders. Cade stood on the rim, his bandaged arms hanging limply at his sides. "Put the pack down and I'll kick it over the lip."

"We're too far away." She could carry the pack a few more steps. He was wounded and still bleeding. She'd carried the damn thing all the way up here and he still didn't trust her.

But when he spoke his voice was gentle. "You're exhausted."

"And you're hurt."

"Don't argue. Take off the pack." He used his *Quait,* forcing her to release the pack from her shoulders.

She slumped to the ground, too exhausted to be alarmed by the heat beneath her. Cade placed his foot through the loop of the pack, tugged until the pack caught on his ankle like a shackle. And then he dragged it to the rim. Kicked it over.

By the time he staggered back to her, she'd recovered a bit of strength. "How long will it take to work?"

Lava burst behind him. In the hellish light, his face appeared grave, his eyes hard. "We may have been too late."

"There's nothing else to do?"

He shook his head.

She never knew where they found the strength to slide down the cone. They couldn't just tumble blindly or they might end up in a fissure, or roll into one of the lava streams. And all the while, the mountain shimmied beneath their feet, threatening to explode.

"Is the ash decreasing?" Shara asked, daring to hope.

"Might be the trees protecting us. I'm not sure." He spoke in a raw whisper, clearly in agonizing pain.

Pain she had caused. And with all her soul she wished she could bear the pain for him. To his credit he didn't blame her. Instead he encouraged her to keep going.

She asked no more questions.

Eventually they reached the base. And breathing became

a bit easier. She peered at Cade, worried about his blood loss. She was certain the average human being wouldn't have still been on his feet.

Jules and Lyle had waited at the bottom and hurried over. Jules hugged Shara. "We lost you in the ash back there."

"The third sphere?" Lyle asked.

"It's done," Shara spoke, using as few words as possible. Speaking took too much effort. "Cade shoved it over the lip."

"But the volcano—" Jules's words were cut off as a huge explosion echoed down the other side of the mountain.

Cade placed his back against a tree to help him stand. Lyle peered at the volcano with scientific curiosity. Jules hid her face on Shara's shoulder. "I can't look."

Red rocks and lava erupted from the peak and poured over the lip. The red flow over the dark volcano looked like a scene from a movie, but it was all too real. Shara wondered if it was the beginning of the end.

Lyle took charge. "We need to move, people. That's lava coming down the mountainside."

Shara refrained from saying there was nowhere to run. It seemed too defeatist, even if it was reality. Haven wasn't that large and while they might escape to her boat, the nearest neighbor was three days away by sea. When Shara wanted to travel quickly to and from Haven, she called a pilot to bring in a seaplane.

"Anyone know how to fly Jamar's plane?" Shara's gaze went to Cade and Lyle. Both men shook their heads. "Then we head for my house, pick up as much food and water as we can carry, and head for my boat."

"Hurry." The urgency in Lyle's tone told her he expected the lava to gush. Or the entire cone to blow.

Turning their backs on the volcano, they took about five steps and a giant fissure opened before them. Only this fissure was different from the others. Right in the middle of the lava flow was a solid looking island. And on the island stood a shiny blue building that had appeared as if by magic.

Shara rubbed her eyes. Was she hallucinating?

"It's the portal." Cade grinned. "The volcano's not going to blow. The energy is keeping the portal open and the automatic machinery is tapping into the ocean to send salt to Rama."

Shara stared at him, confusion and hope swelling in her chest as she tried to take in what was happening. "The volcano's not going to blow? The portal's already working?"

"Yes. Look at the cone. The ash is much less, the rumblings almost gone. And the portal works almost instantly through the folds of space and time. Rama is already receiving the first salt shipments."

The signs of the volcano settling down were apparent—even to her. Cade was telling the truth. The volcano wasn't going to explode. Earth was safe. She was safe.

Relief flowed through Shara. They'd done it. The volcano was returning to dormancy. Haven would be fine. The Pacific Rim wasn't going to set off a chain reaction that tore apart the planet. Cade's people now had a chance to live better lives. She was certain the government could eventually work out a trade balance for the salt. And what of her and Cade? She glanced at him but he was staring at the portal, his eyes shining with satisfaction.

"Where did the building come from?" Lyle asked Cade.

"The portal is like a tunnel through space. Once it opened, my people sent the building through, and our lasers dug tunnels to the ocean to bring the salt to the portal where it's refined, then sent to Rama."

"I'd love to study the science behind your machines." Lyle stared in awe.

"That can be arranged." Cade grinned at Shara. "I still have to work out a long-term lease with Haven's owner."

Shara couldn't quite meet the heat in Cade's eyes, didn't dare to hope he'd forgiven her. She glanced back at the volcano. The explosions had halted. The lava flow had stopped near the cone. Without more pressure to feed the eruptions, the ash in the air slowly settled and the sky lightened.

Jules's prediction had almost come true, but they had survived. Earth would remain whole. Cade would save his people. Trevor would get his story. And from the look on Jules's face as she embraced Lyle, her friend had found a new love.

Shara should feel elated. Perhaps she was too tired. Right now she felt drained.

She wanted to brush her teeth, bathe, and sleep for a week in Cade's arms. His *arms*. She'd shot both of them. Betrayed him. She had no right to expect him to ever hold her again.

As if reading her gloomy thoughts, he walked beside her, strolling slowly behind the others so they had privacy. Cade kept his tone even. "You okay?"

"I should be asking you that question."

"I'm in pain but I'll live." He stopped and turned to face her. "I would have accepted you shooting ten bullets into my body to save both our peoples."

"I tried to destroy the spheres."

"You didn't."

"It's not that simple."

"It can be that simple if we let it be that simple."

Her eyes burned. "Why do I always hurt the people I love?"

"Shooting me was . . . the right thing to do. And perhaps from your perspective, so was trying to stop me."

But that she had hurt him sickened her and her heart swelled at how he was willing to forgive her as he stood there bleeding. But could she forgive herself? "I'm not sure I even know who I am."

"You're strong and courageous. You did what had to be done—even when it was painful. And I love you."

She jerked her head up to see the heat in his eyes. And she saw the truth. He did love her.

And she loved him. Jules had been right again. Bruce had been a once-in-a-lifetime love. But that didn't mean he was her only love. Her love for Cade was different, deeper, broader, more mature, more passionate.

She allowed a pleased smile to reach her lips. "So you don't blame me for—?"

"You didn't want to hurt me."

"Actually, I did when I shot you. I wanted you to hurt so

badly that your *Quait* would kick in and save us all." She reached up and placed her hands on his jaw, tugged his head down to kiss her. "*Quait* or no *Quait*, you're a good man, Cade."

"Is that so?"

She read doubts in his eyes. "You don't agree?"

"I suppose I'll have to or you might shoot me again," he teased.

"Not funny." She kissed him, careful not to touch his wounds. "On the volcano, you trusted my judgment, so do it again."

"All right."

"You're a good man, Cade," she repeated. "And your *Quait* makes you even better."

23

❂

Shara lounged on a towel in the shade of her tiki hut on the beach while right beside her Cade soaked up rays. After a doctor had stitched Cade's wounds, they'd returned to Haven to allow him to recover.

"Has Trevor's story hit the wires?" Cade asked.

"It's tomorrow's front-page news." Shara enjoyed the isolation while they could get it. "Are you prepared for the press invasion?"

"The press isn't exactly one of my favorite Terran occupations."

She wrinkled her nose. "Wait until you meet our politicians."

Shara's satellite phone buzzed. She'd turned off the ringer because it had been chiming nonstop. But when she recognized Teresa's caller ID, she answered. "How's it going?"

"My face should be back to normal once the bruises and swelling fade. The plastic surgeon you sent me to does great work."

"And how are *you*?" Shara asked.

"Seeing a shrink and healing. The best part is . . . I have a surprise for you." Teresa's voice had regained her former enthusiasm. "I found Jamar's ship stashed on a small island."

"Thanks." Shara ended the call and grinned at Cade. "Teresa's found Jamar's spaceship. We can head to Rama whenever you like."

Cade peered at her above his sunglasses. "Are you still certain you want to go?"

"Absolutely. By tomorrow this paradise will be ruined. Haven will be crawling with press, military, and politicians. I'm not certain you realize that billions of people will be focusing on your every word. Television crews will bring our story to the world."

Cade reached over and took her hand. "If you stay by my side, they'll all be looking at you." His eyes sparkled with heat, reminding her this afternoon and evening might be the last alone time they'd have until they left for Rama.

She squeezed back his hand. "Don't kid yourself. Celebrities are commonplace. You are one of a kind." She passed him a bowl of potato chips and shot him a sassy grin. "Eat up. I intend to enjoy you while I have you to myself—and you need your strength for what I have in mind."

"Have I told you lately how much I adore your mind?" Cade turned onto his side and stroked her hair back from her face.

"And I love yours—all of it." She chuckled at his expression. He still hadn't fully accepted his *Quait*, but he no longer argued with her.

"What's so funny?"

"Do you think our child will have *Quait*?"

"I don't even know if it's possible for us to have children together."

"Trust me. It's possible."

"Are you saying . . ." He coughed, almost choked on a chip. "You and I . . ."

"We're pregnant. I hope your spaceship works better than your birth control."

Cade let out a whoop of joy. "The salt must have altered my body chemistry." Then his smile faded a bit. "Is the baby—"

"My doctor tested the baby's DNA. Everything is fine. But I won't bring our child to Rama if you're about to start a social revolution."

"Not a problem. I'll arrange for us to be in the advance party that colonizes the new world." He dug into the pocket of his shorts and shot her a sheepish smile. "I guess I should have given you this ring sooner."

In his palm, he held out the tanzanite-and-opal ring she'd admired so long ago back in Hawaii. "Oh . . . Cade. When did you buy this?"

"Last week. I've been waiting for the perfect moment to give it to you." And then his mouth angled down and claimed hers, sealing their love with a kiss.

Coming from Tor Romance
in July 2007

Kiss
Me
Deadly

BY SUSAN KEARNEY

(0-765-35667-8)

Turn the Page for a Preview

An intuitive warning prickled the fine hair on the back of Mandy Newman's neck.

Danger.

Her finely-honed instincts kicked in, halting her forward progress. She wished she was closer to the safety of her car. In the gloomy solitude of the parking garage, she made out the silhouette of a man half hidden, his shoulders hunched behind a column. She tightened her grip on her briefcase handle.

Perhaps she should turn and flee. Perhaps she was overreacting. *Give a man enough time and he'll show his true colors*, was one of her mom's most annoying sayings. Mandy hated to admit it, but too often Mom was right. After growing up with her mother's brainwashing that men were scum and spending several years in divorce court representing women against abusive spouses, greedy husbands, and cheating bastards, Mandy yearned to march over and smash the dude upside the head with her briefcase just for intimidating her.

She didn't, of course. The man, wearing an over-sized trench coat that was much too warm for a balmy Tampa May evening, stared back with enough venom for her to fear he might turn violent. The baseball cap pulled low on his forehead emphasized his hostile stare. At the menacing scowl of his thin lips, her anger turned to wariness. If he took just one step in her direction, she would cut and run, but after a final glare, he opened the door to a scratched and dented silver pickup truck, climbed in, started his engine and drove away.

Pumps striking a quick beat on the pavement, Mandy hurried to her car and tried to shake off the tension in her neck and shoulders. She'd been working too hard, and the resulting fatigue had her imagining things. Perhaps she should accept her partner and best friend Danna Taylor's invite to LA next week and take a few well-deserved days off. After working a mind-numbing number of back-to-back divorce cases where hostility often overflowed into hateful and bitter behavior, giving in to paranoia was easy. However, just because a client had recently revealed she'd seen her husband scrub the toilet bowl with her toothbrush before replacing it on her bathroom counter didn't mean that all men were rotten or that someone was out to get Mandy. She had to keep her perspective.

After slipping into the leather Beemer seat, Mandy nevertheless slapped down the locks. Feeling overly dramatic, but safer, she snapped on her seatbelt and promised herself a vacation. Soon.

She pulled into street traffic and a light afternoon shower forced her to turn on her windshield wipers. A familiar silver pick-up truck swung around the corner and hugged her rear bumper.

The slime ball from the parking garage was apparently back. Why was it so difficult to get rid of the jerks and yet so hard to find a keeper? She peered into her rear-view mirror, but couldn't see the driver through the truck's dark tinted windows, making it difficult to decide whether to phone the cops on her cell, or ignore the s.o.b. While similarities between the silver truck in the garage and the one behind her might only be a coincidence, her gut clenched. Sweat beaded on her forehead and the AC had nothing to do with the shiver of apprehension that made her grip the steering wheel to stop her fingers from trembling.

Deep down, she knew the guy on her bumper was trouble.

If only she could lose the silver pick-up in the city rush-hour traffic, but delivery trucks and commuters boxed her in. The idea of abandoning her car and bolting among the passersby on the rainy sidewalks seemed foolhardy.

With her gated condo only a few blocks away and convenient to downtown, she stayed in her car, inched through the traffic and kept a wary eye on the rear-view mirror. Security guards on Harbor Island wouldn't allow strangers to pass through the gate. Another few blocks and she'd be safe.

Once she turned at Channelside Drive onto the bridge leading to Harbor Island, the traffic unclogged. Below the two-laned bridge, the Hillsborough River flowed out to Tampa Bay between Harbour and Davis Islands and she picked up speed. So did the silver pickup.

One moment Mandy was driving in the rain, the next, the pickup was ramming her rear fender.

Bastard. She should have followed her instincts and clobbered him with her briefcase when she'd had the chance.

Now, she spun sideways toward the guardrail.

In crisis mode, determined to stay on the road, she slammed on the brakes. *Bad move.* Her tires squealed and skidded on the slick pavement. Clenching the wheel, she fought the spin. But her Beemer careened sideways, smashing into the guardrail. Concrete rumbled. Horns blared.

Her airbag exploded in her face.

Dizzy, she slapped it down, choking on the powder in the air. She opened her eyes.

A view of the river filled her front windshield.

Oh . . . my . . . God.

Pitched downward, her car dangled about twenty feet over the water below.

An engine roared. She craned her neck and glanced over her shoulder, praying help was coming.

Wrong again.

The silver pickup rammed her car a second time. The jarring thud and the fact that someone wanted her dead struck at the same time.

Behind her, the guardrail cracked and metal pieces rained into the river. Mandy, her throat too tight to scream, again slammed her foot on the brakes. Her car slid, teetered. Yet, again, the truck crashed into her, this time shoving her Beemer all the way over the lip.

No. Please . . . no.

She had no time to release her seat belt. No time to escape.

Her car plummeted toward the water, flipping, somer-saulting.

Terrified of the impact, she braced her hands on the wheel, held her breath, closed her eyes, and prayed she would live to hold her precious baby girl, Gabrielle, again. And even as Mandy's ears roared and the water rushed up to smack her, she vowed to survive. For Gabrielle.

The Beemer punched through the water, slamming the air from her lungs and jarring her back. She prayed the car would float long enough for her to escape, but the vehicle didn't remain on the surface. It sank in a giant sucking noise.

Stunned, Mandy fought to keep her wits. Hissing like a deadly sea creature, cold water cascaded over her. She couldn't see in the dark and panic rose up to choke her. Dizzy, confused, and wet, she finally realized her car was upside down and plunging toward the river bottom.

She had to get out or she'd drown and the car would become her tomb. Fighting her seat belt, she finally found and released the buckle. Just in time, she placed her hands above her head to break her fall. Toppling sideways, she ended up sitting on the ceiling in a deepening pool of water.

Unable to see, Mandy reached for the door. She touched smooth leather, then remembered the handle was upside down from this angle.

Think. Everything's backwards.

Finally, her fingers closed on the handle and with desperate strength, she yanked and shoved the door with her shoulder. But it wouldn't budge.

Too much water pressure from outside.

Water poured in. Her air bubbled out. And the car kept plunging. Finally, with a moan of tortured metal, it settled on the bottom, the roof denting beneath her. Water rose past her feet, her waist, her neck.

Her best chance to escape was after the pressure equalized—after the car's interior totally filled with water. So she had to wait for the water to come inside. Keep her wits about her.

As water rose past her chin, she lunged upward and

banged her head. Ignoring the pain, tilting her head back, she clamped her mouth shut and breathed in through her nostrils. Terrified, she waited, every cell in her body urging her to go right now.

For Gabrielle's sake, she refused to panic. For Gabrielle, she stayed and allowed the water to swallow her alive, waited with her nose pressed against the floorboards, snagging in the last of the air.

Water closed over her mouth, nose and eyes, filled the entire car, trapping her in wet blackness.

Now. Make your move now.

Mandy dived down to the handle. Shoved. The door wouldn't move. She refrained from beating her bare fists on the windows in frustration; she knew she didn't have the strength to break the glass. Every good lawyer had a plan B. And she was a damn good attorney.

Think.

She needed leverage.

Yes.

Grabbing the wheel with one hand, the handle with the other, she planted her feet against the door. Straining every muscle, she thrust with her calves and thighs.

Finally, the door gave with a pop.

About damn time.

Rushing out, she banged her shoulder on the doorjamb. Lungs already burning, head aching, she kicked hard for the surface.

I'm coming, Gabrielle. Mommy's coming.

Mandy's lungs burned, but she fought against the urge to open her mouth for air.

Keep kicking.

Overhead, rays of light beckoned with tempting promise. So close. So far . . .